PATRICK

A member of the ____ ____
Outfit and right-h____
Hondo gun wizar____
Counter was a ma____ ____ with.
Well-born, wealthy, charming and
popular with the ladies, he was also a
skilful man with a gun, and a matchless
friend to his fellow hands in the Floating
Outfit.

MARK COUNTER – a giant of a man
whose second name was trouble.

Also available from Corgi Books:

.T. EDSON OMNIBUS
Volume 3

TROUBLED RANGE
THE WILDCATS
RANGELAND HERCULES

CORGI BOOKS

J.T. EDSON Omnibus Volume 3
A CORGI BOOK 0 552 13604 2

TROUBLED RANGE and THE WILDCATS originally published
in Great Britain by Brown Watson Ltd.

PRINTING HISTORY – TROUBLED RANGE
Brown Watson edition published 1965
Brown Watson edition reprinted 1966
Corgi edition published 1969
Corgi edition reprinted 1972
Corgi edition reprinted 1978

PRINTING HISTORY – THE WILDCATS
Brown Watson edition published 1965
Brown Watson edition reprinted 1966
Corgi edition published 1969
Corgi edition reprinted 1972
Corgi edition reprinted 1976

PRINTING HISTORY – RANGELAND HERCULES
Corgi edition published 1968
Corgi edition reprinted 1970
Corgi edition reprinted 1974
Corgi edition reprinted 1981

Corgi Omnibus edition published 1990

Corgi Books are published by Transworld Publishers
Ltd., 61–63 Uxbridge Road, Ealing, London W5 5SA, in
Australia by Transworld Publishers (Australia) Pty. Ltd.,
15–23 Helles Avenue, Moorebank, NSW 2170, and in New
Zealand by Transworld Publishers (N.Z.) Ltd., Cnr. Moselle
and Waipareira Avenues, Henderson, Auckland.

Printed and bound in Great Britain by
Cox & Wyman Ltd., Reading, Berks.

Troubled Range

*For Major 'Digger' Radford, R.A.V.C., Rtd.,
who had the horrible job of putting up with
me in two countries.*

PART ONE

THE BOUNTY ON BELLE STARR'S SCALP

CURSES crackled around Calamity Jane in a profane cloud as she stood, hands on hips, looking at the left front wheel of her wagon which had sunk through the caved-in roof of a prairie-dog hole; then slowly raised her eyes to study the setting sun.

With all the west to pick from as digging ground, trust that blasted, fool critter to sink his tunnel right in the route her wagon was taking. Of course it might be claimed that the prairie-dog had been on the range first and she ought to have avoided its hole, but Calamity had never been a girl to admit she might be in the wrong.

'Dad-blast your ornery, worthless hole-grubbing hide!' she spluttered. 'The hosses'll never haul it out and night's near on here. I may as well make camp and cook up a meal, so keep out of sight, prairie-dog, or you'll be that meal.'

Calamity Jane had reached the mature age of eighteen and already bore a name fast becoming famous. Soldiers in the Army's string of forts claimed her acquaintance. Freighters boasted of having been the one who taught her to wield a blacksnake whip. More than one dancehall girl now knew to sing low when Calamity Jane swaggered into a saloon.

Her red hair had a natural curl to it, hung medium long, and carried a U.S. Cavalry *képi* perched on it. The face framed by the hair was pretty, freckled and tanned. A merry face with lips made for laughter or kissing, but capable of turning loose a blistering flow of invective should she be riled. Her figure had matured early and now at eighteen the breasts rose round and full. They forced hard against the dark blue Cavalry shirt, its neck opened far enough to give a tantalising glimpse of the

7

opening of the valley between her breasts. The shirt, like her buckskin pants, seemed to have been bought a size too small and shrunk in the wash. The pants clung tight to her hips which swelled out and down to sturdy but shapely legs with Pawnee moccasins on the feet. Round Calamity's neck hung a string of freshwater pearls, her sole concession to feminine jewellery. Her arms, exposed by the rolled up sleeves, looked more muscular than a lady of fashion might have liked—came to a point. Calamity had never laid claim to being a lady of fashion, or any other kind. Nor would a lady of fashion be likely to wear a gunbelt, with a .36 Navy Colt butt forward in a fast draw holster at her right side. Calamity wore such a rig and knew how to use it.

'I'll light a fire afore I unhitch you, boys,' she told her two-horse team. 'Maybe somebody'll see the flames and come lend us a hand.'

Collecting wood and buffalo chips from the rawhide possum-belly under the wagon, Calamity built a fire. She took water from the butt on the side of the wagon, filled her coffee-pot and set it to boil on the flames.

All in all, Calamity made an attractive picture as she prepared to make her camp. She attracted the attention of the rider who topped the rim behind her and halted his horse to drink in the scene below.

Sitting his seventeen-hand stallion lightly, no mean feat for a man who topped six foot three in his bare feet and had the muscular development of a Hercules, the man looked down at Calamity. He shoved back his costly white, low-crowned, wide-brimmed Stetson from his curly golden-blond hair. The blue eyes looked out of a strong, tanned, almost classically handsome face. Knotted and tight rolled at his throat, the scarlet silk bandana trailed long ends over the expensive tan shirt. He clearly bought the shirt, and all his clothing, made to his measure. Few stores could supply clothes to fit him off their pegs. His shoulders had a great spread to them, the arms showing their enormous biceps even though the shirt's sleeves had been built generously. Tapering down to a lean waist, the body rested on long powerful legs clad in levis which hung outside

8

his boots and had their cuffs turned back. His boots had the look of good workmanship and the gunbelt, with a matched brace of ivory handled 1860 Army Colts in the holsters, bore the marks of a master craftsman's hands. Whoever tooled that belt knew just what a man needed in the interests of drawing his guns very fast.

The big man might look something of a dandy dresser, but he had an air of quiet self-reliance. He seemed to be at home on the range, although his home range would lie some distance to the south of Montana Territory.

A touch of the Kelly spurs on the heels of his fancy-stitched boots started his bloodbay stallion moving. Before the horse had taken five steps Calamity heard its hooves and turned, hand hovering the butt of her gun.

'Texan,' she mused, studying his hat, then the low horned, double girthed saddle between his knees. 'Cowhand. A good 'un or I've never seen one.'

Despite her thoughts, Calamity did not relax until the Texan halted his horse before her and doffed his hat in a gallant gesture, then nodded to the wagon.

'Howdy, ma'am. You-all having trouble?'

'*Naw!*' she scoffed. 'I just naturally like sitting here with the wheel all bogged down and the wagon stuck. 'Course I'm not in trouble.'

'That being so,' he replied calmly, his voice a deep, cultured southern drawl, 'I'll be on my way again. *Adios.*'

Calamity stared at him for a moment. Then a curse ripped from her lips as he started the horse moving, setting his hat on his head once more. Her hand turned palm out, closed on the butt of her Colt and brought it from the holster. Its hammer clicked back under her thumb.

'Hold it!' she snapped. 'You come back here and lend me a hand to get the wagon out, or I'll put lead into you.'

Turning, the blond Texan surveyed her gun with calm detachment. He twisted in his saddle to do so and made no attempt to turn the bloodbay around.

'Say please,' he answered.

'Do you know who I am?'

'No, ma'am.'

'The name's Canary! Martha Jane Canary. Which, if you're so damned all-fired un-eddicated, spells Calamity Jane—and means I'm Wild Bill Hickok's gal.'

If Calamity expected her words, or fear of the famous Wild Bill Hickok's name to bring the Texan to a condition of servile obedience, she was to be disappointed. Tapping his Stetson to the correct 'jack-deuce' angle over his off eye with the forefinger of his right hand, the Texan answered:

'Which same's as good a reason as any I know not to help you. I never took to Wild Bill in any size, shape or form.'

Once more he started the horse moving and Calamity's temper popped right over the boiling point.

'Hold it, damn you!' she howled and fired a shot, the bullet hissing by the big Texan's head.

This time she got a reaction, although not the one she wanted. Barely had she fired when the Texan turned—only he held an Army Colt in his left hand.

Calamity had not been watching his left hand. She knew that most men only carried two guns to have twelve shots handy instead of six. The Army Colt might be one of the finest percussion-fired revolvers ever made, but it still took time to reload with combustible cartridges or powder flask and ball. Only a few men could handle the left side gun worth a damn. It was in keeping with her lousy luck that she should tie in with a jasper who not only could, but just had showed remarkable skill when using his good left hand.

Flame spurted from the Texan's Colt and dirt erupted between Calamity's feet causing her to take a hurried, if involuntary, step to the rear.

'Leather it!' snapped the Texan, cocking his gun on the recoil, 'or I'll blow it out of your hand.'

He could likely do it too. Calamity had not failed to notice the smooth ease with which he threw lead at the end of a very fast draw. It struck between her feet, but she was willing to bet the bullet went within an inch or two of where the big feller aimed it to go.

'Wild Bill's not going to like this,' Calamity warned, twirling

10

her Navy Colt on the trigger-finger, twisting it around and thrusting it back into the holster. Her attitude was one of 'that showed him how to handle a gun.'

'Which same, looking at your wagon, you won't be headed anywhere to snitch to him about me,' the Texan replied.

The gun in his hand spun in a flashing arc, pinwheeled up into the air and slapped its barrel into his palm, curled around his hand like a trained pig on a barrel, rose into the air once more, was caught and went back into the holster.

Calamity stared, her eyes bulging like organ-stops. Having seen a number of prominent gentlemen of the gun-fighting fraternity, she felt she could speak with some authority on the new and honourable art of pistol-juggling—which was not a show-off stunt, but a method of strengthening the wrists and improving the ability to handle the weapon. One thing Calamity knew for sure. The display she had just seen equalled the best it had ever been her privilege to witness.

'What do I have to do afore you help?' she asked.

'Like I said, say please.'

'Wouldn't want me to say pretty-please, would you?'

'*Adios,*' drawled the Texan and started the bloodbay moving.

'All right, blast you!' Calamity wailed. 'Please, damn you, please!'

'Now that's a heap better,' grinned the Texan, swinging his horse towards her. 'World'd be a happier place happen we all asked each other polite.'

'I hope Wild Bill asks you polite when he blows your ears off for what you done to me!' Calamity howled.

'That'd be the only way he could do it, gal,' the Texan told her as he dismounted and looked around him. 'There's nothing handy we could use as a lever?'

'Which same I saw hours back, you danged knobhead!' gasped the infuriated Calamity. 'What're you fixing in to do about it?'

'Think first,' answered the Texan calmly. 'What'd Wild Bill do?'

'He'd lay hold of that wheel and heft the whole blasted wagon up!'

11

'Would, huh? Have you any more logs under the possum belly?'

Reaching into the rawhide carrier, Calamity hauled out two thick logs.

'These do?' she asked, having decided sarcasm would get her nowhere.

'Why sure. Get set to slide them in under the wheel.'

'How?' she snorted. 'Or are you kin to that prairie-dog and aim to dig the wheel out with your paws? Some pesky varmint stole my shovel back in Hays.'

'Wasn't Wild Bill there to watch it?' asked the man.

Only with an effort did Calamity prevent herself throwing the logs at the Texan. She had considerable knowledge of men, far more than a girl her age in conventional circles would have gained in a life-time, but that Texan sure licked the bejeesus out of the others when it came to riling a girl and getting her pot-boiling mad.

After waiting for some comment for a couple of seconds, the big Texan walked to the wagon. For a moment he stood looking at it, then turned his back to the trapped wheel, bent his legs slightly and gripped the spokes.

'Quit trying, feller,' Calamity said. 'Not even Wild Bill could lift that wagon.'

The handsome blond giant did not reply. Standing with his back to the sunken wheel, he took a firmer grip and slowly put on the pressure in an attempt to raise it.

For almost thirty seconds nothing happened, except that the Texan's face showed the strain, twisted into determined lines and became soaked with sweat. Calamity opened her mouth to make some comment about the foolishness of a lesser mortal attempting something which would have been beyond the power of even the mighty Wild Bill Hickok.

Her words never came. Before her eyes the wagon began to rise, lifting a fraction of an inch at a time, but going steadily upwards. Calamity stopped thinking about Wild Bill Hickok and grabbed a log ready to thrust it under the wheel.

'Just a lil mite higher, friend!' Calamity breathed, kneeling by his side and lowering the log into the hole. The wheel rose a couple of inches higher. 'Easy now! Can you hold it?'

With his breath hissing through his teeth and every muscle and fibre of his giant frame concentrated on the effort, the Texan made no attempt to reply. But he braced himself firmer and held the wagon. He looked like he might be posing for a painting of some legendary classic hero performing a super-human feat, like Hercules carrying out one of his labours, or Atlas limbering up to heft the world on his shoulders once more. Calamity did not have a classical education, in fact beyond being able to read slowly and write a painful, childish scrawl, her schooling had been remarkably poor. To her the big Texan sure looked a heap of man.

Not that she wasted much time in staring. Calamity was an extremely practical young woman, if hot-tempered and hot-headed, she knew there would be limits to the giant Texan's strength and that she must get the supporting log under the wheel before the wagon's weight proved too much for him.

'Lower away, friend!' she said, satisfied the log under the wheel would hold.

Slowly the Texan bent his legs, letting the weight settle down gradually, not dropping it as most men would have, not that most men could have performed the task of lifting the wagon's weight. Calmity watched it sink, biting her lip in anxiety. If the log did not hold she would be to blame, not the Texan, and she could imagine the Texan's blistering comments if she failed in her side of the business after he had succeeded so well in his.

The log held, and Calamity breathed a sigh of relief. Springing to the heads of her horses, she looked at the big Texan. He had moved away from the wagon, turned to face it and now stood with his head hanging, chest heaving as he sucked air into his lungs.

'Giddap!' she yelled, pulling on the horses' head stalls. 'Come on, you no-good, slab-sided, spavined, wored-out worth-less apologies for crowbait. Pull.'

Throwing their weight into the harness, the two horses pulled. The wagon rolled forward, stuck for a moment as its wheel hit the rim of the hole, lurched, rose up on the rim and forward. Calamity grinned broadly. She aimed to show——

'Hold it! Throw back on those horses, you fool female!' An angry bellow left the Texan's lips and, without meaning to, Calamity obeyed the order and stopped her team. Hot and angry words bubbled inside her. She did not take to any man, even if she maybe owed him thanks for helping her out of a tricky spot, talking that way to her.

'What's eating you?' she asked, deciding to start the horses moving again and to hell with him, but not doing it until she had asked the question.

'Leave us not drop the back wheel into the hole,' the Texan answered dryly. 'Where in hell did you learn to handle a wagon?—from Wild Bill?'

'You wait, mister. You just wait!' Calamity said, but she said it under her breath for she was writhing with shame at having forgotten something the rawest cook's louse in a freighting outfit would have remembered. Being Calamity, she blamed the Texan's attitude for causing her to forget the important detail of ensuring the rear wheel did not follow its leader into the hole, miss the log and bog the wagon down again.

Stamping her feet down angrily, Calamity stormed towards the wagon and studied the hole. The Texan's warning had come just in time. Another second and the wheel would have sunk down into the hole.

Taking the second log, Calamity packed it into the hole alongside the first. Grubbing some earth from the sides, she piled it over the logs, then stood up.

'That do it?' she asked.

'Reckon it might. Give her a whirl.'

The Texan's cool, relaxed attitude almost pushed Calamity to the bursting point. Turning on her heel, she threw herself at her horses' heads and gripped the nearest reins. Common sense returned the moment she touched the reins. Instead of giving the word and making the horses jerk, she eased them forward inch by inch. The wagon advanced steadily, its wheel rolling on to the logs, with Calamity Jane holding her breath, leaning to one side so she could watch it roll on to the logs.

'Keep it going easy, gal,' the Texan said, also watching the

14

wheel.

At the edge of the hole, the wheel stuck for an instant, then lifted and passed over on to solid ground. Calamity was clear of the stoppage which had delayed her. Bringing the team to a halt, she walked towards the big stranger.

'Thanks, feller,' she said.

'Think nothing of it,' he replied. 'That coffee smells good.'

'Tastes the same way. Set and rest up a spell while I unhitch my team. Then I'll cook us up a mess of vittles.'

'Never could stand by and watch a lady work. So I'll just tend to my horse while you're unhitching and cooking.'

While she worked, Calamity threw interested glances at her rescuer, trying to decide who he might be. One prominent Texas name fitted his appearance and strength, way other *Tejanos* boasted about it, only that one wore his guns butt forwards for a cross-draw, or so she heard tell. This big feller's matched Army Colts were real fine weapons, with the deep blue sheen of the Hartford factory's Best Citizens' Finish; they rode in contoured holsters which hung just right, but those holsters had never been designed for cross-draw work.

After tending to his horse, the Texan walked back to the fire and laid his saddle carefully on its side. No cowhand worth his salt ever chanced damaging his rig by resting it on its skirts. Without a saddle he could do no cattle work. He set down his saddle so the butt of the Winchester Model 1866 rifle in the boot remained on top and ready for a hurried withdrawal should one be necessary.

With this done, the Texan walked across and started to help Calamity unhitch her horses. Her first inclination was to tell him she didn't need his help even though she could use it. Only she knew if she did he was likely to take her at her word and leave her to it.

'Going to say something?' he asked.

'Sure,' she replied, then to hide her confusion. 'I told you my name.'

'Yep.'

'*Yep!*'

'And now you're wanting to know mine?'

15

'Me! Heh!' snorted Calamity, tossing her head back in an entirely feminine manner which brought no reaction from the man. 'All right then, I want to know.'

'Name's Counter, my pards call me Mark.'

Calamity cut down her whistle of surprise. Mark Counter. That figured, happen a half-smart lil range gal came to think about it.

Although his father ran a big spread down in the Texas Big Bend country, and Mark himself had a fair-sized fortune left him by an eccentric maiden aunt in her will, he still rode as a hand for Ole Devil Hardin's O.D. Connected ranch. More than that, he belonged to the élite of the ranch crew, the floating outfit, and was the side-kick and right bower* of the spread's segundo, the Rio Hondo gun wizard Dusty Fog. When debating to herself who Mark might be, Calamity had thought of Dusty Fog—only if Dusty Fog was bigger and stronger than Mark, it would make him a tolerable big and strong man.

During the War Between The States, Mark rode as a second lieutenant in old Bushrod Sheldon's regiment where his ideas of uniform were much copied by the bloods of the Confederate Cavalry. Now Mark's taste in clothes dictated cowhand fashions in the range country, for he was an acknowledged master of the trade. His strength and ability in a rough-house brawl were spoken of with awe by all who saw him in action. Having just seen an example of that strength, Calamity reckoned for once the Texans were not exaggerating even a little mite as they talked of this particular son of the Lone Star State. Men said Mark could handle his guns well. The few who *knew* claimed him to be second only to the man they called the fastest gun in Texas, Dusty Fog himself, in both speed and accurate placing of his shots.

'Glad to know you,' she said, not wishing him to guess that she felt impressed by being in the presence of a man Wild Bill Hickok studiously avoided meeting when the O.D. Connected brought a trail herd into Hays.

*Right Bower, originally a Euchre term for the highest trump card.

Actually Wild Bill had left town on a buffalo hunt the day before the O.D. Connected herd arrived—he said. Calamity had taken his word for it, content to bask in Hickok's reflected glory. Only now she came to think about it, there had been no buffalo herds seen around Hays at that time. Even the professional hunters had commented on the lack of the shaggy critters on the range.

No matter that she was hot-headed, Calamity could cook up a meal fit to set a man's mouth to watering. One of the few things the nuns at the St. Louis convent—where Calamity's mother left her children before disappearing into the unknown —had managed to teach the girl was how to cook.

They ate their meal without much talk. Then, after cleaning up the dishes, Calamity walked to where her guest stood. She reckoned it was high time they had a show-down and learned who was boss around the camp-fire.

'You sure cook good, Calamity,' he said, grinning down at her. 'Don't tell me Wild Bill taught you?'

'I'm Wild Bill's gal,' she replied and whipped the flat of her hand across his cheek with all her strength.

It was a good slap, Calamity admitted to herself, maybe even a little harder than she ought——

Mark's hands shot out, clamping on her shoulders and jerking her forward. He bent his head and his lips crushed down on hers. With a muffled gasp, Calamity tried to twist her head away. Her hard little fists beat at his shoulders, but Mark ignored them. Twisting his body, he took her knee on his thigh as it drove up. Then he released her, shoving her backwards. For a moment Calamity stood gasping for breath. Then she came forward with another slap and a repetition of the fiction that she was Wild Bill's girl.

Again Mark caught her, hauled her to him and crushed a kiss on her lips. She struggled, though not as hard as before. On being released, she staggered a pace or so to the rear and stood gasping for breath.

'I'm Wild Bill's gal!' she said, her breasts heaving, and she lashed out another slap, only it did not have the power of the first two.

17

On the fourth, fifth and sixth kisses and slaps Calamity's struggles grew weaker. The slaps became more feeble and on the sixth time she found herself starting to kiss back.

'I—I'm st—still W—Wild Bill's g—gal!' she gasped after the seventh kiss, staggering on wobbly legs and landed a slap which barely touched his cheek.

Once more Mark scooped her into his arms. This time her lips sought his, hungrily answering the kiss. Her tongue crept through her lips. Her arms, no longer flailing, crept around him. Clinging to Mark, her fingers digging into the hard muscles of his back, Calamity threw all she had into her kiss.

The night was dark. The stars shone brightly in the heavens. Only the range noises broke the silence; the stamping of Mark's big stallion as it heard the distant scream of a cougar; the thrashing as one of Calamity's team horses rolled in the grass; the squeaking of insects.

Under the wagon a large black mound separated into two smaller black mounds. A masculine voice spoke from the larger of the mounds.

'What do you think of Wild Bill Hickok now?' it asked.

A feminine voice, dreamy, satisfied and contented came from the smaller.

'Wild Bill Hickok,' it said. 'Who *is* Wild Bill Hickok?'

The sun crept up and peeped over the horizon. A cold grey light of dawn began to creep out into the blackness of the night sky.

Beneath Calamity's wagon, Mark Counter opened his eyes and lifted his head from the pillow he always carried in his bedroll. Beside him, the girl stirred sleepily, her bare arm around his equally bare shoulders. Putting up his hand, Mark felt at the oval lump on the right side of his neck. Well, the bandana would hide it and he reckoned he was big enough to handle any adverse comments on his honourable wounds.

Two arms closed around his neck and a hot little mouth crushed against his, worked across his cheek and to his ear.

'Mark!' Calamity breathed into his ear.

'It's time we was up and on our way,' he replied.

18

'Please—pretty please.'

Like the man said, a feller's sins always bounced right back on to his fool head happen he stayed around long enough after committing them; and Mark *had* taken a firm stand on the subject of politeness bringing its own reward when he first met Calamity.

Half an hour later Mark sat drawing on his boots and at his side, smiling contentedly, Calamity buttoned her shirt after tucking it into her pants.

'Yes sir,' she sighed, rising to make the fire. 'World's sure a happier place happen we all ask each other polite.'

There had been a time, back the first time it happened, when Calamity would have expected the man to marry her and spend the rest of his days in a haze of devotion to her.

Only he had not. The feller had been a handsome young freighter and Calamity a naïve sixteen-year-old girl fresh out in the harsh, cruel world. When she woke the morning after it happened, she found him gone and felt that her heart would break. It did not. Fact being Calamity had discovered her heart could stand plenty of jolting around without showing any signs of fracture. From the first time, she built up the belief that no man was so much better than the rest that he was worth busting a gut over when he pulled up his stakes and left. There would be another feller come along, so she went her own way, enjoying life to the full in good times and bad. Only she no longer grew starry-eyed when a man showed appreciation of her feminine charms.

Sure, last night had been swell, but that did not make her a potential Mrs. Mark Counter. Likely they would part in Elkhorn City and never meet again. Although she had never heard the word, would not have understood it if she did, or know how to phrase it, Calamity figured their destinies lay in different directions. While last night had been an enjoyable experience, and one she would not soon forget, nothing serious could come of it.

So Calamity cooked breakfast, while Mark used some of the contents of her water-butt for his wash and shave. They ate their food with a good appetite and prepared to move on.

After saddling his bloodbay, Mark helped Calamity to hitch up her team to the wagon. When all was done Mark mounted his horse and Calamity swung up on to the box of her wagon, taking up the blacksnake whip.

'Giddap!' Calamity yelled, swinging her whip and making it pop like a gunshot in the morning air.

The two horses put their shoulders to the harness and moved forward, starting the wagon rolling. Side by side Calamity and Mark headed across the range, following the faint wheel ruts which marked the way to their respective business affairs in Elkhorn City.

'How come Cap'n Fog's not along with you, Mark?' she asked.

'Had some business to attend to in town and couldn't leave Then he got this telegraph wire from a feller up in Elkhorn wanting to pay off some money he owed Ole Devil. Sent me along to collect it.'

'I'd sure admire to have met Cap'n Fog. How come he took his herd to Newton not Hays this year?'

'Saved two days driving, brought in the first drive of the year. Happen the railroad keeps pointing the way it is, we'll likely be delivering to somewheres around Fort Dodge next summer. You figure Wild Bill scared us off?'

'Like I said last night. Who's Wild Bill?' she grinned. 'Sure would like to see Cap'n Fog though. Is all I hear about him true?'

'Such as?'

'How he stands taller'n you, is stronger, faster with his guns.'

'Would you believe me if I told you Dusty Fog stands only about five foot six at most?'

'Nope—Hey, you're not jobbing me. You're serious, aren't you?'

Mark nodded his head. When he said Dusty Fog stood only five foot six, he told the simple truth—but to Mark's way of thinking, and to many others with whom he came in contact, Dusty Fog could not be measured in mere feet and inches, he stood the tallest of them all.

'I allus heard——!' Calamity began.

'Sure,' Mark interrupted. 'I've heard it too.'

For a time they travelled on discussing Dusty Fog, the Ysabel Kid and the other well-known members of the O.D. Connected. Then Calamity swung the conversation to an item of news which had been the main topic in Newton during Mark's visit.

'Did you hear anything new about the bank hold-up that Belle Starr's gang pulled in Newton?' she asked.

'Belle Starr's gang!' Mark snorted. 'Just 'cause some old biddy who had been swigging corn-toddy reckoned she saw a woman holding the gang's horses, everybody's howling about Belle Starr.'

'You reckon it wasn't her then?'

'No more her than Big and Lil Harpe and they've been dead for over a hundred years.'

'They put a tolerable sized bounty on her head though,' Calamity replied. 'It happened near on a month back, remember. Sheriff's posse run down the four fellers who pulled the raid, plumb shot them to doll-rags and killed 'em all. Which same came out to be plumb foolish 'cause they hadn't the money with 'em, not so much as a red cent, and they was all past telling where it'd gone.'

'Yes,' Mark agreed. 'And now every durned fool in the west allows Belle Starr knows where the money's hid out and are looking for her to make her tell.'

'Kind of like to meet her myself,' remarked Calamity.

'Never took you for a bounty hunter, Calam,' Mark answered, a hint of disapproval in his voice.

'And I ain't one. But they do say she's a real tough gal. I'd like to see just how tough she is.'

'From Missouri, huh?'

'Huh?' Calamity replied, putting a world of puzzlement into the grunt.

'You've got to be shown.'

'I've never yet met the gal who could lick me at riding, drinking, shooting or going at it tooth 'n' claw,' Calamity stated, trying to sound modest. 'And I don't reckon I ever will.'

Calamity did meet a woman who was more than her match, but the meeting was not to come for three years.*

'Not interested in getting your hands on the reward the bank has offered for the recovery of the money?' asked Mark.

'Naw. Anyways, I go with you, I don't reckon Belle Starr was tied in with that raid. Hell, I know the sheriff in Newton, he couldn't catch water in his hat if he stood under a waterfall. He wouldn't have picked those boys up so easy had Belle Starr been running them.'

'What brings you up this way?' Mark asked.

'Load of freight for a spread half a day past Elkhorn. Owner had it shipped into Hays from the east and I caught the contract to deliver it. What's this Elkhorn City like? I've never been this way afore.'

'Nor me. But they do say it's thriving, growing big and fast, what with gold-miners, ranchers and all.'

'Are you fixing to be there for long?' she inquired.

'Day, couple of days at most, depends on how soon I get to see that feller for Ole Devil.'

'I'll maybe see you on my way back then,' she suggested. 'We can have us a whing-ding and tree the town a mite.'

The town known as Elkhorn City was, as Mark claimed, growing big and fast. It sported no less than four thriving saloons, including the Crystal Palace, a place which would not have disgraced the best part of Trail Street, Hays City, or the better part of any rail-head trail-end town. One good, and a couple of indifferent hotels catered for the needs of transient visitors. Various shops which usually found combination in a general store in smaller, less prosperous towns, graced Beidler Street—called after John X. Beidler, leader of the vigilantes who wiped out the Plummer gang which once terrorised the Bannack area. Wells Fargo maintained a large office, stage-route and telegraph service, testifying to the importance of the city. Further amenities showed high standard. A stout building housed the county offices, sheriff's department, town marshal's premises and a substantial jail. In addition the town had the usual run of livery barns, undertaker's shop and stable, bath-

*Told in *The Wildcats* by J. T. Edson.

house and all the rest of the things which made life worth living on the range.

Bringing his horse to a halt before the open double doors of a large building inscribed 'POP LARKIN'S LIVERY BARN. Use it, I'm too old to start working', Mark looked at Calamity, winked and raised his hat. She waved a hand, keeping her team going forward.

'Don't you forget now!' she called. 'You got a date when I come back.'

Swinging from the saddle, Mark watched Calamity's wagon roll on along the street, then turned and led the bloodbay towards the open doors. He did not know if he would be in town when Calamity returned, but felt tempted to stay over. Something told him a night on the town with Calamity Jane would be worth having and be an highly entertaining experience, more so since he missed most of the fun at Newton by coming north to handle the chore for Dusty Fog.

Inside the barn it was cool, light and clean looking. There were a couple of empty stalls at the end of the line across the room and Mark walked towards them, his horse following on his heels.

A man had just finished tending to his horse in a stall down the other end of the line. Turning slowly, he looked Mark over, starting at his gunbelt, dropping his eyes to the high-heeled, fancy stitched boots, then roaming them up to the top of Mark's head. Mark noticed the way the man looked, like a rancher studying a prime bull and wondering if it would bring any profit to him should he buy it.

For his part, Mark gave the man a quick, all-embracing glance and did not like what he saw. The man stood around six foot, had a lean, rangy build and a gaunt face stuck on a neck with a prominent Adam's apple. The face's expression seemed to be one of arrogant contempt, and hinted that he must be able to handle any objections to his attitude should they be made. His clothes told a story to eyes which knew the west. Sure he wore a Stetson hat, bandana, calf-skin vest, shirt, and levis with their cuffs turned back, like a cowhand. He wore a gunbelt with a brace of walnut handled Army Colts in fast-

23

draw holsters, but so did many cowhands. On his feet were Sioux moccasins. That was what made him different. No cowhand ever wore moccasins, they would be of no use to him in his work.

For a long moment the man studied Mark, then, in the manner of a rancher who had decided a prime bull would not bring him any profit, he turned away. Slinging the saddle over his shoulder with his right hand, the man took up the double barrelled, ten gauge shotgun which leant against the wall of the stall. Gripping it with his left hand closed on the small of the butt, forefinger lying alongside the trigger-guard, the man walked out and kicked the stall gate closed behind him.

Without appearing to, Mark watched the man walk out of the barn. Caution paid when a proddy hard-case like that feller prowled around holding a scatter-gun in his hand. The man did not look back, but walked out into the street and started across its wheel-rutted width.

'Ain't sorry to see him leave.'

The words came from a door at the side of the building. Turning, Mark saw a leathery old-timer stumping towards him.

'You know him?' the old-timer went on.

'Nope. Should I?'

'Not less'n you got a wanted poster on ye some place. And you ain't, or likely one of you'd be dead by now. That there was Jubal Framant, mister.'

'Is, huh?'

Once more Mark turned to look after the hard-case. He stood on the far side of the street, talking with a big, burly man who wore a marshal's shield on his vest and carried a heavy old Colt Dragoon hung low at his right side. Mark did not look down on a man who carried one of the old four pound, one ounce thumb-busting Colt giants. The Ysabel Kid toted one and could handle it with some precision when needed.

'Yes, sir. That's Framant,' the old-timer went on, following Mark's gaze. 'Wonder what brings him to Elkhorn?'

'There's only one thing takes him any place,' Mark replied.

Framant's name was not unfamiliar to Mark. The man was

24

a bounty hunter, said to be as mean as a stick-teased rattle-snake. Roaming the range country like a buzzard circling in the sky, Framant hunted down men for the price on their heads. Rumour had it that Framant had killed fourteen men and claimed the bounty their scalps bore.

A man like Framant usually came to a town for the purpose of finding some wanted outlaw. When he found his man he would kill, for Framant never took in a living prisoner.

'Who's the feller with him?' Mark asked.

'Joel Stocker, town marshal. Real nice feller,' replied the old man and turned his attention to the bloodbay stallion. 'R over C. I never saw that brand afore.'

'Nope?'

'Know every danged brand within five hundred miles.'

'Maybe the R over C's five hundred and one miles away.'

A cackle left the old-timer's lips. 'Must've moved South Texas north a helluva ways if that's how close the R over C is.'

'It's Rance Counter's spread.'

'Tall feller, that Rance Counter, so they say. Likely sire tolerable tall sons.'

'I'm the little one of the family.'

'Mark Counter, huh? Pleased to know you. Pop Larkin's the name. I keep this place, leastways, it don't keep me.'

'You look right poorly done by,' Mark drawled, following his horse into the stall. 'Wonder what Framant wants here?'

'I asked you first, and it ain't what he wants, it's who.'

Mark turned to his horse and started to remove the saddle. A shadow fell across the doorway and feet crossed the barn to halt behind Mark at the gate of the stall.

'Howdy, mister,' a gentle voice drawled.

For a big man Joel Stocker moved light on his feet, Mark thought, turning to look at the marshal as he leaned a shoulder against the stall's gate-post and chewed in meditative manner on a plug of tobacco. There was a deceptive lethargy about the marshal which might have fooled some folks, but not Mark Counter.

'Howdy,' Mark replied, continuing the off-saddling.

'New around here?'

'Only just now rolled in.'

'With Calamity Jane?'

'Sure.'

'She's Wild Bill Hickok's gal, way I heard it.'

'Has Wild Bill heard it?' Mark drawled.

'Don't reckon it'd scare you none happen he had,' Stocker replied in his sleepy voice. 'It'd worry me some, though. I'm a duly appointed officer of the law and duty-bound to keep the peace. Which same I don't want no bulls locking horns in my town.'

'Reckon Calam and me's just passing acquaintances. We met on the trail in and I'll likely see her tomorrow—if I'm still here then.'

'Might not be, huh?'

'Not if I see Tom Gamble.'

The look of watchful suspicion left Stocker's face. Straightening up, he held out a big hand and raised his eyes a couple of inches to meet Mark's, something he rarely needed to do with any man.

'Sorry, friend,' Stocker said. 'Reckon Framant being in town's got me spooked up a mite. Are you Cap'n Fog?'

'Mark Counter.'

'Cheez! If Cap'n Fog's got more heft than you, he's a tolerable tall gent.'

Mark let the remark pass. He felt no resentment at the words and it had been many years since he last felt surprised that anybody should mistake him for Dusty Fog, or persist in thinking of Dusty as a tall man. Maybe what caused the confusion was Mark looking like the kind of man one expected somebody of Dusty Fog's reputation to be. Mark did not know if this was true, and was not worried.

'Do you always look your visitors over like this?' he asked.

'Find it saves fuss to know who-all's in town,' Stocker replied. 'And I'm a man who likes to save fuss. There's some less welcome here than others.'

'Like that bounty hunting Jubal Framant, heh, Joel?' asked the old-timer. 'Air ye running him out of town?'

'Nope. I ain't saying I'm not doing it 'cause he scares me, even if he do. But he's got his rights under the Constitution—and knows 'em. I can't run a man out of town just 'cause I don't like his line of work.'

While the men talked, Mark tended to his horse. He removed the saddle and bridle, then hung a hay-net on the hook over the manger. Larkin ambled off to return carrying a bucket of clean water and another full of grain. Showing sound horse-savvy, he did not enter the stall, but handed the buckets over the gate.

'Got me a burro in the back if you'd like to leave your saddle,' he said.

'Thanks, I'll do that. Thought you didn't have one when I saw Framant tote his rig out of here.'

'There's them who I'd let use me burro, and them I wouldn't,' grunted the old man. 'Tote her this way.'

Following the old man, Mark entered the storeroom at the rear of the stable and hung his saddle on the inverted V-shaped wooden rack known as a burro. If possible a cowhand would rather leave his saddle on a burro than lie it on its side; especially when among people which brought the danger of some heavy-footed yahoo stomping on the laid-aside rig.

Mark took his bedroll from behind the cantle and the rifle from the saddleboot. Not that he mistrusted the owner of the barn, but his change of clothing, spare ammunition and toilet articles lay in his warbag within the bedroll; and a man did not leave a loaded rifle in a saddleboot where kids might get at it.

After paying for the stabling and keep of his stallion, Mark joined Marshal Stocker at the door of the barn.

'Which's the best hotel in town?' he asked.

'Ryan's Bella Union down there, right next to the Crystal Palace. Say, Tom bust a leg riding a bad one. Sent word down that somebody from the O.D. Connected'd be along and for them to ride out and see him.'

'How far out is it?'

'Two, three hours' steady ride. Could make it by nightfall.'

Mark grinned. 'I'll leave it until morning. What's the Crystal

27

Palace like? Speaking as a duly appointed officer of the law, that is.'

'Fair place, well-run, got some purty gals in there, and you'll walk out with any money you don't spend, or lose trying to lick the blackjack game.'

'My mammy told me never to buck the dealer's percentage at any game, especially blackjack.'

'It's not the game you buck in there, it's the dealer.'

'What makes him so special?' Mark inquired.

'Being a her,' grinned Stocker. 'And a mighty purty lil her, too. Was I not a married man, which I ain't, I'd sure admire to stake a few myself on beating her game.'

'As good as that, huh?' drawled Mark, ignoring the left-handed statement made by the marshal.

'Better. Not the kind you'd expect to find working a table even in a decent saloon like the Palace.'

'They never are. See you, Marshal.'

'I'll be around,' Stocker answered and slouched away, looking like he was about to fall asleep on his feet.

Mark booked a room at the Bella Union hotel and a boy in a fancy bell-hop's uniform shot forward to grab his bedroll. The boy escorted Mark up to his room, frank hero-worship plain on his face as he lugged the heavy bedroll.

On seeing his room, Mark decided it would be worth the money. The bed had a comforting thickness and would lick using the world for a mattress and sky for a roof. For the rest of the furnishing, the room had a table and two chairs, a clothes-closet with a key in its door; a wash-stand that had a large pitcher of water on top and a couple of clean white towels hanging on its rail.

Tossing the boy a coin, Mark told him to find a shoeshine man if the town had one. The youngster replied that he doubled in shoe cleaning and said he would be back as soon as he got rid of his dad-blasted, consarned monkey-suit the boss made him wear.

Mark took a bath in the hotel's private bath-house, had his hair trimmed, a barber's shave, changed his clothes, ate a good meal and then rested in his room until after dark. From the noise outside, he judged the town had woken up and begun to howl, so he rose from his bed, doused the light, put on his hat and gunbelt, then headed from the hotel, making for the Crystal Palace.

The girl caught Mark's eye as soon as he entered the saloon. Not because she had blonde hair that curled its ends under neatly and framed a truly beautiful face, for there were three other blondes almost as beautiful among the female workers of the saloon. Nor was it because she wore a daring and revealing costume. Compared with the others she looked demure and modest, for she did not wear the glistening, knee-long red, green, yellow, blue or other shade of dresses which clad the others, cut low on the bosom and leaving, apart from the supporting straps, the shoulders and arms bare. Her white blouse had full-length sleeves, a frilly front and buttoned up to the neck. Although it tried, the blouse could not hide the rich fullness of her breasts or the slim waist, any more than the shoe-length plain black skirt concealed the fact that under it lay richly curving hips and shapely legs. Her attitude did not draw attention to her. Unlike the other girls she did not pass among the customers, laughing, joking and making herself pleasant. Standing at the busy blackjack table, she looked calmly detached, smiling at one of the players and yet not offering him any come-on encouragement.

Yet, of all the girls in the room, she took Mark's eye the moment he entered. Anyway a man looked at her, she was one of the most beautiful women he had ever seen; five foot seven of undiluted voluptuous femininity trying to hide itself under those plain clothes.

For a moment Mark thought of crossing to the table and trying his luck—with the cards, not the dealer. He decided to take a drink first. If the liquor should be in keeping with the rest of the furnishings and equipment of the room, it would satisfy even the most discriminating taste.

At the bar Mark ordered a whisky, ignoring the invitation flashed in his direction by one of the girls. The drink proved to be mellow, of good standard and in keeping with the look of the saloon. From all appearances the owners had put plenty of money into the furnishing, equipping and stocking of the place. Mark hoped the town stayed booming long enough for them to show a profit. From the look of the crowd inside, they would likely make it.

A long board, nailed to the wall opposite to the main bat-wing doors, attracted Mark's attention, so he strolled over to examine it more closely. Reward posters were thumb-tacked to the board and the central sheet caught his eye.

WANTED
$5,000 REWARD
ALIVE ONLY
BELLE STARR.

There followed a drawing of a beautiful woman with shoulder length black hair framing her face, a Stetson hat perched on the back of her head, and a tight rolled bandana knotted at her throat. Beneath this followed a brief description. Mark wondered how accurate the drawing and description were, for he doubted if Belle Starr had ever been captured to be measured or sketched and nobody was likely to do it while she stayed free.

Under Belle Starr's name on the poster, and over the drawing, somebody had scrawled the words, 'The Toughest Gal In The West' in a sprawling hand. Mark grinned as he read the comment, wondering what Calamity Jane would say when, or if, she read it.

As he turned away from the board, Mark became aware of somebody watching him. His instincts told him at least two sets of eyes, one on either side, studied him with more than casual interest.

To Mark's right, seated alone and ignored even by the girls paid to entertain the guests, Jubal Framant, the bounty hunter, dropped his eyes towards his whisky glass as Mark glanced in his direction. The watcher at the left appeared to be one of a quartet of scrubby-jawed, gun-hung hard-cases who wore cow-hand clothes but who, in Mark's considered opinion, had never worked cattle—at least not for their legal owner. On seeing Mark turn towards them, the four men resumed their drinking and talking.

Wondering a little at their interest, and not attributing it to admiration of his up-standing, manly figure, Mark walked on. He had not failed to notice that Framant had the ten gauge lying on the table before him and wondered if the man always carried the gun with him.

Putting aside thoughts of Framant's habits, Mark headed for the blackjack table. Before he reached it, Mark saw the blonde signal and a man wearing a dealer's eye-shield, white shirt, black open vest and black pants, crossed the room to take over her seat. Giving the players a dazzling smile, the blonde crossed the room towards where a door led out to the alley between the saloon and the hotel, and a flight of stairs rose to the upper part of the building.

Mark watched her go, then he saw the four hard-cases also watching. As the blonde approached the side door, one of the quartet thrust himself up, but sank back into his chair as she walked by the door and up the stairs.

Interest in the blackjack game waned and the swarm of players faded away to leave only a handful of devotees around the table. Mark himself lost his desire to sit in on the game, and strolled over to the chuck-a-luck table where he won three dollars, took them and lost them at faro. Approaching the poker game at one of the high-stake tables, he studied the play for a time. From all he could see the game, like the others, was run fairly and the house relied only on the percentage to show them a profit.

Sitting in on the poker game, Mark played until nine o'clock. He held his own even though the company consisted of talented players, for Mark was no mean hand at the art of poker.

The blonde came into sight at exactly nine o'clock and walked down the stairs. Shoving the pile of chips to the cashier of the game, Mark told the other players he was finished. A man wearing the dress of a professional gambler gave a grin, for he had seen the direction Mark looked before making the

31

decision.

'How can the simplicity and crudity of blackjack appeal to a man of refinement when he could have the pleasure of our company, the fascination of mathematical studies and the employment of the art of bluffing while playing poker?'

'Well, I'll tell you,' Mark replied to the gambler's flow of rhetoric. 'If you gents looked like that blackjack dealer, I'd stay on.'

'Philistine,' sighed the gambler. 'Meaning no disrespect, sir. My dear mother always told me never to make unfavourable comments about a man as big as you, and I believe her words. But you'll never get rich playing blackjack.'

'Who wants to get rich?'

'The poor people do,' the gambler replied. 'Good luck with Miss Marigold Tremayne, sir. In every way.'

'I might even need it,' Mark replied, picking up the money the cashier passed to him. 'My apologies for leaving, gents.'

Crossing the room, Mark halted at a vacant place by the blackjack table and looked down at the familiar lay-out with the legend 'BLACKJACK Pays 3 to 2. Dealer Must Stand On 16 and Draw to 17'; followed by a list of bonuses which could be won by holding various combinations of cards which added up to no more than twenty-one; and finally came the warning, 'ALL TIES STAND OFF,' meaning that if the dealer and the player held the same score on their cards the bet did not count.

'What's your limit, ma'am?' he asked, buying a stack of chips and thrusting his wallet back into the pocket built on the inside of his shirt.

'Twenty-five cents to twenty-five dollars, sir,' she replied. 'This-all's a friendly little game.'

Her voice held a gentle Southern drawl which conjured up a hint of blooming magnolias, mint juleps on the lawn of some plantation mansion and coloured folks singing their plaintive songs.

'You-all from the South?' Mark asked.

'From Memphis. And you?'

'Texas, ma'am. Or may I call you Miss Tremayne?'

'Feel free,' she said, flipping the cards out to the seven men fortunate enough to get seats. 'Make your bets, gentlemen.'

A couple of saloon men moved in to take seats on either side of Marigold, acting as her look-outs and pay-off hands. Not only would the seven men be playing, but the kibitzers and on-lookers could join in, betting on the players' hands although having no say in the way the hands were played.

Watching the girl's hands flip out the cards, Mark could see no hint that she might be trying to manipulate matters in her favour. Her fingers were innocent of rings which might have tiny mirrors attached, through which she could see the value of each card as she dealt, or a spike with which to mark the cards during play. A black satin vanity bag stood on the table by her right hand, it looked a trifle larger than a lady usually carried and its jaws were open.

For a time Mark played, winning a couple of dollars, losing a couple. A plump, attractive brunette came to his side and slipped an arm around his neck, leaning on to him.

'Let me bring you some luck, handsome,' she suggested.

Then she straightened up and Mark opened his mouth to say something. An icy voice, still retaining its Southern drawl, but losing all visions of magnolia, mint juleps and singing, cracked from across the table.

'Hand it back, Lily!'

The brunette took a pace away from the table, eyes flashing angrily. She looked straight at Marigold and spat out:

'What's eating you, sister?'

'The gentleman's wallet, Lily,' Marigold answered, coming around the table and standing facing the saloon girl. 'Just hand it back, and stay away from my game in future.'

'Yeah?' Lily sneered, bristling like an alley-cat and curving her fingers so the nails stuck out like claws. 'You go to hell, you Sou——'

Without giving the slightest warning of what she meant to do, Marigold folded her right hand into a fist and lashed it around, driving the knuckles upwards underneath Lily's jaw. Lily's mouth snapped shut with an audible click that ended her speech abruptly. She might have considered herself fortunate that her tongue had not been between her teeth when the blow

33

landed, but Lily was in no condition to consider anything other than stars and flashing lights around her head.

Following Lily up as the brunette shot back and landed with a thud on her rump, Marigold bent down. She gripped Lily's ankles and lifted upwards, standing the tubby girl on her brunette head. Jiggling Lily, causing her skirt hem to slide down and expose a pair of shapely, black stocking clad legs to view, Marigold shook the wallet from the bosom of Lily's frock. Thrusting Lily's legs away from her so the brunette landed on the floor once more, Marigold bent and picked the wallet up.

'I apologise for this, sir,' she said, returning the wallet to Mark. 'The owner and the floor manager don't allow the girls to li—steal wallets from the customers. Lily only started here this afternoon and doesn't know the ropes yet.'

'I felt it go,' Mark admitted. 'But I reckon I might have had a mite more trouble getting it back than you did.'

'The feminine touch can work wonders,' smiled Marigold, her voice returning to how it sounded before speaking to Lily. 'Shall we continue the game?'

The game resumed to admiring grins and congratulations. Mark watched the girl called Marigold Tremayne with more interest for he guessed she was not all she first appeared to be. Behind them, the floor manager helped a whimpering, jaw-nursing Lily to her feet and warned her that any further pocket-picking would see her looking for another saloon where her talents would be more appreciated. She limped away, rubbing her rump and glaring over her shoulder at Marigold.

After returning his wallet, Marigold gave no sign that Mark was any more important to her than the other players. She laughed at his comments, but no more than at the other men around the table's remarks. Her attitude set the players at ease and even the losers did not seem to care about their losses.

At half past ten Marigold folded the cards and slid them into their box. She smiled at the players and waved aside their objections to the game ending.

'Why, gentlemen,' she said in a voice that would charm a bird out of a tree. 'You wouldn't want a lady to miss her beauty sleep, now would you?'

From the way they looked at her, if she asked them every man at the table would have stood guard around her hotel room to make sure nobody disturbed her rest and would have counted the task an honour to perform.

Leaving the men to cash in the chips and fold up the game, Marigold swept across the room and upstairs. Mark took his money and walked across the floor to the bar. He noticed that Framant still sat alone and was watching Marigold ascend the stairs. Thinking of Framant caused Mark to look for the four hard-cases, but they had left their table and did not appear to be in the big room.

Just as Mark ordered a drink, he saw one of the men reflected in the bar mirror. The man stood on the sidewalk before the main batwing doors, watching the inside of the saloon. He seemed to be looking for something and Mark wondered what, or who, that something might be.

Mark did not overlook the possibility that the man and his pards had decided that he, Mark, might be a profitable target for a robbery. If they felt that way, Mark reckoned they would be welcome to every red cent, or whatever else they got.

For almost fifteen minutes nothing happened. The man remained outside, never looking in Mark's direction. Mark noticed this, he also became aware that the man's eyes never left the right side of the room. Suddenly the man stiffened like a bird dog catching quail scent. Turning, he walked off to the right, disappearing from the reflection in the mirror.

Looking in the direction which appeared to have interested the man, Mark saw Marigold coming down the stairs. She wore a wide brimmed, fancy looking hat, had a shawl draped around her shoulders and carried the vanity bag hanging from her arm.

Then Mark remembered the way the hard-cases reacted when Marigold crossed the room towards the stairs earlier in the evening. Finishing his drink, Mark strolled across the room and out of the main doors. He glanced back to see Marigold wave a hand to the patrons of the saloon, then open the side door and pass through it into the alley beyond.

A muffled gasp, a startled exclamation, a thud and an angry,

35

pain-filled yelp came to Mark's ears as he approached the alley which separated the saloon from the hotel. Swinging around the corner, Mark saw two of the hard-cases gripping Marigold by the arms and trying to drag her towards the rear of the building. The third man hopped on one leg, nursing his other shin and mouthing curses.

That accounted for three of the quartet. The fourth man ought to be——

Mark side-stepped fast, twisting his body and ducking his head forward. He heard the hiss as something whistled down behind him. Not expecting to miss with his gun butt's blow, the fourth man lost his balance and stumbled forward with a startled curse. He found himself headed straight for the big Texan's back. Mark drove his elbow behind him, feeling it ram into the man's middle. To the man on the receiving end of the elbow it felt as if he had been kicked in the belly by a mule. Letting out a croak of agony, he staggered back a few steps holding his stomach and gasping.

The third man saw Mark avoid the blow, deal with their lookout and head in his direction; releasing his injured shin, but still bending forward, he hurled himself at Mark, ramming his head into the big Texan's stomach. Mark grunted, went back a couple of steps under the impact, then he bent, locking his arms around the man's body from above. Straightening up, Mark hoisted the man into the air and landed him, with legs kicking futilely, on a broad shoulder. For a moment Mark held the man, then bent his knees, straightened them and pitched the man over to smash into the hotel wall from where he collapsed in a limp pile on the ground.

A hand caught Mark's shoulder from behind and dragged him around. The fourth man had not been so badly hurt as Mark imagined for he completed the turn and smashed a fist against the side of Mark's jaw, sending him sprawling into the wall of the saloon. While the man threw a good punch, he lacked science, which was a bad deficiency when dealing with a fighter of Mark's capabilities.

Hitting the wall with his shoulders, Mark braced himself. He wondered why Marigold was so quiet. By all rules of feminine conduct she ought to be screeching her head off, screaming for help. Yet she had not made a sound, apart from that gasp and the hissing of her breath as she struggled with the two men holding her arms.

However, Mark did not have time to give much thought to Marigold's silence. His braced legs held him erect and he thrust himself forward to meet the attack of the fourth man.

Throwing up his right hand, Mark deflected the man's wild, unscientific blow over his shoulder. Almost in the same movement, Mark launched his left fist viciously into the same spot where his elbow hit earlier in the fight. The man let out a squawk of agony, folded over and presented his jaw to Mark's right hand blow, which ripped up at it like iron-filings to a magnet. Lifted erect by Mark's right hand, the man stood open and asking for a left cross to finish him completely.

Mark did not have time to throw the blow, although it would not be necessary for the man was already going down. The sound of footsteps coming at his back caught his ears. He took it to mean one of the men holding Marigold had left her to his pard and moved in to the attack.

This was only partly true. One of the men had released Marigold, swung in Mark's direction and dropped his hand to his gun butt. The girl's foot came up, rested against his rump and thrust hard. Taken by surprise, both by the push and the strength Marigold showed, the man staggered towards Mark, his gun falling from his hand.

Turning fast, Mark shot out his right hand, catching the staggering man at the side of his jaw and propelling him head first into the side door of the saloon. From the limp way the man collapsed, Mark knew he had no more worries in that direction and could concentrate on dealing with the last member of the quartet.

Swinging around, Mark prepared to move forward but saw that Marigold had the situation well in hand.

After shoving the man towards Mark, Marigold turned her attentions to the other hard-case who still stood holding her right arm. Before the man knew what to expect, Marigold launched a kick against the man's shins. He yelped in pain and

37

relaxed his hold on her enough to allow Marigold freedom to make her next move. Twisting around towards the man, she drove her right knee up to where it would do most good, or harm depending upon which end of the knee one was at.

The man's pain-filled curses died off in a yell of sheer torment. Clutching at the point where the knee struck him, he folded over like a closing jack-knife. Marigold had not finished with him. The vanity bag still swung from her arm, but she slid it free, gripped the top in both hands, pivoted and brought it around then up like a baseball batsman driving for a home run. Mark heard the solid, far too solid, thud of the bag's collision with the man's face. The hard-case spun around and piled up over the legs of the man Mark had thrown against the wall.

Light flooded into the alley as the saloon's door flew open. The floor manager and a couple of burly bouncers burst out, skidding to a stop and staring at the sight before them.

'What the——!' began the manager.

Marigold leaned against the saloon's wall, her hat awry and her shawl lying at her feet. Bending, she took up the shawl, then waved a hand to the groaning quartet.

'It's all right, Mr. Cahill,' she said. 'These—er—gentlemen—must have been drinking and became a little too impulsive.'

'Do you want for me to send for Joel Stocker and have 'em jailed?'

'No. I don't think that will be necessary. They've learned their lesson. Take them around the back, douse them with water and send them on their way.'

'Sure,' the manager agreed, nodding to the bouncers. 'Do you want one of the boys to walk you to the hotel?'

'I'm going that way myself,' Mark said, stepping forward. 'May I have the honour of escorting you, ma'am?'

'Why thank you, sir,' she replied, dropping a graceful curtsy. 'I gratefully accept your kind offer.'

After setting her hat right, Marigold offered Mark her arm and they walked together to the hotel. On learning his name, Marigold gave Mark a long, appraising glance, then suggested they had supper together.

After the meal Mark and Marigold went upstairs to the bedroom floor. Mark's room lay to the left of the stairs, but Marigold made no attempt to loosen her hold on his arm and steered him to the right.

'I don't suppose you'd care to come to my room for a few moments, would you, Mr. Counter?' Marigold asked, then her hand fluttered to her lips and she dropped her gaze to the floor. 'My, doesn't that sound forward of me? I realise I should never invite you unchaperoned to my room—But you *are* a *Southern* gentleman, aren't you?'

'Why sure, ma'am,' Mark replied. 'Darned if I'm not.'

Marigold took a key from her vanity bag and passed it to Mark. Unlocking the door, he followed her into the room, crossing to the table and turning up the lamp's wick to give better light. The room looked much like Mark's along the hall, except that it had three chairs at the table and a sidepiece as well as a closet.

A click came to Mark's ears. Turning, he saw Marigold had closed the door and twisted the key in the lock. Feeling his eyes on her, Marigold swung towards him. The demure expression and wide-eyed innocence stayed on her face, but not in her eyes.

'It blows open unless I keep it locked,' she said, coming towards the table. 'Now, what can I do to entertain you?'

Mark had a few ideas, but kept them to himself. Although puzzled at Marigold's actions, he decided to go along with her for a time. It could be the old badger game—where an irate 'husband' or 'fiancé' dashed in to demand money or satisfaction for the alienation of his woman's affections—but Mark doubted if Marigold would be involved in such a game. Or if she was involved, Mark gave her credit for being too intelligent to believe he would make a profitable victim.

Crossing to the window, Marigold looked out, then she drew the curtains and turned to walk to the side-piece. After rummaging in the top drawer, Marigold took out a deck of cards. Mark had been watching her and something told him she had picked the deck out of several in the drawer.

'I know,' she said, crossing the room towards where he sat at the table and tossing her vanity bag on to the bed. 'Teach me to play poker.'

'Here it comes!' Mark thought.

Without removing either her hat or shawl, Marigold sat facing him across the table. She opened the card box, tipped out the cards, shoved the jokers back into the box and tossed it aside. Without offering the deck to be shuffled or cut, she began to deal. This puzzled Mark for he knew she had enough card-savvy not to forget two such basic, but important, details. However, he kept his mouth shut and waited to see what happened next.

Five cards landed on the table before him and Marigold set down the remainder of the deck in the centre of the table. Mark took up his cards, watching her pick her own hand up. Fanning out his cards between his fingers, Mark blinked at what he saw. Ace, king, queen, jack, ten—all hearts.

Studying the cards, Mark felt even more puzzled. Three obvious conclusions leapt to mind: first, she had made a mistake and dealt him the hand from the cold deck intended for herself; second, that the deal was fair enough and the straight flush came out, as it might be expected to do once in 649,740 hands; third, she deliberately dealt him the hand for some purpose of her own, although he could not imagine what the purpose might be.

Whatever the answer, Mark held an unbeatable hand as the jokers, which were sometimes played as wild cards—and made it possible to have four of a kind and a joker which beat a straight flush—were in the box and out of the game.

'What stakes?' he asked, watching her face, but failing to read anything on it.

Marigold looked horrified at the suggestion.

'Land-sakes a-mercy!' she gasped. 'You surely don't think a lady would play cards for money with a gentleman—alone in her room?'

'I apologise, ma'am.'

'I think you could call me Marigold, if I may be permitted to address you as Mark.'

'Reckon we have known each other long enough for that,'

Mark agreed. 'What now, Marigold?'

Studying her cards for a moment, Marigold removed her hat and dropped it on the third chair.

'Just for fun, I'll open with my hat,' she said and lifted her eyes to his face, an open challenge in them. 'It's not like playing for money—now is it?'

'Nope,' remarked Mark, taking his Stetson from where it hung on the back of the chair. 'I'll see the hat, and raise you my bandana.'

'Are we playing table stakes?' she asked, looking coyly at him.

'It's the only way. Your bet.'

'Hum! My shawl to cover the bandana.'

Lifting her right leg on to the chair which held the stakes, Marigold drew up her skirt. The leg was strong, had shape to it under the black stockings. Mark was willing to concede that it was as good a leg as he had seen—well since early that morning. Marigold unclipped suspender fasteners and slid the stocking down, removed it and the shoes, then repeated the process with her left leg.

'My shoes and stockings to raise,' she went on. 'A gentleman would have looked the other way.'

'I was always taught never to look away from the table when playing poker,' Mark replied, hooking off his boots. 'I'll see that bet and raise.'

The raising and re-raising went on for a few more rounds and at last Marigold stared wide-eyed at the chair which held the stakes.

'Why I do declare! I just haven't another thing to raise with. Unless I can go to the closet and——'

'Huh huh! When you play table stakes, you just play for what you bring to the table with you. That's the rules, according to Hoyle.'

'Is it though? But if neither of us have anything with which to bet, what do we do?'

Mark grinned. 'Turn the cards and have us a showdown.'

Flipping over his cards, Mark exposed them before the girl's gaze. She stared down at them with complete innocence in her expression.

'Heavens to Betsy,' she said, turning over her own cards, 'You have just the same hand as I have.'

'Sure looks that way,' he agreed and reached out to turn the lamp's wick down so its flame guttered away and was gone.

'You know, Mark,' Marigold said, her chair scraping back. 'There are actually men who would take advantage of an unprotected, defenceless girl at a time like this.'

'The dirty dogs,' he replied. 'No Southern gentleman would do such a thing.'

He sensed rather than saw her, felt her hand close on his, pulling at it gently but insistently.

The night outside was dark and still. The bright stars did not show through the curtains at the windows and the room lay pitch black.

'What's that swelling on your neck?' Marigold's voice asked.

'Something bit me,' Mark replied.

Silence for a moment, then Marigold said gently, 'You mean like this?'

Laying down the razor he had collected during the night, Mark Counter washed his face. He looked in the mirror above the wash-stand and touched the oval-shaped lump on the left side of his neck, comparing it with its mate at the right. Luckily they were about level in height and his bandana would cover them. His honourable wounds might attract some attention, but he reckoned he stood big enough to handle it.

'Mark,' Marigold said, sitting on the edge of the bed and looking as sedate and demure as ever, as she fastened the top button on her blouse. 'What are we going to do today?'

Which same Mark had also been wondering about. He had his business to attend to and, despite the time being almost nine o'clock, hoped to have it done by four or five in the afternoon. By that time Calamity Jane would be back in town and Mark couldn't see her taking kindly to Marigold's competition.

'I have to go out to the Gamble spread,' he said.

She gave him a long, worried look, then smiled and brightened up a little.

'May I come along? We could hire a buggy and take a picnic basket with us.'

'That'd be great,' Mark replied. 'I'll go hire a buggy from Pop Larkin right after breakfast, and you get the basket from the kitchen.'

'Come on then,' she said eagerly, jumping to her feet and holding out her hand. 'Let's go.'

'Slow down there, gal,' he grinned. 'Let me at least put my shirt on first. We don't want folks to think anything has been going on in here, now do we?'

On his way to the livery barn, Mark saw the town marshal ambling towards him along the sidewalk. Much to Mark's surprise, Stocker did not speak, or even appear to notice him.

'She must be some gal,' Mark said.

'Huh?' Stocker grunted, halting, then he grinned sheepishly. 'Sorry, Mark, I was thinking.'

'Yeah, and when a feller's thinking that thoughtful, there's usually a right purty lil gal at the end of it.'

'For you danged Texas rebs, maybe, but not for us serious minded Montanans.'

'That being the case, how do you come to keep on having any little Montanans?' Mark asked.

'We know there's a time and place for everything,' Stocker replied. 'Right now I'm thinking about a killing.'

'Anybody I know?'

'You had a nodding acquaintance with him last night—or should I say a throwing-at-a-wall acquaintance with him?'

'That went right by me without me drawing bead on it.'

'He was one of the four yahoos you 'n' Miss Tremayne tangled with in the alley last night,' Stocker explained and, before Mark could ask the question which rose to his lips, carried on. 'Why sure, I saw it all. Was just fixing to butt in and help the lady when you arrived. Saw you could take 'em and didn't want to spoil your fun.'

'Why bless your good lil Yankee heart,' grinned Mark, then he became serious. 'Who killed him?'

'Framant.'

'Fair fight?'

'Looks that way,' Stocker admitted. 'It happened down in the Black Cat Café where that feller was having breakfast. Framant come in and told him he wanted to see him outside. The feller got up and went for his gun, started first. Framant didn't even use his shotgun, drew his Colt and put one through the feller's head.'

'I'll buy it,' Mark drawled. 'Who was the feller?'

'Don't know what name he was using in town. Framant had a wanted dodger on him under the name of Wicker. Stands to collect seven hundred dollars on him.'

'Reckon he's the reason Framant came here?'

'Maybe,' Stocker grunted, looking sleepily towards the hotel. 'Had three pards with him in the Crystal Palace when I looked in last night.'

'I never saw you,' Mark drawled.

'You was too busy a-drinking, gambling and carousing. Saw Framant sat near to them four, but he didn't make a move.'

'Like you said, there was four of them. Maybe he didn't like the odds.'

'Could be,' Stocker admitted. 'Went around looking for Wicker's three pards, but they've left town. Feller down to the livery barn on Clark Street says they pulled out right after the shooting. Wonder what they wanted from Miss Tremayne?'

'Likely figured she'd be carrying her cut of the game and figured to relieve her of it,' Mark suggested.

'Yep! Well, I got me an office to run. You fixing to ride out to Tom Gamble's place today?'

'Soon as I hire a buggy. I'm taking Marigold along and we aim to have a picnic on the way back.'

Stocker studied Mark with admiration. No other man in town, and plenty had tried, even got to the stage where they could call the Crystal Palace's lady blackjack dealer by her first name.

'How'd you do it?' he asked.

'Us rebs have to stick together in the hostile north,' Mark replied. 'And now sir, you-all causing me to keep a lady waiting.'

44

'See you,' grunted Stocker and ambled away whistling.

A grin flickered across Mark's face for he recognised Stocker's tune to be 'Dixie'.

That slow-moving, sleepy-looking marshal had a far quicker set of wits than a man would think just by looking at him. Mark knew Stocker had something on his mind. Something to do with the shooting that morning. Maybe Stocker was wondering, as Mark wondered, why a man holding a shotgun, and in the right, should take time out to draw a revolver.

On his return with the buggy, Mark found Marigold standing before the hotel. A picnic basket covered by a clean check cloth lay on the sidewalk at her feet. In her right hand she held her vanity bag, but in her left——

'I thought you might like this along,' Marigold said, tossing his Winchester to him. 'Don't look so surprised. I asked the hall clerk for your key, told him you had forgotten something. The closet seemed the most likely place for you to have left your rifle.'

'And I've got the key in my pocket,' he pointed out.

'Yes,' she replied in a tone which hinted the subject was closed.

Jumping down, Mark helped Marigold into the buggy, went to the other side and swung in beside her.

'I'll take the reins, if you wish,' she said.

This had long been the accepted western convention. The woman handled the team and left the man free to use his weapons in an emergency. Marigold appeared to be fully capable of handling the spirited horse Pop Larkin had guaranteed to be the best buggy-hauling critter in Montana and one which would eat the trip to Tom Gamble's ranch.

For the first couple of miles Mark and Marigold talked of this and that, and the girl showed a surprisingly wide range of knowledge. She clearly had done a good bit of travelling around the west. Somehow or other the conversation turned to the hold-up in Newton.

'Way I heard it,' Mark said. 'Those fellers hadn't much of an idea how to handle the job. They hit the bank at evening, when there was only one teller in it. Then they only took thirty thousand, although there was nearly three times that in the vault.'

'Maybe they didn't have time to get more,' Marigold replied.

'That's what the teller said. Allows their lookout yelled that somebody was coming and they took off like the devil after a yearling. Only when he got outside there wasn't anybody in sight and he had to go and yell for help.'

'That sounds like the gang spooked, or bad management.'

'I bet you could have handled it better.'

Just why he said it, Mark would never know. It may have been a clumsily worded compliment, meant to show his appreciation of her ability. Or it could have been a blind flash of intuition. Certainly he meant little enough by the words.

A low hiss left Marigold's lips. Her right hand dipped into the vanity bag, came out again with something in it. Mark felt that something boring into his side.

'How long have you known?' she asked; her voice sounding as it did when she saw the girl steal Mark's wallet.

'Known what?' Mark replied, looking down.

'That I'm Belle Starr.'

For a long moment Mark did not reply. He looked down at the gun boring into his side. At first glance it looked like a Navy Colt. Marigold—or Belle Starr—held it like she knew which end the bullet left from. She held the hammer back under her thumb and her forefinger curled around the trigger.

'I didn't know,' he said. 'But come to think of it, that explains a couple of things which have been bothering me since we met.'

'Such as?'

'Like why the four hard-cases were watching you last night. Why you didn't scream for help when they jumped you in the alley. If you had, and they'd been caught, they might have told Joel Stocker who you are. And like why you wanted me around last night, so they couldn't slip in on you while you slept.'

'That wasn't the only reason, Mark,' she answered. 'But it was one of them and I don't think you've cause to complain.'

'I'm not complaining. What're they after? Do they reckon

46

you know where the money from the Newton bank job is?'

'*They* reckon I know,' she agreed.

'And do you?' Mark asked innocently.

The gun bored a little harder.

'I do not!' she snorted. 'Land-sakes, Mark, do you think I'd be working with a fool bunch of green hands like that lot must have been? I wasn't even near Newton when the hit happened.'

'Where were you?'

'On the way here from my folks' place down in the Indian Nations.'

'Why here?' he went on.

'Elkhorn's growing,' she replied. 'The banker here is a fat, bulging-eyed pillar of the church with more money than it's decent for anybody but a Southern gentleman to have. So I figure to relieve him of some of it—but not with a gun. His kind fall easy, get them in the right conditions. Only he's gone east on vacation and so I'm getting things set up ready.'

'You've done it real well,' he smiled. 'Maybe just a little mite over-done, but just right for the audience. Put the gun away.'

'Why?'

'You aren't going to use it, Marigold—or can I call you Belle?'

'Feel free, if you're so sure I won't use the gun.'

'You won't use it for two reasons. One, you know I wouldn't turn you in.'

'And the other?' she asked; not moving the gun, but keeping the buggy rolling across the range.

'Those three yahoos from last night are following us.'

'Soskin's bunch?' she breathed and looked back.

Mark's left hand stabbed down, closing over the cylinder of her revolver. He dropped his thumb so it lay between the hammer and the percussion cap. The move was done only just in time. On feeling her revolver grabbed, Belle's finger closed on the trigger and she released the hammer. Instead of it striking the percussion cap and firing the chamber's contents, the hammer landed harmlessly on Mark's thumbnail.

A sudden twist plucked the gun from Belle's hand. She

47

clenched her fists and glared at Mark, then dropped her eyes to the gun.

'Oh, Mark!' she gasped, reaching out to draw the hammer back to the half-cock position. 'I'm sorry.'

'My fault,' he replied, changing his hold and placing the hammer down after turning the cylinder so the striker rested between two of the percussion caps.

For the first time Mark saw the revolver was not a Navy Colt. It appeared to be one of the copies produced by various little companies during the Civil War, when the relaxing of patent restrictions gave them a chance to sneak in and grab a quick profit. The gun looked better made than many of the copies and its cylinder had only five chambers, instead of the Navy Colt's six.

'A Manhattan, isn't it?' he asked, offering the weapon butt forward to the girl.

'Yes. I like its balance,' she replied. 'Is Soskin and his bunch on our trail, or were you only bluffing?'

'Take a peek and see.'

She obeyed, and saw.

'They're following.'

'Would a Southern gentleman lie to a lady?' Mark grinned. 'Who are they?'

'Two-bit long riders,' she answered. 'Must have seen me down in the Nations some time and recognised me. Soskin, he's the one who jumped you first, he runs the bunch. Wicker was the one you splattered against the wall. Varney's the one I used my knee on. And Carter—hey, there are only three of them after us.'

'Framant killed Wicker this morning.'

A shudder ran through Belle's frame and she moved closer to Mark at the mention of the bounty hunter's name. Ordinary men did not scare Belle Starr, but she knew Framant would kill her without thinking twice about it; shoot her in the back, if he thought he could get away with it, rather than take a chance.

'Does he know who you are?'

'No. That wanted poster in the saloon is flattering, but nothing like me,' she replied. 'What about those three?'

'What about them?' Mark countered.

'Mark,' she said quietly. 'I had nothing to do with that hold-up in Newton. I give *you* my word on that.'

'And I believe you, gal,' he replied, bending to take up the rifle. 'Let's show them we know they're there. Stop the buggy.'

Without argument, she obeyed, nursing the Manhattan on her lap as she brought the buggy to a halt. Mark stood up in the buggy and turned to face the men. His action caused them to bring their horses to a halt and show some consternation at finding their presence discovered. Taking off his hat with his left hand, holding the rifle in his right, Mark gave the men a wave 'round.

In the sign language of the range country to take off the hat and wave it from left to right around the head when looking at approaching riders meant keep away, you are not wanted. If the warning should be ignored, the next move came from Mark's rifle in the shape of a flat-nosed .44 bullet powered by twenty-eight grains of powder.

The three men clearly understood the sign. One of them reached down towards the butt of his rifle.

'Get set, gal!' Mark warned.

'I'm set,' she replied calmly. 'Anyways, they won't make a fight of it.'

If Belle did not know the men, she judged their characters correctly. Before the man reached his rifle, one of the others stopped him. They sat their horses for a moment, pointing and talking, then turned and rode away.

'You called the play right,' Mark drawled, not relaxing his hold of the rifle's foregrip and small of the butt; he had put his hat on his head after giving the wave 'round, so as to be ready for action.

'Sure. I know their kind. Especially that bunch. Cheap, nasty and not brave. They saw me at my folks' place and know how far they can push me. And they'll reckon that wherever you are Captain Fog and the Ysabel Kid won't be far away. So I don't reckon they'll fix to tangle with us.'

Mark guessed he could take Belle's summing up of the

situation as being accurate. She had been raised in the Indian Nations, Oklahoma Territory, a haunt of badly wanted outlaws of all kinds. Growing up among such men, Belle had learned to know them. Some were lions, afraid of nothing, honest within their code and lights. Others, like the trio following them, were coyotes, sneaky, treacherous, deadly if they had the other side at a disadvantage. Thinking that Mark's very able friends Dusty Fog and the Ysabel Kid might be around, those three would not risk an attack which might end in Mark's death.

This belief that where Mark Counter was, his two *amigos* were sure to be, saved Mark and Belle from trouble, just as in a future meeting it would again save their lives.*

'Told you so,' Belle remarked calmly.

'You told me,' Mark agreed. 'Let's get on our way.'

She looked at him, her face troubled.

'Are you sure you still want me to go with you?'

'Why not. You're still the girl I brought out with me—'Sides which, you-all carrying the picnic basket.'

A merry smile took the place of the troubled look. The old Marigold Tremayne tone came into her voice once more.

'Shall we go, sir?'

'It'd be my pleasure, ma'am,' Mark replied, taking his seat and putting down the rifle.

'Then we will.'

While watching Belle put the Manhattan into her vanity bag, a thought struck Mark.

'Say, weren't you scared of busting your gun when you hit that feller with your bag last night?'

'Nope,' she replied and held out the bag. 'Look.'

The inside of the bag, apart from a few inches at the top which could be drawn together and fastened, was lined with leather. More, a holster had been built into the bag so she would always find her Manhattan's butt pointing towards the bag's mouth and protected against getting the other items in the bag entangled with its mechanism.

'I wondered why that bag didn't show the gun,' he said ad-

*Told in *The Hard Riders* by J. T. Edson.

miringly. 'That's a neat bit of work.'

'My pappy made it. Let's go.'

Although Mark kept a watch on their back-trail, he saw no sign of the three men following. It seemed that they had either given up the chase, or waited for a chance to hit at the buggy on their return to town.

Mark collected the money from Gamble. The rancher and his wife insisted he and Belle stayed for lunch and Mark had been amused at how thoroughly Marigold Tremayne replaced Belle Starr in the presence of the Gambles. She charmed Mrs. Gamble, even though the rancher's wife did not look the kind of woman to treat a saloon worker as a friend, or have the cowhands of the ranch hanging around to try to win a smile from her.

Not until they were on their return trip was any mention of the previous night's episode made.

Mark reached up a hand to adjust his bandana and Belle glanced at him, a merry twinkle in her eyes.

'Who bit you?' she asked.

'You did,' Mark grinned.

'I mean first.'

'Calamity Jane.'

A smile flickered across Belle's lips as she studied his face, then died off again and a frown creased her brow.

'You're funning me,' she said, then shook her head. 'No, you're not. *Did* Calamity Jane do that to you?'

'Why sure. She's quite a gal,' Mark answered. 'Came through yesterday and she'll likely be back tonight.'

'Will she?' Belle sniffed.

There Belle let the matter drop. Her attitude showed that she did not intend to discuss the matter of Calamity Jane further. Yet Mark's instincts warned him he had better try to keep Calamity Jane and Belle Starr well separated that night.

Belle continued to talk about various things and drive the buggy. Both she and Mark kept alert for signs of the three men, but saw none. Either the trio had decided to call the game off when they saw Belle's escort, or they were lying low and waiting until conditions favoured them. Whatever the reason, Belle and Mark saw no sign of the men and reached Elkhorn without any incident.

In town Mark saw something. Calamity Jane's wagon stood behind Larkin's livery barn and her team horses in Larkin's corral. Hoping he would not come across Calamity in the street and while escorting Belle, Mark headed for the hotel.

'I'll expect to see you tonight,' Belle told Mark as they stood in the passage of the hotel's upper floor. 'You can bring a friend, if you like.'

Reading the challenge in Belle's voice, Mark groaned silently. From the way Belle looked, and what he had seen of Calamity Jane, Mark guessed one thing. Happen they got together, it wouldn't be bulls locking horns that Marshal Joel Stocker had to worry about.

'I'll see you,' he promised.

'Make sure you do,' Belle purred. 'I'd hate to have to come looking for you-all, Mark honey.'

Kissing him lightly on the cheek, Belle turned and walked towards her room. Mark watched her go and grinned as he went along the passage to his. Maybe Calamity would not find him. She might even have found herself another feller by this time.

Just as he unlocked the door, Mark heard a faint scuffling noise in his room. Almost without thinking about it, his right hand dipped and lifted his Colt from leather. Gripping the door knob, Mark pushed hard. The door swung inwards and thudded into something which gave a startled gasp. Mark had been right, he did have an unexpected visitor inside. Stepping into the room fast, Mark thrust the door closed behind him and lined his gun—on Calamity Jane.

The girl stood with her back to the wall, a look of amazement and fury on her face as she put a hand to her nose. However her eyes dropped to the barrel of the Colt lined on her and the anger left her face.

'Easy there, Mark!' she gasped. 'I forgot what you come up here to collect.'

'Huh?'

'That money. I should have known better than fool around

52

like this when you're carrying it.'

Now Mark understood. Calamity put his reaction down to his expecting trouble, or at least being prepared for trouble, while carrying the money he collected from Gamble. He did not disillusion her any, figuring the later she learned about Belle Starr the better for all concerned.

Even as he holstered his Colt, Mark found Calamity close to him, her arms around his neck and her mouth crushing against his. She moved back a shade after the kiss, cocked her head on one side and grinned at him.

'Boy, I sure put my brand on you. Right under your right— Hey! That's not on the right side! Mark Counter, what've you been doing?'

'Would you believe me happen I told you I cut myself shaving?'

'Nope,' she snorted.

'Now what do you reckon I've been doing, Calam?' he went on.

'I just wouldn't want to guess.'

There did not seem to be any point in standing talking. So Mark did the next best thing. He scooped Calamity into his arms and kissed her. While it had nothing to do with the subject under discussion, it sure ended Calamity's curiosity faster than a whole heap of lip-flapping would have.

'Let's hooraw the town tonight, Mark,' Calamity suggested when he released her and went on innocently. 'That's a swell looking saloon next door.'

'There's a couple of other nice places——'

'Sure,' Calamity interrupted, 'but they don't have blackjack games.'

'Blackjack?' Mark asked, sounding nonchalant and innocent.

'Blackjack!' Calamity repeated. 'They do tell me the dealer totes a real mean picnic basket.'

Standing back from Mark, Calamity put her hands on her hips and grinned, her even white teeth flashing. He grinned back. There was something infectious about Calamity Jane's zest for living. Maybe she did not conform to the rigid conventions imposed on women of her day, but she enjoyed every minute of her life.

Then Mark remembered how Belle Starr smiled when she invited him to bring Calamity to the saloon that night. They were two of a kind, those girls. A man couldn't judge them by the same moral standards which affected other women. Each girl lived her life the way she felt it ought to be lived, and stuck to certain rigid codes. The main difference between Belle and Calamity was in the way their lives had gone. Calamity stayed on the right side of the law, Belle strayed over its line and went against it.

'How'd you get to know?' Mark asked.

'You know how folks talk,' Calamity grinned.

'Old Pop Larkin!' Mark snorted. 'Darned old goat, never knew a livery barn owner who wouldn't talk the hind-leg off a hoss. How did you get in here?'

'Bet my door key'll open every room on the floor,' Calamity answered. 'Did she do that?'

'She's a Southern lady,' Mark replied, spreading his bandana to hide his honourable wounds.

'Does that mean yes or no?' grinned Calamity. 'Go wash up, then we'll head for the Crystal Palace and play us some blackjack.'

Mark's hopes of keeping Calamity and Belle apart did not seem very great. They sank to zero as he and Calamity prepared to go down to the hotel dining-room and have a meal before visiting the Crystal Palace.

Even as he stepped into the passage with Calamity at his side, Mark saw the door to Belle's room open. It appeared that Belle had been waiting for his appearance, for she walked towards him. They met at the head of the stairs and Belle directed a dazzling smile at Calamity.

'Why, Mark,' she said, in her Marigold voice. 'You-all never said the Ysabel Kid was in town.'

While the light in the passage was poor, it was not *that* poor. Mark knew it; Belle knew it; and, if the way Mark felt the girl's body stiffen and bristle at his side was any indication,

Calamity knew it too.

'Miss Tremayne,' Mark said, for he had not let Calamity into the secret of Belle's true identity. 'Allow me to present Miss Martha Jane Canary. Miss Canary, this is Miss Marigold Tremayne.'

Belle showed well-simulated shock and embarrassment at her 'mistake'. Her hand fluttered to her mouth and her eye took on an expression of horror as she looked Calamity up and down.

'Landsakes!' Belle gasped. 'How *could* I have made such a mistake? Why I hear the Ysabel Kid is good looking.'

Hearing the sudden intake of breath at his side, Mark prepared to grab Calamity before she jumped Belle. He did not know Calamity very well. The girl might lack some formal education, but she had a quick set of wits sharpened by her contacts with men and women of all kinds.

'That's real swell blonde hair you have, honey,' she replied. 'Why do you dye the roots black?'

'Perhaps you'd like to try to see if they are black?' Belle replied.

'Any time. Right—right nice of you to invite me and Mark to join you for supper, Miss Tremayne. We'll accept.'

The change in Calamity's speech came due to a man and woman emerging from one of the rooms. Before either girl could say another word, Mark gripped them by an arm each and hustled them down the stairs.

Mark enjoyed his supper. His worries that the girls might start a brawl in the dining-room died away. Neither Calamity nor Belle cared greatly for public opinion, but they did know any brawl started in the hotel would be ended quickly. So they contented themselves in firing barbed, biting, catty comments at each other. On the face of it, honours appeared about equal when Mark took their arms and walked them to the saloon.

Interested eyes watched them enter the saloon and cross to the bar. None of the people in the saloon failed to notice that Belle—or as they thought of her, Marigold Tremayne—did not follow her usual procedure of going upstairs to remove her hat. Also they all knew that Marigold Tremayne never accepted drinks, or went near the bar. An eagerly expectant air ran through the room, following the whispered information that the other gal was Calamity Jane.

'What'll it be, ladies?' Mark asked, resigned to the fact that there would be a clash and that he could not stop it.

'Whisky for me,' Calamity replied.

'I'll have a brandy, Mark,' Belle went on.

'*Brandy?*' Calamity gasped. 'French hawg-wash!'

'A *lady* doesn't drink whisky,' Belle replied; and getting no reaction of her emphasis of the word lady, tried another attack 'It's fattening. Of course, darling, with a figure like yours, what have you to lose?'

'You're so right,' Calamity purred back. 'At my age you can eat and drink what you like. But not when you get as old as you are.'

Once more Calamity had come back with a cat-clawing answer that evened the score with Belle. Angrily Belle's fingers drummed on the bar top while she sought for a suitable comment. Calamity grinned at her, enjoying the duel of words and not wanting it to end for a spell.

Twisting her whisky glass between her fingers, Calamity turned her back to the bar and leaned her elbows on its mahogany top. She looked around the room and her eyes came to rest on the board with the wanted posters. Crossing the room, Calamity came to a halt and studied the centre poster, cocking her head to one side and looking at the addition to the official wording.

'The toughest gal in the west!' she read in explosive, snorting words. 'Now that's not right at all.'

Watched by everybody in the room, Calamity dug a stump of pencil from her pants' pocket. She leaned a hand on the small table somebody had placed before the board and reached out to write '2nd' between the first two words of the message.

'That's better,' she said.

At the bar Belle clenched her hands into fists and started to move. Mark's hand caught her arm and held her.

'Easy, Belle,' he whispered. 'Calam doesn't know who you are. At least, I haven't told her. And Framant's sat over there watching.'

For a moment Mark thought Belle would show enough sense to at least wait until Calamity came back to the bar, then find some other excuse to start a fight. Maybe she would have, for Belle had put time and money into setting herself up in Elkhorn ready to pluck dollar-sign marked feathers from the local banker's tail, except for Calamity's next action.

'Let's just pretty old Belle up a mite while I'm at it,' Calamity went on and began to pencil in a moustache on the picture's top lip.

Calamity did not notice Belle had crossed the room to her side. Mark knew she had, for his shin hurt where she kicked him and caused him to release her arm. With a shrug, he leaned on the bar. Things had gone too far now, he could not stop the inevitable.

All eyes went to the table, watching Belle reach out and take the pencil from Calamity's fingers. Everybody, with the exception of Mark, wondered what their lady blackjack dealer meant to do and why.

Placing her hip against Calamity's, Belle thrust hard and sent the red-head staggering a few paces. Then, as Calamity caught her balance and stopped, Belle put down her vanity bag and leaned over to score out Calamity's addition to the poster.

'I've never met the lady,' Belle remarked, ignoring the interest her action aroused among the people in the room. 'But I'm sure the statement was correct.'

At his table, Framant leaned forward, studying Belle with cold eyes.

Unbuckling her gunbelt, Calamity put it down on the table by Belle's bag. She dipped her shoulder and charged Belle, sending her sprawling. Belle caught the wall and prevented herself falling, but her hat slid back and she brushed it from her head. By this time Calamity had picked up the pencil which Belle dropped and turned to the poster once more.

Belle sprang forward and Calamity twisted to face her, sitting on the table and raising her feet ready to thrust the blonde away. Only Belle did not come in range. Shooting out her hands, she grabbed for Calamity's ankles and caught hold of the cuffs of her pants instead. Calamity let out a yell of anger and surprise as Belle threw her weight back and heaved. Although she tried to grab something, Calamity failed to find anything she might grip and prevent herself being dragged from the table. She landed on the floor with a thud, but Belle had not finished. Backing away, Belle dragged Calamity across the floor, the other girl bending her legs and thrusting, trying to force herself free and grabbing at chairs or table legs to avoid being hauled along.

To the tune of laughter and shouts of encouragement, Belle dragged Calamity across the floor. There was only one way out for Calamity, although not a way a more modest young woman would have cared to take. Unbuckling her waist-belt, she tried to slide out of her pants. Their tightness held her and she grabbed the leg of the faro table as she passed it. This proved firm enough, and the table heavy enough, to anchor her down. Belle grunted and threw her weight back to try to tear Calamity free. Too late she realised what Calamity had done. The pants started to slide and Calamity gave a heave which freed herself. She left her pants in Belle's hands and lost her moccasins.

Taken by surprise, Belle staggered back, lost her footing, and sat down hard, still clinging to Calamity's pants. Calamity, still wearing her kepi, made a pretty picture, her shirt tail flapping around her shapely bare legs and giving glimpses of the new white, lace-frilled combination chemise and drawers she had bought that afternoon to prove to Mark Counter that she was a real lady at heart. They were the latest fashion among show people, short legged and daring, and Calamity had the sort of figure to set them off to their best advantage.

Coming to her feet, Calamity flung herself at Belle, landing on the blonde before she made her feet. Grabbing down Calamity gripped Belle's skirt and heaved at it with all her strength. Belle gave a yell, tried to twist herself free and in doing so threw the final pressure on the tortured cloth. With a ripping sound, the skirt tore from waist almost to hem. Rearing back, her trophy firmly gripped in both hands, Calamity tore the skirt away, rolling Belle right over and leaving her black stocking clad legs, with frilly red garters, and black drawers as brief and attractive as Calamity's own, exposed by the hem of her blouse.

Once more Calamity sprang into the attack, her hands closing on Belle's blouse. Belle forced herself up, her own hands gripped Calamity's shirt neck and her eyes met Calamity's.

'Try it!' Belle hissed. 'And I'll peel you raw.'

For once in her life Calamity Jane backed down from a challenge. Nothing she had seen about the blonde told her Belle would not carry out the threat of stripping Calamity naked, even if it meant losing every stitch of clothing she wore in the process. Modesty did not prevent Calamity from calling Belle's bluff. She knew that if they did start to remove more clothing, the owners of the saloon would stop the fight. A hair-yanking brawl between two women was common enough for the owners to let one go on, it was regarded as being a bit of added entertainment for the customers. But there were limits to how far the owners dare let such a fight go.

So Calamity released her hold of Belle's blouse, for she did not want what promised to be a good fight stopping. Not until she had handed that blonde hussy the licking of her life as a warning to stay away from Calamity Jane's man.

While releasing Belle's blouse, Calamity made up her mind how to handle the situation. She had been taught to fight by soldiers and freighters, men who showed her the value of a fist over hair-yanking. In more than one saloon brawl this knowledge had given her a decided edge over the other girl.

'First one into her belly,' Calamity thought. 'Then the next to her jaw.'

The fist drove into the stomach. Up came the other hand and caught the down-dropping jaw——

And Calamity hit the floor on her rump, her head spinning. She had learned an important lesson. The other girl also knew how to use her fists.

Now it was Belle's turn to become over-confident. She sprang forward and drew back her foot. Calamity showed that she had learned other lessons in the art of self-defence. Quickly she hooked her left foot behind Belle's left ankle, placed her right foot on Belle's left knee, pulled on the ankle and pushed on the knee. Caught with her other leg raised for the kick, Belle could not stop herself going over, but she broke the worst of her fall with her hands.

They came up and flung themselves at each other. For a time it might have been two men fighting. They used their fists, wrestling throws and holds, none of the usual tactics of a pair of fighting women. The watching crowd yelled their encouragement and already the house gamblers were taking bets on the results. Not that they had any clear indication of which girl would win for they seemed evenly matched.

'Howdy, Mark,' a sleepy voice said.

Turning from watching Belle drive Calamity back into the crowd with a battery of punches, Mark looked at the speaker.

'Howdy, Joel. What're you fixing to do about this? Speaking as a duly appointed officer of the law that is.'

'Ain't doing nothing,' Stocker replied, watching the crowd scatter as the two girls spun round and through them. 'My job's to keep the peace and I wouldn't reckon anybody's breaking it.' He paused and eyed Mark with that same sleepy gaze. 'How do you figure in on this?'

'Could say I brought them together,' Mark admitted. 'But, knowing Calamity, she'd've come in here and tangled with somebody, and B—Marigold's the most likely one for her to pick from.'

'Huh huh!' Stocker grunted. 'Figured it that way meself. Only I wouldn't have expected Miss Marigold to be the one. Allus struck me as being a real lady.'

The 'real lady' was at that moment swinging Calamity around by the hair and sent her sprawling across the room to hit the wall. Calamity seemed dazed by the impact and stood with legs apart, back braced against the wall.

'Best stop——!' Stocker began as Belle moved in towards Calamity.

His words stopped for Belle did not deliver a crippling kick at her helpless opponent. Instead she stopped and started to slap Calamity's face, alternating hands and swinging the other girl's head from side to side. The pain of the slaps revived

Calamity and she thrust forward, her hands tangling into Belle's hair. If Belle's yell of pain was anything to go by, the grip Calamity had on her hurt.

The fight developed into a more female brawl with Calamity's hair-yanking opening. Reeling backwards, the two girls spun across the room in a flailing tangle of arms and legs, pulling hair, swinging slaps and punches. One piece of feminine fighting was denied them. Calamity's work did not tend to allow her to grow long nails, and Belle knew men objected to playing with a gambler who had long enough fingernails to make identifying nicks on the cards.

Even without scratching, the two girls put on a tolerable example of the art of bar-room brawling. On their feet, or rolling over and over on the floor, they went at it for almost fifteen minutes without a pause.

Then Belle was flat on her back and Calamity dropped to kneel astride her with the intention of grabbing her hair and bouncing her head on the floor. Belle knew as well as Calamity what the red-head intended to do. Bringing up her legs, Belle hooked them under Calamity's armpits from behind, almost as if she was trying to perform a full nelson with legs instead of arms. Calamity gave a yell as she went over backwards, but carried on rolling to land on her feet and dropped down. She landed on Belle's raised feet, felt them against her chest and knew what to expect even if she could not prevent it happening.

Thrusting up with her feet, Belle sent Calamity flying backwards across the room to land on a table top. Calamity saw Belle coming at her and rolled back off the table, throwing it over. It landed on Belle's right foot, the edge thudding down on her toes. Belle squealed in pain. She was still hopping on her other foot when Calamity rounded the table.

Calamity swung herself around, her fist coming in a circle which ended on the side of Belle's jaw. The crowd scattered as Belle went sprawling across the room, hit the bar and clung to it. Dazedly Belle watched Calamity come forward, a chair gripped in her hands ready to strike. The blonde sobbed for breath, she tried to force herself from the bar to avoid the blow.

'We'd better stop Calam,' Mark said to Stocker.

'Ye—Dabnad it, look there.'

Instead of lifting the chair and crashing it on to Belle, Calamity threw it to one side. She staggered to the bar and Belle crouched ready to fight back.

'H—hold it!' Calamity gasped.

'H—had e—enough?' Belle replied in surprise.

'No—no—Feel like a drink.'

'A—and me. Fred, whisky and brandy.'

'What do you make of that?' Stocker asked.

'Those gals sure must be enjoying the fight. Belle could have finished Calamity against the wall there, and Calamity could sure have sung B—Marigold to sleep with that chair. There's been other times when they could have used a knee, or foot and didn't.'

He hoped Stocker had not noticed the slip he made in his words. Not by a flicker of emotion did Stocker's sleepy face show he had noticed Mark say 'Belle' instead of Marigold. However, Mark would have been surprised if he had seen anything on the marshal's face even if he noticed the slip.

The girls finished their drinks. Watching them, the crowd grew expectant once more. Most of the onlookers had felt disappointed when they saw the fight come to such an indecisive end. Now they realised that the fight had not ended, but that the opponents were just taking a drink while regaining their strength for a resumption of hostilities.

From his place at the end of the bar, Mark watched the girls and felt puzzled. While he could understand Calamity grandstanding in such a manner, it surprised him that Belle would act in the same way.

'My turn,' Calamity said, slapping her empty glass on the counter. 'Same again, Fred.'

'Here's looking at you,' Belle replied, raising her glass. 'Not that you'd be seeing much with that eye.'

'If it's worse than yours, it's bad,' Calamity grinned. 'Whooee, that was a mean one you caught me with at the beginning. Say, where'd you learn to wrestle?'

'From an Indian. Have you finished?'

'Sure.'

Setting down her glass, Calamity lashed out her fist, driving it into the blonde's jaw and spinning her in a circle to hit the bar. Belle swung her arm sideways, the heel of her hand driving into Calamity's ribs and stopping her forward rush.

For thirty minutes by the bar-room clock the fight raged, from start, to when the two girls, tottering on legs which looked like heat-buckled candles, gave Stocker cause to think he might have to end the fight.

'I'll have to stop 'em if they go any further, Mark,' the marshal said as Calamity staggered from a push and left her torn shirt in Belle's hands.

'Looks that way,' Mark replied, for Belle had lost her blouse.

It could not go on. The girls were on their last reserves of strength. Where their slaps had sounded like whip-cracks on landing, they now barely made a sound and on reaching flesh seemed more in the nature of a gentle push.

Hooking a leg behind Calamity, more by accident than design, Belle tripped her. They were locked in each other's arms and could do nothing to stop themselves falling. However, Calamity managed to twist herself so they both hit the floor. Their arms relaxed and they rolled apart, lying flat on their backs, breasts heaving, mouths hanging open.

'Get the doctor,' Mark said. 'I'll get the gals to their rooms.'

'Sure,' Stocker replied, 'I'll—Man, just look at that.'

Incredibly, in view of the gruelling brawl they had just fought, Belle was trying to sit up. Beside her, Calamity rolled over and forced her hands against the floor. Belle did not look the elegant creature who dealt blackjack. Her once immaculate hair now resembled a tangled, dirty, blonde wool mop. The face was streaked with sweat and dirt, its left eye blackened and puffed almost shut, the nose bloody. Her most serious injury was a bite on the left hand, gained when the fight was at its height. She had lost one stocking but the garter remained, a slash of colour against the white of her leg. The other stocking had little foot, no knee and hung in tatters. Calamity was just as badly bruised and battered, dirty and exhausted.

Sensing a climax approaching, the crowd fell silent. Quite a lot of money depended on the outcome of the fight.

Through the whirling mists that seemed to surround her, Calamity saw Belle sitting up. Drawing on her last ounce of strength, Calamity thrust herself forward, shooting her fist at Belle. Everything went black for Calamity the instant before her fist landed. Carried by the impetus of her body, the fist caught Belle at the side of the jaw and Belle flopped on to her back. Calamity's limp form dropped on to Belle's and they lay there without a move.

'What'd you call that, Mark?' Stocker asked.

'I'd say a stand-off. Go get the doc, I'll tend to the girls.'

Excitement burst over the crowd, cheers and shouts of laughter ringing out. The floor manager called for drinks on the house and there was a rush to the bar. Mark did not join it. He crossed to where the saloon-girls, eight in all, stood in a group, knowing they were not included in the manager's largesse.

'How'd you gals like to earn five dollars each?' he asked.

'*All of us?*' gasped the boss-girl, a big, beautiful black-haired woman, eyeing Mark with doubt and admiration.

'Not for that,' Mark replied. 'I want you to tote Marigold and Calamity to their rooms at the hotel.'

'Sure we'll do it,' grinned the boss-girl. 'I'm not doing anything important after that though.'

'I wish I wasn't,' drawled Mark and took out his wallet. 'Take them in the back way.'

Four girls took Calamity by the arms and legs, raising her from the floor, while the other four lifted Belle. To admiring cheers the battered girls were carried out of the saloon's rear door.

'Here, Mark,' Stocker said, coming over with a couple of glasses in his big hands. 'I fetched you a drink along. Being a duly appointed officer of the law, I don't get the give-away stuff.'

One sip at the contents of his glass told Mark that Stocker spoke the truth. Like most saloons, the Crystal Palace kept a stock of cheaper whisky to be used when the boss announced drinks on the house. The liquor in Mark's glass tasted like best stock. It seemed that, like Mark, the owners of the Crystal Palace were not fooled by Stocker's sleepy-acting ways and knew how to show a good lawman their appreciation.

'Man, that came from a customer's bottle,' Mark said, then noticed Stocker looking around the room. 'What's wrong?'

'Nothing much. I was wondering where Framant has gone.'

Setting down his glass on the nearest table, Mark looked around the room. He had last seen the bounty hunter before the fight started and Framant was showing considerable interest in Belle's actions.

Without a word to Stocker about his fears, Mark turned on his heel and headed across the room towards the main doors of the saloon.

There was considerable excitement at the hotel as Mark entered its reception hall. Although the girls had carried Belle and Calamity in through the rear door, they still had to bring their groaning burdens to the front and up the stairs. In doing so, they attracted attention, their chatter bringing residents from the dining- and sitting-rooms to see what was happening.

Shoving through the crowd, Mark found the desk clerk, a plump, pompous young man, blocking his path.

'May I ask just what is going on, Mr. Counter?' the clerk said as Mark started up the stairs. 'This is not the sort——'.

His words trailed off as Mark's hands gripped him by the lapels of his coat then lifted. The man's feet left the floor and kicked futilely as Mark set him aside. Gurgling incoherently, the clerk turned and stared after Mark as he went up the stairs. It shook a man to be picked up as if he was a baby and set aside in so casual a manner.

'Just set the blonde down, you calico cats,' a voice said from the passage above. 'I'll tend to her.'

Three strides brought Mark to the head of the stairs and he turned the corner. It seemed he had not come a moment too soon.

'Hold it, Framant!' Mark snapped.

Standing with his shotgun in his left hand, Framant looked towards the big blond Texan. The saloon-girls had laid Belle down and fallen back, flattening themselves against the walls and stared in fear at the bounty hunter.

'Keep out of this, cow-nurse,' Framant replied. 'I'm taking her down to Newton with me.'

'How long have you known who she was?' Mark replied, watching the hand which gripped the small of the shotgun's butt, its forefinger on the trigger.

'Had me suspicions since I come in,' Framant growled.

'And left it until now to take her?'

'I don't take chances,' Framant answered. 'Now just get out of my way.'

Framant bent down, reaching for Belle's arm.

'Leave her lie,' Mark said quietly.

'Yeah!' the bounty hunter replied, straightening again. 'Why? 'Cause you want to take her in?'

'Nope. But you hadn't the guts to stack against her while she was on her feet and you'll leave her now. Or take her through me.'

A grin twisted Framant's lips as he studied the big Texan.

'That can be done easy enough.'

He made a gesture to lift the shotgun in his left hand. Mark watched the move—then remembered something. Another man had faced Framant that day, and he died with a revolver bullet not a charge of buckshot in him.

Dipping his free hand, Framant closed his fingers around the butt of his revolver and started to lift it. Just like all the others, that big Texan had been watching his shotgun, not the revolver, and would shortly pay the penalty for crossing Jubal Framant.

Too late the bounty hunter saw his mistake.

Mark's right hand dipped, the Army Colt flowed from the holster in a liquid smooth move. Cocking back the hammer as the gun lifted, Mark sent a bullet into Framant's head; holding his gun waist high and using instinctive alignment for he did not have time to take aim in any other way.

Shock, amazement and terror warred among themselves for expression on Framant's face an instant before Mark's bullet struck between his eyes and wiped off all expression. In that last moment Framant knew he had met a man who saw through his trick and beat him.

A girl screamed. Another turned, hiding her face in her hands. Framant's shotgun fell from his left hand, the revolver slipped from between the fingers of his right. Its barrel had barely cleared leather and it clattered to the floor, beating Framant's lifeless body by a split second.

Feet pounded on the stairs behind Mark. Stocker appeared at the stair-head, travelling with a speed which belied his usual lethargic pose. Holstering the big Dragoon, Stocker looked down at Belle, then towards Framant.

'What happened?'

'Framant threw down on me,' Mark replied. 'And I found out what he toted the shotgun for.'

Turning, Stocker ordered the people who started to flock upstairs back down again. The cold tone which replaced his sleepy voice warned the crowd that they had best do as he told them without argument.

'How'd you mean, Mark,' he said, after Mark had carried Belle into her room where she and Calamity now lay side by side on her bed. 'You know why he toted the shotgun.'

'It was a plant. Kept the other feller watching his left hand, while his right fetched out the gun. It near on caught me, only I remembered that feller he shot this morning and wondered why in hell he'd chance drawing a revolver when he held the scatter.'

The local doctor arrived, having pushed his way through the crowd, showing a complete disregard for social standing as became the only medical man in almost five hundred miles.

'I'd best see about moving Framant,' Stocker remarked, as the doctor went into Belle's room.

'Sure,' Mark replied. 'I'll go pick up the gals' belongings from the saloon. They'll not be feeling like bothering, way they're all tuckered out.'

'Go ahead. You leaving town in the morning?'

'Sure,' Mark agreed.

'Nothing personal, but I'll not be sorry to see you go. Be pleased to have *you* back any time—but come alone.'

Mark grinned. Having served under Dusty Fog as a deputy marshal, he could appreciate Stocker's point of view.

At the saloon, Mark gathered up Belle's vanity bag and Calamity's gunbelt. The owner of the saloon himself came over, grinning broadly.

'You sure brought our Miss Tremayne out, Mark,' he said.

That the man knew his name did not surprise Mark. A saloon-keeper always tried to keep in touch with important people who used his establishment, and without false modesty Mark admitted he was well enough known to warrant such interest.

'I've got their clothes bundled up back of the bar,' the man went on. 'Reckon they might need them, although apart from Calamity's pants and moccasins and Miss Marigold's shoes, there's not much they'll be able to wear.'

'I'll take them anyways,' Mark grinned. 'What they don't want I'll have built into the suggan I had made after the battle in Bearcat Annie's.'*

'Was you—sure, that was while Cap'n Fog was town marshal in Quiet Town.'

The battle in Bearcat Annie's saloon, where three female deputies fought it out with the saloon-keeper and her girls to allow Dusty Fog, Mark and the other male deputies a chance to enter the saloon and arrest a bunch of gunmen, had become a legend in the west. Mark had gathered the remnants of clothing and had them made into a suggan, a thick patchwork quilt, which he now carried in his bedroll.

Mark intended to have Calamity's shirt and Belle's blouse and skirt added to the other material, as a memento of the occasion.

For a time Mark stayed at the saloon, talking with the owner and a number of prominent business men of the town. The doctor arrived with word that neither girl had sustained any really serious injury, although Belle's hand would always carry the mark of Calamity's teeth.

'Reckon I've lost my blackjack dealer for a spell,' grinned the owner. 'But, man, what a fight.'

*Told in *Quiet Town* by J. T. Edson.

Soon after Mark left the saloon, carrying the girls' belongings with him. On his way to the hotel, Mark thought of Stocker's apparent lack of interest in why Framant should be in the building. This did not fool Mark. If Stocker guessed the truth, and Mark reckoned he did, he was holding off until Belle had recovered from the brawl before seeing her.

How long Mark had been asleep, he did not know. Lying in bed in the darkness of his room, he waited for a repetition of the sound which woke him. Reaching out his right hand, he drew a Colt from where his gunbelt lay on the chair.

The door of his room inched open and he could see a shape, darker than the surrounding blackness, at it.

'Mark!' a voice whispered.

'Come ahead, Belle,' he replied, swinging from the bed and reaching for his levis.

Belle entered the room and closed the door behind her, standing still until Mark drew the curtains and lit the lamp. In its light, Mark studied Belle and a grin of admiration flickered to his lips. She wore a flimsy robe he had seen her in the previous night, but her hair and face still bore traces of the fight even though the doctor had tried to clean her up. The admiration came as a tribute to her courage, not her appearance. After that brawl, Belle could still get up and walk, if hobbling painfully.

'I'm in trouble, Mark,' she said, limping to the bed and flopping down to sit on it.

'You sure look that way,' he agreed.

'Framant saw me. I'm sure he knows who I am. And so does Joel Stocker.'

'Don't worry about Framant,' Mark said gently. 'He was waiting up here for you.'

Which explained itself to anybody who took a minute to think about it. The fact that Mark was still alive, and she still had her freedom, told Belle all she needed to know.

'Joel Stocker knows,' Belle went on. 'He's not as du——'

Her words stopped abruptly as the room door opened. Mark caught up his Colt ready to use, and Belle reached towards the second gun.

'I thought I'd find you here!' Calamity said from the door-way.

She stood for a moment, eyeing Belle with a mixture of anger and admiration. The last thing Calamity felt like doing was going visiting in her present state of health.

'Shut the door and keep your voice down, Calam,' Mark snapped. 'Belle's in trouble.'

'I'll say she is,' Calamity replied, closing the door. B—Belle?'

'Belle Starr, the moustached lady,' Belle grinned.

'You mean—you—I—you're——'

'Whatever that means, I'm still Belle Starr.'

Crossing the room, Calamity flopped down beside Belle, staring at the other girl and holding the blanket draped around her shoulders.

'Belle Starr!' she said wonderingly, then held out a hand. 'I'm sorry, Belle, I didn't know about it when I went to the poster. Shucks, if I had, I'd've kept away and found some other way of starting the brawl so I could hand you your needings. Say, who won?'

Both girls looked at Mark expectantly, for neither could remember the details of the final stages of the fight and each felt sure she had been beaten.

'It was a stand-off,' he replied. 'With both of you plumb tuckered out.'

'That's a good way to be,' Belle said and took Calamity's hand. 'No hard feelings, Calam?'

'Not if you haven't. Say, was you ever in Fort Baker? There's a gal——'

'Let's leave old home week until later,' Mark put in. 'Belle's got troubles enough without that.'

Possibly for the first time in her life Calamity looked contrite.

'Gee, I'm sorry, Belle. It's all my fa——'

'Forget it, Calam. It's as much my fault as yours. I didn't have to let you needle me right then.'

'Framant won't forget it,' Calamity pointed out.

'He's no worry,' Belle replied. 'I'm thinking about Joel

70

Stocker. He knows I'm Belle Starr now, and Joel's too good a lawman to overlook it. He might not like doing it, but he'd take me and send me back to Newton.'

Clapping a hand to her forehead, Calamity groaned. 'And I'm the darned fool who caused it all. We'll just have to pull out of town tonight.'

'Neither of you are in any shape to ride,' Mark pointed out. 'Even if Belle had a hoss.'

'Which I haven't.'

'You couldn't handle my bloodbay, the condition you're in,' Mark went on, looking at Belle. 'And even if you could, the saddle's locked in Larkin's office.'

'Will the marshal be coming after you tonight?' asked Calamity.

'Not if I know Joel. He'll be around in the morning when I've had time to get around to talking and walking.'

'Then we've a chance,' Calamity grinned. 'All we need is a feller with a strong back—which same we've got right here.'

On hearing Calamity's plan, the other two agreed it might work. They wasted no time in preparing to put it into action.

'Calam, honey,' Mark grinned, putting on his shirt. 'You pair know of more ways of making me lose sleep than anybody I know.'

Mark was just boosting a sick, sore and groaning Calamity on to the box of her wagon ready to leave town when Marshal Stocker strolled up. It was morning and the wagon stood ready to roll, Mark's bloodbay stallion waiting saddled for its master to mount.

'Morning, Miss Calamity, Mark,' he greeted. 'See you're fixing to leave.'

'Why sure,' Calamity grinned, settling down on the seat and reaching for the reins. 'Say, have you-all seen that blonde gal around? I bet she's still in bed after the whupping I handed her.'

A sleepy smile twisted Stocker's lips as he looked at Calamity.

'Sure was a whupping,' he grinned. 'She never laid a hand

on you.'

'Then why'n't you stop the crowd, somebody knocked hell out of me. You tell her she'll know better'n tangle with Calamity Jane next time.'

'I'd do that. Only she's up and gone.'

'Gone?' Calamity gasped. 'How'd you mean, gone?'

'Must've left during the night. Took her trunk and belongings and gone. Are you travelling empty, Calamity?'

'Just some of my own stuff is all.'

Walking to the rear of the wagon, Stocker lifted the cover and looked inside. Apart from a fair sized oblong object covered with a buffalo hide, the wagon contained nothing. Turning back, Stocker stepped over a pile of buffalo chips and logs lying between the wagon and the corral fence. Calamity looked back at him.

'You don't reckon I'd be hiding her in the back of my wagon after what happened last night, do you?' she asked.

'Nope, I reckon not,' Stocker answered. 'I'll drift along and see if I can find her around town. See you, Mark.'

'Yeah, I know,' Mark drawled. 'You'll be around.'

Throwing a warning glance at Calamity, Mark swung aboard his saddle and the bloodbay walked forward. Calamity closed her mouth, took up the reins and started her wagon moving. For a few seconds Stocker stood watching them go, then he grinned, kicked the buffalo chips with his toe and slouched away.

Five minutes passed. Then three men came from a side alley where they had been watching the corral. Soskin, the leader of the trio of hard-cases walked to the corral and looked around him. Behind him, Varney and Carter stood with puzzled expressions on their faces.

'Looks like Belle's slipped out of town,' Varney growled.

'How?' Carter replied. 'You saw Calamity, she could hardly stand. Reckon Belle'd be in any better shape?'

'She went all right,' Soskin put in, pointing down. 'And that's how, only Stocker was too dumb to see it.'

'What're we going to do?' asked Carter.

'Trail that wagon from well back. Then when they make

camp for the night move in on them.'

For three miles Mark and Calamity held an even pace, leaving the town behind them. They did not hurry, but Calamity repeatedly twisted around to look at their back trail. She noticed that Mark took no such precautions and grunted.

'What's wrong, Calam?' he asked.

'Reckon the marshal won't be following us?' she replied.

'He'll not. His jurisdiction ends on the edge of town.'

'We sure put one over on him,' she chuckled.

'Reckon we did, huh?'

'Don't you?'

'Nope.'

They were approaching a ford over a wide, though shallow river. Grinning at Mark, Calamity hauled back on the reins and slowed her team's pace.

'Shall I stop here or the other side?' she asked. 'I reckon I'll go through——'

'You do and we'll take up where we left off last night!' Belle's voice yelled from under the wagon.

Laughing, Calamity brought the wagon to a halt, applied the brake and slowly climbed down from the box. Bending, she looked under the wagon to where Belle's face showed from inside the possom belly; a sweat and dirt streaked face for the rawhide sheet had never been meant to carry passengers.

Unlike Calamity, Belle had not changed clothes, but wore a blanket over the outfit she had worn the previous night, or rather ended the fight in. She left the possum belly and groaned.

'Whooee!' Calamity grinned. 'That's a right fetching perfume you're wearing, Belle gal.'

'*Eau-de-*buffalo chips they call it,' Belle replied. 'The sooner I have a bath and change, the happier I'll be.'

'Take the wagon across, Calamity,' Mark ordered. 'Then I'll ride circle while you both have a bath.'

'Yo!' Calamity replied. 'Are you riding over, Belle?'

'Not me. I'm going straight in.'

That night Calamity and Belle looked much better as they sat around the camp fire. They had bathed and combed out the

73

tangles of their hair at the river, and Belle put on black shirt, a pair of levis and dainty high heeled riding boots collected from her trunk which Mark brought to the wagon from the hotel in the small hours of the morning.

'How about coming into Hays with me, Belle?' Calamity asked. 'You'll have to pick up a horse.'

'That's not a bad id——'

'Just sit right where you are!' a voice interrupted, coming from the blackness beyond the fire. 'We've got you under our guns.'

Sitting down, Mark could not have reached his guns quick enough to do anything other than get himself killed. Calamity's hip hurt from some part of the fight and she had removed her gunbelt, it lay just too far for her to reach it. Closer lay her blacksnake whip, but she knew better than make a move for it until the person on whom she meant to use it came into range. Belle had her vanity bag hanging from her wrist, but she doubted if she could get her Manhattan out fast enough to give the others a chance.

Soskin and his two men prowled forward into the fire-light, their guns in their hands.

'Stay still, Counter,' Soskin ordered. 'We want Belle.'

'You won't get her,' Calamity replied, and started to rise.

'Stay down, Calamity!' growled Soskin. 'I ain't the sort to worry about shooting a woman, especially one who can handle a gun like you can.'

'Do it, Calam!' Belle snapped. 'He means what he says.'

All the time the others spoke, Mark watched for a chance, but it did not come. While Soskin and his men would have made one of the big-name outlaws retch, they knew enough about the basic details of their trade to avoid giving chances to the people they covered. Faintly, yet distinctly, Mark heard the distant sound of hooves. Two riders at least and it sounded as if they were coming this way. As yet none of the others appeared to have heard the sound. Mark wondered who the approaching travellers might be. They came from the south, yet they might be friends of Soskin. Or they could be outlaws who would throw in with Soskin for a chance at the mythical loot of the Newton bank job. Even if they were just chance drifters, Mark did not care to have them horning in, for there would be no telling which way they would turn if they rode in and learned that Belle Starr was here.

'You know what we want, Belle?' Soskin asked.

'No.'

'Don't play smart!' Varney snorted. 'We want the money you stashed away after the Newton job.'

'All of it?'

'Naw,' Soskin answered. 'We'll play fair with you. Split it four ways.'

'And these two?' Belle went on.

'We'll have to leave 'em so they can't bother us any.'

'Sounds a good idea,' Belle said quietly, getting to her feet. 'How about Captain Fog and the Ysabel Kid?'

A grin creased Soskin's face. 'We circled Elkhorn yesterday and never saw hide nor hair of them. Happen he is Mark Counter, he's working alone.'

'You could be right at that,' Belle purred, then looked at Calamity. 'Sorry about this, Calam, but I just never could stand playing the losing side.'

Sudden fury boiled up inside Calamity and she looked at Belle. They had been on the best of terms all day, laughing and joking, discussing the high points of the fight, talking over their lives. Now Belle was calmly going to side with the three men who planned to kill them.

'Why you cheap, lousy, double-dealing——!' Calamity began.

Watching Belle move towards Calamity, Mark tensed slightly. He saw the trio of hard-cases were paying more attention to the girls than to him. Mark did not know what Belle's game might be, but he guessed something more than a change of sides lay behind her words.

Stepping towards Calamity, Belle drew back her foot. 'I owe you something from last night,' she said.

Just in time Calamity saw Belle's good eye close in a wink. Then the foot lashed out at her body. Yet it did not come as fast as it might and Calamity had time to shoot up her hands, catch Belle's ankle and twist.

'Get clear of her, Belle!' Soskin bellowed, suddenly seeing the danger.

He saw it a full five seconds too late. Calamity twisted Belle's ankle and caused Belle to stagger. At the same moment Calamity released the ankle, rolled right over and grabbed up her whip.

'It's a trick!' Varney yelled, his gun lining on the staggering Belle.

Several things all started to happen, shattering the group around the fire into sudden and violent action.

Mark flung himself to the left, landing on his side with his right hand Colt drawn and cocked. Varney's revolver was already lining on Belle when Calamity brought her hand sweeping forward. The lash of the blacksnake whip curled out to wrap around Varney's ankle. Still lying on her side, Calamity heaved back on the whip handle and Varney felt his foot jerk upwards. He fired a shot, but it went harmlessly into the air.

Snarling in a mixture of rage and fear, Carter threw down on Calamity; but Belle had her Manhattan out of her vanity bag's holster. She regained her balance and fired a shot which caught Carter in the shoulder, spun him around and put him out of the fight.

Which left Soskin. Never the quickest of thinkers, the man stood hesitating and trying to decide who to throw lead at first. When dealing with a man like Mark Counter such a show of indecision could prove dangerous. Mark's Colt roared while Soskin's still wavered uncertainly. The gun was batted from Soskin's hand for Mark had time to take careful aim and did not wish to shoot to kill.

For a moment Varney stood gun in hand, for he had not fallen when Calamity caught his ankle. The whip's lash writhed away, curling behind Calamity as she prepared to strike again. At the same instant Varney found himself facing the barrel of Belle's Manhattan and Mark's Army Colt.

Out drove the whip's lash again, this time with Calamity on her knees and able to get full power behind it. Varney howled as the lash curled around his wrist. He felt as if the bones had been crushed and the gun fell from his hand.

'Which just about ends that,' Calamity drawled, shaking free her whip. 'Why in hell didn't you wig-wag me, Belle gal, let me know what you aimed to do?'

'I reckoned you'd react better without,' Belle grinned. 'And I was right.'

Then they heard the thunder of rapidly approaching hooves.

'Hey, Mark!' yelled a voice. 'Any more of them around?'

'Hundreds,' Mark called back. 'That's why we're stood out here all lit by the fire. Come on in and stop that yelling.'

Two men rode into the light of the fire. One was a tall, slim, almost babyishly-innocent faced youngster dressed all in black, with a walnut handled Colt Dragoon at his right side, an ivory hilted bowie knife at the left. He sat on a huge white stallion with an easy, almost Indian grace, a Winchester rifle in his hands. The other was smaller, not more than five foot six, with dusty blond hair, a handsome, though not eye-catching face. Belted at his waist were a pair of white handled Army Colts, their butts turned forward for cross-draw. He rode a seventeen hand paint stallion with two letters burned on its flank; an O and a D, the edge of the O touching the straight line of the D.

'Howdy, Dusty, Lon,' Mark greeted, 'wasn't expecting to see you up here.'

'We got through our business in Newton early,' Dusty Fog replied, swinging from his paint's saddle. 'So we reckoned we'd ride up and find out how you were doing.'

'Which same it looks like you're doing all right,' the Kid went on, tossing a leg over the saddlehorn and dropping from his white stallion.

Calamity stared at the Rio Hondo gun wizard, Dusty Fog, for a long moment. It seemed Mark had told the truth when he claimed Dusty Fog was a small man. After knowing Dusty for only a few minutes, she never again thought of him as being small.

'What started all this?' Dusty asked. 'We saw the fire and rode over to ask if we could camp the night. Saw you were in a

77

tight spot, but you handled it before we reached you.'

While Calamity patched up Carter's arm, Mark told Dusty everything. The small Texan threw a look at Belle, then to where Calamity stood working on, and cursing, the groaning man. From the look of the girls, it had been some fight, yet they appeared to be friendly enough.

'So they wanted you to show them where the loot of the Newton bank job is hidden, Belle,' he said. 'How'd they plan to get you there?'

'We brought Wicker's hoss along. It's with our'n out on the range,' Soskin replied.

'Go and find them, Lon,' Dusty said, then turned his attention to the three hard-cases. 'That would have taken some doing, collecting the money.'

'How d'you mean?' asked Soskin sullenly.

'The marshal in Newton isn't as dumb as the sheriff,' Dusty explained. 'He didn't like some of the signs about the hold-up. So he watched the teller, caught him boarding a stage out of town, one that connected with the overland route to the south. The teller had a nice carpet-bag, with thirty thousand dollars inside.'

'*What!*' Soskin yelped.

'Sure. When the gang spooked, they dropped the bag with the money in it. So the clerk picked it up, hid it and then gave the alarm.'

'And the sheriff's posse shot four men for nothing,' Belle said quietly.

'Sure,' Dusty agreed. 'Then the story about a girl being with the gang came out. Maybe the sheriff was just trying to justify the killings, maybe he believed what he heard. Anyway he put out the dodger on you, Belle, and the story that you had hidden the loot got out.'

'Four men died,' Belle said quietly. 'A bank teller takes a chance and grabs the loot they dropped, and they died.'

'Five counting Framant,' Calamity Jane put in.

'I wouldn't say that, Calam,' Mark drawled. 'What killed Framant was the bounty on Belle Starr's scalp.'

PART TWO

THE CODE OF THE MOUNTAIN MEN

MARK COUNTER had been trail boss and brought in a thousand head of long-horned O.D. Connected beef to the town of Brownsville. As a drive it could hardly be compared with running three thousand head up the great inter-State trails to the Kansas railheads, but it had had its moments. Enough of them to make Mark grateful that he had Johnny Wade along with him as segundo.

Normally Dusty Fog would have been the trail boss and Mark the segundo, but Dusty and the Ysabel Kid were handling a chore for Ole Devil in the town of Holbrook,* and could not make the drive. Not that Ole Devil had need or cause to worry, for Mark was a master hand with cattle and delivered the herd safely. Now, with the buyer's certified bank draft in the special pocket let into the top of his left Justin boot, Mark was free to have a celebration in the Texas sea-port before he and Johnny attended to some private business.

'You should see the place, Mark,' Johnny said enthusiastically as they walked towards a saloon away from the dock area. 'I was up there for three months last year before I came back to the O.D. Connected. It sure is a swell lil spread, and I can make it grow. Never thought Uncle Zeke would leave it to me, though.'

'We'll ride up there and look it over comes the morning,' Mark replied.

Johnny was a good hand with cattle and had rode for the O.D. Connected for almost three years, except for brief spells when he wandered off to see what the rest of the world looked

*Told in *The Half-Breed* by J. T. Edson.

like. However, an uncle had died and left him a small ranch up in the San Vegas hills about fifty miles from Brownsville.

With his characteristic generosity, Ole Devil sent Johnny as segundo on the drive, which gave him extra pay that he could use, and told Mark to go out to the ranch with Johnny and see him settled in on it.

'The Last Battle Saloon,' Johnny grinned. 'It's as good as any, I'd say. Well, I've bought my supplies, hired me a rig to tote 'em. Now I want to howl.'

'We'll go in and howl, then,' Mark agreed.

The saloon was one of the better places in Brownsville and drew its custom from a cross-section of the town's residents and visitors. Cowhands gathered at tables; blue clad soldiers mingled with both U.S. Navy and merchant sailors; dock workers and townsmen rubbed elbows. It could be an explosive mixture when the whisky flowed free, but at this early hour of the evening all seemed quiet and peaceable enough. The faro layout, the chuck-a-luck and blackjack tables all had clients and the wheel-of-fortune drew a small crowd.

'Not for me,' Johnny drawled. 'There's no hope in bucking the house percentage in a game.'

'Let's try that poker game then,' Mark replied. 'And let's get sat in on it afore those two gals by the bar come over and eat us.'

'What a way to die,' grinned Johnny, throwing a glance at the pair of painted saloon-girls who looked them over with predatory gaze.

The girls' interest was understandable, for every woman in the room gave the new arrivals more than just a casual looking over.

Johnny stood six foot one, was handsome with curly black hair and a neatly trimmed black moustache. He wore good range clothes and had the build to set them off. Around his waist hung a gunbelt, a matched brace of walnut handled 1860 Army Colts butt forward in the low Cavalry draw holsters.

In any company Johnny might be expected to catch the eye, for he had wide shoulders, a slim waist, and a great muscular development which most men might have envied.

However, Johnny stood two inches shorter than Mark and Mark possessed even wider shoulders and greater muscle development, as well as being even more handsome. All in all it had been a long time, if ever, since two more eye-catching, female-attracting, men walked into the Last Battle Saloon.

Before the two girls could cross the room and reach them, Mark and Johnny walked to the table where a poker game was in progress.

'Is there room for players, gents?' Johnny asked.

'Settle in and get your feet wet,' the tall, slim, well dressed gambler replied, waving a hand towards the empty chairs. 'Game's straight stud, no dealer's choice, no wild cards—and no limit.'

'Then she's the game for me. How about you, Mark?'

'Three things I never could stand are dealer's choice, wild cards and a limit. Let's sit a spell and take instruction in how it's done.'

None of the four players in the game raised any objection to Mark or Johnny sitting in. The gambler's warning about the lack of a limit had told the cowhands what to expect. They were men grown and as such ought to know whether they could afford to sit in and play under those conditions.

Mark could afford to play in the game. An eccentric maiden aunt left all her money to him when she died and the greater part of the money lay on deposit to him in the Polveroso City bank back in Rio Hondo County.

While not being rich, Johnny had managed to save some of his pay—a thing that came as a surprise to all who knew him—and had drawn his savings from the bank before leaving to help on the trail drive. So, even after buying supplies for his ranch, he could afford to chance a few hands of stud even in a no limit game. If the worst came to the worst, he had the deeds to the ranch with which to cover his losses. Not that Johnny wanted to lose the place. He was a cowhand, a tophand at his work, but like most cowhands he tended to live for the moment and let the future take care of itself.

As he sat at the table, Mark studied his fellow players. He knew the gambler to be honest, though obviously an expert at

81

the game or he could not make a living gambling. The man at the gambler's right looked like a senior teller at a bank, or maybe in the county offices. He was fat, stodgy looking, yet he gave the impression he knew the time of day when it came to playing stud poker. To the fat man's right sat a leathery old Army sergeant, short, stocky and tanned to the colour of old oak. Nothing about him suggested he would be a rabbit in the game.

That left the fourth player. He sat hunched in a chair facing Mark. A peaked uniform hat rested on the back of his head. His face looked harsh, weather-beaten and the nose bore testimony that the glass of liquor on the table before him was not the first, nor the thousandth, drink he had ever taken. In dress he looked like an officer of a boat, either master of a small trading craft, or a mate on some larger vessel. The butt of what appeared to be an Adams revolver showed in his waistband. His white shirt looked dirty, the string tie unfastened. His white trousers were tucked into heavy sea-boots. All in all he looked as mean as hell and, while not drunk, carried enough of that sickly-smelling liquor to slow down his perceptions.

Behind the seaman stood a young woman and at first glance Mark dismissed her as one of the saloon workers. She stood only about five foot two and her mass of long black hair hung down well below her shoulders. It framed a pretty face, a face tanned almost as brown as a Mexican's. She had dark eyes, almost Oriental in appearance, this was emphasised by her rather high cheek-bones and the clothes she wore. Mark had seen the style of dress before, on Chinese girls in cat-houses at the end-of-trail towns, or in Quiet Town while he served as a deputy under Dusty Fog there just after the War Between The States. The dress was shiny material, green in colour, fastened high to the neck and slit from hem to thigh. Yet the girl did not look Chinese. Oriental maybe, but no Chinese ever had skin that colour and very few showed a round, firm bosom such as forced against the material of the dress. Her arms were bare, brown and undecorated by any of the jewellery a dance-hall or saloon-girl usually sported.

'This's Ben Goff,' the gambler introduced, waving a hand to

the fat man, 'Sarge Killet of the 12th Infantry and the Cap'n. Gents, meet Mark Counter from the O.D. Connected and——?'

Under other circumstances it would have been regarded as a breach of range etiquette to ask such a question. However, it could be asked in the informal setting of a card game and the one questioned did not have to give his correct name.

'Johnny Wade,' Johnny finished for the gambler, looking at the girl behind the seaman with interest.

'She don't work here, cowboy,' the seaman growled. 'She's mine.'

Not by a flicker of her face did the girl show any interest in either Johnny's frankly admiring glance, or the man's words.

'No offence, mister,' Johnny replied quietly.

Mark, the gambler, the soldier and the fat man exchanged glances. All knew that when a cowhand called a man mister after being introduced he did not like the man. Not that they blamed Johnny, the seaman's comment had been uncalled for. The young cowhand had done no more than look at the girl and could not be expected to know she did not work in the saloon.

Riffling the cards, Packer, the gambler, placed them down for Mark to cut.

'Cut 'em light, lose all night,' Mark drawled. 'Flip 'em out and let's see who's going to take it from me.'

Out flipped the cards, the first face down and then the second exposed.

'And it's the ace to bet,' Packer remarked.

'I'll open it with ten,' Johnny, who held the ace, replied.

From the start two things became clear to Mark; that the standard of play would be high; and that the seaman was out of his depth in such a game. So would Johnny have been, for he played the way he lived, on impulse more than sound judgment.

Where the other three closed a hand that did not show firm hope of being worthwhile, Johnny and the seaman clung to it, staying in the pot and hoping for a last card miracle to save the day. This was not, and never had been, good poker, as the seaman found out to his cost. Johnny might have found it also, but he seemed to be in the middle of one of those flows of luck which made gambling so fascinating to most people. Time after time he would sit with poor hands, betting on them and the last card brought off a winner, or he would run a bluff and scoop the pot.

The seaman was the heavy loser. None of the others took such chances and held their own, or lost a little, knowing the law of averages would in the end crack the run of luck.

After the game had been going for an hour, Johnny glanced at the girl. She still stood behind the seaman's chair and he had not given her as much as a glance as he played his hands and drank glass after glass of rum without it showing any effect.

While the fat man shuffled the cards, Johnny came to his feet, fetching a chair from another table.

'Here, ma'am,' he said, putting the chair behind the girl. 'Have a seat.'

Swinging around, the seaman glared up at Johnny, his drink-reddened face going a shade or two deeper coloured. For a long moment he studied Johnny's big frame, read the challenge in the cowhand's eyes and shrugged.

'Sit down!' he growled.

Obediently the girl sank into the chair, sitting primly on the edge of it and folding her hands on her lap. She gave Johnny a look of silent gratitude as he returned to his seat and took up his cards.

A few hands went by and the seaman grew more surly with each one. His losses had been heavy and his consumption of rum almost continuous. Fumbling into his coat's inside pocket, he took out a stiff white sheet of paper and tossed it towards Johnny with an angry gesture.

'Here, the bill of sale for Jaya, give me two hundred on it!'

'Two hundred?' Johnny replied, wondering why the man would offer his ship for such a small sum.

'She's worth it.'

'Reckon she might be to you,' Johnny agreed, then he shrugged. 'Sure, two hundred it is.'

Easy come, easy go, that was Johnny. He had no use for a ship, but could always let the seaman redeem the bill of sale after the game. Way Johnny saw it, a man who had suffered from such stinking luck in the game deserved a chance to break even.

'Let's call this the last hand, shall we?' the fat man asked, watching Mark riffle the cards.

None of the others objected, although the seaman muttered something under his breath. The other players in the game, poker addicts though they were, did not like the seaman's attitude enough to want to continue playing with him. All had played enough poker to know such a man in his present condition might make trouble that could end up in gun play. So, rather than wind up with a corpse and cartridge affair, they would break up the game.

'I'll do it!' the seaman growled as Mark passed the cards to Johnny for the cut.

Under the rules of poker any player could ask to cut the cards before the deal. Yet the seaman's attitude annoyed Mark, brought a frown of disapproval to the gambler's face, an angry grunt from the soldier and a worried look to the fat townsman. Johnny's hands clenched, but he caught a warning head-shake from Mark and kept his thoughts to himself. Only he sure hoped that loud-mouthed made some remark after the game. It would give Johnny pleasure to bounce that sullen yahoo around the room.

Out sailed the cards, landing face down on the table, followed by the next turned face up for all to see. The seaman peaked at his hole card, the king of hearts and he had the ace of spades showing. Across the table Johnny sat with the four of hearts showing.

'I'll open,' growled the seaman.

Mark threw his cards in, the three of clubs and nine of diamonds did not have enough possibility of improvement to make it worth his while staying in on them. The others stayed in and Mark dealt them their third cards. The seaman caught the queen of diamonds and Johnny received the nine of hearts. After seeing the card he received, the fat man followed the other players out, leaving the pot between Johnny and the seaman.

On receiving a ten of spades, the seaman pushed up the betting and Johnny drew the seven of hearts. Again they bet and the last cards flipped to them from the deck. Nobody spoke, but every eye went first to the jack of clubs before the seaman and the six of hearts which lay on Johnny's hand.

'Ace to bet,' the gambler said quietly.

Indecision showed on the seaman's face, a trickle of sweat ran down his brow and he brushed it aside. Although he held as high a straight as a man could get, one little heart in the hole would give Johnny a flush; and that would beat any straight no matter how high.

Having seen how Johnny's luck ran through the game, the seaman felt uneasy. Nothing in the young cowhand's face or attitude showed any hint of alarm, or sign that he might be running a bluff.

'I'll check,' the seaman said.

'Then she's loose for a hundred,' Johnny answered.

Once again the man paused and studied the cards. He lifted his face to look at Johnny. The other players stayed silent, waiting to see the outcome of the game.

Slowly the seaman reached out a hand. He looked at the money before him and gave an angry scowl.

'I'm in!' he snarled and folded his cards.

With a broad grin, Johnny scooped in the pot and thrust back his chair. He looked at the other players.

'Drinks are on me, gents,' he said. 'Let's head for the bar.'

All but the seaman rose to accept Johnny's invitation. They left the cards on the table just as when the deal finished. The seaman leaned over and lifted up Johnny's hole card. A snarl of fury came from the man's lips. He dropped the two of spades face up on the table. Johnny had run a bluff and the seaman knew he had fallen for it.

Coming to his feet and throwing his chair over, the seaman drew the Adams revolver from his waistband.

'Look out!'

The girl had not moved from her chair, nor had her eyes left

86

Johnny since he accepted the bill of sale from the seaman. Now she came to her feet and screamed a warning.

It came almost too late. The Adams's bullet missed Johnny by inches as he started to turn, thrusting the gambler and fat man aside and twisting his right hand palm out to hook around its gun butt.

Mark also turned, saw the seaman and acted. Faster than Johnny moved, Mark brought out his left hand Colt, his right hand shooting out to send the old soldier staggering to safety. Flame ripped from the barrel and the seaman reeled back under the impact of the lead. He still held his gun and tried to shoot, swinging the Adams in Mark's direction. It gave Mark no choice. He fired again, sending the bullet into the man's head and tumbling him in a lifeless heap on the floor.

The girl screamed, twisting away from the sight and standing with her hands clenched at her sides. Everybody in the room swung around, preparing to take cover. Smoke dribbled up from Mark's Colt and Johnny thrust his weapon back into its holster.

'Thanks, Mark,' he said. 'Looks like the feller saw I'd run a bluff on him and didn't like it.'

'Sure looks that way,' Mark replied. 'I figured you hadn't filled the flush at all.'

'I hadn't. Reckoned to give him a chance to win his boat back. I'd best go thank the lady, she saved me for sure.'

'Go to it,' Mark answered. 'I'll send for the marshal.'

Crossing the room, Johnny halted by the girl and looked down at her. She turned a frightened face to him.

'Thanks for the warning, ma'am,' he said. 'I'm sorry about what happened to your man.'

'He is not my man,' she replied. 'You are.'

'*Me?*' Johnny asked, his voice rising a shade. 'How'd you make that out?'

'My name is Jaya Hara. You won me from the captain. I saw him give you the papers.'

The town marshal arrived and heard the details of the shooting, declared it to be self-defence and that no action need be taken against Mark. In Texas at that time people took the sensible view that a man could defend his life, or the life of a friend, even to the extent of killing an aggressor should it be necessary. Mark had not sought a fight, but he shot to prevent the seaman killing Johnny and the law rightly found no fault in his actions.

Leaving the marshal to attend to the removal of the body, Mark crossed the room and joined Johnny at the bar. The little girl stood with Johnny and from the expression on Johnny's face, he was trying to explain something to her.

'I can't own you, Jaya,' Johnny was saying as Mark joined them.

You do,' she replied and Mark could detect a faint accent in her speech. 'The captain sold me to you. I saw him.'

'Mark,' Johnny groaned, turning to his big *amigo*, 'tell Jaya that a man can't sell a gal to anybody.'

'Let's get out of here first,' Mark replied. 'Like the marshal says, that feller might have friends, and he doesn't want a shooting war between the cowhands and sailors.'

Turning, Mark headed for the door. Johnny watched him go, then followed, for he could see the wisdom in the marshal's suggestion. If the dead man had friends they might come looking for revenge. Johnny and Mark could handle their guns and take care of their end in any man's fight, but the sailors would tend to side their kind. This in turn would bring the cowhands in to help Mark and Johnny and could blow the whole town apart at the seams.

'Give me my bag, please,' Jaya said to the bartender. 'The smaller one.'

'Sure,' he replied, bending to lift a canvas duffle-bag from the floor. 'How about the other one?'

'I do not want it,' she answered, swinging the bag to her shoulder and hurrying across the room after the departing men.

'What were you saying in there?' Mark asked as he and Johnny left the saloon and walked along the sidewalk.

'That lil gal, Jaya she says her name is, she reckons I bought her off that sailor.'

At that moment Johnny sensed rather than heard the girl and turned towards her. Mark also swung around, looking at the bag the girl carried.

'What in hell?' Johnny snapped. 'Look, gal, I don't own you.'

'Yes you do. You have paper——'

'Durn the paper!' Johnny interrupted. 'I'll give you the——'

'Let's get off the street and talk this out!' Mark put in urgently, for a few people were looking in their direction, attracted by Johnny's rising voice.

'Yeah, we'd better,' Johnny replied. 'Come on—and give me that durned bag, gal.'

Jaya looked at Johnny in surprise as he took the bag from her hand, slung it on to his shoulder and turned to walk away. For the first time her full lips parted in a smile. Her mouth looked just a shade too large for some tastes, but the teeth were firm and even, without the gold filling so many Chinese girls sported. She fell into line behind him and followed on his heels.

Stopping, Johnny looked back at the girl. 'Come on up here and walk between Mark and me, gal,' he ordered.

'It would not be correct for me to do so,' she answered.

'Dad-blast it, gal, this's Texas. You come between us.'

Somehow they attracted less attention walking that way, although several people threw knowing looks at them. The looks annoyed Johnny for some reason. On more than one occasion he had escorted a girl through the streets and received the same sort of looks, only then the looks had been justified. This time he had no ulterior motive; and, strangely, the thought of the implied suggestion about Jaya's morals riled him.

On reaching the hotel where they had taken rooms, Johnny went to the reception desk and jerked a thumb towards Jaya. The reception clerk, a plump, pompous dude with spectacles and side whiskers, looked at the girl, then turned an indignant face to Johnny.

'This isn't the sort of hotel——!' he began.

'They never are,' Johnny replied. 'The lady's taking my

room and I'm bunking with my *amigo*.'

'Yes?' sniffed the clerk.

'*Yes!*' Johnny barked, his hands slapping palms down on the desk top and causing the clerk to take a hurried pace to the rear. 'Any objections?'

'N—no, sir. None at all!'

Actually the clerk had several objections, but he remembered that the big blond cowhand had appeared to be on friendly terms with the hotel's owner, so kept his views to himself. Besides, he knew cowhands. One wrong word would cause more trouble than the clerk reckoned he could handle.

On reaching the door of his room, Johnny unlocked it and handed the key and her bag to Jaya.

'Say,' he said, 'do you have any other clothes in that bag?'

'Of course.'

'You'd best put another dress on. That one sure attracts attention.'

'Yes—may I call you Johnny? I heard your friend call you Johnny.'

'Sure you can, Jaya,' Johnny replied. 'Come give me a knock when you're changed, then we'll go eat.'

'You not wanting me to cook for you?' she gasped.

'Not today,' Johnny grinned. 'Let's say you're on holiday.'

'I never had a holiday before,' Jaya sighed, opening the room door and stepping inside. 'I like belonging to you, Johnny.'

Sitting on his bed, Mark grinned at Johnny when the young cowhand entered the room.

'What's amusing you?' Johnny asked. 'That's a nice gal there.'

'Sure is,' Mark agreed. 'What're you fixing to do with her?'

'Me?'

'You,' Mark agreed. 'She reckons you own her.'

Johnny flung his hat on to the small dressing table angrily. 'You know that isn't possible, Mark.'

'Why sure,' Mark agreed. 'I know it, you know it. But does *she* know it?'

90

'I'll explain it to her while we're eating,' Johnny drawled. 'It's allus easy to explain things to a gal when she's full fed.'

At that moment the door of the room opened and Jaya entered. She wore a different dress. The sight of it lifted Johnny out of his chair and even Mark, who reckoned to be blasé about females, stared.

From waist to ankles the dress looked normal, no slit through which shapely legs could peek seductively, the sort of thing any good woman in town would wear. Above the waist—well, it would raise a dead Indian, happen one had been close at hand. The material clung so tight that it seemed moulded to her and left her arms and shoulders bare, apart from the two straps. The neckline of the dress had been cut down lower than even a dance-hall girl in a wide-open town would chance wearing, and showed that Jaya wore nothing but the dress.

'I have changed my dress as you say,' Jaya announced unnecessarily.

'Land-sakes, gal!' Johnny gasped. 'Is that the only one you have?'

'No, I have others, but they are smaller than this one.'

Under different circumstances Johnny would not have cared how scantily a girl dressed. Yet somehow he felt differently about Jaya. She looked so small and helpless, happen a man kept his eyes on her face. He did not feel she should dress in anything so revealing when men could see her.

'Go put a coat on,' he said. 'I'll take you to the store and buy you a couple of dresses.'

Left alone in the room, Mark lay back on his bed and grinned up at the roof. He knew Johnny very well and had been surprised at the cowhand's behaviour towards the girl. With any other girl, or any other girl he had met in a saloon, Johnny would never have thought of handing over his room, or worried about how she dressed. Yet he had taken the little girl in and was spending money to buy her clothes more suited to the ideas people had about how a young woman ought to dress.

Maybe the chance meeting would have its use, Mark thought. While Johnny was a tophand with cattle, ready to work all hours of the day and night, or give his life blood for the brand he hired to, he never accepted responsibility. He would need to if he hoped to make the ranch he inherited pay. What Johnny needed was a steadying influence, a wife—but would that girl make him the right kind of wife?

When Johnny returned, he presented Jaya clad in a gingham dress of modest, conventional pattern. A parcel he carried contained two more, and various articles of underclothing the storekeeper's wife insisted Jaya would need, for her scanty wardrobe did not contain any such luxuries.

'Let's go eat and talk things out,' Mark suggested.

Over the meal, with Jaya attracting little attention in her new clothes, the girl told her story.

Jaya was born in a seaport on the Siam coast, although Mark had only a vague idea, and Johnny none at all, where this might be. Her father had been a German trader, her mother a Javanese dancing girl. Not that her father had been a very successful trader, the girl admitted, in fact he spent so much time drinking that he rarely had any business to support an ever-growing family.

Four years ago her father needed money and sold her to the man Mark killed, the captain of a small trading ship. From the calm way Jaya spoke of the matter, it did not appear to be an unusual transaction in her home land. The captain kept her on the ship as his cook and servant, strangely he had treated her as nothing worse—probably because he planned to sell her to some brothel keeper when she matured and knew he would gain a higher price that way. Then for some reason not unconnected with piracy, but into which Jaya did not go, the man sailed for the United States. He brought his ship around the tip of Southern America to make for the eastern sea-board rather than chance recognition on the west coast. On arrival at Brownsville, the captain had been in urgent need of money. He brought the girl ashore to try to sell her, however, the card game at the Last Battle Saloon gave Jaya a stay and Mark wrote a finish to the man's plan.

'I did not want to be what he would sell me for,' she finished, looking at Johnny with her luminous black eyes and pleading that he believed her. 'I am good girl. I cook good, mend clothes or make them. I am strong, work very hard for you all the time, Johnny.'

'But I don't own you,' Johnny groaned.

'You do. You have the papers.'

'Dang the papers!' Johnny yelled, then dropped his voice. 'They don't mean a thing. You can go any time you want.'

'I not want to go,' she said. 'You good man, you own me. I not leave you.'

Nor would any amount of arguing shake the girl. Mark tried to help out by explaining the impossibility of Johnny owning her, but she brushed aside every suggestion that she was free.

'Blast it, Mark!' Johnny growled as they followed the girl upstairs after the meal. 'How do—say, I've an idea. Let's me and you go out and have us a time. That way she'll see that I don't care.'

'I'll go along with you,' Mark replied. 'It may work.'

Not until they had reached the saloon nearest to the hotel did Johnny remember he had left his saddle, bedroll and war bag in the hotel room that he loaned to Jaya. Yet he did not worry for his every instinct told him his belongings would be safe.

It had been Johnny's intention to get drunk, which he did, then pick a gal as unlike Jaya as he could find and take her back to the hotel with him. That ought to show Jaya he wanted no part of her. He even had the right girl picked out, a large, buxom blonde beauty who would make two of Jaya in size and heft. The girl would have agreed to Johnny's proposal, but did not get a chance.

Just as Johnny started to walk towards the girl and suggest they made a night of it, he seemed to see another face before him. One with a mass of long black hair, dainty, pretty features and luminous, yet sad, black eyes. Suddenly Johnny wanted no part of the big blonde.

Instead he drank more than he meant to. Whisky never made Johnny aggressive. The only effect it had on him was to make him sleepy. After a time Mark steered Johnny back to the hotel. In their room Johnny gravely thanked Mark, shak-

93

ing his hand and telling him that he was the best damned *amigo* a man ever had. Then Johnny undressed and headed for his blankets which lay on the floor at the side of the room. Mark had done some drinking himself, though not as much as Johnny, and certainly not enough to make him lose his memory. Yet he could not remember Johnny bringing the bedroll into the room and spreading it out ready for use.

Mark was still thinking about the matter of Johnny's bedroll when he went to sleep. Light sleeper though Mark usually was, he did not hear the door open. A dark shape entered, spent a few minutes in the room and left as silently as it came.

'Where in hell's my clothes?'

Daylight streamed in through the room's window as Mark woke to Johnny's wail of anger. Sitting up in bed, Mark looked across the room to where Johnny sat on his blankets and stared around the room.

'Is this your fool idea of a joke?' Johnny growled, seeing Mark sit watching him. 'Come on, Mark, where in h——'

His words died off as the room's door opened to admit Jaya carrying a cloth covered tray. Johnny let out a startled yelp and ducked under his blankets, drawing them around his naked torso.

'I have brought you coffee,' the girl said, setting the tray on a chair. 'Shall I bring your breakfast to you?'

'Huh?' Johnny gasped. 'Hey—No! And you shouldn't come in here like this, Jaya. I'm not dressed.'

'I will fetch your clothes,' she replied and left the room.

An amazed looking face stared at Mark as the door closed behind the girl. Mark could not hold down his grin, for he had never seen Johnny so completely at a loss for words.

'D—did she——?' Johnny croaked.

'Not that I know of,' Mark grinned. 'I never saw her when we got back here. You undressed yourself and went to sleep, like a baby when its mother sings a lullaby.'

'How'd you like me to sing you a lul——'

Once more Johnny's words died off as he stared at Jaya. The girl came into the room carrying a neat pile of clothes. Johnny's Stetson, freshly brushed and with the silver conchas

94

of its band gleaming, lay on top of the pile. His spare shirt, undershirt and underpants, all clean and pressed, his levis, tidied up after their wear, and boots showing an unaccustomed shine, completed the girl's load. Placing the clothes down, Jaya reached into one of the boots and took out a clean, darned pair of socks which certainly had not been clean or darned when Johnny last saw them.

'I have packed your old clothes away to be washed when I have time,' she said. 'Can I——'

'No!' Johnny yelped as if the words had been stung out of him by a bee. He held the blankets tighter to him. 'I can dress myself.'

A gentle smile played on the girl's lips.

'I only wanted to know if I could pour out the coffee for you.'

Mark grinned and spoke up. 'I'll take a cup, if I can, ma'am.'

Whisking the cloth from the tray, Jaya poured out two cups of coffee and looked at Johnny.

'How do you like it?' she asked.

'Black and sweet,' he replied, sounding dazed.

'I will remember in future,' she promised.

Although Johnny thought up some comment about her having no need to remember, he did not use it. The aroma of the cup of coffee Jaya handed to him made him forget the speech.

'No hotel cook ever threw up Arbuckle's like this,' Mark drawled, accepting the cup Jaya carried to him after serving Johnny.

'I made it myself,' the girl answered. 'Please get dressed now so you can go and eat the breakfast I have cooked for you.'

'Sure, Jaya gal,' Johnny replied. 'Just you go and let us dress.'

Not until he was dressing did Johnny realise his wallet and money-belt had been among his clothes. Before he could mention this to Mark, he found them under the pillow. Johnny, who had known enough saloon-girls to have few illusions left, never even thought of checking that the money be intact.

'Where in hell did the bed come from?' he asked.

Mark rose, and began to dress before he answered.

'Jaya must have brought it in for you. What're you going to do about her?'

'I don't know,' Johnny admitted. 'I can't just turn the gal loose down here. She'd never get by. I reckon I'll take her up to the ranch until she knows her way around.'

'Why not marry her?' Mark replied.

Johnny was climbing into his pants as Mark spoke. He stopped with one leg in the air, twisted around and almost fell.

'Marry!' he howled. 'Mark, you-all been falling on your lil pumpkin head too many times. Why in hell should I get married?'

'Why not?' Mark countered. 'You're all set to settle down and be a rancher. Which same, you're going to need a woman to run the house.'

'Nah!' Johnny snorted. 'A gal'd just be a drag to me. I'll take her up to the spread, happen she wants to come. But when she knows her way around, waal, I'll stake her to wherever she wants to go.'

There the matter rested for the time being. The two men washed and shaved, finished dressing and went downstairs to eat a good breakfast served to them by Jaya. She seemed to be surprised when Johnny insisted she join them, and sat watching him with smiling lips and happy eyes.

Before they left the hotel Mark saw its owner, a friend from his Army days. He learned that Jaya had worked until long after he and Johnny went to bed, at washing Johnny's clothes, sewing tears and replacing missing buttons, darning his socks and cleaning his boots and hat.

Mark did not tell Johnny of his findings. He paid the hotel bill and they took Jaya to collect the hired wagon, then drive to the store and load the ranch's supplies.

'You stack and I'll load,' Mark told Johnny on reaching the store.

'Any way you want, *amigo*,' Johnny replied.

Neither of the men noticed Jaya, who had rode alongside Johnny on the wagon box, climb down and walk on to the sidewalk. The girl followed Mark into the store and watched him pick up a sack of potatoes, sling it on his shoulder and stroll out of the door with no more apparent effort than a kid toting a bag of candy.

'I thought I'd tote all the heavy stuff out first,' he told Johnny who took the sack from him.

'Any way you——' Johnny began, then glanced at the store's door. He came erect fast, his eyes bulging wide open. 'Great blistering horned-toad! Will you take a look at that?'

Swinging around, Mark saw what had startled Johnny. Came to a point the sight rocked him back on his heels too.

Jaya came through the door and across the sidewalk, toting a heavy sack of sugar on her back. She walked forward, bowing under the weight, but keeping moving with it.

To his credit, Johnny reached the sidewalk even before Mark. He sprang over the side of the wagon and took the sack from the girl's back.

'Land-sakes, gal!' he grunted. 'What're you trying to do, kill yourself?'

'It was not heavy,' she replied.

Johnny could have given her an argument about that. The sack *was* heavy, far heavier than he would have believed the girl's small figure capable of bearing.

Coming from the store, the owner looked worriedly to where Johnny stood heaving the sack on to the wagon.

'I'm sorry, friend,' he said. 'The lady came in and asked me which was your gear. I showed her, and next thing I knowed she'd picked that sack up and toted it outside. I never even thought she could heft it from the floor.'

'And she'd best not heft any more,' Johnny replied grimly.

'I do not please you, Johnny?' Jaya gasped, looking worried.

'Sure you do,' he replied with a grin and gently laid a hand on her head to ruffle her hair. 'Only there's no call for you to go hefting the heavy stuff around. You lend a hand with the lighter gear if you like.'

By the time the wagon was loaded, Jaya had proved she knew how to stack a load, spread a tarpaulin over it and lash the tarp home securely. She showed embarrassment when

97

Johnny pressed some money into her hand and told her to go buy a present.

'Man'd be a fool to let a gal like her slip through his fingers,' Mark drawled as he and Johnny watched Jaya skip lightly into the store.

'Likely,' Johnny agreed. 'Only I'm not the marrying kind.'

Normally Mark would have accepted, probably applauded, his friend's decision to avoid the bonds of matrimony. However, on this occasion he figured he should break his rule. Johnny needed a good wife, and Jaya showed signs of being a better girl for the job than the sort Johnny would pick given first and free choice of the remuda. Jaya needed a husband, there were too few ways a woman could earn a decent living in the west; and Johnny would make a good husband once he settled in to the idea. Only if Mark knew Johnny, and he reckoned he did, he didn't figure the cowhand would want him handing out advice on the subject of matrimony. More so when thinking of Mark's views on the subject as it affected him personally.

There was one way to make Johnny see the light though; and Mark reckoned he was just the boy to do it.

Jaya used the money Johnny gave her to buy a Stetson hat. When she sat by his side on the wagon box, her eagerness to have pleased him by the purchase started Johnny worrying. The last thing he wanted was for her to get too attached to him. Sure, she was a great little gal, but it was just that Johnny did not think he could make a marrying man.

'Pass it down this way, Jaya,' Mark said, riding his bloodbay stallion at the side of the wagon. 'I'll shape it Texas style for you.'

Glancing hopefully at Johnny, who pretended to be too busy handling the reins and make sure his big dun horse followed the wagon, to the tail of which its reins were fastened, Jaya handed Mark the hat.

'See you bought a good hat,' Mark went on, altering the Stetson's crown to meet the dictates of Texas fashion. 'It's always worth the money.'

Johnny looked towards the girl, now facing Mark and engrossed in his words of wisdom on the subject of hats. Having seen Mark in action around the ladies before, Johnny felt a hint of relief. He did not forget how Mark cut the ground from under his feet one time with the best looking girl in a Newton saloon. From the way things looked, Johnny reckoned Mark to be using the same technique with Jaya.

'Good ole Mark,' he thought. 'You're sure taking that lil gal off my back.'

Then another thought struck him. In a way he was responsible for Jaya. If he had not brought her out here there would be no need for Mark to take her off his back. What about after Mark got the gal interested? Johnny knew Mark too well to reckon anything more serious than a flirtation could come with Jaya. So what would she do after Mark rode on?

For the first time Johnny began to think of Jaya's many good points. He also decided he had best try to stop her becoming too involved with Mark. Not that he cared one way or the other, of course, but he did not want to see that innocent little gal get hurt.

So Johnny tried to regain Jaya's attention. Woman-like, Jaya's feelings had been hurt by Johnny's apparent indifference to her choice of hats—when she made the choice because she felt it would please him and instead of buying some cheap, rather gaudy jewellery which attracted her. So she intended to make Johnny suffer a little for his indifference.

For the rest of the day, while they travelled across the range heading towards the San Vegas hill country, Johnny tried to get into the conversation which went on between Mark and the girl. He met with little success.

When they made camp for the night, Mark allowed Johnny to slip in and show Jaya how to handle the unhitching and care of the wagon horse. The girl cooked a meal for them and they prepared to settle down for the night.

'You can use my pillow and blankets, Jaya,' Mark said.

'There's spare blankets on the wagon,' Johnny put in. 'We'll make Jaya a bed under the wagon and we'll sleep by the fire.'

'Where else?' Mark replied.

He found that Johnny spread his bedroll on the side of the fire nearest to the wagon. Nor did Johnny go to sleep until he saw and heard the rhythmic breathing by which he assumed that Mark had already settled down for the night. Mark looked across the fire at the now sleeping Johnny and a grin came to his lips. Turning over, Mark drew his blankets up higher. It looked like old Johnny was beginning to point the way Mark wanted him to go.

They moved on at dawn, after a good breakfast and some of Jaya's coffee. What that girl could do with Arbuckle's coffee had to be tasted to be believed. Johnny had always liked good coffee and he could not remember any that tasted just as good to his palate as the kind Jaya made.

Once more Johnny missed his chance. Mark's praise of the coffee brought a smile to Jaya's lips and she turned to Johnny.

'Do you like it?' she asked.

'Huh? Sure, it's all right.'

Straight off Johnny could have cursed himself. With an annoyed toss of her head, Jaya turned and carried the coffee-pot away, pouring a good cup full that Johnny would have liked over the fire's flames.

Once more Mark monopolised the conversation with the girl and Johnny scowled to himself, concentrating on driving. His few attempts to say anything found the girl attentive, but each time Mark cut him out.

Towards sundown they came into sight of the ranch buildings and Johnny brought the wagon to a halt. He did not notice that Mark dropped back and left him alone with the girl and the view.

'There it is, Jaya,' Johnny said, a note of pride in his voice.

'I think it is beautiful, Johnny,' she replied and her voice sent a thrill through him.

Compared with the O.D. Connected's great two storey main building, the house below did not appear very grand. Yet Johnny did not care. After all, he did not own the O.D. Connected but he did own that house down there and a fair slice of the surrounding land.

The house was stoutly made of logs, with a good strong roof

over it, glass at the windows and a porch on which a man could sit and rock in the evening while his wife made supper for him. There was a good sized, well-made barn, a blacksmith's forge, a backhouse and a couple of stoutly constructed pole corrals. His uncle had built to last and it would be long, given reasonable care, before Johnny would need to start rebuilding.

'Let's go take a look inside,' Johnny suggested eagerly and the girl, clutching his arm, agreed.

Watching the wagon roll down the slope, Mark smiled. He had not failed to notice how Johnny and Jaya acted. Give them a couple of days, and Johnny a little more of the treatment handed out the last couple of days, and Mark reckoned he could leave his two friends in each other's care.

A pump and empty horse-trough stood before the house. Mark swung from his bloodbay's saddle and went to the pump, starting to fill the big trough. A woman could likely do her wash in it, or even take a bath on warm days when her man and the help worked the range.

Side by side Jaya and Johnny ran from the wagon, across the porch and to the door. When Johnny's uncle rode into Brownsville for the last time, he had locked the door and taken the key. Apart from the sheriff's deputies checking in once in a while, nobody had been near the house since that day. Johnny unlocked the door and he and Jaya entered.

The house had a simple lay-out much used in the west. The front consisted of one room, serving as dining-room, sitting-room, lounge, library combined. It was furnished, the furniture not new, but still in good condition. Three doors led off at the rear, two to bedrooms, one into the kitchen.

The dust of a month of emptiness lay everywhere, but apart from that the place appeared to be untouched.

'Tomorrow,' Jaya said, looking around her, 'we start to clean everything.'

'Whatever you say,' Johnny replied.

Mark came into the room, halting and looking around him. Turning, Johnny looked at his *amigo* and grinned, finding it impossible to stay annoyed.

'How'd you like it, Mark?'

'Great. A stout little house with all the furnishings. You've got a good home here, Johnny boy. I'll go tend to the horses, unless Jaya wants another lesson in horse-handling.'

'She don't!' Johnny grunted, before the girl could answer. 'I want to show her her room——'

'And I want to see my kitchen,' Jaya went on.

On finding her kitchen, Jaya chased Johnny off out to help Mark with the horses while she started the stove and prepared a meal for them. Johnny joined Mark outside and worked in silence, which Mark knew to be unusual for Johnny.

'Jaya says we're starting house cleaning tomorrow,' Mark remarked as he turned the harness horse into one of the corrals. 'Reckon she's the boss on that end of the spread.'

'Reckon she is,' Johnny replied. 'You figure it'll be all right for you to stay on here, Mark? Ole Devil might have something for you to handle.'

'Nope. He told me to take a few days vacation. So I might as well do it up here, lending you a hand. I wonder if Jaya's got everything she needs in the kitchen?'

'I'll go see,' Johnny grunted.

Watching Johnny walk away, Mark grinned broadly. He attended to the horses and when finished, walked to the house. Johnny and Jaya appeared to be getting on much better.

'Johnny boy,' Mark thought as he joined them at the table, 'you've one foot in the hole and the other on a greasy slope. Just a lil mite more pushing and I'll leave you set up for life.'

So Mark kept on the pushing. When he wished, he could talk fascinatingly about a number of things. Jaya listened to his descriptions of the pre-war south, of Maximillian's court in Mexico; and Johnny sat watching the girl, getting more and more sure that he must protect her from Mark.

Not that Johnny cared about her himself. He just did not want to see her hurt—or so he told himself.

The girl showed off another accomplishment, although not one Johnny approved of her doing in mixed company. From her bundle of belongings, she produced a scanty sleeveless blouse and a skirt which seemed to be made of grass, hanging to her knees. Wearing these, and barefoot, she began to dance. It was a dance like the two men had never seen before, with swaying hips, sensuous writhing body movements.

Johnny felt hot under the collar as she sank to her knees in the dusty room and faced him, leaning her torso back as she writhed and her arms moved gracefully in the pagan dance. He enjoyed every movement of it, but swore she would never again dance like that before another man.

'That is how the native girls dance in the South Sea Islands,' she said, rising to her feet. 'Did you like?'

'I've never seen better,' Mark answered.

'You go put your other dress on now,' Johnny put in, for the grass skirt revealed more of the girl's legs than even the Chinese frock had. 'You'll catch a cold in that outfit.'

Once again Mark could cheerfully have kicked Johnny across the room. The girl wanted his praise, and instead of giving it, telling her how he enjoyed her dance, the durned fool had to make a remark like that.

A very indignant Jaya stormed out of the room, to return wearing the gingham dress. Ignoring Johnny, she began to ask Mark questions about the range, things a woman should know about and which Johnny wished he could be discussing with her.

'It's time we were getting to bed!' he growled, unable to stand it any longer. 'You use the bedroom, Jaya. Me 'n' Mark'll bunk down in the barn until we get the place cleaned up.'

Not until they had spread their bedrolls in the barn, with Johnny getting between Mark and the door, did the young cowhand speak to his blond *amigo*.

'Take it easy on Jaya, Mark,' he said.

'How do you mean?' Mark asked, straight-faced but enjoying every minute of the situation.

'Shucks, she's not used to being around fellers. She might—you—that is—it's——'

'I thought you hadn't any claim on her,' Mark drawled.

'I don't have!' Johnny snapped. 'It's just that I feel

103

responsible for her after fetching her out here.'

'Do, huh?'

'Sure, I do!'

'I'll mind what you say,' Mark said calmly. 'Now let's get some sleep. We've got a big day ahead of us.'

And with that, Mark undressed and climbed into his bed. He went to sleep almost immediately, knowing Johnny was willing himself to stay awake until sure he had nothing to fear.

Dawn brought a fresh problem for Johnny. Jaya came to tell them that she had breakfast ready for them.

'What're you wearing that dress for?' he yelled indignantly, for it was the one into which she had changed at the hotel and which caused him to buy her new clothes.

'I have much work to do,' she replied. 'It is not good that I should dirty my good clothes.'

'Yeah, but——'

Sitting up, Mark looked at the girl and interrupted Johnny's protests.

'Man, you look prettier than a June-bug, Jaya,' he said.

'Thank you, Mark,' she replied. 'Johnny thinks I should wear my good dress to work in.'

'That'd be real foolish, was you to ask me,' Mark drawled.

'Nobody did,' Johnny growled.

'I have breakfast ready,' Jaya said, in a tone which showed she considered the matter of her dress closed. 'Hurry, before it gets cold.'

Not even the mood of 'to hell with her, let her make a durned fool of herself over him,' could last in the face of Jaya's coffee and breakfast. Johnny ate well and even managed to compliment her on her cooking, and her appearance.

With the breakfast over, Jaya gave her orders, and from the way she spoke the men saw they were going to have a hard and busy morning. On leaving the house, Mark removed his shirt and undershirt, putting them with his hat and gunbelt on the wagon box.

'You can't go around like that!' Johnny objected.

'Why not?' Mark replied. 'Jaya's been on a ship and likely seen a man's bare chest before now, so why should I get my

104

clothes mussed up?'

'Johnny!' Jaya called, coming to the cabin door. 'Will you and Mark come and move the furniture for me?'

'Sure,' Johnny replied, stepping hurriedly before Mark in the hope of hiding his naked torso and saving Jaya embarrassment.

'Why don't you take off your shirt, too?' she asked. 'It will save me some washing.'

For a moment Johnny thought of ignoring the advice. Then he thought why the hell should that big blond bladder of lard get off showing his physique to Jaya. Maybe Mark was a mite bigger, but Johnny reckoned his own build was not exactly so puny that he need be ashamed to show it off. So he stripped off his shirt and left it, hat and gunbelt with Mark's on the wagon.

Not that Johnny had time to stand around and let Jaya admire his well-developed body. If she noticed it at all, Jaya gave no hint. Instead she had the two men working hard, carrying all the furniture out into the space before the house while she heated water.

'She sure has some go for a lil 'un,' Johnny said admiringly, looking towards the house.

'Yep, she sure has,' Mark agreed. 'Let's go clean out the barn while she does her chores in the house.'

Despite all his suspicions of Mark's intentions, Johnny went along with the idea. They heard the sound of scrubbing and Jaya's voice as she sang a song in a lilting tongue neither could understand, but which sounded mighty sweet to a man's ears. It made him think of the way Jaya looked in that frock, or how she danced the previous night. Johnny watched Mark, trying to read something in the big blond's face, but could not.

Johnny threw himself into the work before him like a man possessed. The barn needed a good cleaning and that was exactly what it got. Between them, Mark and Johnny did four men's work, lifting, toting, moving bales of hay and straw, and by noon they had cleaned the barn.

By noon Jaya had finished scrubbing the house. She stood in the centre of the main room and looked around her. If that did not please Johnny, she thought, nothing would please him. Perhaps she had been too friendly with Mark, she could not say, but Johnny had only himself to blame if she had. At that moment Jaya heard the sound of horse's hooves. She wondered who might be calling and, not wishing to disgrace Johnny before his neighbours, she decided to take a moment to tidy her appearance before going outside.

The sound of hooves brought Johnny and Mark's attention to the visitor, as they walked from the barn to the house to fetch Jaya and allow her to inspect and comment on their work.

'Going to need some chickens for Jaya to tend,' Mark drawled, then he heard the hooves and turned.

Johnny also turned, saw the on-coming rider and felt suddenly sick in his stomach. Of all the folks he had met during his last visit to the spread, the visitor was the last he expected to see—and the last he wanted to come calling under the circumstances.

Springing from the shaggy scrub horse's bare back, the newcomer dashed forward to throw arms around Johnny's neck and crush a hot little mouth to his.

The newcomer was a girl of about five foot five. Her tawny, curly hair hung in a tangle around a pert, pretty, naïve, dirty face. She had a full, rich, magnificent body which a sleeveless, tight fitting, man's old shirt did nothing to conceal, especially as it hung open at the neck and half-way down her round, full bust. The old, patched jeans clung to her hips like she'd been moulded into them, were about knee long and her legs and feet were bare.

'Hello, Tilda-Mae,' Johnny said, pushing the girl back to arm's length for her body gave off a stench of stale sweat and lack of soap which had always turned him from her.

'Johnny!' she replied. 'I done saw your smoke and come a-running.'

She tried to move closer, but he held her off, his hands on the greasy shoulders of her shirt.

'Won't your husband mind you coming over?' he asked.

'Naw! Never gotten married. That feller he took up and

106

run. The boys plumb chased him down to the gully country and let holes in his side. So I'm all free and ready to marry you-all.'

'*Me!*' Johnny yelped.

'Why sure. Figured it'd be fittin', us going to be neighbours 'n' all.'

At that moment Tilda-Mae's eyes caught a glimpse of Mark, jerked towards him and looked him over appraisingly, hungrily.

'Who-all's this here?' she asked.

'My *amigo*, Mark Counter,' Johnny answered hopefully.

'Johnny.'

Jaya could not have timed her arrival at a worse moment. Five seconds later and Tilda-Mae would have been throwing herself at Mark with the same reckless abandon that characterised her association with every presentable man who came along.

Whirling from Johnny, Tilda-Mae faced Jaya, suspicion and anger glowing in her eyes.

'Who-all's she?' the girl spat out.

'That's Jaya,' Johnny replied, which left a lot unexplained.

'She's your wife?'

'No——' Johnny answered, meaning to say he hoped she would be soon.

'Then she's going now!' Tilda-Mae screamed. 'No dirty furrin gal's going to come here and steal my man!'

With that she hurled herself forward, fingers crooked ready to snatch at Jaya's hair. Jaya fell back a couple of paces before the fury of the other girl's rush, a look of numb shock on her face at the words.

The wildly furious mountain girl did not reach Jaya, did not even set a dirty bare foot on the porch. Johnny had been standing staring, suddenly scared at the thought of what Tilda-Mae's words must mean to Jaya. For once in his life Johnny, who had acted fast in emergencies many times, could not think of what to do.

Springing forward, Mark caught Tilda-Mae around the waist from behind, just as she reached the edge of the porch.

107

He clamped his left arm around her pinning down her arms as well to her waist. Instantly she began to scream and curse, her strong little body thrashing and struggling against his, her legs thrashing and hacking back.

'Le'me go!' she screamed. 'I'll scratch her eyes out! I'll yank her bald-headed! The dirty, stinking furrin calico-cat! Come here and glomming on to my man!'

'Honest, Jaya!' Johnny gasped, turning to the girl as Mark dragged Tilda-Mae backwards. 'I never——'

With a strangled sob, Jaya turned and ran into the house, slamming the door behind her, not even offering to listen to his explanation.

One of Tilda-Mae's heels caught Mark on the shin. Having never worn shoes, the girl's feet were hard enough to pack some power behind them. Mark grunted in pain and annoyance. Then he swung the girl up from her feet, gripping her by the hair and pants seat, hoping the material would hold out. In that manner, keeping her bucking, writhing body at arm's length, Mark carried Tilda-Mae towards the horse-trough. One way or another that foul-mouthed, dirty little mountain girl needed cooling off and a bath. Mark reckoned he was the man to attend to that.

Tilda-Mae gave a scream as she hit the water and disappeared under its surface. Coming up, she started to scream curses so Mark shoved her under again. This time he held her under until he figured she ought to have learned her lesson. A gasping, sobbing, water-spitting girl sat up in the trough, but she neither struggled nor cursed. While never having received any formal scholing, Tilda-Mae knew she had best yell 'calf-rope' and give in, or be ducked under again.

Seeing the girl had quit struggling, Mark stepped back and allowed her to drag her soaking little body from the trough. She glared across to where Johnny stood trying to decide what to do, how to explain things to Jaya, how to stop Jaya leaving him.

'Bring that dirty furrin gal here, will you?' Tilda-Mae screamed. 'Just you wait 'til my kin hears what you done, Johnny Wade. They'll fix your wagon, but good, see if they don't. Then I'll get that furrin gal and beat her so ugly she'll never steal another American gal's man.'

All the time she screamed at Johnny, Tilda-Mae was backing away and keeping a wary eye on Mark. She saw the anger in his eyes as he started towards her, so spun on her heel and went afork her horse with a lithe bound. Her final threat to Jaya came as she sent the horse running up the bush-covered slope down which she came on her arrival.

Not until the sound of the horse's hooves had died away did either man make a move. Johnny let out his breath in a long, hissing sigh and turned on his heel towards the house. The only thing he could do was go in, explain things to Jaya and hoped she believed him. Before he could take three steps, Johnny felt a hand clamp on his arm and pull him around. He could never remember seeing Mark so angry as the big blond appeared to be at that moment.

'Why didn't you mention the gal?' Mark snapped.

'Why should I?' Johnny replied. 'Hell, I didn't but meet her a couple or so times last time I was up here. We had some loving, not much, I like mine washed and not smelling like a Kiowa wickiup. You saw how she looked at you, that gal's plumb man-hungry. Anyways, one day she came over and told me she wouldn't be seeing me again as she was marrying up with a travelling salesman who was working the county. I never even mentioned marrying her, and right after that I came back to the O.D. Connected. But I never said, or even gave Tilda-Mae cause to reckon I'd marry her.'

'Didn't, huh?'

'No, I damned well didn't!' Johnny answered, his temper and voice rising. 'What the hell is it to you? Reckon it'll give you a better in with Jaya?'

Mark looked at Johnny for a moment. Then he made a reply which he hoped would show his *amigo* that he (Mark) had no designs on Jaya, and doubted if she would give a damn even if he did have.

'I don't need a chance with Jaya,' was what Mark said.

Then Johnny hit him.

Taken anyway a man looked at it, except on the receiving end, Johnny could throw a good punch. His right arm whipped around, he ducked his shoulder behind the punch and drove his knuckles against the side of Mark's jaw. Mark spun around and only with an effort did he manage to keep his feet.

Coming in, Johnny ripped his left fist into Mark's stomach and smashed up the right at Mark's jaw, for he packed enough muscle and heft to fold Mark with the first blow.

The blow sent Mark backwards but did not put him down. Only just in time he caught his balance and clenched his fists for Johnny was coming at him again.

'Jaya's a good kid!' Johnny spat, closing with Mark. 'I'm going to make sure you stay away from her.'

He threw his right at Mark's head, but this time Mark was ready. Up came Mark's left, his wrist deflecting the right past his head. Then Mark drove out his right, smashing it into Johnny's mouth and knocking him backwards. Johnny hit the dining-room table, which fortunately had been stoutly built. Instead of it crumpling under Johnny's weight, the table took it and Johnny went straight over.

'It's time you woke up!' Mark growled, coming forward. 'Jaya isn't——'

With a snarl of rage, Johnny came to his feet and threw the table over in his eagerness to get at Mark. There was no avoiding a fight. Mark knew it. He also knew he would not have an easy time fighting Johnny, the cowhand was almost as big and strong as Mark and had learned many of Mark's fighting tricks during their friendship.

Mark snapped Johnny's head back with a right hand, stopping him in his tracks. Instantly Johnny's left flashed out like a diamond-back rattlesnake striking. The knuckles caught Mark in the mouth and Mark felt the salty taste of blood on his soft palate. He saw how Johnny stood, perfectly balanced, his left held out maybe just a little low, but his right cocked in front of his shoulder in the way Mark had taught him.

'You're learning, Johnny,' Mark said.

Feinting with his right, Johnny threw another left, but Mark moved his head far enough to let the blow slip over his shoulder. Johnny brought the stiff edge of his arm against the side of Mark's neck, knocking him off balance and then slugged his left into Mark's ribs bringing a grunt of pain. Shooting out his right, Mark drove it hard into Johnny's stomach, ripped a left after it and hooked a short left viciously to the side of Johnny's jaw. The force of the blow dropped Johnny to his knees.

Even as Mark moved in, Johnny flung himself forward, tackling the big blond around the knees and ramming him backwards. Mark felt himself going down and as Johnny lunged forward hooked his feet under the other's belly and heaved. Looking as if he had taken wings, Johnny sailed through the air to land on his back. He rolled over and came up fast, reaching his feet as soon as Mark did.

Once more Mark moved into the attack, wanting to keep Johnny away from the furniture. Sure Johnny wanted a fight, but that did not mean they should wreck his home having it.

The two men closed, fists stabbing out, ripping into each other. Mark took a savage hook to the floating ribs and went down to his knees. Up lashed Johnny's knee, driving under Mark's chin and throwing him on to his back. Johnny leapt up into the air, meaning to land on Mark with his knees. Too late he saw Mark roll, he missed but managed to break his fall. Without rising, Mark flung himself on to Johnny and they rolled over and over, fists thudding into flesh. Breaking apart, they rolled away from each other and made their feet once more.

Driving out his fist, Mark crashed it into the side of Johnny's head and Johnny went down. Instead of attacking immediately, Mark stood back and allowed Johnny to make his feet. They were both breathing hard, blood ran from Mark's mouth and Johnny's nose seemed to be twice its normal size. Yet Johnny still was not done. When Mark moved in, Johnny caught him with a left jab which landed under his eye, then closed with a two-fisted, slugging attack. Mark fought back, for almost five minutes they slugged it out like that. Then Johnny twisted around, getting his arms under Mark's armpits from behind, curling them around to clamp fingers behind Mark's neck.

They were locked in a struggle of strength, Johnny applying pressure with his full nelson and Mark fighting it off. Mark tried to twist free, turn and catch Johnny in the same hold. Both his body and Johnny's arms were soaked with sweat and coated with dust, so he could not escape that way.

The pain of the hold was intense. Drawing forward his stomach, Mark suddenly jerked it back again. His rump drove into Johnny's body and Johnny lost his hold, shooting back and doubling over. Turning, Mark drove up his left, the knuckles smashing into Johnny's jaw. The force of the blow lifted Johnny to his heels and tilted him over backwards to land in a cloud of dust on the ground.

Moving forward Mark dropped astride Johnny, kneeling on him. Desperately Johnny arched his back, trying to lift and roll Mark. It appeared that Johnny was not ready to listen to reason yet. Mark cocked his fist, drawing it back, his eyes, or his good eye, for his right eye had started to swell up and close, aiming at the point of Johnny's chin.

Something crashed against Mark's head. He heard a dull clang and he pitched sideways from Johnny to land on his face. Mark lifted his head; through the spinning mists and whirling lights, he saw Jaya, a furious-faced Jaya, standing above them, holding a shovel in her hands.

'Th—thanks—h—honey!' Johnny gasped and sat up.

The shovel came around and down as Johnny reached for Mark. It clanged on Johnny's head and he landed flat on his back again.

'Keep still!' she hissed and the concentrated fury in her voice, as much as the blow, made both men obey. 'What were you fighting over, who should have me and who should take the other girl?'

Neither man made any reply. Their fight, and her intervention, had left them in no condition to make flip answers, or any other kind.

'What do you think I am, Johnny Wade?' Jaya went on, her voice throbbing with emotion. 'Am I just your property? Do

112

you think I did not know that bill of sale was worthless? I saw you were a good man in the saloon. No other man had ever bothered about me enough to get me a chair. I wanted you to win me and when you did I could have cried. I hoped you would bring me with you, that I could make you care for me, marry me. I was willing to work for you, to live or die for you. Now I find you have another woman. I hate you! I never want to see you again!'

Throwing down the shovel, Jaya turned and ran blindly towards the house. She disappeared inside, slamming the door behind her. Gasping for breath, Johnny weakly forced himself to his feet. He opened his mouth to call after Jaya, but left it too late.

'Boy, we sure loused that up.'

Mark's words brought Johnny around to face him. The big blond stood rubbing his aching head which had a sizeable bump that had not been present when he rose that morning.

'You've sure put me in wrong now,' Johnny growled back.

'Me?'

'Yeah, you. If you hadn't been sweet-talking Jaya all the way up here I'd've told her how I felt about her.'

'The hell you would,' Mark answered. 'You shied away from her like a horse fresh caught on the range every damned time she tried to get close to you. So I figured to show you what you was missing.'

'You sure showed me,' Johnny groaned. 'Of all the lousy luck. I act about as dumb as a man can get—and then that man-hungry she-cat from the hills rides in and busts everything to hell and gone. I'm going to the house. Jaya'll listen to me, let me explain.'

'Not the way she feels right now,' Mark drawled.

'She'll list——!' Johnny began and turned.

Mark's right fist drove out, smashing into the side of Johnny's jaw with the power of a knobhead's kick. The blow took Johnny completely by surprise, it flung him from his feet and flat on to his back. This time Johnny would not be getting up. At least not for a spell. Mark hoped he would have time to do what needed doing before Johnny did get up.

113

'Sorry, *amigo*,' he said. 'It's the only way.'

Walking to the horse-trough, Mark pumped water over his head, clearing the dizziness out of it. He would need a clear head if he hoped to pull Johnny and Jaya out of their tangle. After sluicing his bruised, aching body, Mark walked to the house and entered.

He heard Jaya's sobs from the bedroom and went to its door. Inside the girl stood at the bed, thrusting her clothes into the bag, but leaving the items Johnny bought her, including the hat, on the end of the bed.

'I'll take you into Brownsville if you like,' he said.

'I'll walk,' she replied without turning around.

'If that's the way you want it,' Mark drawled. 'I reckon you're doing the right thing, leaving Johnny. See the way he's been acting over you when you dressed up and danced for him, and other times. Hell, he's been acting like a man in love with a gal, instead of his old self. Just shows how deceitful he is.'

No reply. The sobs had ended and Jaya no longer forced her clothes into the bag, but she did not turn.

'He's a worthless cuss at best,' Mark went on. 'And a hell of a liar. Why he told me that gal used to chase him last time he was up here, but that she took out to marry some other feller, not that Johnny ever wanted to marry up with her any old way. Fact being, old Johnny reckons he never wanted to marry up at all until he met you. But like I say, he's a li——'

Swinging around, Jaya flung herself at Mark, pushing him backwards.

'Where is Johnny?' she asked.

'Knowed you wouldn't want him bothering you,' Mark replied. 'So I left him lying out there with a busted jaw.'

'You brute!' she screamed and dashed from the room.

'Johnny boy,' Mark said quietly, 'Happen you've come round, just use your fool head for once with that gal and she's yours.'

By the time Mark left the house, Jaya had reached Johnny and knelt by him, pillowing his head in her lap.

'Johnny!' she gasped. 'Speak to me! I love you! I will not

leave you!'

Picking up a bucket, Mark filled it with water from the horse-trough. There was no use Jaya spilling her heart out to Johnny unless he happened to be able to hear and appreciate it.

'You big bullying brute!' Jaya spat as Mark came up.

He barely had time to set down the bucket before she landed on him with little fists swinging. After catching a couple of blows on the chest, Mark managed to grab the girl's arms and hold them. He twisted his body and caught a kick on the hip, then saw Johnny, behind the girl's back, raising his head and grinning.

For once it seemed Johnny had used his head around the girl.

Giving out a heart-rending groan, Johnny let his head flop back again. Jaya tore herself free from Mark's hands, forgot all about him, flung herself back to Johnny. Lifting his head and shoulders, she cradled them in her arms and kissed his battered face.

Johnny slid his arms around the girl and kissed back. For a long moment they stayed locked in each other's arms. At last they separated to catch their breath.

'Johnny,' Jaya breathed. 'I love you!'

'Jaya gal,' he replied, 'not as much as I love you.'

'Yes I do!'

'We're getting married, even if I have to whup ole Mark to——'

Jaya ended the threat with a kiss, then said, 'Mark never meant anything to me. Nor I to him. He acted as he did to make you jealous, so you would notice me as a woman.'

For a moment Johnny did not reply. Although every muscle and fibre of his body ached, he could hardly see through his right eye and his nose felt twice its normal size, Johnny had never felt so happy in his life. Nothing else mattered except that Jaya loved him.

'Reckon old Mark did just that,' he said.

Then they were locked in each other's arms once more and Johnny could hardly force himself to wait until they could find a preacher and get married. With any other girl he would not even have tried to resist.

'Where's Mark?' he asked, easing himself free from her arms.

'I don't know,' Jaya replied in a tone which implied she did not care either. 'Oh Johnny, you're hurt!'

'I asked for it,' he grinned, getting to his feet and helping her rise then feeling at the knot she had raised on his head with the shovel. 'Don't know as how I'd want to marry a gal that handy with a shovel—unless she knew how to dance in a lil bitty grass skirt.'

'You wait until our marriage night,' she answered. 'Then I will show *you* how the maidens really do it—where are you going?'

'To find a preacher,' he grinned.

'I help you,' she said eagerly, taking his hand.

Instead of looking for a preacher, they walked to where Mark sat on the anvil in the forge. He turned towards them and showed simulated surprise when Johnny told him of the impending marriage.

'I'd never have expected it,' he grinned.

'We want you to be best man,' Jaya said, squeezing Johnny's hand in a gentle warning that he had best agree.

'Sure we do,' Johnny agreed whole-heartedly. 'I know that's the only part you ever want to play in a wedding ceremony.'

'Do I get to kiss the bride without having a fight on my hands?' Mark asked.

'That depends,' Johnny grinned.

'On what?'

'How long after the wedding it is when you kiss her.'

Jaya looked from one man to the other. They were the first two men who had treated her decently, cared for her and showed her respect. She almost wished she had not been so free with the shovel head when they were fighting.

A flash of light flickered up on the slope above them. Just a brief flick and then it disappeared. Mark only saw it from the corner of his eye, but his brain sent out a warning.

'Duck it!' he yelled, shoving Jaya into Johnny and staggering them to one side.

116

His move came only just in time. A bullet hissed down from the slope, but not from where Mark had seen the reflection of the sun on some part of a weapon. Even as the crack of the shot reached their ears, Johnny had Jaya in safety, between him and the wall of the forge.

Two more shots, from different spots, came down. One struck the top of the anvil as Mark dropped behind it, then ripped off in the vicious whine of a ricochet. The other struck the top of the forge throwing brick chips into the air.

'Wade! Johnny Wade!' yelled a voice. 'You come on out here and take your needings.'

'Who is it?' Mark asked, looking at the wagon before the house and wishing either he was there with his guns, or they were here with him.

'Sounds like Big Tup,' Johnny replied. 'Tilda-Mae's oldest brother.'

That figured, happen a man knew hill-folks and Mark reckoned he did. The girl had returned home with word of the affront to her person, and all her male kin took down their rifles to avenge her. Only it should be the head of the clan who did the talking.

Watching the slope, Mark had three men spotted, the three who had fired at them. One lay up just on the rim, not far from where a dried-out water-course ran up the slope. The second appeared to be dened up between a couple of rocks out on the rim to the first's right. From the flash and smoke, Mark figured the third man further to the right, down behind that big old chestnut tree. The speaker had been still further along.

'How many are there in the family?' Mark asked.

'Four boys and Tilda-Mae,' Johnny replied, feeling the girl's warm body writhing at his side. 'Their mammy died just after Tilda-Mae was born, pappy got killed hunting a silvertip grizzly a couple of years back.'

'What do they want, Johnny?' Jaya asked.

'Nothing much, honey,' he lied.

'Wade!' yelled the voice again. 'Talk up. Air ye ready to do the right by our lil Tilda-Mae gal?'

'Come on down and talk it out, Tup!' Johnny called back.

117

'There ain't no talking out to do. You marry our lil sister, or we plant you out back of the house.'

'Johnny!' Jaya said, looking up at him. 'Did you ever tell the girl you would marry her?'

'No, honey. Honest, I never did.'

'That is all I wanted to know.'

Saying that, Jaya pushed past him, wriggling free and darting across the forge. Johnny sprang forward, three bullets cut the air around him and he flattened down again. The girl ran out towards the slope and from it burst Tilda-Mae on the shaggy mountain scrub horse.

Once more Johnny came to his feet, a fourth shot came down and ripped across his shoulder, tearing through flesh, but luckily not striking bone. The wound, on top of the fight he had fought, proved too much for Johnny and he dropped to the ground.

Springing to his *amigo*'s side, Mark dragged him back into cover for another bullet sprayed dirt up between Johnny's feet. Then Mark looked to see what Jaya was doing.

Tilda-Mae had left her horse and stood before Jaya.

'Please,' Jaya said. 'I will leave, but you must promise not to harm Johnny or Mark.'

'You're going to leave, you little furrin slut!' Tilda-Mae replied. 'But not 'til I've done with you. I don't take no furrin gal's leavings.'

And with that she lashed her hand around, the palm slapping across Jaya's cheek. Jaya staggered back a few steps, caught her balance only to take another savage slap.

'Dirty furrin whore!' Tilda-Mae hissed. 'Don't you have the guts to try and fight back?'

Again her palm lashed out, straight into the grip of Jaya's hands. Catching the other girl's wrist, Jaya carried it up over her head, pivoting around under the arms, then bringing her hands down. Tilda-Mae howled, her feet left the ground and she thought the world had suddenly spun around. The thud with which she landed on her back jarred the wind out of her.

Before Tilda-Mae could draw breath, she thought she had

been jumped by a bobcat. Jaya sprang forward, landing on Tilda-Mae, hands lashing, clawing, tearing at hair, slapping, punching and gripping flesh. For a moment Jaya had it all her own way. Then Tilda-Mae caught her breath. The attack and throw had taken the hill-girl by surprise, now that surprise was wearing off, those hard little hands, ramming, squeezing legs and sharp teeth driving it away.

Watching the girls roll over and over, Mark saw his chance. He glanced up the slope and saw the three men he had located earlier. They were all in plain sight now and yelling encouragement to their sister.

Mark was reminded of the battle at Bearcat Annie's saloon in Quiet Town, both by the wild savage way in which the girls went at it, and in the way the men up the slope stood watching. Maybe he could turn Jaya and Tilda-Mae's brawl to his advantage as Dusty Fog used the fight between the three female deputies and the saloon girls to let him get his male deputies inside the saloon and take a bunch of gunmen without firing a shot.

'You all right, Johnny?' he asked.

'I'll live!' Johnny replied weakly and thickly. 'Go help Jaya afore Tilda-Mae kills her.'

A glance at the girls showed Mark that Johnny's fears were, if not groundless, at least not urgent. From the way Jaya went at it, they were on their feet now, she looked like she could take care of herself. Mark had not forgotten the different ways Jaya had shown her strength, both at the store and since. She might be smaller and lighter than Tilda-Mae, but he would not say she was weaker or less able to take care of her end in the hair-yanking brawl.

'She doesn't need help. But you stay put here, or they'll make wolf-bait of you. I'll do what I can.'

Turning, Mark slipped from the cover of the open-sided blacksmith's forge building and darted across the open land. At any minute he expected to feel lead either slap by him, or drive into him. Yet none came and he lit down in the comparative safety of the mouth of the water-course.

119

'Go at her, Tilda-Mae gal!' a voice screeched from above him.

Looking upwards, Mark saw one of the brothers, a tall, gangling youth in a torn old shirt and bib-overalls. The youngster, for he seemed to be young, stood on the rim, waving his rifle over his head as he encouraged his sister.

Mark started forward, keeping in the water-course and climbing up over the rocks on its bottom. Under other conditions this would have been a suicidal route, but happen the fight lasted long enough, and it showed no sign or sound of abating in fury, he might reach the top unseen by the youngster.

'Yank her bald, sister!' howled the youngster.

So engrossed had he become that he did not see the shape inching through the bushes towards him. Mark had reached the head of the slope and now crawled forward on his stomach, using every bit of cover he could find. His path brought him to a halt behind the young man and his hands reached out.

The first sign the youngster had of his danger came when a pair of hands clamped hold of his ankles and heaved. Letting out a screech like a drunk Sioux Indian, the youngster landed on his face and felt himself being hauled down off the rim. His rifle had gone as he felt the hands grip him and he twisted around, fanning his right hand towards the butt of his bowie knife. Mark took aim and hit with all his skill. His fist caught the youngster's jaw, snapped his head to one side and dropped him in a limp heap on the ground.

Moving on, keeping to what cover he could find, Mark advanced towards the second brother, knowing this one would be harder to take. He looked maybe four or five years older than the one Mark had silenced. There seemed to be a hard, mean look about him and he cradled the Henry rifle with a negligent ease that did not deceive the big Texan. Give that feller half a chance and he would come spinning around with the rifle ready for use.

Yet there was no way to move in on him from behind. A feller with his looks did not pick a place where he could be sneaked up on. He leaned against one of the rocks, a coonskin cap on his head and wearing dirty buckskins, right out in the open, clear of anything even an ant could hide behind.

Bending, Mark took up a lump of rock about the size of a baseball. Then he started forward, hoping the girls kept the hill-man's attention for long enough to let him get in close.

Mark took three steps, then the man glanced back. He must have been expecting one of his brothers, for he just glanced at Mark, then turned back towards the fight—and whirled around again. The rifle started to come from his arm. Mark whipped back his arm and hurled the rock. It shot forward and caught the man on the front of his coonskin cap. From the thud, Mark knew he had put the man out of mischief, but hoped not too permanently. Without a sound, the man crumpled up and flopped to the ground.

Instantly Mark went back into cover. He thought he would be shot at, but the remaining brothers must have been too absorbed in what sounded like a humdinger of a fight to see what was happening on the rim.

This proved to be the case with the third brother. In age he seemed to fit between the first and second. Leaning his back against the chestnut's stout trunk, his rifle resting at his side, the third brother gave the girls his full attention, ignoring the possibility of an attack.

A big hand came around the tree trunk and clamped on the brother's shoulder. He let out a startled squawk, grabbed down at and missed his rifle, then shot around the trunk to catch Mark's other fist full on the side of his head. He went down as if he had been boned.

Which only left Big Tup, always provided the second man had not been he. There should only be the four of them. Mark reckoned Tilda-Mae's honour would be strictly family business, so only the direct kin should be along.

'You move nice, stranger,' a voice said.

Mark halted, he had been moving towards a clump of bushes where he suspected Big Tup to be hiding. The man sat in front of the bushes, his rifle on his knees, not aiming at anything in particular. In size he equalled Mark and looked like he weighed maybe ten—fifteen pounds heavier. Given that he was fresh and fit, Mark could have taken Big Tup, maybe after a hard fight. In his present condition he doubted if he could.

'Must have hill-blood in you,' Big Tup went on. 'Didn't hurt none of the boys bad, did you?'

'Beaned the one with the Henry with a rock, maybe bust his head,' Mark replied, wondering if he could get in close and jump the other before he rose.

'That'd be Lenny. Serve him right. He allows to know it all about hunting. The young 'uns all right?'

'They'll likely not feel like chewing raw beef for a couple of days.'

'Happen you put 'em off their food, I should be thanking you,' Big Tup grunted. 'Set a spell and let's see how that fracas 'tween Tilda-Mae and the lil furrin gal comes out. Boys'll be tolerable riled that you made 'em miss it. Ain't seed a cat fight as good as this since Maw caught Paw with that medicine show gal one time.'

Then Mark got it. The code of the hills, the code of the mountain men. Tilda-Mae brought her brothers to deal with Johnny, make him marry her, but when she went down and took Jaya on it made the matter personal between the two girls and the family would not intervene as long as nobody else did. Tilda-Mae must stand or fall alone. Mark could have saved himself some time—provided Jaya licked Tilda-Mae in the fight.

'Reckon I'd best get down and see how Johnny is,' Mark said.

'You 'n' him been fussing?'

'A mite.'

'That boy must be able to fight, happen he stood up to a feller like you,' Big Tup said soberly. 'Hope Tilda-Mae licks the furrin gal, we could use some good fighting blood like that in the clan. He hurt bad?'

'Caught him a bullet in the shoulder just now.'

'Land-sakes!' Big Tup grunted, coming to his feet. 'Why'n't you-all say so at first. Go on down to him. I'll look to the boys, then come on down myself.'

122

Mark did not know how far he could trust the big hill-man and so watched as Big Tup, moving faster than one might have expected of a man of his size, went to examine his brothers. He showed no great concern about any of their conditions and waved Mark down the slope.

It must have been some fight if the girls' appearance was anything to go by. Tilda-Mae had lost her shirt and her face carried marks. Jaya had come off better in the matter of clothes. Her skirt was torn from hem to hip and trailing behind her, her long hair in a dirty tangle, her face bruised and bloody.

Even as the men reached the foot of the slope, Tilda-Mae fell against the corral rails, hung there and reeled forward. Jaya braced herself and kicked up. While visiting New Orleans, Mark had seen French *savate* fighters and was reminded of them in the way Jaya kicked, except that they wore shoes and used the toe while Jaya's feet were bare and she kicked with the ball of her foot. The result was just as effective. Caught in the pit of the stomach, Tilda-Mae gave a scream and dropped to her knees. She landed on to Jaya's other knee as the little girl leapt forward and brought it up. Coming erect again, Tilda-Mae went backwards, hit the corral rail and hung there, then her knees buckled up and she crashed forward on to her face. Reeling forward, Jaya fell against the corral fence and held herself up on it.

With no more concern than he showed when looking at his brothers, Big Tup walked forward, bent and dug his hand into Tilda-Mae's hair. He lifted the girl's head from the ground, looking at the dirty, bruised features and glazed unseeing eyes. Releasing Tilda-Mae, he let her flop to the ground once more and turned to look at Jaya who supported herself by the corral rail, gasping for breath, sobbing and trying to hold the ripped top of her dress together.

'You whupped her fair 'n' square, lil furrin gal,' Big Tup said. 'She won't bother you or your man again.'

Bending, he lifted his sister and carried her to her horse, draping her face down over its back.

At the same moment Johnny came up, limping and with his

123

wounded arm hanging limply at his side. In his good hand, he held a Colt.

'Let it lie, Johnny!' Mark snapped, stepping into his line of fire.

'Look at what she did to Jaya!' Johnny growled, turning his eyes to the little girl who had sunk to her knees.

'You should see what Jaya did to her,' Mark grinned. 'Boy, when you're all married off to her, you do what she says. That gal fights like Dusty, uses a lot of the same tricks.'

At another time Johnny might have been interested to know of somebody who could use the fighting techniques so ably practised by Dusty Fog. Right now his only interest was Jaya.

Dropping the Colt, Johnny sprang to the girl's side. She turned her face to his.

'I—I would have gone away—rather than let them hurt you,' she said.

With his good arm, Johnny lifted the girl to her feet and supported her as he headed her for the house. Mark turned to watch Big Tup leading the scrub horse and its burden up the hill and saw two of the brothers on their feet. The youngest turned and jumped to where his rifle lay, but Big Tup bellowed and waved a hand to Tilda-Mae. Lowering the rifle without lining it, the young man moved down to meet Big Tup and his sister.

Picking up the Colt Johnny had dropped, Mark looked at it, then turned.

'Hey, Johnny!' he called. 'The next time you decide to throw a gun around in the dirt—do it with one of your own.'

Mark looked at the other two occupants of the room and grinned as he sank stiffly into a chair at the breakfast table.

'What's so funny?' Johnny growled, limping up and taking his seat.

'I was thinking what a sorry looking bunch we look,' Mark explained.

Hobbling stiffly around with the food and coffee, Jaya looked at the two men's faces and smiled.

'Do I look like you?' she asked.

124

'Worse,' Mark replied.

It was the morning after the day of the fights. Although none of the three meant to, they had slept in late and Jaya, first awake, now served them their food. On taking her seat, she looked at Johnny and Mark, then started to giggle. Her merriment started Johnny chuckling, for he too now saw what amused Mark.

After the departure of the hill family, Mark helped Johnny to care for Jaya, then patched his *amigo*'s wound up, using a basic knowledge of such matters gained in years of hectic life. The wound proved to be more messy and painful than dangerous, but Mark put Johnny's arm in a sling to prevent him using it too much.

With Jaya and Johnny's help, and his own terrific strength, Mark unloaded the supplies and stored them in the root cellar under the house. Then he moved as much of the furniture back into the house as he could manage. After that Mark was only too willing to go to sleep.

Jaya had bathed the previous night, combed the tangles out of her hair and now, with a couple of additions, looked her usual self.

'Where'd you learn to fight like you did?' Johnny asked her. 'I never saw anybody but a French-Creole kick like you did.'

'It is an old Siamese fighting trick,' she replied. 'I was a wild child and learned to defend myself from the native children.'

'You sure did,' Mark grinned. 'If you hadn't tangled with her, we'd likely still be out there, or dead.'

'They would have killed us all?' she gasped.

'They're hill folk, mountain men. Don't go by the same standards as other people. They've lived to that code ever since their kind moved in from the east. Cut one hill feller and all his kin bleed. They live by the rules their fathers and grandfathers laid down for them. That's why they didn't shoot after you and the gal tangled. She'd made the fight a personal thing and they couldn't cut in.'

'Then she won't come here again?' Jaya asked.

'Not after Johnny,' Mark replied. 'That's for sure. Under the code of the mountain folk she was whipped fair and square and she's got no claim on him.'

'She never had,' Johnny growled.

'I feel a little sorry for her,' Jaya put in, ignoring Johnny's comment.

At that moment they heard hooves outside and the snort of a horse, then a voice called: 'Hello, the house!'

'Tilda-Mae!' Johnny snapped, thrusting back his chair.

The girl sat her horse before the house. Although she wore a shirt it was not clean and she had made a very poor job of cleaning the results of the fight from her face and those parts of her body which showed; nor had she done anything about her dirty, tangled mop of hair.

'Can I see the furr—your woman, Johnny?' she asked without dismounting.

'No you c——'

Before Johnny could finish his denial, Jaya came from the house and pushed between him and Mark, stepping from the porch.

Tilda-Mae squinted down at Jaya, then looked at the two men. 'Can we make women talk?'

'Of course. Get off your horse. Come in and have some breakfast. We only just rose.'

Slipping from her horse, Tilda-Mae stood by it. She raised her right foot against her left calf, looking embarrassed. She made no attempt to walk towards the house and Jaya turned to tell the two men to go inside.

'It's all right, Johnny,' she said when he showed signs of hesitation. 'Go in, please.'

Once left alone words rushed out of Tilda-Mae's mouth.

'I want you to help me! I want to know why it is I can't never get a man who'll stick to me. And I don't mean Johnny. Sure I went after him, but he never said he'd marry me. But I want to know why I can't get a man.'

'How would I know?' Jaya smiled.

'You furrin gals know about things like that.'

Looking at the other girl, Jaya felt pity for her. Tilda-Mae was lonely and needed affection. Her brothers were kind enough in their own lights, but they did not give the girl the

126

love and affection she craved for. So she had tried to find it with other men, and never with happy results.

'I'll help you,' Jaya promised, looking the other girl over. 'The first thing we do is get you a bath——'

'A *bath!*' Tilda-Mae gasped. 'You mean all over, without any clothes on?'

'Of course. A man likes a girl to smell nice. Come, I found some clothes belonging to Johnny's aunt, they might fit you, and there are other things that we can use.'

'Yeah, but——' Tilda-Mae groaned, hanging back at the awful thought of having a bath.

'It's the only way,' Jaya warned, taking Tilda-Mae's grubby little hand and leading her gently towards the house.

Neither Johnny nor Mark knew what Jaya planned. She gave them orders to go out and find some work, but not to come in until she called for them.

At noon, still with no sign of the two girls, Johnny saw something which took his mind temporarily off thoughts of what Tilda-Mae might be doing to his Jaya.

A large party of people were coming towards the house. Four buggies carrying neighbouring families rolled in the centre of some twenty or more men. In the lead of the party, spurring his horse forward, rode Big Tup.

'Howdy, Johnny,' he greeted, sliding the horse to a halt. 'Real sorry about your arm. That big feller near on cracked Lenny's head and raised lumps on Sam and Jeb. Reckon we can call it evens?'

'If that's the way you want it,' Johnny replied, throwing a puzzled look at the approaching party.

'Preacher's in town,' Big Tup remarked. 'So I sent the boys out to gather in your neighbours. Figured you and the fu— your gal'd like company on the way in to see him.'

By that time the others of the party had arrived and broad grins came to every face as they studied Johnny.

'Where-at's your gal, Johnny?' asked a stout woman. 'We didn't know you'd got here or we'd've come over to lend a hand.'

'Jaya!' Johnny called.

The house door opened and Jaya came out. There were mutters of admiration and surprise at her appearance, but what the crowd saw following her really made them sit back and stare.

'Is that you, Tilda-Mae?' Big Tup gasped.

His surprise had good cause. The girl behind Jaya was clean, her hair still curly but soft looking and tidy, and she wore a gingham dress of modest pattern. During the morning Jaya had searched through the drawers of the side-piece and found clothes belonging to Johnny's dead aunt; she died some eighteen months before his uncle. For the first time in her life Tilda-Mae wore clean underclothes instead of old flour-sack drawers and she liked the feeling. She also liked the admiring looks several young men threw her way, but remembered Jaya's advice about not throwing herself at men so stood demure and unspeaking.

'Jaya,' Johnny said. 'There's a preacher down at Bagley's Corners. Do we want to see him?'

'Yes, Johnny,' she gasped. 'Yes, please!'

And she threw her arms around his neck, kissing him, then moved away with a blush on her cheeks as the watching people laughed. Her embarrassment did not last for the women of the party bore down on her, sweeping her and Tilda-Mae back into the house to do the things women must always do before a wedding.

It made a pretty picture. The bride standing blushing shyly at the side of the very nervous groom. The best man and bridesmaid in their places, the guests seated on cracker boxes, chairs and the bench brought in from its usual place on the store's porch. Bagley's Corners had not yet grown in size to the point where a preacher could live as a permanent thing, or to where a church became a necessity.

Standing with his back to the assembled crowd, the preacher prepared to start the ceremony. When the rustling and shuffling died away behind him, he turned to face the congregation.

First he looked at Jaya's puffed and swollen left eye and

128

scratched cheek. Next his eyes went to Johnny's swollen nose and almost closed right eye. From there his gaze took in Tilda-Mae who sported two blackened eyes and a lump on her forehead and Mark whose left eye matched Johnny's right and whose top lip looked twice its normal size. After that the preacher looked at the crowd, to Tilda-Mae's three brothers who each bore signs of how the big blond Texan handled them; and finally to a pair of young men who carried more recent signs of a discussion as to who should escort this new, clean Tilda-Mae to town.

After travelling the Texas range for nearly twenty years in a vain attempt to save unruly souls, the preacher reckoned he could not be surprised any more. If the sight before him had not been a surprise, it would do until one came along. However, he rallied quickly.

'Dearly beloved,' he said. 'It sure looks like you had a hard time convincing each other it was time to come to church.'

For a moment Jaya and Mark's eyes met and the girl smiled.

'We did,' she breathed. 'But we made it in the end.'

PART THREE

THE KIDNAPPERS

A SUDDEN crash! The batwing doors of the Indian Nations Saloon burst open and the citizens of Guthrie, Oklahoma Territory—or such of them as chanced to be in the vicinity at that moment—were treated to the spectacle of Fatso Kinnear erupting into the street. He came out all doubled over, like a man who had been kicked in the belly by a mule; or hit there by a real powerful fist. On the street he dropped to the hoof-churned dirt and lay writhing in agony upon it.

An instant after Kinnear's arrival on the street, the batwing doors flew open once more and his partner, Lou Rushton, came into sight running backwards; or so it seemed. At least his stubby fat legs moved as if running, although they continued to do so after he left the sidewalk. Then he lit down on his feet and flopped backwards to crash down across Kinnear's bloated form.

Again the doors opened, although with less violence, as Mark Counter and his cousin Beau emerged. They halted on the sidewalk and looked down at the recumbent forms of their attackers with dispassionate gaze.

'It looks like they're plump tuckered out, Cousin Mark,' said Beau, calmly setting right his grey cutaway jacket, for he was a professional gambler and always liked to appear neatly dressed when his funds ran to it.

'Looks that way, Cousin Beau,' Mark agreed. 'I take it you'd won some and they didn't like losing.'

'Amazing deduction. They sat in the game half an hour back and I warned them I intended to pull out at ten o'clock. But when the time came they objected to my going.'

Beau's accents sounded different to Mark's deep south drawl for he had spent several years in England and picked up the speech of the upper-class folks he mingled with.

'Happen they'd known you, they'd've been pleased to see you go,' grinned Mark. 'It might have given them a chance to win.'

'My dear old cousin, that pair couldn't count to eleven without taking off their shoes—I won't say socks, they probably don't wear any. Come along the street a piece, I've something for you.'

A few people had gathered around, looking at the groaning shapes on the ground. One of the crowd wore the badge of a deputy town marshal, but he made no attempt to stop Mark and Beau as they walked away. Bounty hunters had never been held in respect by lawmen of the better kind. Kinnear and Rushton were even viler than most of their breed. The deputy knew they had come into Guthrie the previous day bringing in three dead outlaws, two of whom had been shot in the back, to make collection on the bounty their heads carried.

Being unmoved by public disapproval, Kinnear and Rushton took their blood money to the Indian Nations Saloon and found a big stake poker game in progress. They sat in and found Beau among the players. Not being skilful poker players, their money soon faded away, most of it going in the mistaken belief that Rushton could fill an inside straight on the draw.

Which was when the trouble started. Beau had already announced his time for quitting the game, both knew of his decision. Yet when the appointed hour arrived they raised violent objections to his going. Their objections brought Mark into the affair for his cousin faced odds of two to one in numbers and almost three to one in weight.

Actually Beau could probably have managed the two men single-handed. Mark definitely could, for neither Rushton or Kinnear had the courage of cornered rats when put to the test. However, Mark cut in and rendered Kinnear incapable of enjoying his food for some time to come, while Beau demonstrated his fistic prowess on the no more able Rushton.

Seeing the local law did not appear to have the intention of taking their part, Rushton dragged himself to his feet. He wore an Army Colt at his side but did not touch it. Not that his scruples would have prevented him shooting a man in the back, but he knew the deputy would intervene should he try.

Helping the moaning Kinnear to his feet, Rushton half dragged, half carried him from the street.

At the hotel Mark and Beau prepared to go their separate ways. Beau intended to catch a stage and Mark wished to collect his horse and head down trail on his business.

'About that thousand you lent me to sit in the game, old son,' Beau said, talking out his wallet. 'I rather improved on it. Here.'

Mark accepted the sheaf of hundred dollar bills and riffled them through his fingers.

'Feels like there's more than a thousand here,' he remarked.

'Two actually. Call the other interest on your loan.'

'You don't need to pay me interest, Cousin Beau.'

'I know. But take it anyway,' Beau replied. 'I'm always luckier if I show a bit of generosity, and I couldn't have got into the game without your help. So put it away and don't argue. I'd force it on you, only I'd get licked.'

Grinning at his cousin, Mark put the money into his own wallet and slid the wallet under his shirt to the special pocket built inside.

'I don't feel like licking anybody today,' he said.

'Where are Dusty and the Kid?' Beau asked.

'They headed straight down to the O.D. Connected. What with the delay we had on the way up, with that trouble on the Lindon Land Grant,* and running the law in Mulrooney, they wanted to get back fast. But I heard Pappy was bringing a herd up the west trail and came this way to see him.'

'If I was staying in town for the night we could whoop things up a bit. I know a couple of young ladies who're just pining for the company of a brace of fine, fit and frolicsome Southern gentlemen. But I've booked a passage on the north-bound stage and there's a big game I want to catch due to start

*Told in *Trigger Fast* by J. T. Edson.

in Mulrooney so I can't cancel it.'

'Sure,' Mark drawled. 'I want to be riding myself. See you, Cousin Beau.'

'Sure, Cousin Mark. Don't take any wooden women.'

'I leave that to your side of the family, *Adios*.'

With that Mark turned and headed for the livery barn where his horse waited for his pleasure. Beau entered the hotel to collect his belongings. Neither noticed the two girls who had followed them along the street, listening to every word they said.

Riding his seventeen-hand stallion at an easy trot along the winding trail from Guthrie, Mark made for the western slope of the cattle drives which came up from Texas. Somewhere on the western trail he would meet his father's herd, visit for a spell, then head back to the O.D. Connected.

The noose of rope came flying from the side of the trail, sent out in a hooley-ann throw to drop over Mark's head and around his shoulders, then draw tight. Although taken by surprise, Mark did not panic. Allowing the reins to fall, he stopped his horse. His right leg kicked free of the stirrup, over the saddlehorn and he dropped to the ground. With a sudden heave of his enormous biceps, he opened his arms. The rope jerked and he heard a startled feminine yelp, then a thud as the one who roped him shot out of the bushes. Mark started to turn, the rope still on him and slowing his move towards his guns.

A bullet kicked up dirt between his feet. The shot, a flat bark of a Winchester carbine, came from the opposite side to where the rope came.

'Just freeze solid, big boy!' warned an unmasculine voice.

Keeping his hands still, Mark turned towards the speaker. She stood at the side of the trail, having stepped from concealment. Working the lever of her carbine, she kept Mark covered.

The girl wore a white Stetson on the back of a mop of close cut, curly black hair. She was a good-loking girl, probably not more than eighteen years old at most, with her skin tanned by much time spent in the open. The tartan shirt she wore, and the jeans with their turned back cuffs, emphasised a slim, but not bony build. She wore high-heeled cowhand boots, and a gunbelt, with a Navy Colt in its holster at her right side, hung around her waist.

Just as slowly, Mark turned to look at his captor. She stood in the trail where his sudden jerk had heaved her, the rope still gripped in her hands. In height she came maybe to her pard's shoulder, but did not have a slim build. Rather there was a rubbery plumpness about her, not fat, but the kind of build which allowed its owner to be as agile as many a slimmer person. Her hair style copied her friend's, was mousey brown, and if anything more curly. Her face bore a warm, vibrant, merry, if naïve charm. Mark put her age at maybe a year less than the other girl's. A black Stetson hung by its storm strap on to her back. The blue shirt fitted tightly to her body, and the jeans looked stretched almost to their limits. At her left side, the holster and gun looking like mates to the one her friend wore, hung a Navy Colt. Her face showed amazement at having been plucked out of her hiding place with no more effort than if she had been a feather.

'Haul that rope tight again, Britches!' the slim girl ordered. 'One wrong move'll see you limping, big boy.'

'Annie could do it, too, mister,' warned the chubby girl, her voice a little high with excitement.

The chance dropped names, if it had been by chance, puzzled Mark. Sure he had heard of Cattle Annie and Little Britches, but he always discounted them as being no more than camp-followers of the Doolin gang. Messengers or lookouts kept around to amuse the male members with their pose of being desperate lady outlaws.

Having met Doolin on two occasions, not connected with the outlaw's professional life, Mark liked the man. It did not fit in with Mark's ideas of Doolin's character that the outlaw would allow Cattle Annie and Little Britches to do the dirty and risky work of a hold-up while he and the other men stayed hidden. In fact it seemed highly unlikely that Doolin would waste time robbing chance-passing strangers. Finally, apart from their friendship, Doolin would not risk antagonising a man as dangerous as Mark Counter; a man with capable, tough and good friends to back him, or take the vengeance trail should Mark be shot in a robbery.

He allowed the rope to tighten, for Cattle Annie held the carbine like she knew how to use it. Remembering Doolin boasting about the girl's sighting eye, Mark knew better than to object.

'Now ease your hands round in front of you,' Annie ordered and Mark obeyed.

Showing skill in the handling, Little Britches sent two coils of rope flipping out to settle around his arms and draw tight. Now Mark remained very still. Given a chance and a few minutes to work up to it, he might have snapped the three strands of hard-plaited Manila rope around him, but not in time to stop the girl in front planting lead into him.

'Cover him, Britches!' Annie ordered, leaning her carbine against a bush. 'And keep that rope tight.'

Stepping forward, Annie lugged a pair of old Bean Giant handcuffs from her hip pocket. Mark tensed himself, but felt something hard and round gouge into his back. Something about right for the size of the business end of a Navy Colt. Doolin allowed Britches to be fair with a carbine and handy with a light calibre Colt. Even if she could not shoot like Dusty Fog, the girl would be highly unlikely to miss at that range, and Mark had heard her cock the Colt as she approached.

Had there been men along Mark could have acted in a different manner. A man could not kick a girl in the guts, then jump her to get a weapon, which he might have chanced with a man. He knew Doolin would soon put an end to such foolishness. Which worried Mark. Where was Doolin?

The handcuffs clicked on to his wrists. They looked like an old pair, probably stolen from some sheriff's office. He hoped the girls had a key, although it did not worry him a great deal if they had not.

'Don't tickle,' he warned as Annie bent to unlash the support thongs on the bottom of his holsters.

Yet Mark felt puzzled. He could not see why the girls would

take the trouble to handcuff him if robbery was their plan. Nor would they waste time in taking off his gunbelt.

Slinging Mark's gunbelt around her shoulders, Annie stepped back. Britches removed the rope with the easy speed of a cowhand and stood grinning at the other girl.

'It worked, Annie,' she said. 'Just like we planned it.'

'Sure,' Annie replied, turning to walk towards Mark's horse.

'Watch him, gal!' Mark ordered. 'He doesn't take to strangers handling him.'

To prove its master's words the big stallion swung its head towards the girl, snorting a warning. Annie showed she knew something about horses. Talking quietly and steadily, she walked towards the horse. Out shot her hand to haul the rifle from the saddleboot, then she sprang clear and avoided a vicious chop from the stallion's jaws.

'What now?' Mark asked, puzzled at the girls' actions.

'You're coming with us,' Britches replied, stepping around him, having holstered her Colt while she coiled the rope.

'Why?' Mark asked.

'Why'd you think?' Annie answered.

Mark did not reply in words, but his smile brought an angry flush to Annie's face and caused Britches to giggle.

'Not for *that*!' Annie snorted.

'You wouldn't need to hawg-tie me if it was,' grinned Mark. 'Why then?'

'We know you, Mark Counter. Your pappy's coming up trail right now.'

'So?'

'So we figure he'll pay a thousand dollars to get you back,' Britches explained and Annie frowned at her for stealing the thunder.

It took Mark almost thirty seconds to get what Britches meant.

'How long's Bill Doolin gone in for kidnapping?' he asked.

'Shucks, this isn't Bill's idea,' Britches replied. 'It's mine— well, mine and Annie's.'

Her amendment came as she saw a frown crease Annie's brow.

136

'Sure,' Annie agreed. 'Bill and the boys went out to pull off a raid and left us at a hide-out. Only we come into Guthrie, saw you, learned who you was and where you was headed. Came out here, laid in wait and caught you. Ole Bill doesn't know sic 'em about this.'

That figured, happen a man came to think about it. Bill Doolin must be far away for the girls to be trying such foolishness. Mark knew Doolin would put an end to the farce quickly enough should he return. So Mark reckoned he might as well go along with the girls. His father's herd would not be close enough for them to deliver the ransom message for several days and by that time anything could have happened to set Mark free.

'On your hoss, big boy,' Annie ordered. 'And no tricks, or they'll be calling you Limpy.'

While Mark swung afork his horse, Annie threw a bullet into his rifle's chamber. Britches hurried off to return with a pair of wiry ponies. She mounted one, jerking the carbine from its saddleboot, after strapping on her rope to the horn. Annie booted her carbine and retained Mark's rifle in her hands to help keep the big Texan under control.

'Get going, and don't try a trick,' Britches ordered.

'Nary a trick, ma'am,' replied Mark, now thoroughly enjoying the unusual experience of being kidnapped by a pair of pretty little girls. 'Where'd you want for me to go?'

'Turn right into the trees,' Annie replied. 'We'll point you from there.'

They rode for a time in silence, Mark in the lead and the two girls like the twin points of the letter V behind him. However as they left the wooded land behind them and wound through the rolling Indian Nations land, Britches could restrain herself no longer.

'Boy!' she said, bringing her pony alongside Mark's stallion. 'Won't this shake ole Bill down to his toes. And Red Buck and the rest. We'll make a thousand on our first chore.'

'Sure,' Annie agreed delightedly. 'And they wouldn't take us with 'em this time in case the going got rough. I bet they take us along in future.'

Mark considered this highly likely, or that Doolin would throw them out on their rumps for pulling such a fool trick. He could imagine Doolin's comments when the outlaw heard the two girls had been stupid enough to think of kidnapping Mark Counter and asking for a ransom from his father, Big Rance Counter. Mark also thought that the girls might find Doolin's reaction far from the one they hoped to receive.

For a pair of bold, daring kidnappers, the girls made a bad mistake. They took trouble to hide their tracks and stuck to country over which the following of sign would be a slow, difficult proceeding. Yet they made no attempt to blindfold him and prevent him seeing where they took him.

After covering some five miles from the trail, the girls pointed Mark down into a wide, winding valley. The slopes rose fairly steep, with a scattering of rocks, trees and bushes covering them, but the bottom lay open and offered good grazing.

Turning a bend in the valley brought them into sight of a small log cabin. A snug retreat well hidden from prying eyes. To one side of it lay a spring which widened into a deep pool and trickled off in a stream which ran through the edges of a couple of pole corrals. Although the corrals had no horses in them, they had been in recent use. All in all the place looked ideal for gentlemen following Mr. William Doolin's self-effacing business.

'Get yourself down, big boy,' Annie ordered as they reached the corrals. 'Watch him, Britches, while I tend to the hosses.'

'You-all reckon you can handle that big bloodbay of mine, Annie-gal?' asked Mark, swinging from his saddle.

Annie bit her lip, eyeing the stallion doubtfully. This was a snag she and Britches had not foreseen when they rode into Guthrie meaning to find somebody to rob as proof for Doolin of their capabilities. Of course, they had not thought of kidnapping anybody, either. The idea came to them after they left town meaning to merely hold Mark up and empty his wallet. Then Annie had her brilliant idea, to pull off a more impressive, and better paying job. Now she found a problem, for her love of horses would not allow her to neglect the big stallion.

Yet she could see no way out of the predicament.

'Happen I give my word will you unlock one cuff and let me tend to him?' Mark suggested.

For a moment Annie did not reply. She looked Mark over from head to foot, then glanced at Britches, seeking advice.

'You'll give us your solemn word not to try anything and let us fasten you soon as you're done?' Britches asked.

'As solemn as they come, and they don't come solemner,' Mark replied, hoping the amusement he felt did not show.

The two girls drew away and went into a huddle, talking and throwing looks in his direction. Mark watched them, leaning against the corral rail and awaiting their decision.

'Don't you try nothing,' Annie warned, taking the handcuffs key from her pants pockets.

'Ma'am!' Mark answered, drawing himself up indignantly, 'if you're doubting a Southern gentleman's word——'

'Shuckens, no!' Britches put in. 'We wouldn't do that.'

Clearly the two girls accepted that he would keep his word, for Annie unlocked the handcuffs without taking any precautions such as handing either Mark's gunbelt which hung around her shoulders, or her own revolver, to Britches. If Mark had wished, he could have drawn the nearest of his Colts and disarmed the girls. He did not. After all, a man should ought to keep his solemn given word to a pair of gallant lady outlaws.

After attending to his horse, Mark carried his saddle to the lean-to behind the house and hung it alongside the girls' on the burro. Then, as solemnly as Lee offering his sword to Grant at the Appomattox Courthouse, he held out his right arm and allowed Annie to secure it.

'March to the house,' Annie ordered.

Grinning, Mark marched. His horse stood in one corral, the girls' mounts in the other. Annie brought her carbine and Mark's rifle along and Britches carried her carbine under her arm.

The door opened into the main room of the cabin, with a stove and cooking range to one side, a rough table and maybe half a dozen chairs as the sole furnishings. A wall split the cabin into two parts, the rear being given over to a couple of bedrooms.

Britches saw the way Mark looked around him and her cheeks flushed a little.

'This's just a lay-off place,' she said. 'You should oughta see our main hide-out, it's got rugs on the floor, even a pianny. Ain't that so, Annie?'

'It sure enough is,' Annie agreed. 'Make yourself to home, mister. We'll fix you a meal, then you can write us a note to deliver to your pappy, telling him what we aim to do to you happen he don't pay up.'

She hung Mark's gunbelt on a peg by the door, and put the rifle and carbine on the racks which lined the walls. A happy smile came to Cattle Annie's face. It sure would be great to show Bill and the boys that they could handle their share of the business.

For almost an hour Fatso Kinnear had been cursing the man who laid him low after rough-handling him. While it never was much to look at, his fat face had an ashy greenish shade which made it even more repulsive.

His partner did not say much, though less from a spirit of Christian forgiving of his enemies than because his swollen jaw did not make for easy talking. So he stood scratching his long, shaggy hair and thinking on much the same lines as Kinnear spoke.

The two bounty hunters stood in the cheap livery stable which doubled as a place to leave their horses and a hotel room for themselves. True Guthrie was a fair sized city with several hotels and rooming houses, but every one appeared to be booked up solid when the two bounty hunters arrived asking for a place to sleep while in town. On hearing of their problem, the owner of the livery barn generously offered to allow them to sleep in an empty stall mostly used for penning his pigs.

'How about the smell?' Rushton had asked when presented with the magnanimous offer.

'Don't worry,' the owner replied. 'The pigs won't mind it.'

Rushton still did not know how to take the remark.

'I'll kill that big blond feller, see if I don't!' Kinnear snarled, showing a remarkable lack in inventive powers as he had made the threat at least six times. 'You see if I don't.'

At that moment the third member of their evil organisation entered the barn and slouched towards the two men. He came silently, for he wore Indian moccasins. Nor did the Indian motif end there. His fringed buckskins smelled like a Kiowa lodge and had been greased and smoke blackened to a pitch where they could be located when down-wind—and up-wind too, happen a man had a delicate nose. His face bore the high cheekbones, the slightly hooked nose and slit-eyed look of an Indian, yet had a sickly pallor. Sunset Charlie Mallalieu's mother had been an Osage Indian who even the Osages regarded as being beyond the pale; his father, a white of French birth, although he always celebrated a festival called *Yom Kippur*. The half-breed inherited the worst characteristics of both races and none of their good points.

'I found-um something,' he said, hitching up his gunbelt, with its Beals Navy revolver at the right and Bowie knife at the left side.

'Who?' asked Kinnear.

'Those two gals who ride wit' Doolin. I found out who they is from Injun feller. Him say they gals who ride with Doolin all right.'

'Got mon' on 'em?' mumbled Rushton.

By this he did not ask if the girls carried money on their persons, but if any interested law-enforcement body had offered a reward for their capture dead or alive, preferably the first.

'No. Them gals not impo't' enough,' Mallalieu replied.

'Then why in hell are you coming bothering us?' demanded Kinnear; his stomach seemed to be trying to crawl up his throat as he caught a whiff of the half-breed's stench.

'Them leave town. I see-um go. Maybe-so they go to Doolin's hide-out.'

Instantly the other two sat up and took notice. Bill Doolin and his bunch carried big money on their heads. Higher than Kinnear and co. had ever made, for they tended to be coyotes rather than buffalo-wolves in their line. If their financial situation had been better they might have passed up going after the Doolin gang as far too risky. But, as Kinnear and Rushton were all too painfully aware, beggars could not be choosers.

'Word has-um that Doolin and his boys away on raid,' Mallalieu went on. 'Maybe them gals lead us to-um straggler.'

'Yeah,' muttered Rushton. 'They could at that. Let's go see.'

They took their horses and belongings, slipped out of town and Mallalieu pointed out the girls' tracks. At first the half-breed found no difficulty in following the trail of the two horses. He led the way to where they left their horses among the trees and read the story left by their feet. It appeared that the girls had set up a hold-up on the trail, although none of the trio could think why, nor could they decide why the man the girls stopped should accompany them into the trees.

'Looks like they met up with the feller to take him back to their hide-out,' Kinnear remarked.

'Let's take after him,' Rushton replied, speaking with difficulty.

However, tracking the three horses became more difficult once they left the trees behind. Although Mallalieu could cling to the trail, it took good and careful sign-reading to do so, and good and careful sign-reading could not be done at a gallop. Their slow rate of progress did nothing to improve Kinnear's and Rushton's tempers, for it prevented them from getting close enough to even see their prospective victims. Had they done so their plan of action would have been simple yet effective; sneak up when the three riders were bedded down for the night and pour a volley of rifle fire from the darkness into the sleeping camp.

'No see-um tracks any more,' Mallalieu announced.

'Leave it until daylight then,' Kinnear answered. 'We'll camp here and move on at dawn.'

The first light of dawn found them with a problem. Rushton's jaw was so swollen that he could barely speak a coherent word. Yet he did not trust the other two enough to allow them to go on without him. They rode on and came to a wide valley with steep slopes covered with rocks, bushes and trees. Here Mallalieu drew his horse to a halt and cocked his head on one side, listening.

'They close,' he said.

Kinnear swung from his saddle and drew the rifle from the boot. He saw the other two had followed his lead and nodded his head.

'Let's move in and take a look,' he said.

Give them their due, Cattle Annie and Little Britches might be no more than a couple of fool kids playing at being outlaws, but they sure could whomp up a mess of hog-jowls and mustard greens fit to set before a king.

Mark ate well, despite the handicap of being handcuffed and having his ankles roped together in an effective hobble which would not permit him to walk at anything faster than a snail's pace. In payment for his meal Mark entertained the girls with jokes and stories, keeping them laughing and making a favourable impression on them both. He noticed the way Britches studied his great spread of shoulders and slim waist with interest. And, although she tried to hide it, Annie was taking in his handsome features, noticing the virile, vital health of his giant physique. This did not surprise Mark, for he was used to attracting the interested looks of females.

With the supper done, Mark suggested he helped Britches wash the dishes. He sensed rather than saw Annie watching them. The elder girl grunted her disapproval as Mark, seemingly by accident, bumped into Britches who began to giggle. When the dishes were done Annie told Britches to watch the big feller and walked from the cabin.

'Ain't she the bossy one though?' grinned Mark.

'Yeah!' agreed Britches. 'Ain't she?'

Only she did not grin and there was a hint of annoyance in her eyes. They said no more until the other girl entered and spread Mark's bedroll on the floor by the wall.

'You sleep there, big boy,' she ordered. 'I'll stand the first night herd on him, Britches.'

'Reckon we need to?' Britches replied suspiciously.

'Sure we need to. We'll look real fools if he sneaks off in the night.'

For a moment the desire to go to bed and suspicion of Annie's motives warred on Britches's pretty little face. Then she turned and headed for the bedroom door, turning towards Annie as she reached it.

'Mind you call me for my watch!' she warned. 'I'll leave the door open in case *you* need help.'

An angry frown creased Annie's face as she watched Britches's fat little rump disappear into the bedroom, but she did not reply. Instead she began to tidy up the cabin while Mark remained seated at the table. After finishing her tidying, Annie took the two carbines and cleaned them. By the time she had finished, the bubbling snores coming from the bedroom told her Little Britches was asleep.

'She snores worse'n a hawg at times,' Annie remarked, bringing the coffee-pot from the stove. 'Are you all right?'

'I've been more comfortable.'

'Shuckens, you can lie down if you like.'

'The night's young. I'd rather sit and talk.'

'Always say a man talks better with a coffee-cup in his hands,' she replied. 'What do you want to talk about?'

'Weather, if you like.'

'Whether I will, or whether I won't?' snapped Annie.

'The thought had crossed my mind,' grinned Mark. 'What'd be the answer?'

'That depends on who asked.'

'Me, I'm asking.'

'Bill and the boys'll be back by night time tomorrow, happen everything goes smooth,' Annie said, speaking rapidly as she changed the subject. 'Won't they be surprised when they find you here?'

Surprised was not the word Mark would have used.

'How come you to get tied in with Bill and his bunch?' he asked.

It all began when the Doolin gang paid a courtesy call to the small village where Cattle Annie and Little Britches lived, the girl explained. The outlaws came to attend a wedding and

144

dance. They intrigued the local kids and made themselves pleasant to the citizens for Doolin knew the value of good public-relations even though he had never heard of them.

To the youngsters of the area Doolin's gang carried an aura of glamour. But Annie McDougall and Jennie Stevens did more than just sit back and watch from afar. When Doolin's gang rode out of the town, the two girls took their horses and borrowed men's clothing and followed. Once Doolin chased them back, but they tagged along and showed up at his hide-out. After that Doolin could hardly risk allowing them to go back.

So they became Cattle Annie and, from the way she filled her pants, Little Britches. They were accepted as the mascots of the gang, for Doolin's bunch had a string of good fortune starting from their arrival. The outlaws treated them with kindness, protected them, and taught them a number of things girls from honest, God-fearing homes only rarely learned about; such as how to handle a rifle or a revolver and how to take care of themselves by using their fists instead of hair yanking. This latter had come in useful when one of the gang brought a calico-cat along to the hide-out and she would not leave after he grew tired of her. It fell on the two girls to take the errant female out and show her the light.

True, Annie went on, Bill had never yet let them ride on a raid, but she bet he would when she and Britches handed him the ransom money from Mark's father.

They talked on for a time and then Annie rose, walked around the table to sit on Mark's lap and wrap her arms around his neck. She crushed her mouth up to his, kissing him with what she fondly imagined to be more passion than he had ever before come up against in a woman.

'How was that?' she asked, releasing him.

'Not bad at all,' Mark replied. 'How's about turning me loose so I can sample it properly?'

For a moment he thought she would. Interest, eagerness and anticipation flickered across her face, to be wiped out in an expression of fear almost. She showed the sort of reaction a man on his first visit to a cat-house might have as he

145

approached the door, then saw one of his neighbours coming along the street.

Gently Mark put his hands on her leg and she sprang to her feet, moving hurriedly away from him.

'Oh sure!' she said, breathing heavily. 'I unfasten you and the next thing I know is you're headed out of here.'

Mark let it go at that. He started to rise and the girl took a hurried pace to the rear. Dropping her hand, she drew the Navy Colt. Mark ignored the move. Turning his back to the girl, he walked across to his bedroll and settled down on it as comfortably as possible to get some sleep.

After a time Mark rolled over and looked to where Annie sat at the table. She had stoked up the stove and range, now she sat with her head rested on her folded arms, fast asleep. Slowly Mark rose, taking up one of his blankets. He went to the girl's side and draped the blanket over her shoulders. Then, grinning to himself, he returned to his bed.

There did not appear to be any point in escaping at the moment, leaving a snug cabin and having to spend the night out on the open range. So Mark went to sleep. One thing he did know. He was not fixing to be around when Bill Doolin came back from the raid and before he left he intended to take a couple of desperate lady outlaws and paddle some sense into their heads, via their seats.

Long practice on trail drives and at other times when setting a watch had been necessary woke Mark. He looked at the clock on the wall, saw it to show time that Britches should take over his 'guard'. Sitting up he began to cough, it took a few loud barks before Annie opened her eyes and sat up. She threw off the blanket and reached for her gun as Mark rose to his feet.

'Can I go outside?' he asked.

'What for?' Annie snapped.

'Guess.'

A slight flush came to Annie's cheeks. She rose, blinking sleepily at the clock, and nodded.

'Go ahead.'

'No peeking mind.'

When he returned, Mark found a sleepy-looking Britches emerging from the bedroom, her hair tangled, her shirt half in, half out of her waistband, ankles and feet bare, and carrying her gunbelt in her hand. Flopping in the chair, she dumped her gunbelt on the table.

'You watch him good now, Britches!' Annie ordered.

'I'll do just that,' the little girl replied, throwing a suspicious look at the blanket draped over the chair back.

However, once Annie entered the bedroom and settled down Britches rested her head on her plump arms and soon began to bubble gently as she drifted off to sleep. Mark, watching her from his blankets, knew she would make no better a guard than Annie had. Rising, he crossed the room, wrapped the girl up, built up the stove fire without waking either girl, then went back to his bedroll and fell asleep.

The first light of day broke through the window and Mark heard Little Britches stirring. The girl padded across the room to stoke up the stove and range, setting the coffee-pot on it. He waited until she had made the coffee before he let her see he was awake.

'Hi!' Britches greeted. 'Come on over and drink some coffee.'

While drinking the coffee they talked of various things and Mark let slip the information that he knew somebody in whom Britches had a great interest.

'You mean you know Belle Starr?' she gasped.

'Why sure,' Mark agreed. 'I met her up to Elkhorn three years back.'

'You know her *real* well?'

Mark grinned, thinking of his meeting with the famous, or notorious lady outlaw. Anyway a man came to look at it, Mark reckoned he could say he knew Belle Starr *real* well.

'As well as they come, gal,' he admitted.

Next moment Britches sat in his lap, her arms around his neck and her mouth thrust to his, kissing him with all the passionate power she could manage. On releasing Mark, Britches stood up, put her hands on her hips, tossed back her head and looked him over in a challenging and provocative

147

manner.

'How does she come up to me?' she asked.

'Nary a comparison, Britches gal.'

Fortunately Little Britches took the statement at its face value and did not ask him to explain it further. Britches was a pretty little girl, gay, happy and cute. Yet to compare her with Belle Starr—well it would be like comparing a pretty, friendly, cuddly little house-cat kitten with the latent, wild and savage beauty of a she-cougar.

'Course, a man can't really tell, not unless he's free to get his arms around the gal,' Mark went on. 'Just cut me loose and we'll try it again.'

For an instant much the same expressions played on Little Britches's face as had shown on Annie's when Mark made the suggestion to her. Then Britches winked and bent over, reaching for the rope hobble on Mark's feet. Neither she nor Mark had seen a sleepy looking Annie emerge from the bedroom and her bare feet made no sound as she crossed the room. Like Britches, Annie had removed her boots and gunbelt before she went to sleep and was not wearing either.

Britches received notice that Annie had woke up when the other girl delivered a round house slap which cracked like a gun shot and landed fairly on the tight stretched seat of Britches's amply filled pants.

'Yeeeow!' Britches yelled, jerking erect and whirling to face Annie. 'I was just making sure the rope hadn't slipped.'

For all that hot anger flooded her face and tears brimmed in her eyes as she rubbed the spot on which the slap landed.

'Yeah!' Annie replied. 'I could see you was.'

'Now easy there, Annie,' Mark put in. 'Choke off, she kisses just as good as you do.'

Instantly the girls were facing each other. Annie opened her mouth to frame an angry, if untrue, denial. She saw the look which came into Britches's eyes and knew she should not have slapped her plump little friend.

Suddenly, without any warning, Britches let Annie have it. Not a slap, but a round-arm punch with her clenched right fist. She swung the blow in the manner Bill Doolin taught her, smashing her fist into Annie's cheek, snapping her head around. At the end of the swing Britches brought the hand whipping back, the knuckles landing on Annie's other cheek and swinging her head over once more.

Mark grunted, wincing in sympathy, for it looked as if Britches knew how to throw a real good punch. With a yell of triumph Britches lunged in, but she was over confident. Annie, who had staggered back a pace or two, recovered her balance and stabbed a hard right into Britches's plump middle and rocked her back a few steps gasping and holding where the blow landed.

The two girls had always been tomboys and since joining the Doolin gang had received lessons in defending themselves. They appeared to have learned their lessons well. Britches backed off hurriedly, avoiding Annie's rush and keeping her fists raised. Annie shot by Britches, hit the table, which stopped her charge.

Giving a squeal of fury, Annie turned and attacked once more. At the last moment Britches side-stepped and hooked her in the stomach, then clipped her over the ear as she staggered by. Annie hit the wall, twisting around to ram head first into Britches's middle and force her backwards. Digging her left hand into Annie's hair, Britches dragged the other girl's head up and started to drive her free fist into Annie's face. Three times she hit, drawing blood from Annie's nose. Then Annie caught Britches by the left wrist, twisted and threw the plump girl over her shoulder. Flinging herself on to Britches, she landed facing the other girl's feet but they rolled and squirmed until they managed to get around and at each other.

Clinging to each other's hair, they rose and reeled across the room. At last Annie forced Britches backwards to hit the table. For a moment Annie held the advantage, yanking at Britches's hair with her left hand, slapping and punching with the right. Desperately Britches wriggled backwards on to the table and Annie followed her. Annie landed between Britches's legs and the little girl wrapped them around the other's slim waist. Crossing her ankles, Britches began to squeeze. From the way Annie howled, Britches's legs packed a fair amount of crushing power.

Squawking in agony, Annie grabbed Britches's hair in both hands, trying to smash her head on the table top. One of Britches's wildly flailing hands touched the handle of the coffee-pot, missed its hold as her head thudded on to the wood, slapped wildly at Annie's cheek, then came down and caught hold of the handle.

That was when Mark decided to take a hand. The coffee in the pot would be hot enough to give Annie a nasty scald and he knew Britches did not mean to do so, yet in her anger she might.

Lifting his feet, Mark placed them under the edge of the table and tilted it over. The weight of the girls turned the table on its edge and they slid to the floor. Desperately trying to avoid Annie's hands, Britches let the coffee-pot fall and it spilled harmlessly on to the floor. Getting her feet under Annie's body, Britches flung the other girl back across the room.

On closing with each other, the girls decided to start using fists again. Annie decided her best hope lay in keeping Britches at range and Mark admired the way the slim girl stabbed out punches which stopped her opponent's rushes and kept her back. For a few seconds she managed to keep it up, then Britches got inside her guard, ripping savage little fists into Annie's ribs. Squealing in pain, Annie trapped Britches's right hand under her arm. Then Annie began to lash her other hand in flat palm slaps and back-hand blows across Britches's face.

Britches took it for a moment, then thrust Annie backwards so she crashed into the wall by the door. The impact not only jarred Britches free, but it knocked the catch off the door. Swinging a round-house punch, Britches knocked Annie staggering through the now open door. Lowering her head, Britches charged out after Annie. The thud of a blow sounded and Britches came in again, landing on her plump little rump.

Coming up with a yell, Britches lowered her head to charge into Annie with head down as the other girl appeared in the doorway. They shot through it and out of Mark's sight, but from what he could hear the fight did not slacken its pace any.

Mark had come to his feet after turning the table over. With the girls busy outside, he set the table on its legs again and prepared to escape. Up until the fight starting Mark had planned to escape some time in the morning, then take the two girls across his knee and teach them not to waylay and kidnap strangers. From what he had already seen, and from the sounds coming in through the door, Annie and Britches were raising lumps on each other and handing out more punishment than he would have.

Raising his hands, Mark brought them down in the direction of the table. The handcuffs struck the wood and, as he knew they would, burst open. As a trained lawman Mark knew better than leave a handcuffed prisoner unwatched, the girls did not know of the danger.

On the impact, the handcuffs burst open and Mark tossed them aside. His powerful fingers made short work of the hobbles and he rose a free man. Crossing the room, Mark took his gunbelt from the racks and donned it while watching the two girls. They appeared to have forgotten their fist fighting and were rolling over and over in a hair-yanking feminine brawl.

After checking his guns were still loaded, Mark took up his hat, set it at the correct 'jack-deuce' angle over his off eye and prepared to deal with the two girls. They seemed to be tempting providence for they had rolled to the edge of the spring and still fought on. Neither had any idea their prisoner had freed himself. Not until they felt a hand clamp on each of their waist-belts and lift them into the air.

Although Mark held the squealing, kicking girls in mid-air, they still clung to each other's hair. He swung them forward and sent them flying out over the spring and they disappeared with a splash and muffled, mutual squeals of surprise. They came up spitting water and spluttering. The ducking in the icy cold water appeared to have ended their aggressive desires and they stood hip deep in the spring, side by side looking dazedly around them. It took them almost thirty seconds to realise their prisoner was a prisoner no more and that they were now at his mercy.

'Come on out!' Mark ordered grimly.

Two dishevelled girls waded towards him. Both had lost their shirts in the fight; Annie's underskirt had been ripped open but she held it together with both hands; Britches wore a man's undershirt that had been torn across one shoulder and which she held up protectively. Both had a blackened eye, bloody noses and numerous bruises. Altogether they looked like a very sore and sorry brace of desperate lady outlaws.

Suddenly the life of an outlaw lost its appeal for the two girls. They found themselves faced with the consequences of their actions. The man they had so merrily kidnapped now stood before them and in a position to send them both to jail for a long time.

Just as they came ashore and started to walk by Mark, a shot ripped through the air. A second bullet kicked up dirt between Annie's feet and the third came so close to Britches it made her yelp in fright and released the vest which collapsed to expose her chubby, naked torso.

At another time Mark might have enjoyed the view.

'Head for the house!' he ordered.

Neither girl needed twice telling. They had been born and raised in Indian country and did not need warning twice when bullets flew. So they took off at a gallop for the safety of the house.

The shots had come from the corner of the valley. Mark knew this and he sprang away from the girls, making a fast, swerving dash towards the slope, hoping to draw the fire from the girls. He had no idea who the attackers might be, but he sure as hell did not intend to stop and find out. Three more shots spattered around him, from two of the rifles unless he missed his guess, for he had heard another shot which must have gone in the direction of the girls.

A rolling dive carried Mark to the first of the cover. He heard the scream of a ricochet as he lit down behind the rock. Turning, he looked to see how the girls fared. Neither lay on the ground, which was a relief, and the door to the cabin slammed to even as he looked.

Then Mark turned his attention to his attackers. Two of

them had found a snug spot, one between two large rocks, the other on the slope side of them. It took Mark just five seconds to recognise the two flabby hard-cases he and Cousin Beau tangled with in Guthrie. It would appear they sought revenge.

At that moment Mark remembered the third rifle. Apparently the two men had brought along a friend to even the odds a mite—or had they come after him at all? Mark remembered the bartender's pungent comments on how Rushton and Kinnear made their money. More likely they came after the Doolin gang. Of course the girls would be worthless to the bounty hunters, for they did not have rewards on their heads. However they would know the location of Doolin's hide-out, so could lead the bounty hunters to it.

Somehow it did not fit with what he had seen of the two men in town that they would risk tangling with the Doolin gang. Maybe they only hoped to pick off a stray. Perhaps they took him for an outlaw—or they may have recognised him and decided to combine business with pleasure and get their revenge.

Carefully Mark scanned the slope. One thing he did know. He must get in a whole lot closer happen he hoped to do any shooting. Maybe if he used both hands, rested his wrists on the rock top and took careful aim he might be able to do something useful at that range. Only while he stayed up there ranging in on the men, they could aim their rifles on him and finish him off; for a rifle was easier to aim over a distance.

With that in mind Mark left his cover and started to move up the steep slope. He wanted to get above the men, always the best place to be in any fight. While not being the Ysabel Kid, who could glide through the thickest cover as silently as a shadow, Mark had taken more than one wary mule deer by stalking it. So he moved from cover to cover, angling up and along the slope.

The man who stalked Mark had Indian blood and knew the secrets of silent movement. Luckily for Mark, the half-breed had never been a very good shot and wanted to get so close he could not miss. Mallalieu's instincts warned him that if his first shot missed, or failed to kill, he would most likely die an instant later. Consequently Mallalieu came to within twenty feet of Mark before he crouched among the bushes and raised his rifle.

In the cabin Britches and Annie, their differences forgotten, knelt by a window, each holding her carbine. From their position they could see the two men by the rocks, Mark moving up and along the slope—and a patch of black where such a colour had not been a few seconds before.

'Hold them two down, Britches!' Annie snapped.

Without questioning her friend, Britches started to throw lead at the rocks and her spirited bombardment caused Rushton and Kinnear, never the bravest of men, to duck hurriedly. Annie rested her carbine on the window ledge, took careful aim and fired.

Mark became aware of a smell as he inched along on silent feet. He did not carry his guns in his hands, keeping the hands free for parting branches and giving him support. The smell wafted down-wind to him and it took him an instant to recognise it. Then he remembered. The stench of grease blackened buckskins and stale, unwashed human flesh which often clung to Osage Indian villages. Yet such a smell should not come to him here unless——

Behind the bushes Mallalieu lined his rifle at the big Texan. His finger curled on the trigger, then Annie's bullet slapped the air over his head. He jerked back and his rifle cracked as its muzzle tilted upwards.

Flinging himself to one side, Mark lit down with a gun in either hand. He fired, left, right, left, right, sending the four bullets hammering into the bushes and spacing them along. He heard a gasp and the soggy thud as his fourth bullet struck flesh, so sent a fifth into the same spot. Mallalieu reared upwards into view, his mouth hanging open, a neat hole between his eyes and no back to his head.

Fifteen seconds ticked by slowly. Mark lay under the cover of a rock, his Colts in his hands. He watched the moccasin clad foot which stuck from behind a bush, but it did not move.

'Looks like he got Sunset,' Kinnear remarked, crouching between the rocks and throwing a couple of shots at the cabin.

'Sure,' Rushton replied, ducking down as a bullet sent rock chips flying into the air. 'But I reckon Sunset downed him at the same time. What now?'

'There's only them two gals and the Texan here. We'll get the gals and make 'em tell us where Doolin and the bunch are. If they haven't pulled the raid, we can telegraph the town they're headed for, warn the marshal and get a cut of the reward.'

A loose-lipped, slobbering grin came to Rushton's lips. 'We'll do more'n . . .'

Yet the problem of how to get at the girls needed some solving, for both had weapons and showed they knew how to use them. Rushton and Kinnear did not aim to take chances, that had been Mallalieu's side of the partnership, they reserved the safe plays for themselves. Neither man had come up with any startlingly brilliant solution when Mark appeared and took cover behind a huge rock some forty yards above them.

Now Mark also had a problem. A similar problem to the two bounty hunters if he had only known. His problem, like theirs, was how to get close enough to take his opponents without also taking a bullet in the belly.

His eyes checked the area ahead of him. It appeared to have been swept by an avalanche at some time, for it lay more open than most of the slope. Then Mark looked at the rock he stood behind. This rested on a level piece of the slope, but did not appear to be part of it or an outcrop rising above the soil.

Turning, Mark holstered his Colts. He pressed his back against the rock, braced his arms and hands against it, bent his legs and began to push. Never had his enormous strength been placed to such a test. Never had so much depended on his muscular powers. Sweat poured down his face, he forced back on the rock, his boot heels gouging into the earth. Joe Gaylin, the El Paso leather-worker who made the boots, always boasted that no power on earth could rip off the heels. Now Mark was giving the boots a thorough test—and they proved Gaylin's boast.

Mark felt the rock move, tilt slightly. He relaxed his hold, seeing that the rock did not settle back again, and turned to look down. Now there was a small gap between the rock and the ground and he knew he could only achieve his aim in one way.

Bending down, Mark put his hands under the edge of the rock, setting his feet a short distance apart and bending his legs. Then he began to lift. Although he felt the tremendous dead weight upon his hands, Mark did not give in. His face twisted in the strain and he felt as if his back would cave in under the weight. Yet he did not give in. Slowly the rock rose and Mark kept on his relentless lifting, moving over a thousand pounds weight by his giant strength.

'Just look at that man!' Britches gasped, forgetting to use her carbine as she watched Mark's efforts.

'Whooee! He makes Bill or any of the boys look like weaklings!' Annie replied, resting her carbine and not firing. 'What a man!'

With a final heave, Mark lifted the rock past its point of balance and it started to tilt forward. Mark gave a final thrust and the huge rock turned over, going away from him, bounding and rolling down the slope. Gasping for breath, Mark sank to the ground, but he knew he might still have need to defend himself.

Not until the huge rock began to roll did the two bounty hunters become aware of their danger. The first warning they received came with a dull rumbling sound that drew their attention up the slope. They saw the huge rock rolling, at an ever-increasing speed, down towards their hide-out.

Rushton, nearest to the rolling rock, flung himself clear and leapt to safety. Perhaps Kinnear would have been safe in the shelter between the two rocks, but he panicked. Rising hurriedly he tried to dive over the rock on the side away from the rolling menace. His right foot slipped and he fell on to the rock he was trying to climb over. A glance over his shoulder told him he was not going to make it. His scream of terror chopped off in a hideous crunching crash as the huge rock smashed down, coming to rest where Kinnear and his cover had been.

Shaken by the scream, Rushton staggered forward. He still

held his rifle and his eyes went up the slope to where Mark stood with hanging head and fighting to recover from his exertion. Throwing up the rifle, Rushton fired a shot at the big Texan, but his nerves had been jolted and he missed. With fumbling fingers Rushton tried to work his rifle's lever.

The bullet missed Mark by inches. It served to warn him of his danger. At that range a man would have to use sights to make a hit and he knew he must hit—or die. He could guess that Annie and Britches would be in no condition to help him after what they must have seen when the rock landed on Kinnear.

Mark's right hand Colt came from leather and lifted. Raising the weapon shoulder high, he gripped and supported his right hand with the left, extending his arms almost straight. Sighting the V notch in the tip of the hammer and the foresight, Mark aimed down at Rushton. He fired four shots as fast as he could work back the hammer. The first three bullets missed Rushton, getting closer all the time, as the bounty hunter finished working the lever and sighted again. If the fourth bullet missed Mark would be a dead man.

It did not miss. Grazing the barrel of the rifle, Mark's .44 bullet whirled off in the buzz-saw action of a ricochet to strike full into the centre of Rushton's forehead. It threw him backwards from his feet, his rifle firing off one wild shot as it fell from his lifeless hand.

Like the circuit riding preacher used to say: he who lives by the gun shall die with lead in his hide. Rushton had killed five men in cold blood for the bounty on their heads. He would never kill again.

Holstering his gun, Mark walked slowly down the slope. He saw the cabin door burst open and waved the girls back inside. Kinnear's body under the huge rock was no sight for a girl to see, even if she was a tough lady outlaw.

Mark counted off a thousand dollars from his wallet and handed it to Cattle Annie.

'Here,' he said, 'I'm in a hurry to get back to the O.D. Connected. So I'll pay you the ransom and save you holding

157

me until pappy gets up here.'

The girls, both wearing new shirts and cleaned up—though showing marks of their fight—stared at the money, then at the big blond Texan. He had buried the two dead bounty hunters and done what he could about hiding all that remained in sight of the third. Now he was preparing to resume his interrupted journey.

'You don't have to give us this,' Annie objected and Britches nodded in agreement, their earlier rivalry forgotten.

'Sure I do,' Mark replied. 'Business is business. Whyn't you girls go off and spend it someplace far from here?'

'That wouldn't be fair to the boys,' Britches explained.

'It sure wouldn't,' Annie agreed.

Mark shrugged. He knew he could not persuade the girls to change their way of life. Still they seemed happy in it and he reckoned Bill Doolin would see nothing serious happened to them. Swinging afork his bloodbay, Mark raised his hat to the girls.

'If I'm ever up this way again, I'll look you up,' he promised. '*Adios.*'

Standing side by side, their arms around each other's waists, Cattle Annie and Little Britches watched Mark riding south. The little girl sighed and turned to her friend.

'Did he—last night—you know—did he?'

For a moment Annie thought of lying. Then she shook her head.

'No,' she said, sounding a little regretful. 'How about you?'

'Me neither,' Britches confessed just a shade wistfully. 'Do you think he knows that we've—that we're——'

'How could he?'

But Mark did know. Which same was one of the reasons he had not accepted their invitation to stay on for another night. Which same was also the reason why he aimed to steer clear of Cattle Annie and Little Britches—well, at least until they got to be a few years older.

The Wildcats

PART ONE

BETTER THAN CALAMITY

THE town's usual crowd of loafers gathered at the Wells Fargo office to welcome the arrival of the west-bound stage. They watched the bouncing Concord stage roll to a halt, then waited to see who travelled aboard the coach. This day trade appeared to be bad, for only one passenger climbed down, a woman.

In height she stood at most five foot four. A dainty, small and stylish hat sat her piled-up red hair. The good ladies of the crowd whispered amongst themselves that the hair must be tinted with henna, although this might have been no more than their catty way with anyone better favoured in the matter of looks than themselves. Her face looked attractive, maybe not out and out beautiful, but still pleasant, with lips which looked like they were used to smiling, and sparkling blue eyes. She wore a black travelling outfit, stylish, costly and in good taste. It did tend to emphasize her plump build, but plumpness, especially the type which sported a large bosom, reasonably slender waist and full hips, was held to be the peak of feminine attraction in male eyes at this time.

Her arrival stirred some speculation amongst the crowd, the more so as she appeared to be meaning to stay in Tennyson for some time. While they watched her baggage, including a large trunk, unloaded, the crowd speculated as to who she might be and why she came to their sleepy little Texas township. A variety of answers sprang to mind. That she was a rich widow come west to find a husband. She might be on the run from the law after some spectacular crime back east. Or she might, studying her calm poised assurance and good clothes, be a famous theatrical lady on a tour, although that did not explain why she stopped in Tennyson which boasted only one saloon and it rarely imported entertainment.

They all studied the woman as eagerly as she ignored them, being more concerned with the unloading of her baggage. The women, still in their catty way, decided her age must be at least forty even though she looked in her middle thirties at most.

From the pile of bags which heaped around the trunk, the woman took a small grip. She stepped to where the Wells Fargo agent stood signing the driver's official delivery receipt book.

'Can you have my gear taken to the Bull's Head, Oscar?' she asked.

'B-Bull's Head?' squawked the agent, a thin, studious looking man whose name might well have been, but was not, Oscar. He heard the talk well up amongst the loafers at her words. 'But that's a saloon, ma'am.'

'I knew that when I bought it.'

She made her reply with calm assurance, in the manner of a woman who knew her way around and cared little for the type of public opinion expressed by the people who stood around the front of the Wells Fargo office.

The watching and listening crowd stood, stared and talked amongst themselves discussing the woman's statement. A small group of dried-up, vinegar faced women; wives, mothers, unmarried sisters or spinsters; gathered like vultures over a kill, clucking their tongues, shaking their heads and mumbling together.

'Disgusting!'

'Shocking!'

'How could she!'

'This is a disgrace!'

If the red-haired woman heard the words – and they were repeated often or spoken loud enough for her to do so – she ignored them. After throwing a cool, contemptuous look at the women and seeing them for what they were, she dismissed them as being of no importance to her future.

'Take hold of that bag there, Charlie,' she said with easy familiarity to one of the loafers, indicating the top piece of luggage. 'Tote it to the Bull's Head and there'll be drinks all night for you tonight.'

Although he noted an expression of disapproval amongst the crowd of women, the man eagerly grabbed the bag. He grunted as he felt its weight, but gritted his teeth manfully and set into the task of toting the bag and keeping pace with the red-head. With the looks of the good ladies of Tennyson bouncing unheeded from her back, she walked along the street, keeping from the warped sidewalk the better to study her surroundings. Her bag-carrier struggled gamely by her side, trying to impress her with his strength.

'You aim to run the Bull's Head yourself, ma'am?' he asked, gasping the words out.

'I reckon so.'

'It's a tough joint. Reckon it got too much for Turner. That's why he sold out.'

For all the notice the woman took she might never have heard a word he said. Her eyes studied the length of Tennyson's main street in one quick glance and then appeared to dismiss it. Not that Tennyson looked any better, or had anything more to offer than a thousand other such small towns which dotted the open range country from the east line of Texas to the Pacific Ocean. The building materials might differ, ranging from stone and logs in the north to pure adobe or adobe and wood in the south. The names on the business premises might change. Yet the layout still looked the same with the same kind of businesses, the bank, the undertaker's shop, the saddler's place of work, stores, town marshal's office and jail, saloon, all in one way or another catering for the cowhand workers of the land.

She saw all this, but mostly her attention fixed on the Bull's Head Saloon. It looked to be a fair and substantial piece of structure, two floors high, with a veranda and rail for the upper floor's rooms, allowing their occupants a chance to step out into the fresh air without needing to walk downstairs. The lower floor looked much as the front of any other saloon. A hitching rail lined the sidewalk edge. The big front windows were painted white over their lower halves so that minors could not see their elders enjoying the pleasures within. The batwing doors gave a main entrance into the barroom.

The red-haired woman looked at all this with the expression of a pilgrim getting his first sight of the promised land, or an immigrant seeing the shores of America for the first time.

'Who's your great seizer?' she asked.

'Huh?' gasped the man, not sure he had heard right.

'Lawman, town marshal, county sheriff, whatever you have here.'

'Tune Counter, ma'am,' the man replied, wondering where this woman with her refined eastern clothes learned a western term for a law enforcement officer.

'He all right?'

'He's square enough, ma'am. Tried to make Turner run an honest place.'

Giving a grunt which might have meant anything, the woman paused for a moment to give the saloon a last long searching look. Then she stepped on to the sidewalk, crossing it with purposeful stride and thrust open the batwing doors.

On the first glance the Bull's Head did not look prosperous or busy. At the bar two waiters and a bartender idly matched throws with dice. Half a dozen girls in dresses which left arms, shoulders and half the swell of their bosoms bare to view and ended just below their knees, sat around a table talking to themselves. So far there did not appear to be a single customer in the big barroom. The faro layout had a cover over its tiger-decorated top, the vingt-un and chuck-a-luck outfits stood silent and unused and the wheel of fortune on its stand by the wall did not spin. For the rest of it, the long bar's mirror showed no reflection of trade in progress and the shelves had few bottles on them. The doors leading to the outside world, the back rooms and the owner's private office, were all closed and the stairs leading to the first floor lay silent.

'Four fours to beat,' said the bartender, from his place on the sober side of the counter. Then he threw a glance at the batwing doors to see who entered at this unexpected hour. He dropped the dice cup to the counter, staring at the door. The expression on his face brought every other eye to the entrance and the shape standing just inside.

'Excuse me, ma'am,' one of the waiters said. 'You got the wrong place. The hotel's down the street a piece, this-here's a saloon.'

'I didn't buy it for a church-hall,' replied the red-haired woman, walking forward and looking around with some interest.

At their table the girls stared. The big, good looking blonde's story of how she had been in Quiet Town during the wild days before Dusty Fog tamed it, died on her lips.

She studied the newcomer with cold and calculating eyes. She saw the others looking at her, read their challenge for her to get up and do something. Shoving back her chair, she rose to meet the challenge. Then she stepped before the red-head with insolence showing in every inch of her frame.

An expectant, tense air filled the room. The workers and the townsman who carried the red-head's bag all knew Viola to be a real tough cookie and the boss-girl by the combined virtue of her skill in a hair-yanking brawl and having been Turner's girl-friend before he left. Viola had been treated with some favour under Turner's wing and she doubted if the same would apply with a female boss.

'You bought this place, did you?' she asked, planting herself full in the other woman's path, standing with hands on hips and legs braced apart, between the red-head and the bar.

Slowly the woman looked Viola up and down. Just as slowly she swung the grip on to the nearest table.

'I did.'

'Well I don't like the idea of taking orders from a dame.'

'Don't, huh?'

Speaking mildly and giving no warning of what she aimed to do, the red-head gave her employees a sign of how things would be run in future. Her right hand folded into a fist and came around fast. She swung the fist like she knew what she was doing. It drove around, she dropped her shoulder behind the blow as it smashed with the power of a mule-kick against the side of Viola's jaw.

In his time the bardog had seen many a beautiful punch thrown and that right swing handed out by the red-head was as good as any he had seen from woman or man.

It landed well and squarely, spun Viola around on her heels, propelled her across the room to crash into the bar. Viola hung there for a moment, eyes, glassy and mouth hanging open. Then slowly she slid to the floor, hanging with one arm draped over the brass foot-rail.

A stunned silence followed the crack of the blow and Viola's involuntary trip to the bar. Everyone in the room watched as the red-head took up her bag and crossed to where Viola sprawled in a limp pile on the floor. For a moment they expected the woman to drive a high-buttoned shoe into Viola's unprotected body. She did no such thing.

Placing her grip on the bar, the red-head bent and hauled

Viola away from the foot-rail and turned her face up. Then she looked at the bartender and said:

'Have you a bucket of water back there, Henry?'

'Yes'm,' he replied, deciding this was not the time to point out his name was Sam.

Reaching down he lifted the bucket of water used for washing the glasses during business hours. He placed it on the bar-top from whence the woman lifted it one-handed, making no strain of it even though the full bucket weighed heavy. She gripped the bucket by handle and bottom, then up-ended it, pouring the water over Viola's head and shoulders.

With a gasp, followed by a spluttering squeal, Viola recovered and forced herself into a sitting position. Her head spun and she put a hand to a jaw which felt a good three times its normal size. Then she sniffed and started to wail in pain and humiliation.

The red-head bent forward, dug a hand into Viola's soaking hair and lifted her to her feet, then shoved her back against the bar. Hands on hips the newcomer studied Viola.

'The name's Madam Bulldog,' said the red-head. 'I'm your new boss. Got it?'

For a moment Viola clung to the bar, sniffing tears and staring at the other woman. Viola might have always been the boss' favourite and real tough in her own right, but she knew when to yell 'calf rope' and surrender. From the look of her, Madam Bulldog was more than ready and willing to wade in tooth and claw, or with those same hard fists to prove her point and make sure Viola 'got it'. After one sample Viola wanted no more.

'I got it,' she mumbled through a jaw which hurt when she spoke.

Madam Bulldog turned to face the other girls, looking them over in the same impersonal manner.

'Anybody else need convincing?'

'No ma'am,' answered the girls in chorus. They had seen Viola yell, 'calf rope' and needed no more convincing.

Turning once more to the bar Madam Bulldog looked around her. 'Where did Turner room?' she asked.

'I'll show you,' Viola replied, working on the sound principle of 'If you can't lick 'em, join 'em.'

'I want to see all that staff here in a couple of hours,'

Madam told the bartender. 'Who's been running things since Turner left?'

'I have,' replied the bartender, thinking of the profit which slipped into his pocket since Turner departed the scene hurriedly and wondering if she would find out about it.

'Then I want to see you and the books in the office when I come down,' she said and pointed to the man who carried her bags. 'See that gent has free drinks all night tonight.'

With that she turned and nodded to Viola who led her upstairs. Viola looked a little guilty and worried as she opened the door to Turner's room, for her belongings lay scattered about.

'I used it after Joe – Mr. Turner left,' she said.

'And while he was here, I wouldn't be surprised,' answered Madam Bulldog dryly. 'And don't try to look shocked or innocent. If you're innocent, I am; and it'd take a damned sight more than that to shock me. Get your gear cleared out this afternoon so I can move in. And I'd better know your name.'

'Viola.'

'You're the boss girl?'

'I was,' agreed Viola, a trifle bitter at her loss of face and station in life.

'You still are. You'll get ten dollars a week over the pay the other girls make and you'll earn it. I expect you to keep the girls in line and see there's no trouble. None of you roll drunks, go on the streets, or make fuss with the town women. Can you handle it?'

Viola nodded. She had never been paid extra, nor had any special duties under Turner's control. However, she reckoned she would be able to handle things the way her new boss wanted them handling.

'Then make a start at clearing the room out,' said Madam Bulldog. 'I'll move in after I've attended to a few things.'

Saying this Madam Bulldog turned and headed downstairs once more, still carrying her small grip. She went straight to the office, halted at the door to tell the waiters to close the main doors and keep customers out, then went inside to interview the sweating bartender. He indicated the safe, its door standing open, and the books which lay on the desk top ready for her inspection.

'I only want to get an idea of what trade Turner did here,' she remarked. 'I expect you made a reasonable profit out of running things. And don't look so pained, you'd have been a fool not to. I only bought the building and fittings. From what I can see you ran the place all right so you're welcome to whatever you made. If you want a drink, go get one. Then let's talk.'

It became clear that Madam Bulldog knew more than a little about running a saloon. She asked pertinent questions about trade, the customers, sources of liquor supplies, how they stood with the local citizens. She also discovered the bartender's name to be Sam, not Henry.

'I don't want any customer to complain of short measure, short change, spiked drinks or anything,' she warned at the end of her check. 'You order what fresh liquor supplies we need this afternoon. Now let's take a look at the games.'

Her inspection of the decks of cards proved she knew more than a little about such things. She examined the cards, studying the designs on their backs, then riffling them through her fingers, watching the designs flip by and alert for any sign of irregularity which would warn her the cards had been marked.

One thing caught Madam Bulldog's eye immediately, the cards lay in two separate piles. After her inspection she waved a hand to the left hand pile.

'Get rid of 'em,' she ordered, watching the bartender's face and ready to take action if he objected.

'Sure, boss,' Sam replied instantly and in a manner which told her he had nothing to do with the ownership of the cards.

She threw a look at the small group of workers who sat around, seeing they all watched her with interest but not animosity. They most likely wondered what changes she intended to make and how those changes would affect them.

'Who handles the gambling, Sam?' she asked.

'Feller called Wallace. Took a percentage cut with Turner.'

'I hope he's another place marked down,' she said quietly.

They went to the chuck-a-luck table but Madam's thorough inspection found nothing in either its operation or dice to meet with her disapproval although the layout of numbers needed their odds correcting to give the players a fair chance. the Vingt-un layouts needed only honest decks of cards to make them satisfactory. However, the wheel of fortune had a concealed control button connected to springs and wires which took all the chance from its operation as far as the house was concerned. A quick rip tore the wires loose and Sam beat his boss to the move. Madam Bulldog nodded her agreement and they headed for the faro layout.

Once more Madam Bulldog showed her remarkable knowledge of such matters. She gave the dealer's box on the table a careful inspection, then stepped back and looked at the table itself, seeing how thick and stoutly made it looked to be. She bent and examined the end where the dealer sat by the case keeping box. Her hands ran along the wood and a panel in the side slid open. With a grunt as if she expected no more, Madam Bulldog removed a second box, one which looked almost the same as the one on the table. Yet it contained certain improvements the box on the table did not have, by far the most important being that the slot through which the cards could be dealt had room for two cards instead of one to pass.

With a grunt she raised one box in each hand, then smashed them down against the table edge, shattering them. Tossing the wrecked boxes to the floor she went on:

'I'll not have a second dealer box in my house, Sam. When my bags get here I've a straight box, with an open top.'

Sam caught the significance of the remark. The two boxes she broke did not have their tops left open, but only a small hole through which the cards could be pushed. The second dealer box allowed the manipulator to put two cards out, then retract the top one if having it played would not be favourable to the house.

'We have a swamper?' she asked.

'Two, they're not here now.'

'I want to see them. I want this floor washed every day before we open and fresh sawdust on it.'

'I'll see to it,' Sam promised.

'Swell,' she said. 'Where's the bank?'

'Down the street. Only the banker's wife wouldn't let Turner do any business in it.'

The news did not appear to distress Madam Bulldog. She waved the hand holding the grip towards the door.

'Let's go see him.'

Her interview with the banker proved once and for all to

Sam that Madam Bulldog could take care of herself in any society. She swept aside the protesting teller and entered Banker Hoscroft's private office with Sam following on her heels.

Before the banker could rise and impose his full pompous power upon her, Madam Bulldog dumped the grip before him and opened it.

'There's five thousand dollars in here,' she said calmly, as if she wished to deposit five dollars. 'I've a further fifteen thousand in the First Union Bank in Kansas City. You can have it here in my account, or I'll open my own bank. It's all up to you.'

Despite his present position in life, and his pompous manner – which was mainly due to marrying a Bostonian lady – Banker Hoscroft was a shrewd man of business. A deposit of twenty thousand dollars would do his bank nothing but good. He might let his wife dictate to him on some matters, but could also put his foot firmly down when necessary. So he donned his most jovial smile and the manner he reserved for his largest depositors, escorted Madam Bulldog to the business section of the building and opened an account for her.

'I'll be expecting to see you in for my grand opening tonight,' she said as she left the bank and Hoscroft agreed he would be there.

From the bank Madam Bulldog passed around the town, visiting such businesses as she would need to deal with, leaving each place with the owners full of admiration for her astute business sense. The owners of the businesses saw they would make profit far in excess of anything Turner put their way and that was one argument to silence the objections of wives, mothers, spinster sister or maiden aunts who might complain.

Actually the complaints never came. Seeing a meeting of the good ladies in the Black Cat Café, Madam Bulldog bearded them in their den. She stated quite firmly she aimed to run her place, but also promised that the conducting of it would be blameless. She spoke to such effect that not only did the ladies withhold their complaints but they accepted her as a social equal.

All the saloon's employees were waiting to meet their new boss. Sam noticed an expectant air and looked to where

Wallace, a small sly man in the usual dress of a frontier gambler, stood by the faro layout and scowling at the wrecked dealing boxes. Wallace turned, looked towards Madam Bulldog and came to meet her, a truculent gleam in his eye. He waved a hand towards the broken boxes which he dropped on the table top.

'Did you do that?' he asked in a threatening manner.

'I did.'

'Why, you fat —!'

That was when Madam Bulldog hit him. She ripped a punch into his belly, just under the watch chain on his fancy vest. It came so unexpectedly and with such power that it folded Wallace over, right on to the other hand as it came up, knotted into a useful fist, to meet his jaw. He straightened out again and went sprawling on to his back, cursing, spitting blood and clawing at the butt of the Second Model Smith & Wesson revolver under his jacket.

'I can copper that bet, too.'

Madam Bulldog gave the warning in a flat, cold voice. She held a Colt Cloverleaf House Pistol in her right hand, drawn from under her coat in a flickering blur of movement. Before Wallace could collect his scattered wits, or get his gun out, the .41 calibre barrel lined on him, the two exposed cylinders of the 'cloverleaf' chamber like two unwinking eyes watching him.

While being a real mean cuss and card cheat, Wallace also had a wide yellow streak in him. He knew better than to call the bet when the other side held a .41 calibre, four shot answer to his play. He let his hand come clear of the gun and backed away, crawling across the floor, fingers feeling at his jaw.

'Have you got a horse?' asked Madam Bulldog.

'Yeah!' Wallace replied in what he hoped would be a defiant snarl, but that came out more of a whine.

'Then get on it and be out of town before the marshal gets back or I'll show him those decks of cards and tell him why I bust the dealing boxes.'

She knew she had won, even without meeting Tune Counter. It showed in the scared expression which came in Wallace's eyes and on his hate-lined face. She guessed the town marshal had been interested in Wallace's little additions to luck without being able to prove what they were. In which case Wallace would not be around when the marshal came back that evening.

'See him on his way, Sam,' she ordered.

Sam needed no second bidding. He had never approved of swindling the customers, regarding it at best as a short-sighted policy which eventually led to trouble with both the customers and the law. He knew Tune Counter would never stand for any crooked play if he detected it and had long expected the marshal to catch Wallace out, then close the saloon down.

Bending forward Sam grabbed Wallace by the jacket collar and hauled him to his feet then hustled him across the room to the side door. One of the waiters, who felt the same way as did Sam on the subject of crooked gamblers, obligingly opened the door through which Wallace departed, helped on his way by a hard-applied boot.

'Git – and keep going!' Sam advised.

Wallace took the hint. He saw that his presence in the saloon would no longer be tolerated. So he headed for his room at the hotel to collect his belongings. If he nursed a grudge against Madam Bulldog and her employees he did not intend to stay around and do anything about it.

The teller at Hoscroft's bank beamed a welcome to Madam Bulldog as she entered through the doors at eleven o'clock on a warm summer's morning something over a year after her arrival in Tennyson.

'Good morning, Madam,' he greeted, using the only name by which anyone in town knew her. He reached for the canvas bag she laid on the counter before him. 'You look to have been busy last night.'

'Fair enough,' she replied, then turned to Marshal Tune Counter as he stood by the teller's cage. 'Hi, Tune. You putting it in too?'

'Sure,' he replied. 'I get paid the same day as the cowhands. My pile looks sort of paltry besides your's though.'

She laughed. 'You don't have my overheads.'

They got on very well together, the marshal and the saloon-keeper. In fact romance had been increasingly hinted at, for he spent some of his time with her and not in duty hours. Certainly Tune liked her, admired her for the way she kept her promise of allowing the place to run smoothly and fairly, relying on the house percentage to make the gambling pay. Nor did Madam ever offend the public good taste by appearing on the streets in her working clothes. To see her around town one might never have known she ran a saloon, for she always dressed in stylish and conventional fashion.

'The trouble with my business,' she went on, 'is—'

The words died on her lips. Behind them the door of the bank had opened and four men stepped inside, fanning across it as it closed once more. Madam Bulldog glanced to see who might be entering, then stood very still, her words dying away unsaid. Tune Counter stood just as still, his hands on the teller's counter top and well clear of the Army Colt at his side. Behind the counter, the teller stayed just where he was. He gave a quick look at the Navy Colt kept under the counter for just such emergencies, but he made no attempt to touch it.

Not with four men standing across the room and lining guns on him and the two customers. Four tall, trail-dirty, mean-looking men. At least eyes held a mean glint, being about all of their faces which showed from behind the drawn-up bandana masks. They handled their weapons like they knew which end the flame came out of. The clothes they wore, even without the dirt, would have been hard to describe and no different to those worn by thousands of cowhands. Except that this bunch were not any kind of cowhands, but master at a line of business perfected by Messrs. Jesse and Frank James of Clay County, Missouri.

From the way the four men stood and acted they had not just started on this line of business, but knew it from A to izzard. A man couldn't take foolish chances with that kind, not and stay alive to boast about it.

'Just stand there nice and easy,' ordered the man at the right. 'That way we won't have any fuss. Now turn around real slow, the lady first.'

On turning, Madam Bulldog studied the four men, not trying to memorize details about them, but to see what sort of opposition she might have to tie into. She saw one of them would be the real danger. The other three looked like older men, competent workers who conducted their business quickly and with as little rough stuff as possible. The fourth was young. His eyes bore a look which told he wanted nothing more than an excuse to throw lead.

'All right, big feller,' said the man at the right. 'Now you.'

Tune obeyed. He had no intention of making a move or trying to go against the guns of the four men. Not that Tune was a coward. He had proved his courage on every occasion which demanded it. But a lawman needed to know when to stand fast as well as when to make his gun-play. To make it now would endanger the lives of Madam Bulldog and the bank teller.

Only the matter left Tune's hand the moment he turned far enough for the youngster at the left of the quartet to see his badge. A low snarl rippled the masking bandana and he swung his gun around. Tune Counter saw the move and flung himself to one side, right hand stabbing at his Army Colt. Flame tore from the young outlaw's gun and Tune took a .36 calibre ball in the left shoulder, went to his knees but got his gun out.

'You fool k—!' yelled one of the others.

Then all hell tore loose in the bank. Madam Bulldog's right hand went under her coat in a fast move. The men had discounted her as a factor until too late. Flame spurted from the Colt Cloverleaf and a hole appeared between the youngster's eyes, slamming him around the instant before he could trigger another shot into the marshal. He hit the man next to him, knocking his gun out of line even as he tried to bring it around and cope with the new menace.

Although hit in the left shoulder Tune Counter drew his gun with the right hand, throwing lead into the man at the right and spinning him into the wall. However, the man still held his gun and Tune acted in the manner of a trained law enforcement officer. While the man still held his gun he could be termed dangerous, so Tune shot him again. At the same moment another of the bunch sent a bullet into Tune. The outlaw did not get a chance to take another shot for the teller grabbed up his Navy Colt and fired. His actions might have been in the nature of a concerned rat, knowing it to be a case of fight or die. This made the gun in his hand no less deadly although more luck than skill sent home the bullet which dropped the outlaw.

The fourth man, seeing his three pards go down, forgot fighting. He made a leap for the door, throwing it open and darting out. The shots had aroused interest and brought people out, people holding guns, for this was a Texas town and every man in it owned a firearm of some kind. Making for the waiting horses, the man made a leapfrog mount aboard his mount as it turned from the hitching rail. He set the pet-makers to work and ran the gauntlet of fire along the street, lead singing around his ears.

He almost made it through without a scratch, then his luck gave out. The agent for the Wells Fargo office cut loose with a short barrelled guard's model ten gauge shotgun. The nine buckshot charge had spread some and the outlaw took three balls in his back. He yelled in agony but managed to stay in his saddle. After the lapse his luck returned. Not only did he manage to keep on his horse but no posse followed him, for the town was disorganized without Tune Counter's strong hand to guide them. The outlaw rode for all that day, through the night and late the following morning dropped unconscious before the door of a rancher who made far more money hiding outlaws than by working his cattle.

In Tennyson, even while the guns roared, Madam Bulldog went to Tune Counter and dropped to her knees by him. She looked at the teller who retained enough of his senses to go forward and disarm the three outlaws.

'Get the doctor!' she ordered.

The teller needed no second order, he went outside and yelled for medical aid. Madam Bulldog stayed by Tune, not touching or moving him. She could see he was in pain, but he stayed conscious and his instincts were those of a lawman. He looked at the three sprawled out forms on the floor and weakly pointed.

'That one's still alive,' he said. 'See to him.'

'Let him rot,' Madam Bulldog answered. 'I'm seeing to you.'

Not until the doctor, followed by the teller, entered, did she go to the wounded outlaw. He was dying and nothing could save him, or could have saved him had she gone to him immediately. His eyes went to her face and he pointed to the youngster who brought the trouble on them.

'That damned fool kid!' he gasped. 'He was kill crazy. Worse than the other Cousins boys.'

Madam Bulldog felt as if a cold hand touched her. She looked down at the dying outlaw and asked. 'Is *he* one of the Cousins family?'

'Yeah. He was Breck. Hank Cousins' youngest.'

Turning her face towards Tune Counter, the woman saw he had both heard and understood. This in itself was not surprising, most everybody in Texas had heard of the Cousins family. They were a close-knit clan of a father and four sons – only now but three sons remained. The fourth son's lifeless body lay on the floor of the Tennyson bank, a .41 calibre hole in his forehead, the back of his skull a bloody, brain-spattered, bone-shattered horror where the bullet smashed out again.

The Cousins family, Hank, the father, a balding, heavily built man with some pretensions at being educated and peering through steel rimmed spectacles at the world, Joe, Tad and Burt, had the reputation of being bad-men, killers with no regard for human life. A sullen wolf-pack full of hate, with but one redeeming quality, their loyalty to each other. Cut one Cousins and the whole stinking brood bled. Now one of their kin had died at the hands of the people of Tennyson, or a section of the population. The rest of the clan would not rest easy, when they heard, until they shed blood, killed whoever shot down Breck and all who might have been near when it happened.

'You mean that there's Breck Cousins,' gasped the teller, having returned in time to hear the outlaw's words.

'The late and not lamented,' replied Madam Bulldog.

Behind her the doctor glared at Tune Counter as he tried to force himself to his feet.

'Lie down again, Tune!' he spat. 'You'll kill yourself afore I get a chance to do it.'

'What about the other man?' Tune replied.

'He got clear, carrying lead,' growled the doctor. 'Now lie easy, blast you, and let me fix those wounds.'

Tune shook his head weakly, still trying to rise. He had his duty to the town, to the badge he wore. Sooner or later, depending on if the wounded man lived or died, word would reach the Cousins clan, the escaped outlaw would bear the word; or the prairie telegraph carry it. Then the Cousins bunch would be riding, hunting the man who killed Breck. That it had been Madam Bulldog not a man who shot him, that she shot in defence of another man's life, would mean nothing to the family. They had killed women before and done worse before killing. Tune knew he must get help, bring

22

in a reliable man or men into town to stiffen the citizens and help guard Madam Bulldog until he could stand on his feet again.

He thought of men who would willingly offer their help. Most of them were occupied on law enforcement work from which they could not easily be spared, although they would come willingly if he asked. He thought of another man, a member of his own family, a nephew.

'Hold it, Doc!' he gasped, then beckoned Madam Bulldog to his side. 'Happen you want to stay alive. Send a telegraph message – to Ole Devil – Hardin. Tell him what happened here!'

He had been three days in the saddle, riding north from the great OD Connected ranch in the Rio Hondo country, headed for the small town of Tennyson in Sand County. Soon it would be night again and he must spend it sage-henning out under the stars, something he never took kindly to doing no matter that he spent a good half of his life sleeping in such a manner. Around noon the next day he ought to reach Tennyson and discover the meaning of the telegraph message which brought him away from the urgent business of gathering a shipping herd for delivery to a fort that had trouble feeding hungry Kiowa tribesmen. It had been almost three years since he last saw his Uncle Tune and so he wondered what need the marshal of Tennyson might have for his services.

Sitting his seventeen hand bloodbay, stallion with the easy grace of a light rider despite his giant size, Mark Counter presented a picture Fred Remington or any other artist would not have hesitated to set on canvas.

Six foot three, even without the aid of his expensive, made-to-measure, fancy stitched boots, he stood and with the physique of a Hercules. His shoulders had a great spread to them, his frame trimmed down to a lean waist and long, powerful legs. Yet in no way did he look slow, clumsy, or awkward, exactly the opposite in fact, and he sat his horse in a manner which took less out of it than would a lighter though less skilled rider.

His costly white Stetson hat, with its silver concha decorated band, sat on neatly barbered golden blond hair. The face, shielded by the wide brim of the low crowned hat, looked almost classically handsome, tanned, intelligent, virile and with strength of character etched upon it. In appearance he looked much like a Greek god of old who elected to wear the dress of a cowhand instead of his formal robes. In all things Mark tended to be a dandy dresser. His tan coloured shirt had been tailored for him, as had the levis trousers which hung with turned back cuffs outside his boots. The tight rolled green bandana around his throat and trailing long ends over his shirt was made of pure silk. Once the Beau Brummel of the Confederate cavalry, now Mark's dress style tended to set cowhand fashion in Texas.

Around his waist hung a gunbelt with a brace of fine looking ivory handled 1860 Army Colts riding in holsters that looked just right and told a story to eyes which knew the signs. The entire rig, expensive though it was, looked both functional and practical, the kind of outfit a real fast man with a gun would wear.

Mark Counter could lay just claim to being a fast man with a gun. There was more than just a dandy dresser to him. He knew the cattle business from calf-down to shipping pen and acknowledged no superior at the cowhand trade. His strength had become a legend and his skill in a roughhouse brawl talked of wherever it had been seen. He could handle a rifle well, though not as well as his good *amigo* the Ysabel Kid. He could handle his matched guns very well, although not quite as well as his illustrious *amigo*, Dusty Fog. Reliable witnesses, men who themselves were no slouches at the art of getting them out and throwing lead through them, claimed Mark Counter ran Dusty Fog a close second in speed and accuracy. The general public, however, knew little of this, for Mark rode in the shadow of the fastest of them all, the Rio Hondo gun wizard called Dusty Fog.

This day, and for the past two days, Mark Counter rode alone. The OD Connected had been very busy and, while Ole Devil would have spared the whole of the floating outfit if need be, Mark suggested he rode alone. On reaching Tennyson he would discover why his Uncle Tune needed his aid. If he then decided the situation called for more men he could send a telegraph message which would bring Dusty Fog, the Ysabel Kid and Red Blaze hot-foot to his aid.

An ear splitting 'splat!' sounded just over Mark's head, a sound he knew all too well. The sound of a close passing bullet as it split the air above him. Even as he heard the crack of the shot to his left Mark went sideways from the saddle to the right. He landed on his feet, holding his right hand Colt with the hammer drawn back ready to use and with the bloodbay between himself and the shooter.

Mark peered cautiously around the horse's neck and across the range. The shot appeared to have came from the small clump of trees out about a hundred yards away; which did not make Mark feel any happier with his present situation. His rifle remained in the saddleboot and the problem would be how to get it from the left side without taking a bullet between his shoulders in doing so. Sure he held the revolver. Sure an 1860 Army Colt would carry and kill at a hundred yards. But a man didn't like the idea of staking his life on it, not when matched against what sounded like a Winchester carbine. True the Winchester Model of 1866 used a comparatively light twenty-eight grain load, much the same as the Army Colt. The carbine, however, gave better range with its twenty inch barrel than did the Colt's eight inch barrel length.

Nothing stirred for a few seconds. Mark wondered who might be shooting at him and why no further shots came. He gave some thought of how he might lure his unknown attacker into a range where the Army Colt could be used with accuracy and deadly effect.

'Yahoo,' whooped a voice he knew all too well. 'Hi, Mark. Mark Counter!'

Giving a disgusted grunt, Mark set his Colt's hammer on on the safety notch and holstered the weapon. He swung into his saddle once more and saw that he guessed the direction of the shot correctly and the make of the gun. Calamity Jane rode from the clump of trees with her Winchester carbine resting across her arm.

In the years since Charlotte Canary left her family in the care of the St. Louis convent and faded for ever out of their lives, the eldest daughter, Martha Jane had travelled far and made something of a name for herself.

The last time Mark saw her she had been riding the box of a freight wagon, wearing an old buckskin jacket, patched pants, battered old hat and scuff-heeled boots. It appeared her fortunes had taken a turn for the better. Now she wore an expensive Texas style black Stetson hat sitting on her shortish, curly red hair. Her face had a tan, was still good looking, friendly and bore its usual reckless grin. She stood around five foot seven, her figure rich and full, maybe just a mite buxom but still firm fleshed and attractive. The rolled up sleeves of her tartan shirt showed arms a mite more muscular than a lady ought to have, but Calamity never set herself up as a lady. The tight rolled silk bandana hung long ends down between the full swell of bosom as the breasts strained against the shirt which hung open one button too many. The levis trousers looked like they had been bought a size too small the way they clung to and emphasized her full hips and thighs. Around her waist hung a new black gunbelt with an ivory butted Colt Navy revolver nestling in the fast draw holster, butt forward at the right side. On another woman this might have looked like an amusing affectation, but Mark knew Calamity could draw and shoot in just under a second and put lead into a man-sized target at gun-fighting ranges at the end of that time.

Calamity charged forward and at the last moment swung her horse with the grace of a polo pony and halted it at the side of Mark's bloodbay stallion. The horse, a fancy, high-stepping buckskin stud, like Calamity's outfit, pointed to her affluence.

'Mark, you ole goat!' she said, booting the carbine and thrusting a hand out towards him. 'Where you headed? Where's Cap'n Fog and the Kid? How you been keeping yourself, you ole coyote? See Belle Starr lately?'

'Ease off and let me answer one at a time,' he replied, finding her hand felt as hard and strong as ever. 'You look like you're in the money.'

'You said it. I've been freighting for the army up north, but we paid off a piece back and some of the boys allowed they could play poker. Which same only goes to show, now don't it.'

'Sure does,' agreed Mark, knowing Calamity fancied her skill as a poker player. 'Where're you headed, gal?'

'Down trail a piece, saw you coming and allowed to give you a surprise. Boy, you sure lit down from that hoss real *pronto*. Where're you making for?'

'Tennyson,' Mark replied, hoping she would be hide-bound for some other town.

'Yahoo!' whooped Calamity. 'Ain't this my lucky day.

Here's me headed for Tennyson myself. We can ride in together.'

Which was just about the last thing Mark wanted. In fact he could not think of anybody he would less want to head for Tennyson with. His uncle ran the law in Tennyson and needed help, most likely in some serious matter pertaining to his office. While Mark could not think why Calamity would be headed for Tennyson he did know one thing for sure, the visit would most likely wind up with trouble. Calamity's idea of fun was to ride in, find a saloon, locate its toughest female employee and pick a fight with her. If in doing this Calamity could also embroil the rest of the saloon in a general free-for-all it made her day and she enjoyed it to the full.

Not that Mark objected to a good fight and had been in more than one free-for-all in his time. Only right now he was on business, serious business, and a saloon ruckus came under the heading of pleasure. He knew that Calamity would do her damnedest to get him involved in a fight if she could, just to see him in action and admire his skill in a brawl.

'Why Tennyson, Calam?' he asked. 'It's nothing but a sleepy lil one hoss town. I'd h've thought you'd be headed for Wichita.'

'Nope, Tennyson,' she replied, then as if it explained everything. 'Madam Bulldog's there.'

It explained plenty and Mark could have groaned at the words. He had overlooked the stories he heard about Madam Bulldog. Now he saw the reason for Calamity's visit and did not care for what he saw. It spelled but one thing – TROUBLE. Might even be the trouble he had been sent for to help handle although he doubted that. His Uncle Tune might not be a spring-chicken, but he could handle fuss between two women even if one of them be Calamity Jane.

'You heard of her?' Calamity asked after they had rode on in silence for a moment.

'Some,' Mark replied.

'They say she can play better poker, out cuss, drink, shoot, fight and spit any woman around. Waal, she can't. Not while old Calamity Jane's still on her feet and r'aring to go.'

Now Mark knew for sure what Calamity's intentions were. Like some men would ride out of their way to meet a fast gun and pick a fight with him, so Calamity Jane sought out, to try conclusions with, any tough woman she heard about.

Calamity felt some pride in her toughness and the notoriety it brought her way. She laid claim to the same talents as legend had it Madam Bulldog showed, so what would be more natural but that Calamity would ride over to Tennyson and see who was the better woman.

Only this did not cause Mark to feel any happier about meeting Calamity. In a tight spot and when guns roared Mark would not object to Calamity at his side, for the girl had sand to burn and could handle her weapons. At a time like this, with some real urgent business on hand. Calamity was about as welcome as a rattlesnake in bed. Yet there didn't seem much he could do about it. Texas was a free country and Calamity could ride to Tennyson if she felt like it.

They rode on together. Towards dusk Calamity took her carbine from the saddleboot and blew the heads from four big jack rabbits which showed such poor sense as to halt in their flight within shooting range. Then as night closed in they headed for a small wood which gave them shelter and through which flowed a small stream. There they made camp. Like Mark, she carried her bedroll on her Cheyenne roll saddle but instead of a Manilla rope had her blacksnake whip strapped to its horn. Mark cared for the horses while she made a fire and prepared the meal. Give her credit, Calamity sure knew how to cook up a mess of rabbit meat in a way that would make a man's mouth water, Mark thought. She also made real good coffee in the true range tradition that a spoon should be able to stand upright in it.

After the meal they sat for a time talking over their last meeting and some of their mutual acquaintances. Calamity also talked of her forthcoming meeting with Madam Bulldog. She had heard of the saloonkeeper during her freighting trip and at its end prepared herself to enter the lists and toss down the gauntlet. Staking her pay in a poker game, she built it into a good-sized roll out of which she bought an eye-catching outfit, a new gunbelt and Colt and a fancy horse. She aimed to show folks what a real tough gal looked like.

'Well,' Mark drawled. 'I'm turning in now.'

Taking his bedroll, Mark opened it out, spreading the seven by eighteen foot water-proof tarpaulin cover on the ground, exposing the two suggans, heavy patch-work quilts and a couple of blankets as well as his depleted war bag which contained ammunition and spare clothing.

Calamity came over and looked down at the top suggan which appeared to have been built around three gingham dresses, several garish frocks and various items of female underclothing.

'That the suggan you had made after the battle at Bearcat Annies,* Mark?' she asked.

'Sure is.'

'From all I heard that was some cat-brawl. I wish I'd been along for it.'

The incident to which Calamity referred had occurred while Mark served as Dusty Fog's deputy in the Montana gold camp called Quiet Town. Three female deputies went into Bearcat Annie's saloon to arrest the owner and create a diversion to allow the male members of the town's police force to enter and take a bunch of hired gunmen. Mark needed a new suggan at the time and had one made from the torn clothing. From the look of the suggan it had, as Calamity said, been some fight.

One thing Mark knew for sure. No matter how Calamity felt on the subject, the law in Quiet Town had had enough on its combined hands without her adding to its complications – just as he had right now.

'Yes sir, I'd sure liked to be there,' sighed Calamity, sounding like a housewife wishing she could have attended some cooking contest. 'What're you headed to Tennyson for, Mark?'

'Uncle Tune's the law up there. He sent a message he needed some help, so I came along.'

'Sure pleased you did,' she sighed. 'Gets to be lonely, sage henning without company.' She threw a glance at him. 'I'm going to turn in.'

'And me,' Mark answered. 'Good night, Calam.'

Mark settled down, drawing the blanket and suggans over him but did not bother snapping the hooks and eyes of the tarp to make himself a waterproof cover, for the sky held no sign of rain. For a time he lay awake, listening to the night noises and the stamping of the horses. He wondered why his Uncle Tune might need him.

'Mark!' Calamity called from the other side of the fire.

'Yes?'

* Told in *Quiet Town*.

29

'I'm cold.'

What could a Texas gentleman, raised in the traditions of Southern chivalry and hospitality, do?' Could he allow a poor girl to lie shivering in cold through all the silent hours of the night?

He most certainly could not!

Rising to his feet, Mark carried his bedroll to where Calamity lay peeping up at him. He placed his own blankets on top of her and sat down.

A few minutes later Calamity whispered, 'I'm so warm now I'll have to take this damned shirt off, Mark.'

'That's the best idea you've had all day,' he answered.

Calamity Jane sat on her blankets and looked across the clearing as she tucked the shirt into her trousers. By the stream Mark Counter stood shaving without the use of a mirror. He had removed his shirt for his morning ablutions and the rising sun's beams played on the muscles which writhed and moved under his tanned skin. Calamity got to her feet and gave a contented sigh.

'Yes sir, Martha Jane,' she thought. 'That Mark Counter's a real hunk of man for sure.'

After breakfast, prepared by Calamity, they rode on once more. On the ride they talked of many things, but love was not one of the subjects they discussed. Neither Calamity nor Mark harboured any thoughts of romance, even after their interlude the previous night. Certainly she did not visualize herself dressed in white, looking virginal and bride-like before the altar and becoming Mrs. Mark Counter. She had known Mark for some time and counted him as being a good friend. Calamity always tried to be generous to her friends.

Shortly before noon they topped a ridge and received their first view of the town of Tennyson. Calamity let out a disgruntled curse as she studied the place, for it did not come up to her preconceived ideas.

'Huh!' she grunted in annoyance. 'What a one hoss town. You reckon there *is* a Madam Bulldog, Mark?'

'*You* reckoned there was,' he replied.

'That was before I saw Tennyson,' she sniffed. 'I'll bet she's nothing but some fat old calico cat who one time got lucky with a deck of cards. Still I've come this far, so I might as well ride the rest of the way. Might even be able to help you and your uncle out.'

Mark did not reply to this. He doubted if his Uncle Tune would thank him for bringing Calamity along. However, Mark could think of no way to prevent her coming and so decided to make the best of a bad job.

A crowd gathered about the building which housed Doc Connel's home, office and what passed for a hospital in Tennyson. Some two dozen or so citizens stood in a sullen half circle before the outside flight of stairs which led up to Doc's office. In the front, acting as a leader of the people, stood Joe Stern, the local blacksmith and a man much admired for his strength, if for nothing else, around town.

Right at that moment Stern faced Connel like a bear confronted by a fighting cock. The description seemed very apt for Doc Connel stood little more than five foot six and had all the aggressive spirit of a game bird. No man in the town had ever succeeded in browbeating Doc or making him back water. From the look of things he did not aim to let them start this day.

'Now you listen to me, Doc!' Stern said in his most blustering manner. 'It ain't that we don't respect Tune Counter. But them Cousins bunch sent a telegraph message sayings they's coming looking for him. And you knows what that means.'

'I know what *you* bunch here are,' Doc replied in his most hide-blistering and insulting tone. 'I suppose if Hank Cousins told you to string Tune up from a cottonwood tree you'd do it.'

A mutter of objection rose from the members of the crowd. None of them paid any attention to the two riders who came towards them, for all eyes were on their leader and the chief of the opposition to the 'run Tune Counter out of town' club.

'Now you know we wouldn't do that, Doc,' Stern objected. 'All we want to do is put ole Tune in a wagon and take him to Sand City where there's a sheriff and deputies and the cavalry at the Fort to protect him.'

'Tune wouldn't make five miles in a wagon,' Connel replied. 'Which same Sand City's over fifty miles on bad roads. He stays!'

Neither Mark nor Calamity Jane had the slightest idea

what the gathering might be about. They brought their horses to a halt and Mark raised his voice, cutting off the mutters of objection which rolled from the crowd.

'Excuse me, folks. Where at's Marshal Counter?'

The crowd turned their scared faces to him, taking in his matched Colts and general air of tough ability and handiness. They next looked Calamity over with some curiosity.

'Who's asking?' Stern asked, taking courage from the fact that none of the Cousins' bunch fitted Mark's description.

Swinging from his saddle, Mark walked forward. The crowd parted to let him pass through. Calamity stayed where she was, leaning forward on the horn of her Cheyenne roll saddle, watching all of them.

'I'm Tune Counter's nephew,' Mark replied. 'Where'd I find him?'

'You find him up here, friend,' Connel answered, jerking a thumb over his shoulder. 'Tune took lead a couple of days back. He's sick and sorry, but he's still living.'

'And he's got the Cousins bunch after him,' Stern went on, for once having to look up to a man. He weighed somewhat heavier than Mark, but stood two inches shorter. 'You kin of his?'

'So my pappy allus told me.'

'Then you talk some sense into Doc there!' yelled Stern, pointing to Connel. 'Get Tune out of here and to Sand City afore the Cousins boys come in after him.'

'I'll tell this feller what I told you, Stern,' said Doc Connel calmly. 'Old Tune's not fit to be moved for a week at least.'

'Which means he stays right where he is,' drawled Mark and stepped forward, meaning to go up and see his uncle.

Never before had Stern seen his wishes flouted in such a manner. He shot out a big hand to clamp on Mark's left bicep – and got himself a shock. Despite having been in the saddle for four days Mark's clothes still retained their costly, and rather dandy, appearance and his voice held the cultured tones of a wealthy, well-bred southerner. Stern made the mistake of thinking Mark to be no more than a fancy dressed kid. Now he felt a bicep which in size and hardness exceeded his own. Only he noticed it too late to stop his words.

'Listen!' he began, as he reached for Mark's arm. 'We're wanting Tune—'

'Just take your cotton-picking hand off my arm.'

From her vantage point on the buckskin, Calamity looked expectantly as she heard Mark's soft drawled reply. The last time she heard him speak in such a manner there followed a brawl she would never forget in which two U.S. cavalrymen were taken off with broken jaws. So she knew the danger signs.

Unfortunately for him, Stern did not.

Releasing the arm, Stern drew back his fist and threw a punch. He had something of a reputation around town as a fighting man of the first water. Against that same reputation most folks around the town felt under a disadvantage from the start.

Only Mark did not live in Tennyson, had never heard of Stern's reputation and most likely would not have been impressed by it if he had heard. All he knew was that this loud mouth wanted a fight, which same Mark sure don't aim backing away from.

Mark's left hand rose fast, deflecting the blow over his shoulder, then his right fist shot out. To the amazement of the watching crowd – and even more to the amazement of Stern – the blacksmith caught a punch with enough power to propel him backwards and knock him from his feet.

After reeling back a few steps, and causing a rapid scattering of the crowd, Stern lit down on his seat in the dust. He shook his head dazedly, then came up fast. Being trained in the old toe-to-toe bare-knuckle boxing school, Stern took a dim view of a man who avoided a blow, then hit back. With a roar like a starving and enraged grizzly, Stern charged at Mark with his fists flying.

He hit nothing but air, for Mark learned his fighting skill in a different, but much more effective school. At the last instant Mark weaved aside and clipped Stern's jaw, snapping his head back, the other hand followed and cracked the blacksmith's unlovely looking nose. Once more Stern retreated, shaking his head and wiping blood from his injured nasal organ.

'Let it drop, *hombre*!' Mark growled.

Instead of taking Mark's advice Stern came into the attack again. He took a punch in the mouth, then threw his arms around Mark's waist then clamped hold his pet hold. Mark let out a sudden grunt, for Stern had developed the crushing bear-hug hold to perfection. To get it clamped on mostly wound up with the one receiving it also collecting a couple or so broken ribs.

Mark felt the power of the crushing arms and then rammed his hands under the other man's chin. The strength in Mark's arms prevented Stern's next surging crush, holding him off just enough to prevent his obtaining full power from it. Now it became a trial of strength and Mark knew that he could hold off the other man, but wanted to get the business over with so he could go up and see his uncle. Mark remembered a trick Dusty Fog pulled once to escape from such a hold.

Raising his hands, suddenly Mark chopped down, the edges biting either side of Stern's neck even before the blacksmith could tighten his hold again. Stern let out a squawk of pain, lost his grip and took an involuntary pace to the rear.

Mark followed him up, stepping in with a fist he smashed into Stern's belly. It thudded home with a boom almost like a struck drum. Stern doubled over, legs caving under him. He did not go all the way down, for by this time Mark was riled. Up lashed Mark's other fist, catching Stern's jaw, lifting him erect, up on to his toes, then straight over on to his back. Stern landed hard, rolled over to his face, tried to push himself up. Then he went limp and collapsed to the ground and lay still.

One of the men in the crowd had long been a crony, sidekick and helper of Stern in anything the big man began. He took a look at Mark's back, forgetting the girl seated behind him, dropped his hand to his gun butt.

Calamity saw the move. Her right hand stabbed down, gripping the handle of the whip and snapping it free from the saddlehorn, she jerked her arm and the lash curled up, then shot out to crack like a rifle shot within an inch of the man's ear.

'Try it!' she warned.

The man had no such intention, being more concerned now with holding his ear and shaking his head to try and clear it of the sounds which seemed to be bouncing around inside it. He twisted around, anger plain on his face. The anger died again as he saw that Calamity still held the whip and looked capable of using it. The man gained the correct impression that had Calamity wished she could just as easily carved his ear off.

'All right, all right!' bellowed Doc Connel, walking to where Stern lay and rolling him over ungently. 'You folks have had your say and seen your fun. Now for the Lord's sake let's us have some sense.'

Turning towards the crowd Mark looked them over. They were the sort he expected to see present, idlers who would join any cause or follow any leader and do anything but work or wash. It would be easy to persuade such men that they represented public feeling and were acting for the best in getting Tune Counter out of Tennyson, especially when their own valuable hides might be endangered by his presence.

'One thing's for sure,' drawled Mark. 'Uncle Tune stays right here – unless any of you bunch want to call it different.'

'In case you bunch reckon all of you agin one's good odds,' Calamity put in, 'I'm siding Mark, so the odds are halved. And in case any of you are wondering, they don't call me Calamity Jane for nothing.'

Once again the crowd muttered, but they saw the cold gleam in Calamity's eyes and read the warning in Mark's. So they broke up their gathering, separating into chattering groups and heading away from the doctor's home. Two of the men helped the groaning Stern to his feet and steered him towards his forge.

'You got a powerful way about you, friend,' Connel remarked calmly. 'Yes, sir, real powerful. So's your lady friend.'

'Whooee!' Calamity whooped. 'I ain't never been called a lady afore.'

'There's always a first time for everything Calam,' Mark replied. 'Say, take my hoss down to the livery barn and give him a loose stall, will you?'

'Why, sure, right next to this here ole buckskin of mine.'

'Another thing, Calam.'

'Yeah?'

'Stay clear until I've seen Uncle Tune and found what he wants.'

Calamity threw back her head and laughed. 'For you,

35

anything. And I do mean anything. I'll book in a room at the hotel and you can buy me a meal there.'

Watching Calamity ride off Mark felt even more sure his job would not be made any easier by her presence.

'Nice gal,' Connel said dryly. 'Even if she does think she's Calamity Jane.

'I think she is, too,' Mark answered. 'And mister, I *know* Calamity Jane.'

Connel threw a look after the departing girl. 'Landsakes, friend, you mean that gal really is Calamity Jane?'

'Yeah. That's just who she is. Now where's Uncle Tune?'

'Up in my office. Come on up, but you can't be spending long with him.'

They climbed the stairs and passed through into the small room where Connel's patients waited until he could see them. The next room had an examination couch, cupboards with medicines and other supplies and had a couple of limp white coats hanging behind the door. Connel led Mark into the small room at the rear of the building and waved a hand to the shape on the bed.

Tune Counter looked at his nephew and managed a grin. He lay in the bed, a sling on his left arm and bandages showing around his chest. He tried to sit up and brought an angry growled curse from Connel.

'Just stay where you are, this feller don't expect you to get up and dance with him.'

'If he's like his pappy, and he looks like he is, he wouldn't want to dance with a man, though I'd sure keep your daughters locked up, Doc.'

'Never been fool enough to have any,' Connel grunted. 'He allows to be kin to you.'

'My nephew, Mark,' Tune introduced. 'Mark, this here's Doc Connel, best dang doctor and biggest fishing and hunting liar in the county.'

Which told Mark that the doctor was an old friend of his uncle's and a man he could rely on in whatever blew wild around Tennyson. He shook hands with Connel and the doctor grinned.

'Cap'n Fog and the Ysabel Kid aren't coming along, are they?' Connel asked.

'Not unless they're needed real bad.'

'Set and we'll tell you,' Tune said.

It took Mark just five minutes to know that the situation was not as bad as he might have thought – it was a damned sight worse. Only that morning Hank Cousins had sent word from a Wells Fargo way station up country that he and his boys aimed to visit Tennyson in the very near future and they did not aim to come peaceable.

'What was that ruckus on downstairs?' Tune asked as Mark reached his conclusions as to the state of affairs.

'Nothing,' Mark replied.

'You never could lie worth a cuss, boy.'

Connel snorted. 'Just a few of the town bums got all yeller bellied and wanted to ship you out to Sand City for safety – their safety. Mark talked 'em out of it though. He's got a convincing way with him. That right hand of his 'minds me of you'n.'

'You say the word and I'll get in the wagon,' Tune replied. 'Sheriff Haydon's got every man tied up out at Sand City and—'

'And you lay easy there,' Connel growled. 'I reckon, from the way he handled Stern, young Mark here can hold down the town. 'Sides he could always deputize Miss Calamity Jane.'

'Calam—!' Tune put in. 'You brought Calamity Jane *here*, boy?'

'Not so's you'd notice it,' Mark answered. 'I met her on the trail and she was already headed here. Apart from shooting her hoss from under her and leaving her hawg-tied I couldn't see any way around it.'

'Why's she here?' Tune growled.

'Why'd you think?'

'Madam Bulldog?'

'Sure,' drawled Mark. 'I could try and get Calam out of town.'

'Would it work?'

Connel looked from uncle to nephew and suddenly the light dawned. He cut in before Mark could reply to Tune's question.

'You mean Calamity Jane's here to tangle with Madam Bulldog?'

'Why sure,' Mark agreed.

'Whew!' Connel let out his breath in a gasp, then went on, 'It'd be a sight to see, only Madam Bulldog's got trouble of her own. She's the one who cut Breck Cousins down.'

Weakly Tune forced himself up on one elbow and gripped Mark's arm. He pointed to the town marshal's badge which lay beside his fully loaded and capped Army Colt on the chair close to the bed.

'Never had no call to take on a deputy, boy,' he said. 'You take this badge to the bank and ask Hoscroft, the owner, to swear you in. He's the mayor as well so he can do it. You'll maybe find him a mite pompous, boy, he acts that way. But you can reckon on him all the way should Cousins come.'

A flat grin creased Mark's face. 'He'll come all right. You know he will.'

'All right, that's enough talk for now,' growled Connel, in a tone which warned Tune he would allow no objections. 'I'll go along with Mark, down to the bank, just in case any other damned fool wants to run you out of town.'

'See you, then, Uncle Tune,' drawled Mark, taking up his hat and settling it at the right jack-deuce angle over his off eye.

'I'm not going any place, boy,' Tune replied.

At the bank Mark found Hoscroft to be affable, friendly and grimly determined to back the law to the hilt. He raised no objections and willingly swore Mark in as temporary town marshal. Nor did his help end with just swearing Mark in. He clearly did not aim to just sit back and allow Mark to face the Cousins gang alone. Opening his desk drawer Hoscroft took out a large map and spread it out before Mark. He tapped his forefinger on a point some distance from the town of Tennyson.

'This's the way station from which Cousin sent his message,' he told Mark and Connel. 'I had the map out and checked on things when I heard of the message. Way I see it the station's a good two days' hard ride from here.'

Mark studied the map and nodded his agreement. 'Even if he started off as soon as he saw the telegraph operator sending the message it'd be two days. I can't see him getting here before noon tomorrow at the earliest.'

'That's the way I see it too,' agreed the banker. 'They'd be lucky and need good horses to make it that early.'

'Couldn't you get help from the OD Connected in time,

Mark?' asked Connel, thinking of all he had heard of the murderous ways of the Cousins family.

'Not a chance of it,' Mark answered. 'It took me near to four days to come.'

'It appears we stand or fall alone then!' boomed Hoscroft. 'There are some of us, quite a few, on whom you can rely, Mark. We'll back you to the hilt.'

'And there's some who might go the other way when Cousins comes,' warned Connel. 'That bunch you had fuss with when you arrived, Mark, some of them wouldn't be any too steady behind us when the shooting starts.'

'You mean like that big feller I had fuss with?'

'Naw!' snorted Connel. 'Stern's not got sense enough to pack sand into a rat-hole, but he's honest. Just hawg-stupid enough to let the bunch with him, some of 'em at any rate, talk him into thinking he was acting best for the town. Stern'd be the last one to want Tune out of town, happen he'd stopped to think it might kill Tune doing it. I reckon he was even convinced that it'd be best for Tune.'

Hoscroft nodded his agreement to the words. He had seen something of the meeting, guessed at its cause and was about to go along to lend his moral support to Connel when Mark's intervention rendered the support-lending unnecessary.

'Tune ran the town with a tight, but fair, hand,' he stated. 'With the backing of most of the people. However, as you may know, Madam Bulldog's presence brings in much extra trade. Other people wanted to cash in on that trade – and I mean cash in. But Tune stopped it. There are some who wouldn't mind seeing him out of town and a more amenable man in his place.'

'Madam Bulldog be one of them?' Mark inquired.

'Certainly not. She runs her place fairly!' barked Hoscroft. 'And as I say, she put lead into Breck Cousins, so she'll be one on their visiting list when they get here.'

'Reckon I'd best go and see her then,' drawled Mark.

'Sure,' agreed the banker. 'But she'll be the least of your worries.'

A grin came to Mark's lips. He thought of Calamity Jane's proposed meeting with Madam Bulldog and doubted if Hoscroft's prophecy would prove to be right. As town marshal even on a temporary basis, his responsibility was to keep peace in the town. Happen all he had heard about Madam

Bulldog should be true, then when she and Calamity met the town's peace looked likely to be disturbed.

After a few more minutes of talk, receiving promises of aid, Mark left the bank. Connel had to return to his place of business and so Mark walked alone to the hotel. He saw the citizens of Tennyson showed some considerable interest in him as he passed. People peered through their windows, or out of doors as he passed. The loafers on the sidewalk also looked him over with interest, nodding towards the town marshal's badge he wore and muttering among themselves, but none offered to try and halt him or speak with him. They clearly did not aim to show their hand one way or another until he proved that he could take his fair share in the defence of the town.

He called in at the hotel's stables and found Calamity had attended to his big stallion as well as her own horse. She appeared to have taken his saddle along with her, for he could not see it on the burro by the wall.

Mark went to the hotel and saw the clerk who gave him the key to his uncle's room, for Mark intended to use it during his stay in town. He had barely entered when a knock came and he faced the door, his right hand Colt drawn and cocked ready for use.

'It's me Mark,' called Calamity's voice.

Holstering his Colt again, Mark opened the door and admitted the girl. She carried his saddle in her right hand, putting it carefully on its side in the corner of the room, then looked at him with a cheery grin.

'See you took on as marshal,' she drawled. 'How'd it go?'

'Uncle Tune's all right. You know what's happened here?'

'Some. I never yet saw a livery barn owner who wouldn't talk the hind leg off a dead hoss. He told me about everything that's happened here since they took the town from the gophers.'

'Way I see it the Cousins bunch'll be in either late tomorrow or the next day, noon tomorrow at the earliest though,' Mark told her.

'I'll side you when they come,' she promised. 'Anyways, I'll have tended to Madam Bulldog's needings by then.

'I was going to see you about that, Calam,' Mark said. 'Are you set on meeting Madam Bulldog?'

'Set as I could be,' she answered. 'Hell, Mark, I've been working like a dawg for nigh on six months freighting to the army. A gal's got to relax and have fun sometimes, don't she?'

Mark shrugged, seeing there would be no way of dissuading Calam from her proposed course. Short of tossing Calamity into jail, or running her out of town on a rail, he could see no way of avoiding the clash between the two women, unless, which he now doubted, Madam Bulldog should prove to be greatly over-rated. He might have asked Calamity on the strength of old friendships and did not doubt she would do as he asked, but he had never been one for using friendship to turn another from a thing they wanted to do. So he decided to sit back and allow things to fall the way the fates dealt them.

'Don't you worry none, Mark boy,' said Calamity. 'After I showed her a thing or two tonight she'll know who's the better woman and that'll have you 'n' me free to hand the Cousins bunch their needings.'

With that promise she headed for the door and left Mark alone with his thoughts. He cleaned his guns, made sure they were ready for use, then lay on the bed fully dressed, to catch a short rest. Something told him that he was going to need it.

The sun had just gone down when Mark entered the Bull's Head Saloon. He saw a fair crowd in attendance and wondered if this was the ordinary way of the place or if word of Calamity's arrival and intentions had gone out, bringing extra folks in to see the clash.

Mark walked across the room, ignoring the glances directed at him and the badge he wore. Knowing these small western towns he did not doubt that everyone knew he was Tune Counter's nephew, *the* Mark Counter who rode with Dusty Fog and the Ysabel Kid. Doubtless any number of them would also be speculating when Dusty and the Kid were due to arrive.

He studied the girls as he crossed the room, wanting to form his own opinion of Madam Bulldog. However, he doubted if the great lady be present. All he could see looked like run-of-the-mill dancehall girls of the kind one met in every town from Texas to California and back the long way.

Not one of them appeared to be the kind to make legends or attract much attention to themselves.

Reaching the bar, Mark looked at the bartender who came towards him. The man grinned a welcome which, if Mark was any judge of such matters, looked sincere enough.

'Howdy marshal,' the bartender greeted. 'What'll it be?'

'Beer. Take one for yourself.'

'This'n's on the house,' Sam replied. 'I saw you up in Quiet Town, didn't I?'

'I was there,' agreed Mark.

'The name's Sam, marshal. I'm Madam Bulldog's house boss.'

Mark took the drink offered to him and nodded his thanks. 'Reckon you know I'm Mark Counter,' he said, 'Tune's nephew.' He glanced around the room while Sam leaned by him clearly aiming to talk and leave his assistant to deal with the lesser clientele. 'Madam Bulldog here?'

'Not just yet. Be down soon.'

Although he talked with the bartender, Mark did not relax. His eyes flickered at the bar mirror, studying the room behind him. This was partly caution and partly training, for he knew better than take foolish chances in a town which contained enemies.

Three men in particular caught Mark's eye. He stayed facing Sam, but watched them in the long mirror's reflection. Two of them had been members of the crowd who wished to run his uncle out of town, which accounted for why Mark spotted them. They most certainly did not work cattle for a living, nor, despite their town suits, did they give the impression that they owned or worked in any business house of the town. To Mark, with a long experience of their kind gained in his travels and time as a law officer, they spelled cheap tinhorn card shark, goldbrick salesmen, or petty thief.

The third man was none of these things – he was much more dangerous. He wore somewhat expensive and dandy range clothes, a thing Mark could hardly hold against him. His face bore a tan, yet he did not strike Mark as being a cowhand. Comparing him with the other two Mark decided he could not be very tall. Yet he had a faintly hidden truculence about him that did not go with his lack of inches. Mark knew the signs, could read them well. This small man had all the markings of a real fast proddy hard-case, which, viewing his lack of inches, meant he relied on gun speed, not muscle, to get him by.

Unless Mark was mistaken, the trio appeared to be giving him much more than casual attention. They watched him enter, cross to the bar and stand at it. Then they thrust their heads together and talked. From the repeated looks they threw his way, Mark guessed himself to be the subject of their conversation.

'Sam,' Mark said quietly. 'Who're those three citizens sitting there to the right of the vingt-un lay-out?'

To give him credit, Sam did not stare directly at the men. He clearly had learned his trade in the saloons which gave support to the law, for he merely glanced around the room with keen, all seeing gaze, not pausing his look on the three men. For all that he answered Mark's question as soon as his quick look around ended.

'The two townies are Wardle and Schanz. Never seen the other, except his type and we've both seen *that*. Them two come here to try and open a saloon, when the town broke open after Madam arrived. Only they didn't have enough money and the bank wouldn't loan any. So they came here, wanted to set up a game and cut Madam in on the profits. She wouldn't have any of it.'

'What do they do around town?'

'Play here some nights, join the cowhand games.'

'Play straight?'

'We never caught them at anything crooked,' Sam replied. 'And Madam keeps her eyes on them. We run a straight place and that's the way she aims to keep it.'

'Then they don't make much here?' asked Mark, watching the men, seeing the small hard-case rise, seeing for the first time that he wore two guns.

'Enough. You know how it is, their kind can lick the pants off most cowhands, even in a straight game,' Sam answered. 'I heard they run another game in their room at the hotel. It's only a rumour though. Nobody talks much about it.'

By this time the short man had reached the bar, halting to Mark's left and a short way along. Mark felt his back hair rise stiff and bristly, the instinct of years of wearing guns warning him of danger.

'Hey, bardog!'

Although the term 'bardog' had much use throughout the west it had never been considered polite to use it to a bartender's face, or when calling for service; the small man did so. Sam scowled, seeing the man's attention directed straight at him. So Sam ignored the small man and waited to be asked in a more polite manner.

'Serve you, friend?' asked the second bartender moving up as Sam turned to talk with Mark once more.

'I want him,' replied the small man, pointing to Sam.

'He's busy.'

Turning to face the second bartender fully, the small man's face twisted into an ugly snarl.

'He's the boss bartender and Al Cordby don't take no dealing with underlings. So get out of the way.'

Sam threw a look pregnant with meaning to Mark, seeing that the name had not gone unnoticed by the big Texan. Over the past couple of years Al Cordby had built something of a name for himself in Texas. Folks spoke of him as a fast gun hired killer. Mean as hell and a hater of any man taller than himself.

This was the man who stood along the bar from Mark. He had come up to the bar for a purpose and that purpose was not just to buy a drink.

Slapping his right hand hard on the bar top, Cordby looked hard at Sam.

'I want you to serve me, bardog.'

'He's serving me.'

Mark spoke quietly. Yet in some way his words reached out around the room. The piano player hit a jangling discord and stopped playing, talk died down, every eye went to the bar, and those nearest to it set down their glasses ready to dive for cover.

For a long moment Cordby studied Mark. He had the true killer attitude, the calm, detached, confident way which served to disturb and scare lesser men when faced by a known fast gun. Cordby made no move. His right hand stayed where it lay on the bar, but the left hand hung hidden by his body. He studied Mark, noting the way the big Texan's guns hung, knowing that here stood a man who wore the rig of one who could draw real fast. That increased Cordby's hate, strengthened his intention of carrying out the work for which he had been hired.

'I want him here, big man!' he said.

'Now you know what it is to want,' Mark replied.

Still Cordby did not turn to face Mark, just twisted his head and looked. A cold, savage snarl came to his lips.

'Big man, huh?' he asked. 'You're the big man who aims to stop Hank Cousins and his boys coming in here and roughing the town up?'

'That's what they tell me,' Mark replied.

'You're setting all these folks up for trouble they could avoid,' Cordby went on, seeing the crowd hung on his words. 'You're aiming to keep Tune Counter here instead of sending him to Sand City where he'll be safe.'

'That's just what I'm going to do,' Mark replied.

'And you reckon you're big enough man to do it?'

'I reckon I'm big enough to do it.'

'Big man, huh?' Cordby sneered.

'Depends,' replied Mark.

'What on?'

'How big a man I'm talking to. There's some around who likely reckon I'm a midget.'

Nothing Mark might have said could have raised Cordby's hate against him more. Cordby felt all too fully his lack of inches and resented any man making even a casual reference to them.

For his part Mark saw the clash coming. He knew Cordby came to the bar with the intention of picking a fight with him and could guess at the reason. The two men sat at their table and watched everything with interest. Only one person in the room moved. A tall, blonde girl went upstairs at a fast walk and disappeared from sight at the top, likely headed away from danger, Mark thought.

'Get me another beer, Sam,' Mark said, taking his eyes from Cordby for an instant, then watching him again.

'Leave it!' the words cracked from Cordby's lips. 'Listen good to me, big man. You get out of this town and take your kin with you. That way Hank Cousins and his boys'll be satisfied.'

'Will, huh?'

'Sure they will.'

Now Cordby was not speaking to Mark, but directing his words to the crowd. Some of them even looked as if they might believe him. Mark now knew why Cordby came to the bar. To force the issue, to either make Mark back-water in which case he would be finished as town marshal, for none would follow his lead, or to terminate Mark's period in office by means of a bullet. Either way he would give strength to the men who hired him, allow them to dominate their will upon the town. The fate of Tennyson City hung in the balance.

All this Mark knew. If he faced the challenge he would bring the town around behind his back. If he failed to handle Cordby, or if he backed down, his Uncle Tune would be on the wagon and headed for Sand City before an hour passed and most likely Madam Bulldog would be run out of town at the same time.

'I said get me another beer, Sam,' Mark drawled.

Against the flat defiance Cordby prepared to make his move. He knew Mark could not see his left hand, knew also that most men tended to ignore the left hand as a faction in a gunfight. There were a few men who could draw and shoot equally well with either hand, but they could almost be numbered on the fingers of a man's two hands. Most men, even men who wore two guns all the time, kept the left hand weapon in reserve, to have another six shots ready instantly in case of urgent need.

Cordby pivoted around fast, his left hand stabbing to his side, dipping, closing on the butt of his gun, and bringing it forth even as he made his turn. Yet before he faced Mark fully, Cordby knew he had called the play wrong.

The significance of the hidden left hand did not escape Mark, for he knew men who handled their guns with ambidextrous skill. So he stood ready for just such a move as Cordby now made.

His right hand dipped, fingers closing about the ivory butt of the Colt in his right side holster, thumb curling around and drawing back the hammer even as he lifted the gun from leather. In slightly over half a second, even as Cordby faced him, and before the man's gun could line, Mark's gun came clear and roared.

For an instant the short killer's face showed amazement, horror almost, as he realized his favourite play had failed him at last. Then Mark's Army Colt roared, the recoil kicked the barrel up and a .44 bullet ripped into Cordby's head, threw him backwards to crash to the sawdust covered floor, dead.

There had been no time to shoot in any other way. Cordby's intention had been to kill Mark and the big Texan acted the only way he dare, by killing Cordby first.

Across the room Cordby's two pards came to their feet. Wardle thrust his hand under his coat to where a short barrelled Colt hung in a shoulder clip. A shot spat out, a lighter crack than the roar of an Army Colt. It sounded from the stairs and splinters erupted from the table between Wardle and Schanz. Looking towards the shooter, Wardle froze, letting his hand stay under the coat but not trying to draw his gun. He saw who had cut in and knew Madam Bulldog's bullet hit the table because that was where she intended it to go.

Mark turned fast, his gun slanting towards the stairs for an instant, then swung back towards the two men as the crowd scattered from them. He watched Wardle's hand come clear of the coat, then turned his eyes once more to the two women on the stairs. One was the blonde who he had seen going up and thought had been headed for safety, only Mark knew he had miscalled her intentions, for she went to fetch help. The other woman clearly must be Madam Bulldog. Looking at her, Mark studied for an instant the Colt Cloverleaf she held. Then he nodded, this surely was Madam Bulldog and she looked like she might live up to her reputation.

However, there would be time to get to know her better when a small matter had been attended to. He nodded towards the woman as she stood watching him, her gun still in her hand.

'Thank you kindly, ma'am,' he said.

The big Colt spun on his finger and dropped back into the holster. He started across the room with long, purposeful strides. The two men watched his coming and moved around to try and keep the table between themselves and the advancing Texan.

Madam Bulldog gave Viola her Cloverleaf and told the blonde to take it to her room. She watched Mark crossing the room, then waved two of the waiters, pointing to Cordby's body. The men knew what they must do and went forward, the town undertaker with them. Before they removed the dead man they stopped to see how Mark handled the other two.

Neither Wardle nor Schanz were brave men. Given a drunk in a side-alley they could handle him with ease. Faced with a big, sober and very angry man their courage oozed out of them. Nor did either have the slightest intention of trying to draw the guns they carried. They had seen Cordby die before the fast drawn Army Colt and knew Mark could handle them both in the matter of gun-play.

Shoving the table aside, Mark reached out a big right hand. He gripped the front of Wardle's jacket and shirt, bunching them up as he dragged the man towards him. A look of relief came to Schanz's face, but did not stay there for long, for Mark wiped it off with a backhand slap which spun the man around, sent him staggering into the wall. In a continuance of the same move Mark brought his arm around and landed a bare-hand slap across Wardle's face, snapping his head back and spinning him the other way.

Coldly Mark looked at the two men. 'You pair tried to set me up for a kill,' he said quietly, yet grimly.

'You – you got us wrong!' Wardle croaked, wiping a trickle of blood from the corner of his mouth. 'We didn't know what Cordby aimed to do.'

Mark's grin looked colder than ice as he replied, 'You're a liar.'

The correct answer to such a statement should have been a fast drawn Colt, for the word 'liar' was regarded as one of the supreme insults in the west. Yet the man at whom Mark directed it made no reply. He made his feet and stood staring at the big Texan. Schanz also stood up, his eyes showed hate, but they showed fear too.

'Tune Counter's staying in town,' Mark went on. 'And if Cousins wants him he'll have to go through me first. But you pair won't be here to see it. If you're in town tomorrow at dawn I'll shoot you on sight.'

'You—!' began Schanz, meaning to stand on his Constitutional rights.

He saw the look on Mark's face and discarded his rights. Turning on his heel he made a rapid dive for the batwing doors of the saloon, beating Wardle to them by a scant half second.

For a moment Mark stood watching the doors, he heard the footsteps fading away along the sidewalk and knew the two men would not be back. Their kind would never face a determined man and they would not dare go against him, not face to face. From behind they might be a danger, but he doubted if they would be in Tennyson when he made his morning rounds.

'I've seen to having Cordby removed.'

Mark turned at the words and found Madam Bulldog standing nearby. He looked her over with some interest and knew that here stood a woman who might even be able to outdo Calamity Jane in the matters at which they both claimed pre-eminence.

He threw a glance towards the bar where the local undertaker and the waiters, seeing there would be no further developments, lifted the body and carried it towards the rear door.

'Thanks, ma'am,' he replied.

'Are all you Counter men tall?' she inquired, studying his six foot three inches of height and the great spread of his shoulders.

'Most of us,' Mark grinned. 'My Uncle Shorty though, he's only six foot tall. We don't talk about him much.'

A laugh changed Madam Bulldog's face, made it look pleasant, friendly and attractive. She lost the smile after a moment.

'Those two set Cordby on to you?' she asked.

'Why sure,' agreed Mark.

'Saw it all. I thought Tune was fast with a gun, but you're faster.'

'You'll be making me blush next, ma'am.'

'The day *you* blush will be a day to remember,' she sniffed. 'Tell you one thing though. You've got the town now.'

Mark knew what she meant. His handling of Cordby, his proof of how fast he could draw and with what skill he could plant home his bullets, had not gone without notice amongst the customers. They knew they had a good man with a gun wearing the law badge and would be the more willing to follow his lead when the time came.

'Those pair, ma'am,' Mark said, 'you reckon they're working with Cousins?'

49

'No. They saw a chance of getting Tune out of town – and knowing he would be unlikely to come back, so they took it.'

'Huh, huh!' grunted Mark. 'Anybody in town likely to side with Cousins and his bunch when they come.'

She grinned. It was a hard, cold grin, without humour. 'Not since you cut Al Cordby down.'

At that moment Madam Bulldog stopped looking and talking to Mark and stepped by him, making for the door. Mark turned and almost groaned aloud as he saw the reason for Madam Bulldog's departure.

Calamity Jane entered the Bull's Head Saloon, shoving through the batwing door as she had done in innumerable places and towns throughout the west. She left behind her the world of the good ladies of a town, entering the protected domain of the dancehall girl. This time Calam took a bare three steps into the room before she found her way blocked, a woman standing full in her path.

'The door's there, girlie,' said Madam Bulldog, indicating the entrance through which Calamity came into the rom.

'Yeah'!' replied Calamity, studying the woman she had ridden almost five hundred miles to meet. Then, although she could make a real accurate guess at the answer, went on: 'Who're you?'

Hands on hips, feet braced apart, stood Madam Bulldog. She read the challenge in Calamity's eyes and knew that here stood no ordinary saloongirl trying to impress folks with how tough she was. To the saloonkeeper's way of seeing, Calamity formed a definite and dangerous menace, more so than the average tough calico cat who came to try Madam Bulldog out and left a sadder, pain-filled and wiser woman. The red-haired girl, for all her fancy, man's clothes, would need different handling than the normal run of challengers.

'I'm Madam Bulldog – and who might *you* be?'

Calamity grinned broadly. 'I might be Belle Starr, or Poker Alice, or Madame Moustache, but I'm none of them. I'm Calamity Jane.'

A matter of interest, anticipation and excitement rose from the watching and listening crowd, for all had heard of Calamity Jane, and all could guess at why she came to Tennyson.

So could Madam Bulldog and in that moment, she felt

grateful to Calamity for making the pilgrimage. Madam Bull-dog could see that all thoughts of danger, all fears of the Cousins' gang, already weakened by Mark's prompt action in dealing with Wardle and Cordby, now became forgotten in the anticipation of the forthcoming clash between herself and Calamity Jane. So, although she did not wish for the clash, Madam Bulldog did not side-step it either.

'Calamity Jane, huh?' said Madam Bulldog with a sniff which might have meant anything or nothing.

Everybody in the room waited and watched. They won-dered if Calamity would land on the other woman with tooth and claw, in a brawl which would make a legend, or if the girl aimed to make her play with guns, which would also be memorable if not as lasting or entertaining.

Calamity herself had the same thoughts. She took in the hard rubbery way in which the other woman stood, noted the powerful looking arms and general air of tough capability.

'Yes, sir,' thought Calamity, 'this gal's worth riding to see.'

She thought also that such a meeting much not be ter-minated too quickly by licking Madam Bulldog physically. First Madam had to learn that her other talents high though they might be, stood second to Calamity Jane's. With that in mind Calamity held off her physical attack until she had showed Madam how a real wild and woolly gal could cuss.

'You know what I reckon you are?' Calamity asked. 'I reckon you're a—'

There followed a string of profanity good enough to turn a thirty year army sergeant green with envy as Calamity poured her vilification on to the other woman's head in a fast flow.

After almost three minutes Calamity stopped, sure she had rocked Madam Bulldog to the toes of her dainty high heeled shoes. Only Madam gave no sign of being either rocked or shocked. Instead she came back with and pro-ceeded to heap on the girl a flow of cursing of equal length, pungency and power of abuse.

For once in her life Calamity looked surprised and taken aback. She grudgingly admitted that Madam Bulldog could pour on the abuse real fast, hard and colourful.

At the end of Madam's flow, she turned and walked back to the bar with Calamity on her heels Mark Counter watched them go, then followed to take up his beer. He grinned as he looked around the silent and still room where the crowd, customers and workers alike, sat in rapt attention. Calamity started cursing once more and a man holding an aces full house, with over two hundred dollars of his money already in the pot, sat staring, ignoring the game. At the faro lay-out the bets lay forgotten. The wheel of fortune came to a halt but the lucky winners did not trouble to gather in their winnings for they stared and listened like men turned to stone.

The rules for a cursing match had long been known throughout the west. Now Calamity Jane tangled in such a match with Madam Bulldog. The girl had learned her business from the inspired utterances of miners, soldiers and bullwhackers. To this she brought and added all her native powers to improve and increase her vocabulary. Yet for all of that she gained the idea that Madam Bulldog commanded just as good a flow.

They matched each other word for word, invoked weird and horrible gods, suggested each other had unmentionable diseases, accused each other of every low act the human body could possibly perform and several for which it would be impossible for any human body to perform. They cursed each other's ancestors, descendants and distant kin. Sweat came to their faces, running down their cheeks. Calamity tore her bandana off and Madam Bulldog's hair came down, hanging around her face while her make-up became streaked and then washed away.

Not a sound came from the room. Every man present would have given all he owned to have those inspired utterings written down so he might read and learn from them.

Then slowly Calamity's voice trailed off. She looked glassy eyed and dazed under the strain. No longer would her mind function and her mouth felt dry, her tongue unable to force another word through her lips.

With a croak of frustrated rage Calamity swung her hand around, fist clenched for a blow and in doing so she admitted her defeat at the cussing match. Only the blow did not land. Mark Counter, watching and listening with the same rapt attention as the others, saw the start of the move and took steps to prevent it. He moved forward and his big hand shot out to catch her arm, holding it before the fist touched Madam Bulldog's face.

'You're licked, Calam,' he said quietly.

The girl nodded her agreement, clinging to the bar and unable to make a single sound in reply. She stared through glassy eyes as Madam Bulldog spat out another flow of curses, driving home the point that Calamity Jane had been out-cussed, over-cussed and cussed plumb into the ground. Although her throat felt raw and she could hardly think or breathe, Madam Bulldog made her final speech. She knew Calamity to be licked at cussing, but doubted if the girl would be willing to let things go with just that.

So Madam Bulldog turned to face the bar, looking at the state of her face and barely holding down a gasp of horror. She nodded to Sam, not wishing to speak and knowing he would understand her needs. Sam did, he poured out a couple of schooners of beer, a drink which at other times Madam would not have thought of touching, but which he knew would be the only thing she could manage at the moment. Placing a schooner before each woman, Sam stepped back, grinning broadly.

Calamity took up the glass and drank deeply, watching Madam Bulldog in the mirror, trying to carry on drinking after the woman finished. However, Madam saw the way Calamity looked and so tilted back the big schooner. Calamity managed three-quarters of her glass before lack of breath caused her to put it down, she watched Madam empty her's and knew the task ahead would be far harder than she at first imagined.

'It's not so easy, is it, Calam?' asked Mark Counter as he watched Madam make for her room to tidy her appearance before attending to her customers.

'It sure ain't,' Calamity replied, mopping her face with the bandana, all the beauty treatment she needed. 'This gal's going to take some licking.'

Half an hour passed before Madam Bulldog returned to the barroom with her face once more made-up ready for business and her hair tidy again. She crossed straight to the bar, making for Calamity and the crowd looked on, wondering at what the two women would clash next. The air of eager expectancy had not diminished after seeing Calamity out-cussed, for all knew she was not the kind of girl to take defeat lying down. Most of the crowd hoped for a fight, but once more they did not get their wish for Calamity grinned and said:

'They reckon you play poker, Madam.'

In this Calamity showed wisdom. Not that she feared a physical tangle with the other woman. At any other time she would have been only too willing to pitch into Madam Bulldog tooth and claw, but she knew it would not be an easy matter to whip the saloonkeeper and wanted to keep out of the fight until after she helped Mark Counter meet the Cousins gang, if possible. Madam Bulldog's motives were the same. She also wanted to be unimpaired by the injuries a fight with Calamity must bring, so that when Cousins and his bunch came she could lend Mark a hand and save her own life, for she knew Cousins would be after her as well as Tune Counter.

'I do,' she replied to Calamity's suggestion. 'Do you?'

'Let's set, deal a few 'n' find out, shall we?'

Madam nodded, then looked towards the bar. 'Sam, a new, unopened deck of cards. That table in front of the bar suit you, Calamity?'

'Why, sure.'

For a long moment Madam Bulldog studied the girl, almost as if she felt she ought to recognize, or at least know, Calamity from somewhere. Sure she had heard of Calamity Jane, there were few in the west who had not. Yet few, a very few indeed, knew Calamity's full name of Martha Jane Canary, for it never received mention when folks talked about her. Madam Bulldog knew her only as Calamity Jane and after the long look shook her head, clearing the thoughts of recognition from it. She led the way to the table and they took their seats facing each other.

'Mark!' Madam called. 'Bring a box of chips, and come on over to act as look out for us.'

'I'll do just that,' Mark replied, taking a new deck of cards and box of poker chips from Sam, then crossing to join the two women at the table.

Once more the other entertainments of the evening lapsed and became forgotten as a crowd gathered around the table, standing in a circle to see the sport. They all knew Madam Bulldog's skill, but also had heard of Calamity's poker playing prowess and so expected a good display.

54

Certainly Calamity would be on her mettle after losing out on the cussing match.

Calamity took the deck of cards, turning it between her fingers, seeing the box carried the mark of a well known firm of card makers and that the Federal tax seal remained intact. This meant little, as she knew well, for crooked gambling supply houses could easily steam off the seal, doctor the cards and reseal it again so as to defy detection. With this thought in mind she broke the seal, took out the cards and flipped the jokers aside.

'When I play,' she stated, 'there's no limit, no wild cards, and no ladies in the game.'

'I play any way the others want,' answered Madam and Calamity's annoyed grunt told her she had scored the point with her words.

She sat back and without annoyance watched Calamity give the cards a quick but thorough check to ensure they had not been marked or, by having the others filed down a minute piece at the edge, certain cards being larger than the remainder of the deck so as to allow them to be located and used during the game. Madam took no offence at the precautions, for they gave her an insight into Calamity's knowledge of the game and left her sure of one thing, Calamity knew more than a little about the art of playing card games for money.

Calamity gave a sweeping glance round the table, making sure that nothing lay on it which might contain a tiny mirror to show Madam the value of the cards as she dealt them. Nor did Madam have either a small bandage on a finger and concealing all but the tip of a thumb-tack, or a ring which might carry a tiny sharp spike either of which could be used for 'pegging'; marking the cards during play by pricking the backs in certain spots to show their value. This was an old crooked gambling method, but one which still brought in profit when playing against the unwary.

Although Madam's hands carried neither bandage nor rings, Calamity knew there were many other ways by which the deck might be marked during play. Nailing, pressing the thumbnail into the edge of the cards, making a tiny mark, dangerous against an alert opponent, but used in some circles. Waving, bending the desired cards slightly, again risky when the other player or players knew anything about their business. Daubing, this offered less chance of detection on the cards, but carried the risk of the opposition seeing the small, concealed spot of dye of slightly lighter or darker hue than the back of the deck, or spotting the tell-tale stain on the thumb or finger used to transfer the dye to the cards.

All these methods Calamity knew of and although she took precautions against them and aimed to keep her eyes open for any kind of crooked play, some instinct told her she did not need to worry, the game would be fair.

She gave the cards a rapid riffle-stack, then thrust them across the table to Madam Bulldog who took them up and also riffled them. Madam laid the cards on the table top and nodded to the girl.

'Cut,' Madam said. 'Draw or stud?'

'Make it dealer's choice,' Calamity said. 'Cut light, lose all night.'

Giving out with the old poker adage Calamity cut deep into the deck and left the completion of the cut to her opponent, watching for any sign that Madam aimed to lay the cards in the same order as before the cut. Madam took up the cards and, deciding to make the first game draw poker, flipped five cards face down to each of them.

So began a card game which would go down amongst the legends of the west. A game of skill, science and bluff which would have made many an acknowledged master of poker look to his laurels.

From the very first hand Mark, no novice at the poker game himself, saw that it would be a hard fought contest. Both women had an extensive knowledge of the game, both its mathematics and, although neither of them had ever heard the word, of its psychology. The early hands saw them playing an almost classic game and in such case, their skill being near enough equal, neither could make any impression on the other's pile of chips.

However, Mark got the idea that of the two Madam Bulldog showed the better poker sense. Calamity's volatile nature led her to pile on the pressure when the cards started falling her way. For a time the cards ran Calamity's way and it seemed that she could do no wrong. At draw she would take one card to two pairs and a third member of one of her

56

pairs would pop up like a trained pig, or she would go for one to an inside straight (which was never good poker) and that required one arrived as if drawn by a magnet.

Against such luck no amount of skill could prevail and even though she played every hand in a manner which would have brought a nod of approval from Hoyle: always working on the widely accepted, but erroneous belief, that Hoyle had played and mastered the game of poker; Madam Bulldog lost heavily. The crowd watched everything, guessing, or trying to guess what each woman held. They groaned their sympathy when Madam lost on a good hand which Calamity's lucky draw, or lucky arrival of a last up-card winner, snatched from her.

At the end of two hours' play Calamity stood almost fifteen thousand dollars ahead and Sam, who knew his boss' business, felt panic, for he watched the way the girl bet. Madam could not stand much more of this kind of loss.

For her part Calamity enjoyed every minute of the game, so did Madam Bulldog, even though losing for, if she could hang on long enough, she knew the cards must change their ways.

'Aw, hell,' drawled Calamity, hauling in a pot. 'Whyn't we move to a bigger table. I've hardly got room to move an elbow for my winnings.'

Mark grinned and Madam Bulldog's face showed an expression at this ancient poker artifice. She sat back, with no sign of worry, or interest in the growing pile before Calamity.

'Deal,' she said.

'Damned if I don't buy into a freight outfit with my winnings,' Calamity went on, scooping up the cards and riffling them. 'Wouldn't want to keep this place going though, never could stand being in one place. Sorry I can't stack 'em better than this, Madam, got so much loot in front of me. Say, Mark, did I ever tell you about the time I took a five thousand dollar pot with three threes?'

For her part Madam ignored the words, playing each hand on its merit, neither being scared out of playing a good hand because the luck went against her, nor trying to make Calamity look small on taking her on an understrength hand. The taunt that Calamity intended to win her place just rolled off her back and she waited.

57

Then:

'Aces full,' Calamity said in a bored tone, as if drawing a full house of three Aces and two nines had become such a regular thing as to bore her. 'You had me worried. I thought you'd filled those fours you were after.'

'That's funny,' replied Madam Bulldog calmly. 'I *did* get them.'

She turned her cards face up and Calamity stared at four threes and a four. It came as a real shock to Calamity who had been betting high, wide and handsome, assuming that Madam Bulldog drew a flush which her hand would beat.

Thinking of the game later Mark decided the earlier run of luck clouded Calamity's judgment. There had been turns when she had pulled a last card miracle at stud during those earlier hands. Then, as almost always happens, the cards swung their favour the other way completely. From being able to do everything right Calamity made the complete circle and all went wrong.

Now Madam Bulldog started to needle Calamity in the same way the girl worked on her while winning and Calamity, while knowing she was being needled, rose to the bait like a hungry rainbow trout after a floating fly.

Having found Calamity's weaker game to be stud, Madam dealt it every time and mocked the girl for changing to draw. Against her better judgment, Calamity tossed out the first cards face down, then turned the second over to bet on instead of all five face down for draw.

The taunting and goading were all accepted as completely fair and honest tactics in the rough-and-tumble of no limit poker and a player who was not a past-master, or mistress, of the art of applying the needle, had no right to be playing.

'Oh hum!' sighed Madam Bulldog, tossing a straight flush face down on the table, into the deadwood, acting as if she had bluffed Calamity on a seven high, no-nothing hand. 'I always reckon you should have the guts to call them when you bet on them. Lucky for me you didn't though.'

Calamity let out an annoyed grunt, not sure whether she could have beaten Madam's unseen hand and wishing she had paid to see. She would not sink to the depths of trying to look at the hand without paying for the privilege.

So Calamity sat back and the next time she felt Madam to be bluffing, she called the bet.

'I've what it looked like,' replied Madam, contemptuously exposing a ten high flush. 'You never called on that hoss-droppings you held, did you?'

The game went on. Calamity's temper crackled, but she knew to allow it to burst would be certain proof that she had met a better poker player and worse in her eyes, would brand her as a poor loser.

At eleven o'clock Mark rose from the table, leaving the saloon to make his rounds of the town. He walked the silent streets and kept his ears and eyes open. He knew Wardle and Schanz would never have the guts to stack against him on even terms, but they might chance a shot from some dark alley. So Mark stayed alert, using the caution he gained while serving as a deputy under Dusty Fog in Quiet Town.

He gave little thought to the big game at the Bull's Head. The meeting had so far come off much more peaceably than he expected. It also had not gone the way he would have bet on it going, for so far Calamity had been licked at cussing and it looked like Madam could lick her at poker, for Mark admitted the saloonkeeper had been the better player of the two, with the wisdom of extra years to back her. That there would be a head-on physical clash Mark did not doubt, but he also doubted if it would come until Calamity lost out at drinking and cards. It might even not come off until after the Cousins bunch arrived, depending on how Calamity felt at losing.

Mark did not hurry his rounds, nor did he waste time in worrying about possible dangers. He called into the jail house, lit the lamp, checked the place, filled the desk log and left. Doc Connel's house lay in darkness and Mark doubted if the good doctor would take kindly to being wakened at this hour to answer pointless questions about Tune Counter's health.

So after almost an hour Mark returned to the Bull's Head. Passing the hotel he came on Viola carrying something he recognized as Calamity's war bag and bedroll. From the look of this, and the fact that customers streamed out of the bat-wing doors, Mark judged the game to be over and that Calamity had come off second best.

In the saloon the waiters harried the last of the customers through the door, driving out the indomitable few who stayed to the bitter end of the game. Madam Bulldog always insisted that the workers cleared everything up before they left at night, that all bottles and glasses be removed from the tables and all be left ready for the swampers to do their cleaning in the morning. Behind the bar Sam had the cash drawer open and counted the night's take. It was heavier than usual for the spectators of the clash spent well as they watched.

'Hi Mark!' called Calamity, taking the bedroll and war bag from Viola and looking to where the big Texan stood at the door of the saloon. 'You need a deputy?'

'I thought you didn't need work, Calam gal,' Mark replied.

'I do now,' she answered with a grin, then turned to Madam Bulldog. 'I'll change into my old gear and leave the rest in there.'

After Calamity left the room Madam Bulldog sighed. 'That girl's good. I would hate to play her in another ten years' time.'

'She lost heavy?'

'Heavy enough. Have a beer, unless you fancy something a mite stronger.'

'Beer'll do.'

When Calamity stepped from the saloonkeeper's office she wore a battered cavalry kepi, an old shirt, patched old pants and worn boots. Her old walnut gripped Navy Colt stuck in her waistband and she carried all her belongings, including the new gunbelt and holster with her. However, for all of losing her fancy duds, the new gunbelt and ivory butted Colt and her buckskin horse, Calamity had not offered to wager the most important of all her belongings, her saddle, carbine, whip and hand-gun. The rest she had lost meant nothing to her. She could always work and earn money to buy new clothes and a new horse. But without a saddle she could not work and without her firearms she could not protect herself while working. The whip too was a part of her stock-in-trade and she clung to it.

'Have a drink, Calamity,' Madam said as the girl handed over her belongings. 'If you want broke money it's yours.'

'Thanks,' grinned Calamity, holding out a hand. 'You play a

mean hand at poker and you licked me fair and square. I'll take that drink though.'

'What'll it be, Calam?' asked Sam from behind the bar.

'Whisky. You drinking with me, Madam?'

Once more Madam Bulldog read the open challenge and did not try to avoid it. She hated drinking in public and would never have a better chance than right now, to show Calamity how well she could handle a bottle.

Sam read the answer to his unasked question and poured four fingers of the house's best whisky into each woman's glass. Calamity took her's up, turned it between her fingers and looked at it.

'This is ten year old stock,' Madam remarked calmly.

'It's not very big for its age, is it?' Calamity countered.

There was a raw challenge in the words which Madam met head on and without a thought of avoiding it. She waved a hand towards the two pint glasses mostly used for beer.

'Fill them up, Sam,' she said.

Sam threw a startled look at his boss, but knew better than raise any objections. So he poured out the whisky, emptying one bottle and starting another to fill the glasses. He threw a look at Mark, hoping for guidance, but Mark stood back and let things go.

'You're not drinking Mark,' said Madam Bulldog.

'I've had all I want for one night,' he replied.

'So be it. Don't let moss grow in the glass, girlie.'

Saying that, Madam Bulldog raised her glass in a cheery salute to Calamity and started to drink. Not to be outdone, Calamity also raised her glass and began to let the whisky flow down her throat. She bit down a gagging cough as the liquor hit her, for Madam calmly held her own glass and drank at it without showing a sign.

Not untill the glasses were both empty did Calamity and Madam Bulldog set them down. Then they looked at each other quizzically. The whisky had not taken its effect yet and they stood erect, watching the other for any sign of weakening. On seeing none Madam nodded to Sam and ordered him to refill the glasses.

'Here's to you,' said Calamity, gripping her glass by the handle and lifting it from the bar-top.

Then the whisky hit her, landing with the kick of a

Missouri mule. Calamity gave a gasp, her eyes glazed over, the glass fell from her hand, her knees buckled and she went to the floor in a heap.

For a moment Madam stood swaying over the girl, then raised her own glass and took a long swallow. She set the glass on the bar, turned to Mark and said in a cold sober tone:

'Don't reckon she could take her likker after all.'

And then Madam Bulldog's legs folded under her and she piled in a limp heap on to Calamity Jane.

Dawn's cold grey light crept through the window of Calamity Jane's room at the hotel. The girl lay where Mark Counter left her, for he carried her home the previous night. Apart from removing her kepi and boots Mark had not troubled to undress her, but rolled her under the blankets of the bed while she still wore her shirt and pants.

Calamity stirred, groaned, opened her eyes, clutched at her forehead and hurriedly closed her eyes again. She gave a moan, her mouth felt like she had been licking up skunk droppings and her head throbbed fit to burst. For a moment she lay on the bed, then her stomach started to turn somersaults, or so it seemed to her.

With a low moan, Calamity rolled from her bed and staggered to the door of the room, opened it and made a hurried dash down the back stairs, out into the cold chill air of the morning, racing for the backhouse and hoping she would make it in time to prevent disgracing herself.

A very sick and angry Calamity came from the backhouse. She felt mean, ornery on top of the sickness, the sort of condition when she had to have a drink, or go and bust something. So it was unfortunate that at that moment she saw the old swamper open the Bull's Head Saloon's side door ready to start his morning's cleaning.

Calamity, who had been in her present condition on several previous occasions, decided that the only sure cure would be a hair of the dog which bit her. Also she decided that her condition stemmed from the liquor at Madam Bulldog's place and it must be Madam Bulldog who served the hair. So, with that thought in her mind, she headed for the saloon.

On reaching the building she shoved open the side door

and walked into the empty, almost deserted barroom. Calamity groaned a little as she looked at the bar and remembered the previous evening. She saw the glass of whisky left by Madame Bulldog, at least, it was a glass half full with whisky and would be just what she needed to satisfy her restless stomach.

The old swamper turned. He also had an eye on the whisky, for only on very rare occasions did he see such a windfall left behind. Sam would have removed the glass the previous night, but had been more than occupied in getting Madam Bulldog to bed, so it lay where she set it down on the bar top.

'Wha' you wan', gal?' asked the swamper, casting avaricious glances at the inviting glass of whisky and licking his lips. 'Ain't open yet.'

'You soon will be,' Calamity replied and stepped forward.

'Cain't come in here!' wailed the man, stepping before her.

'Don't rile me pappy!' growled Calamity.'Or I'll ram you feet first and head deep into the wall so we can use your ears for a hatrack.'

With that she pushed by him and headed for the bar. He stood staring at her, then let out a moan of annoyance as he saw the girl take up the glass and raise it to her lips. The threat did not worry him, but this drinking of what he regarded as his private property hurt his tenderest feelings. His sense of duty was outraged and his stumpy, bowed old legs headed him across the room, then upstairs where he would find people to help him attend to the matter.

Calamity held the glass in a shaking hand. The raw smell of the whisky came up to hit her, causing her to gag and her stomach to make a violent heave. She fought down the nausea with an effort, knowing that the whisky would still her troubled insides. She drank and felt a shudder run through her, then set the glass down on the bar top again. After standing for a few hours the whisky had a bitter bite to it and she felt she could use a cold beer to balance its effects.

Raising her hand Calamity banged it down hard on the bar top. The sudden noise jarred her head and she let out a moan. The whisky might have settled her stomach but it did nothing to improve her temper. The pain in her head caused her to bang again and lift her voice in a yell.

'Hey! About getting this lousy joint open?'

'We're closed!' answered a sleepy but annoyed female voice from upstairs.

That did not make Calamity feel any better. She pounded on the bar top once more and repeated her yelled demand for service. A sound from the head of the stairs brought her attention to where Viola and two more girls, tousle-haired, sleep eyed, with housecoats dragged over their night wear, stood glaring down at her with hostile gaze.

'Why don't you go where you came from?' asked Viola, never at her best or most friendly when wakened from her sleep in the small hours of the morning.

'Why don't you come down and try to make me?' Calamity answered truculently.

An angry curse came from Viola's lips. She studied Calamity and weighed up her chances of a single-handed tangle with the girl, then discarded the idea as being out of the question. However, her two friends also felt riled at having their beauty sleep despoiled and ruined. Between the three of them they ought to be able to hand even Calamity Jane her needings.

'Let's go down and toss her out, Viola,' suggested the chubby brunette at her right.

'Yeah,' agreed the slim blonde at her left. 'Hell, it's only after seven and we were late getting to bed.'

The three girls started down the stairs and Calamity saw that she would have to defend herself. She put down the glass which she had taken to sip at, clenched her fists and moved to face the stair head. Taking on these three girls would whet her appetite and prepare her for dealing with Madam Bulldog when the time came.

'Hold it, Viola!'

Madam Bulldog's voice cracked out from the top of the stairs, just as her boss girl tensed ready to throw herself bodily at Calamity. The voice held the torment of the damned in it and told that, like Calamity, its owner suffered from the effects of a previous night's drinking.

Looking up the stairs Calamity focused her eyes on the owner of the Bull's Head saloon. Madam Bulldog did not look her usual cool, friendly and immaculate self on this early morning. Like Calamity, she had gone to bed fully dressed except for her head-dress and shoes; Sam, being a man of moral standing, had done no more than get his boss to her room and left her on the bed. Now she stood at the head of the stairs, bleary eyed, make-up smeared, hair hanging straggly and uncombed, not looking at all her usual self. Nor did she feel her usual self and one thing she did not want was to have her sleep shattered at this hour. The swamper had woke her by pounding on her door, he delivered an incoherent burble about some tough dame breaking into the saloon and drinking all the stock, so Madam came to investigate and found her girls already on the way down to deal with the invader.

'Come on down here, you fat old cow!' Calamity bellowed. 'Can't a gal get a drink of your rotgut whisky without having to knock herself out trying to get some service?'

'You get out of here,' replied Madam Bulldog, no less heatedly. 'And when we open, come with a civil tongue in your head, or don't come at all.'

Up until that moment Calamity had been firmly determined to leave her fight with Madam Bulldog until after she helped side Mark Counter against the Cousin's bunch. Only having a hangover always tended to make her temper as touchy as a teased rattlesnake, or even touchier.

Which was unfortunate, for having a hangover had roughly the same effect on Madam Bulldog and at the moment she, too, suffered from a hangover.

Any way one looked at it things were rapidly building up to a brawl.

'Keep out of it, you three!' growled Madam Bulldog as she started down the stairs and passed her girls. 'I've got my guts full of her and her yapping. It's time we found out who's the better woman.'

Silence fell on the room as Madam Bulldog carried on down the stairs to where Calamity waited with clenched fists and a mocking grin. Calamity stood ready, her eyes on the other woman's face and a feeling of eager anticipation in her heart, for this was the thing she came to Tennyson to do.

Suddenly, as Madam Bulldog came towards her, without giving any hint of what she meant to do, Calamity lashed her right fist around. The knuckles cracked against Madam Bulldog's cheek, snapping her head around and sending her staggering back into the banister at the bottom of the stair. Calamity let her breath out in a hiss, for that had been a beautiful blow.

Eagerly Calamity moved forward, ready and willing to finish off the other woman as quickly as possible. Too late she saw Madam push her plump frame from the support of the banister and shoot out a punch. Calamity walked full into it, catching the hard fist full in the face and the next instant she went reeling back, feeling and tasting the hot salty touch of blood from her lips even as she went down between two tables. She shook her head and gasped a little, for she had never before run across a woman with such a powerful punch. It looked like once more Madam Bulldog would prove to be a tougher nut to crack than she airily imagined as she rode south to try conclusions with the other woman.

Calamity came up with a bound and rushed in, fists flying. It was a tactic which carried her victorious through more than one rough-and-tumble brawl with a tough dancehall girl or cavalry camp-follower. Only this time she was up against a woman who knew more than a little about the fighting game herself. At the last moment Madam Bulldog side-stepped, rammed her left fist into Calamity's middle, then clipped her across the ear with the right as she doubled over. Calamity went down again, landing at the foot of the stairs.

'Stomp her, Madam!' howled Viola. 'Hand her her needings.'

Rubbing the blood which trickled from the side of her mouth, Calamity forced herself up, shaking her head. Madam was at her, one hand shooting out to dig into the girl's short hair and hold it, the other lashing in back and open palm slaps at her face. Calamity's head rocked from side to side and her own hands drove out to tangle into Madam's longer hair. The pain must have been intense if the howl Madam let out could be anything to go by. They staggered backwards across the room, both alternating between tearing at hair, swinging punches and slaps and kicking out, although as neither wore shoes this did not prove to be very effective.

It took Calamity just ten seconds to know she had tangled with a woman as strong as, and with as much fight-savvy as herself. Calamity had learned her fighting from soldiers, bull-whackers and mule-skinners and they had taught her to use her fists like a man. Wherever Madam Bulldog learned to fight, she also learned that a clenched fist proved more effective in a brawl than any amount of hair-yanking.

On the stairs the three excited saloon girls watched, gave their vocal and moral support to their boss, for Madam Bulldog had endeared herself to them all and they held her in the greatest respect. Besides Calamity Jane was not one of them, she belonged to the world outside, the world of 'good women' who looked down on and sneered at the painted workers of the saloons, or caused them much trouble and inconvenience. So they wanted to see their boss hand Calamity a whipping, to uphold the high traditions of their place.

The noise brought the other girls out, sleepy-eyed and complaining until they saw what caused the fuss. Then they also settled down to enjoy the brawl. None of the male saloon workers lived on the premises, an innovation since Madam Bulldog took over, and the old swamper was hustled indignantly into a room and locked in by one of the girls. So no man saw the great battle between Calamity Jane and Madam Bulldog.

Despite the lack of witnesses, which did not bother either fighter in the least, the two women put on a brawl which neither would ever forget, nor would the few girls who saw it.

At first they fought with their fists, like two men, then closed and started hair yanking, tearing and kicking at each other, crashing to the floor and rolling over and over, still tearing at each other. They rolled apart and came up again with Calamity attacking even before Madam made her feet. She came into a punch which knocked her backwards, on to a table top. Madam rose, caught up a chair and swung it over her head, charging forward to bring it down at Calamity who rolled from the table and dropped to the floor just as the chair splintered above her and where her body had been an instant before.

With a spluttering curse Calamity dived under the table, locking her arms around Madam's legs and bringing her crashing down. Calamity clung to the legs as she fought her way to her feet, then leaned forward to grab at Madam. Too late Calamity realized she had made an error in tactics for Madam managed to get her feet under Calamity's body. She started to thrust and Calamity, clawing desperately for a hold, caught the top of the green satin dress. With a powerful heave of her legs Madam threw Calamity backwards and from her. There sounded a harsh ripping noise as Madam's dress, tight on her figure and not meant for such strenuous activities, parted at the seams. Calamity lost her hold and shot backwards, on to a chair which broke under her and deposited her on the floor.

When Madam rose she found her torn frock impeded her free movements. She tore it from her and charged at the girl clad only in her underwear and stockings.

While still on her hands and knees, Calamity saw Madam coming into the attack. Calamity threw herself forward, her head ramming into Madam's middle and bringing a croaking gasp. Calamity locked her arms around the plump waist and bore Madam backwards. Then a hand dug into Calamity's hair, bringing forth a howl of pain. Madam's other hand caught at the back of Calamity's shirt, tearing at it, dragging it from under the waistband of her old pants and ripping it. At that moment Madam realized such methods would do her no good and drove two hard blows into Calamity's back. The girl lost her hold and caught Madam's knee as it drove up to stagger her away. Now it was Calamity's turn to get rid of a torn garment, for the shirt got in her way. She wriggled and tore out of it without a thought for not having a stitch of clothing under the shirt. When Calamity attacked she was naked to the waist.

For a full fifteen minutes they fought like enraged wildcats and without a pause. Their clothes had suffered still more. Madam also fought bare to the waist now. In a wild thrashing attempt to grab Calamity, Madam had caught the patch on the seat of her pants, torn it away and got a hand into the exposed hole, then tore from the seat to the bottom of the right leg. Nor were clothes the only things to suffer. Neither woman had long nails, but their hard fists left bruises or drew blood, while their teeth had found flesh and both bore marks to show how effective the teeth had been. Yet, bloody, bruised, half naked and battered though both were, neither would give way or call the fight off.

Once they went down, laying gasping for breath, then slowly rose, but when they made their feet they fought on with the same ferocity which marked the fight from start to finish. They used fists, back-hand and open hand slaps rained on faces and bodies, their elbows thudded into ribs, they kicked, using the sole of the foot, they drove knees into each other, tore hair, butted like a pair of Rocky Mountain rams, threw or swung chairs at each other. Blood ran from their noses and lips, sweat soaked them, but neither gave a sign of finishing.

'Reckon we ought to stop them before they kill each other?' asked one of the watching girls as Madam and Calamity rolled off the faro lay-out on which they had landed and thrashed over and over in their fight.

'You can try if you like,' answered Viola, watching the two women, clinging to each other still, crawl to their feet and fight on. 'I sure don't aim to.'

'They'll stop themselves soon,' another girl, face flushed with excitement, answered. Then she shuddered as Calamity swung a roundhouse punch at her boss. 'Ouch! I felt that one.'

Viola also winced in sympathy as Madam took the punch. It sent the plump woman stumbling back. She hit the side of the vingt-un table and clung to it for a moment, then slid down. A moan of disappointment rose from the girls as Calamity, tottering but still on her feet, started towards their boss.

'H – had – enough?' Calamity croaked, hoping the other woman would say she had.

Weakly Madam put her hand on the seat of a chair and used it to lever herself up. Her other hand gripped the edge of the table and with this to help she made her feet. She had to cling to the table, but she stood there and gasped in breath as she watched Calamity come closer.

Madam released the table and brought around her fist. The blow caught Calamity and stopped her in her tracks, for she had never thought the other woman capable of such a blow. She stood there, dazed and unable to stop the next swinging blow Madam launched against her. For a moment Madam stood staring, then swung again, this time with all her strength Calamity's head snapped back, she reeled away, hit a table and fell over on to it, laying there.

Still Calamity was not beaten. She saw Madam coming at her and lashed out with her foot. With a flat 'splat!' the foot caught Madam in the face and stopped her advance. She shook her head, another kick caught her and she stumbled forward, gripped the edge of the table and heaved it upwards. Calamity yelled as she felt herself slipping. She twisted and rolled sideways from the table as it turned over, landing on the floor and rolling over on to her back, laying there with arms thrown wide and one knee raised, her eyes glassy, her breasts heaving. On the other side of the overturned table Madam Bulldog sank to her knees, rested a hand on the floor and then flopped on to her side.

'Wowee!' gasped a girl. 'They're both done for.'

It certainly looked that way, for neither woman offered to try and get up for almost a minute and Viola opened her mouth to tell the others to get their boss up to her room. Before she could they all saw a movement. Only it came from the far side of the overturned table. Calamity had rolled over and braced her hands on the floor as she tried to force herself up.

'It's Calamity!' groaned one of the watching girls.

'Looks that way,' agreed Viola, bitterly disappointed, for she knew that if Calamity rose she would be the winner.

Now Calamity knelt on the floor, gasping and sobbing for breath as she weakly reached her hands upwards towards the edge of the overturned table. On the other side of the table, weakly but definitely, Madam forced herself up on to her hands and knees. She could hardly think straight and wondered why Calamity had not ended the fight. She could see no sign of the girl, only the legs and bottom of the table she tipped over. The warning yells of her girls seemed to be far off and she could not make out their meaning, something about somebody getting up, pulling herself up on the table. Madam shook her head to try and clear it, then she saw a hand grip the edge of the table and another hand. Something clicked, the meaning of the yells she had heard. Although she felt like collapsing, ached in every muscle, bone and inch of flesh, although the top of her head seemed to be on fire where hands had torn at her hair, Madam Bulldog braced herself on her knees and one hand, watching the top of the table. Calamity Jane was getting up that she knew.

Calamity gripped the edge of the overturned table and used it to help drag herself to her feet. It proved to be a mistake. The moment Calamity's head came into view over the edge of the table Madam Bulldog shot out a bunched fist which crashed into the girl's jaw and sprawled her once more to the floor. Calamity rolled over and slowly tried to force herself on to her hands and knees. Just as slowly Madam rose to her feet and, staggering in exhaustion, she moved in. Bending down she took a handful of Calamity's tangled red hair and hauled her to her feet. On being released. Calamity tottered dazedly and almost fell. Before the girl's legs could collapse under her, Madam brought around a right fist with a full swing of her body, smashing it into the side of Calamity's jaw. Calamity spun around like a child's top, then crashed down. From the rag doll limp way she fell one thing was for sure – this time Calamity would not be getting up.

Stepping forward Madam sank to her knees, straddling Calamity's body, then she gripped the girl's hair in both hands, lifting the head ready to bang it against the floor. Seeing how limp Calamity's head hung in her hands, Madam released it and it flopped to the floor. Madam rested her hands on the floor by the side of Calamity's head and stayed where she was. She heard the excited chatter of the girls as they crowded down stairs and came towards her. Hands gripped her arms and helped her to her feet, for she had not the strength to rise under her own power.

'You licked her, Madam!' Viola whooped eagerly. 'Come on, gals, get the boss up to her room.'

Though whirling mists of pain filled her and the room seemed to be flying in a circle around her, Madam clung to consciousness. She gasped in breath to her aching, tortured lungs as her girls held her on her feet. Weakly she managed to point down to Calamity's still form as the girl lay with breasts heaving and mouth hanging open.

'G—get—her—to—her room at—h—hotel!' Madam gasped and went limp in their hands.

Mark Counter sat in the room at Doc Connel's, eating breakfast and talking over the events of the previous evening with the doctor and his uncle. Mrs. Connel, a small, pleasant woman who had many of her husband's good points, such as an ability to get things done, entered, bringing Viola with her.

'Doc,' the girl gasped, she wore her street clothes and

showed signs of having dressed hurriedly. 'It's the boss.'

'What happened?' Connel replied, thrusting back his chair and rising from the small table where he and Mark sat.

'She tangled with Calamity Jane. They fought for nearly an hour and Madam licked her in the end.'

Which showed how legends could grow. The fight lasted just over thirty minutes and had already been almost doubled in duration.

'Where's Calam now?' Mark asked, also rising, for he knew something of the ways of dancehall girls with their enemies.

'We took her back to the hotel,' Viola replied. 'The boss told us to.'

Mrs. Connel glanced at her husband. She knew and liked the boss of the Bull's Head but did not have any illusions about her toughness. If she and Calamity Jane had fought both would likely be needing medical aid. She looked at her husband and gave her orders.

'You go to the saloon and do what you can for Madam Bulldog, George. I'll take the hotel and do what I can for that Calamity Jane woman.'

'I'll come along with you, ma'am,' Mark offered. 'Like to see how bad ole Calam's hurt, then I'll make my rounds of the town.'

'You start thinking about Cousins and his bunch arriving, Mark,' warned Tune grimly. 'They might be here today, or they might not. But it won't hurt none to be ready for them.'

'You lie easy and I'll tend to it,' Mark replied. 'Say, you'll be alone for a spell. I'll put your gun under the pillow where it'll be handy.'

At the hotel Mark started to follow Mrs. Connel into Calamity's room, but was ordered out before he got beyond the door.

'Tell the manager to send up some hot water,' she said. 'And stay out. This gal's in no state yet to have male visitors.'

Mark guessed as much from the brief glimpse he'd got of Calamity before being chased out. He knew she had been wearing her sole remaining items of clothing the previous night. Which meant she would hardly be in any shape to appear in public until she obtained some more clothes.

'You'd best give me an idea of what size clothes she'd want, Mrs. Connel,' he said. 'Shirt and jeans.'

'She a friend of yours?'

'You might say that.'

'Huh!' sniffed Mrs. Connel. 'There's no accounting for taste.'

Mark grinned. 'You're not seeing Calam at her best right now. And she's a damned good friend to have in a tight corner.'

The rebuke was plain in Mark's voice and Mrs. Connel smiled. 'You're right. I'm not seeing her at her best. Go tell the manager and when you get back I'll tell you the size of clothes to buy.'

After delivering Mrs. Connel's message and collecting the sizes from the woman, Mark headed for the general store where the owner studied the list Mark gave him. The items attracted some excited comment from the storekeeper who could tell at a glance the shirt and levis would never fit Mark, nor would the big Texan be likely to wear the other items of clothing on the list.

'You mean Madam 'n' Calamity Jane tangled this morning?' asked the storekeeper, sounding disappointed at missing the fight.

'That's just what I mean.'

'Hell, and we never got to see it. Who won?'

'Madam, way I heard it,' drawled Mark.

'Yeah, that figures,' said the storekeeper, then remembered the other item of interest and speculation in Tennyson. 'Say, Mark, do you reckon Cousins'll come today?'

'Today, tomorrow, the next day. He'll be here. I'll see you, Herbie.'

Leaving the storekeeper loading his old ten gauge scatter gun with a dose of nine buckshot, Mark headed back to the hotel with his purchases. He went up to the first floor and tapped on the door to Calamity's room.

'How's Calam?' he asked Mrs. Connel.

'Well, one eye's closed, the other looks a mite black. Reckon she won't feel like eating anything solid for a spell way her jaw's swollen. She's got a few bites, a few lumps raised and it's easier to see bruises than skin on her body, but she'll live. That gal's sure tough as leather. She's conscious, but I've given her a dose of laudanum to ease the aches. Go in and look her over.'

Mark entered the room and found a battered but clean

73

Calamity lying on her back in the bed. By now the laudanum was taking its effect, but the girl managed a very faint attempt at her usual grin and even tried to wink through her good eye.

'You look like you tangled with a bobcat, Calam gal,' drawled Mark, laying the new clothes on the chair by her bed. 'And a mule or two.'

For all her aching body, dulled by the laudanum's action, Calamity still tried to tell Mark what she thought of him. However the effort was too much and after an incoherent mumble she lay back and glared at him as best she could.

'Leave her be, Mark,' said Mrs. Connel. 'She needs rest.'

'Why sure,' agreed Mark and looked down at the girl. 'Don't go away, Calam.'

With that he left the room and found Doc Connel in the hall, having come from attending to Madam Bulldog's injuries. Mark stopped to learn how the saloonkeeper had faired in the fight.

'That must have been a hell of a brawl,' Doc said. 'Madam sure looks a mite peaked. I hope Cousins holds off until she gets on her feet.'

'When'll that be?' asked Mark.

'I gave her laudanum to ease her aches, enough to make her sleep until noon, but she'll be stiff as a dead polecat when she recovers and in no shape for fast moving.'

'Damn that fool Calam!' Mark snapped. 'Why in hell couldn't she have waited a day or so. I'll take a switch to her hide, see if I don't.'

After delivering the threat Mark turned and left the hotel. He walked along the sidewalk, making for the marshal's office, nodding in answer to the greetings called by passers-by and owners of business premises as they opened for the day's trade. From the look of things none of them seemed unduly bothered by the threat of Cousins' arrival. Just as he was about to enter the office he happened to look towards the Wells Fargo office. He saw Viola, Madam Bulldog's boss girl, enter the building and wondered if the girl might be booking a seat, or seats, on the stage which passed through that evening headed for the west, from Sand City. He doubted if it would be Madam Bulldog running, although the injured woman might be trying to escape before Cousins arrived. Mark decided to go and see her, warn her that she could be running into more danger by leaving, for Cousins possibly would have men watching the stage coaches out of town.

Deciding he would go along to the saloon as soon as he had checked at the jail, Mark turned into the marshal's office of the jail building. His eyes went to the rack of weapons, three Winchester rifles and three double barrelled, ten gauge shotguns supplied by the town for use of the marshal and his deputies, if he ever found call to need deputies. Mark crossed to the rack and took the rifles out one after another. Much to his surprise he found they were clean and only needed loading to be ready for use. He realized that he knew little about the running of his office and would need to find out.

A check of the desk log showed his uncle had a temporary deputy, the old retired marshal, who acted as a jailer and up until the day of Mark's arrival had kept the jail and its weapons cleaned. Mark decided to pay the man a visit as he had not met him yet.

Before Mark could do this he received a visitor. The agent for the Well's Fargo office entered carrying two telegraph message forms and looking worried.

'This here's from Cousins!' he said, slapping one down before Mark. 'It just now come in.'

Mark took the form and read, 'To the people of Tennyson. I will be coming soon. I want only Tune Counter and Madam Bulldog. Let me have them. Keep clear of me and you won't get hurt, Hank Cousins.'

'Where'd it come from?' asked Mark, putting it on the desk.

'Gopher Hole way station.'

'Where's that?'

'About half way between here and the place he sent the last from,' replied the agent worriedly. 'And that means—'

'That he could be here by noon if he pushed his horse,' Mark interrupted.

'What do you want me to do with this?'

'Take it and show Mr. Hoscroft, ask him to bring the Town Council to see me.'

All the time they spoke Mark watched the man's face. Something warned the big Texan that his visitor was hiding something from him. The agent turned, walked slowly towards the door, halted and came back again. His face worked with a variety of emotions as he looked at Mark. Then, as if making a difficult decision, he laid the second form on the table.

'Viola, that's Madam Bulldog's boss girl, sent this off, just afore Cousins' message came in.'

'Kusin, Sand City,' Mark read. 'Come as soon as possible. Madam Bulldog.'

He put the form down on the desk top and looked at the man. 'So she's sending a message to somebody to come. What makes it so important?'

'I was on a way station with a feller called Svenson for a year,' replied the agent. 'We were miles from anyplace and he taught me Swedish to pass the time. I never forgot it, a man working for Wells Fargo needs to know a little of language with all the folks coming west.'

'Well?'

'It never struck me, not until I got the message from Gopher Hole.'

'What never struck you?' growled Mark.

'*Kusin* is Swedish for cousin.'

The man looked almost sick with worry as he said this. Mark did not speak for a long moment as he thought over the import of the words. He looked down at the message form and frowned.

'Has Madam Bulldog or Viola ever sent a message to this Kusin before?' he asked.

'Nope. Only messages Madam ever sends is to likker salesmen and gals like Viola don't send telegraph messages all that often,' answered the man. 'What do you reckon it means?'

'I don't know.'

'Why would she be sending word to Hank Cousins?' asked the man.

Mark thrust back his chair and came to his feet. The cold expression on his face caused the man to take a rapid step backwards.

'We don't know this is to Hank Cousins,' Mark warned grimly. 'So don't go talking about it around town.'

'I didn't even aim to tell you,' replied the agent indignantly.

Not for the first time since his arrival in Tennyson did Mark marvel at the devotion, friendship and respect with

76

which many of the citizens regarded Madam Bulldog. The agent did not believe that Madam would be sending for Cousins and had clearly been undecided what he should do for the best. He had told Mark about the mysterious message as a last resort and wanted reassuring that the owner of the Bull's Head Saloon was not betraying her friends. Only Mark could not give that reassurance. From the little he had seen of Madam Bulldog he doubted if she would do such a thing as send for Cousins.

'Why would she send word to Cousins?' groaned the agent when Mark did not reply. 'If it was anybody else I'd say they wanted to do a deal to save their own hide. But not Madam Bulldog.'

'That's the way I see it,' Mark answered. 'There's nothing about the Cousins bunch to make Madam reckon they'd do a deal with her, or that they'd stick to their side of it if she made one with them.'

He could see the look of relief which came to the man's face. The agent did not waste any more time, but, after stuffing away the telegraph form concerning Madam's mysterious friend in Sand City, headed out into the street to collect the town council for a meeting with Mark.

The town council came quickly. Hoscroft as mayor, the old storekeeper Mark bought Calamity's clothes from earlier, the town preacher, two more men who ran businesses in town and, although not a member of the council, the old-timer who acted as jailer.

Quickly Hoscroft introduced the council to Mark, for he had met none of them the previous day. The jailer went under the name of Corky and was a leathery old hard-case with a pair of twinkling and surprisingly young looking eyes. He hitched up the worn old Dragoon Colt slung at his side and stoutly affirmed that he stood by Mark no matter what the rest decided on doing.

'How about this message, Mark?' Hoscroft asked.

'It tells us only what we know already,' Mark answered. 'All it gives us more is that Cousins is nearer than he was yesterday.'

'And the message itself?' put in the storekeeper. 'There's some might say we ought to do what Cousins wants, stand pat and let him make the play his way.'

'Which's just what he wants,' drawled Mark. 'You give

in to him this time and he'll walk over you, or the next bunch who wants an easy town to ride will.'

'Cousins has played this hand before when he's been after somebody,' Hoscroft interrupted. 'Sent word ahead that he was coming and I know of one case where the town turned a man out to Cousins. This time let's show him he's bucking a town that's got guts enough to face him down.'

'That's the way I likes to hear you talk, Ted,' Corky growled.

'I say barricade the streets and keep men on watch ready for him!' stated the storekeeper.

'And how long could we keep them out there watching?' asked Mark. 'Cousins won't be here today most likely. He wants to get folks spooked, give them time to think. Nope, we can't barricade the streets or have men on guard. There's a hundred ways Cousins and his bunch could get in here after dark and we can't cover them all so as to stop them, that'd take near on a regiment of sentries and look-outs.'

'What do you suggest, Ted?' the preacher asked.

Although it had become the usual thing for the town council to look to Hoscroft for suggestions, this time he did not have an answer available. He frowned and paced the room for a long minute. Mark watched, waiting to hear what the other men wished to do before he put his plans into words.

At last Hoscroft came to a halt and faced the big young Texan across the desk. Drawing in a deep breath Hoscroft put forth his thoughts and his ideas came very close to what Mark intended to ask them to do.

'What I suggest is that we appoint four special deputies to be on watch at all times in the jail under Mark and ready to go should Cousins arrive. That will give Mark a well armed fighting force at his disposal ready to stand off an attack until the rest of the town can organize.'

The other members of the town council exchanged glances then looked at Mark for his views.

'That's about what I was going to ask for,' Mark drawled.

'I don't have no work on,' Corky grunted. 'You can take me on full time if you like, Mark.'

'You can be first deputy then, Corky,' Mark answered. 'I'll see Doc Connel and Madam Bulldog, find out if they want guards at their place.'

'If I know Madam I can tell you the answer,' chuckled Hoscroft. 'And you'll get the same from Doc. They'll not want to take your men.'

'Don't reckon we could keep it up indefinitely either,' Mark said quietly. 'We'll just have the four men here all the time and on the first sight of the Cousins bunch we'll get two men to the Bull's Head and two more to the doctor's. The rest of the town had best to keep off the streets, we don't want the deputies to have to wait to find out if it's a friend or not coming towards or behind him.'

'I'll see to that for you,' promised the gaunt owner of the Tennyson newspaper. 'For the first time since I started I'll run an extra edition.'

No more time was wasted in talk. The council headed out of the office to carry out their part of the business of organizing Tennyson's defence. They agreed to get volunteers to take four hour tours of duty as deputies and that, with the exception of the preacher, they should take their turn.

For the first time Mark gave his office building a thorough examination to see how it would stand as a defensive point. After the big establishment at Quiet Town with its line of cells, large front office and a room which quartered the six man police force, Tennyson's jail looked small and puny. It had been built of stone and amounted to no more than one large room partitioned by a wooden wall. At the front side of the wall, with two windows and the double doors facing the street, lay the marshal's office. Mark passed through the partition door and found himself in a narrow passage, facing the steel barred doors of the two small cells, separated by a stout wooden wall, each with two double bunks which had been secured to the floor and each of which had a small window with two stout iron bars instead of glass.

The jail had been built for a town which could not keep a large police force and so the only door giving access to the building lay on the front street, facing the marshal's desk. Mark noted this with approval, it would save the need to have a man fully occupied with watching a rear entrance.

'It'll do,' he said as he came from the cell section and found Corky seated at the desk loading the shotgun with powder and buckshot. 'Seeing's how I can't get a seat at my own office I'll make the rounds. Don't you go shooting yourself in the leg.'

Corky's reply, which followed him to the door, came hot, pungent and blistering and covered the entire Counter family in its spread. Mark turned and grinned at the old-timer.

'You've been listening to Madam Bulldog,' he said and left before Corky could think of an adequate reply.

Mark first went to the livery barn. He attended to his own and Calamity's horse, forgetting the girl no longer owned the big buckskin. After taking them out to the two empty corrals behind the barn and telling the owner of the establishment he would be back at nightfall and stable them, Mark went on to Doc Connel's house to see his uncle. Tune knew the town much better than did Mark and agreed with the arrangements made for its defence. Doc Connel bristlingly asserted that he did not want his office cluttered with men and that he and Tune ought to be able to take care of themselves.

'I've got a shotgun here,' Doc stated grimly. 'And to hell with the Hippocratic oath in Cousins' case. I didn't waste time patching this worthless cuss here up to have some murdering skunk shoot him and give me more work.'

'All right, Doc,' Mark grinned, seeing his uncle to be in good hands and knowing that Tune could handle his Colt if need be. 'But if you hear any shooting get the house door locked. I'll be along as fast as I can.'

'Sure, I'll do that,' promised the doctor grimly. 'I tried to get Milly to go and stay with the Hoscrofts but she won't. Danged woman, gets more ornery 'n' balky every day.'

'They reckon a woman starts to take after her man,' drawled Mark and left the room.

He had reached the door of the consulting room when he heard Doc's enraged yell and knew the meaning of his words had sunk in. In the sickroom Doc looked at Tune with a wry grin.

'There ain't one of you Counters to improve on the others.'

'Sure ain't,' answered Tune cheerfully. 'That Mark's growed into a real smart man.'

From the doctor's home Mark went along to the Bull's Head. He found the place open and a few customers already in. Sam left the bar and came to join Mark on catching the big Texan's signal.

'Now there's no need for you to worry, Mark,' he said when Mark told of the idea for defending Madam Bulldog. 'I got a ten gauge under the bar and all the waiters are heeled. The only way Cousins and his lousy bunch can get at the boss lady is through us.'

'All right,' Mark replied. 'As soon as I hear a shot I'll bring the deputies along on the run.' He grinned at Sam's surprise. 'Sure, we've got deputies, a regular city police force.'

'Say, I've just got a meal on order, why not set and join me?' Sam said.

Mark looked at the wall clock and found, to his surprise, the time had reached noon. He accepted Sam's offer and joined such of the saloon workers as were present at a table for a meal brought over from the café along the street. Viola was not on hand and none of the others seemed to know anything about the mysterious telegraph message the blonde sent to Sand City. Mark asked no questions about the message, for he did not want all kinds of rumours to start circulating until he got to the bottom of the matter.

A boy entered the saloon bearing a thick sheaf of newspapers fresh from the *Tennyson Herald*'s press. The arrival of an edition at this unprecedented time of the week attracted much interest and the boy sold all his copies. Mark bought one and found the editor had given the council meeting full treatment and that their advice to the citizens for when Cousins came had been printed. Mark only hoped that when the time came folks would remember and stay off the streets. If he and his deputies could pin the Cousins bunch down someplace, they could use the town's help, but not until such time.

From the talk which welled up around the saloon and the offers of help Mark received, Tennyson's citizens intended to extend a strenuous hospitality to the killer and his family. However, Mark emphasized his desire that only he and the four deputies met the first attack and folks agreed to it.

On his return to the jail Mark found his first group of special deputies gathered and waiting for him. Much to his surprise he found Stern, the blacksmith, one of the party but the burly man appeared to hold no grudge over the incident of the previous day. In fact Stern shook hands and apologized for his actions, then stated his willingness to obey orders. From what Mark saw of the man during the period they spent together the more he decided Doc Connel had been right. Stern was the kind of man who would be easily persuaded that some action be for the best and then would let himself be talked into leading the movement.

Five o'clock came around with no sign of the Cousins bunch and Mark left the jail to walk along to the Wells Fargo office and see the stage arrive. It came in a few minutes late and Mark, leaning on the wall at the end of the building, watched the door open. A big, heavily built woman climbed out. From the look of her she was a townswoman, respectable and not too well-to-do, though not poverty-stricken either. She took the big carpetbag handed to her by one of the passengers who stayed in the coach, nodded to the driver and walked along the street. Mark gave her little more than a glance, being less interested in the big blonde woman than in any other person who might climb from the coach. In this he had no luck for only the woman got down.

Mark strolled along to where the driver and agent stood talking.

'No more getting off here, friend?' he asked.

'Nope.'

'Drop anybody off within a couple of miles from town?' Mark went on.

'Nope, Olaf Cussing's missus was the only one who booked anywhere near here, marshal.'

'That was the blonde woman who got off?'

'Sure, her and her husband run the bath-house in Sand City. You thought I might be bringing in some of the Cousins' bunch?'

'It was a thought,' agreed Mark. 'See any sign on the way to town?'

'Nope, kept looking, so'd the guard,' answered the driver. 'Sheriff at Sand City said for me to tell you he's holding all his deputies ready to come and sit in, but he'd rather you handled it alone if you could. He's got a big gold shipment at the company office and wants to keep all his men on hand if he can.'

'We'll manage then,' Mark promised and was about to

walk away when a thought struck him. 'Say, if any of your passengers want to get off within four miles of town, make damned sure what they're fixing to do and if they can't give a real good reason for getting off hawg-tie them and come back on the run.'

'I'll see to it,' the driver promised.

Feeling puzzled Mark turned and headed back to the jail. It looked like the telegraph Viola sent to Sand City did not have any result. He found a fresh batch of deputies on hand, told them their duties and went to the café and had a meal. After that he headed for the livery barn to stable his and Calamity's horse for the night. With this done he headed towards the hotel to collect his bedroll, for he would be spending the night at the jail and did not see why he should spend it in discomfort.

Mark was opening his door when he heard noises from Calamity's room. He wondered if the girl's pain made her give the squeals and gasps which sounded. Mark walked to the door and listened. Calamity's crackling, profanity, interspersed by slapping sounds, squeals and little yelps of pain came to his ears.

Not knowing what to expect Mark prepared to investigate. He wasted no time in knocking, that could be dangerous both to the girl and himself if something should be wrong beyond the door. His right hand brought out its Colt, then he lowered a shoulder and rammed into the door, bursting it open. Mark flung himself through the door with his revolver held ready for use.

Then Mark stood still, amazed at the scene before him. Viola staggered back a pace or two with a look of horror on her face. The woman at Calamity's bedside straightened up with a gasp of horror, her right hand still holding Calamity's ankle. On the bed, naked as the day she was born, lay Calamity. The big blonde woman who had come in on the stage let the girl's bent leg fall and took a hurried pace backwards. She no longer wore the suit she travelled to town in, now she had on an old blouse and skirt, the blouse's sleeves rolled up to show brawny arms which went well with her rather big, strong looking hands.

'Yumping yiminy!' she gasped. 'What's this?'

'You all right, Calam?' Mark asked, still holding his revolver.

His words seemed to shake them out of their trance. Viola took a step forward and the big woman's face turned slightly red, her hand dropping to the neck of a bottle full of oily looking liquid which stood on the chair by the bed.

'I reckon so, Mark,' Calamity replied to the question, grinning and not showing the slightest embarrassment at her lack of clothing. 'If Madam Bulldog can take it I reckon I can.'

'It's all right, Mark,' Viola went on. 'Let's you and me go out into the passage and I'll explain everything.'

For a moment Mark hesitated and Calamity grinned again.

'Go on, Mark. I'm all right and you'll be making me blush next.'

Holstering his Colt, Mark walked from the room and Viola followed, closing the door. From behind them came the slapping sounds, gasps and squeaks which told that the woman had started to do whatever she had been doing to Calamity all over again.

'What's this all about?' Mark asked.

'It's all right. That's Mrs. Cussing from Sand City. Madam sent for her to come here and rub her down. She's a massager.'

'A what?'

'A massager. You know, one of them Swedish dames who give you a massage.'

Mark grinned. 'It's always been a man when it happened to me.'

'Yeah, well the boss has her around once a month or so, says it keeps her schoolgirl figure. Anyway after the fight Madam decided she needed a rub down and told me to send for Mrs. Cussing. Then after she was done Madam figured that Calam'd like need some help and told me to bring Mrs. Cussing down here and tend to her.'

'How do you spell Mrs. Cussings name?' asked Mark.

'K-u-s-i-n,' she replied. 'Why?'

'Just a thought,' grinned Mark, cocking an ear towards the door through which Calamity's curses and squeals still sounded. 'They always allow you have to be cruel to be kind.'

He left the girl and walked to his own room. For all his grin, Mark felt relieved. Now he saw the reason for Madam Bulldog's message and the mistake in the name. In the friendly, though arbitrary way of the old west Mrs. Kusin's name became Cussing, pronounced that way by the people who saw it. That *kusin* should be Swedish for cousin amounted to nothing more sinister than coincidence, yet Mark knew how suspicion, fear, panic even, might have been spawned from the telegraph message had word of it been spread around the town. He knew his first task after he collected his bedroll must be to see the worried Wells Fargo agent and relieve the man's mind of its troubles over the message.

After satisfying the Wells Fargo agent that his trust and respect of Madam Bulldog remained unsullied, Mark went along to the jail and found his night detail of deputies present. He told them to make themselves comfortable and then made his first rounds of the night, taking Banker Hoscroft with him.

It looked more like a scene from Dodge City at the height of the trail season than the main street of a very small cowtown, to see two shotgun armed lawmen on the prowl. However the town carried on as usual, cowhands from the nearby ranches coming in and the usual assortment of drifters, visiting the Bull's Head Saloon or doing business with such stores as stayed open to catch this transient trade. The night passed without incident and the dawn came without any sign of the Cousins bunch making their arrival.

Time hung heavily on Mark's hands as he made his rounds and waited for the Cousins bunch to arrive. He hated this waiting and watching and wanted action, to get the business settled one way or the other so he could head back to the OD Connected and his friends. He did not let his nerves get on edge and kept a careful watch on the people around town to see that they did not either. He knew that nervous tension was what Cousins wanted and that the killer waited for a moment when the townsfolk were jumpy and scared, then he would strike. Only that looked as if it would be a long time in coming.

Certainly the man who rode from Tennyson shortly before noon thought the coming had been delayed long enough. So he took his horse and headed out to try and speed matters up. Although he wore a town suit he had never worked in a store or any other kind of business premises,

85

other than a saloon or a gambling house. He came to Tennyson with Wardle and Schanz in the hope of finding the pot of gold at the end of the rainbow, or at least a town full of folk ready willing and delighted to be bilked at games of chance in which no chance was allowed on his side. The promised land did not materialize, for Tennyson had taken wise precautions against him and his kind. He stayed on even though the proposed saloon did not arrive. There were pickings for the vultures, happen a man knew how go about it and avoided coming into conflict with the law. The pickings were not great and on the day Tune Counter took lead this man had been thinking of seeking pastures new. Then he, along with Wardle and Schanz saw a chance of getting rid of Tune Counter and the strong hand which controlled the town, as well as moving Madam Bulldog from their path. By methods known to such as them, they got in touch with Cousins, notifying him of the death of his son and offering their help. In return they received word that Cousins aimed to come and take revenge and told where to look for him on his arrival. The man rode towards that place now.

For three miles he rode across country making for a large bosque well known for its qualities as a hide-out amongst men of Cousins' kind. Nor did the man from Tennyson ride blindly along. He kept a sharp watch on his backtrail, making sure no one followed him. He knew Cousins to be a most untrusting soul who would not regard the sign of approaching men with equanimity. Cousins' tricky mind might lead him to believe the leading rider had sold him out to his enemies and his answer to such an action would be effective, if crude.

At last the man, who went by the unimaginative name of Smith, halted his horse thirty yards from the edge of the woods. He scanned them for some sign of life and saw none. Being a town dweller who spent but little of his time in travelling and that time being spent in a stage coach if possible, the man called Smith thought nothing of the silence of the woods, or the lack of bird sounds.

He took out a gaudy handkerchief and mopped his face with it. Then, just as he was about to turn his horse, a thought struck him. He looked towards the silent woods and called:

'It's all right. I came alone.'

Silence again, not a sound in the woods. The man licked his lips, some instinct warning him that cold eyes watched his every move. He debated to himself on the possibility of Cousins not being at the *bosque* yet and started to turn his horse to make for town.

'You'd've been dead five minutes back if you hadn't been alone.'

The words came so unexpectedly that Smith almost jumped from his horse. He stared towards the *bosque* and the tall, gaunt young man in cowhand clothes who stepped from behind a tree, cradling a Winchester rifle across his arm.

'I'm a friend of Charlie Wardle,' Smith said hurriedly, smiling what he hoped was a warm and winning smile. 'You with Hank Cousins?'

'You might say that.'

'Charlie told me where to come,' Smith explained.

A cold, wolf-savage smile split the young man's face and he gestured with his rifle. 'Come and come easy. I'd as soon shoot you as not.'

With that friendly advice given the young man turned on his heel and walked away into the trees. Smith swung down from his horse and led it as he followed the lead of his guide.

After winding through the trees of the *bosque* for a time they came at last to where, in a hollow on the banks of a stream, a small, rough camp had been made. Five men were by the small campfire and they came to their feet, hands reaching to their guns as they looked with suspicious gaze at Smith. Three of the men showed a strong family likeness, the burly man with steel rimmed spectacles being Hank Cousins. Next to him stood the oldest son, Burt, a mean looking unshaven man. Ted and Joe, the look-out, were twins and neither would have won any prize for having a kind or gentle facial aspect. The remaining two men had all the marks of hard-case outlaws, men who would follow any leader as long as he paid well and would stay loyal to him until it came to a time when loyalty no longer paid them.

'What're you wanting?' Hank Cousins asked, coldly surveying Smith through the plain glass of his spectacles.

'I was in with Wardle and Schanz,' replied Smith.

'Why didn't they come themselves?' growled Cousins, then

looked at Joe and didn't wait for Smith's reply. 'Was he followed?'

'Naw.'

'I made sure of that,' Smith stated. 'Wardle and Schanz got themselves run out of town and I thought I'd come along to let you know how things stand.'

'Did you?' asked Cousins with a chilling lack of interest.

'Sure. The folks there are standing fast, all of them are solid behind the marshal.'

'The marshal's hurt bad,' said Cousins, 'or so we was told.'

'His nephew come in and took over. A big *hombre* toting a brace of white handled guns that he's real fast with. He beat Al Cordby to the shot in a fair fight, which same Cordby was drawing first when he got it.'

A low rumble of talk came from the men and a quick exchange of glances which told Smith he had interested the others. They all knew Cordby's reputation and were wondering who this fast-drawing nephew of Tune Counter's might be. Then one of the two non-Cousinses recollected something.

'Counter,' said the man, Potts by name, 'he wouldn't be a real big, handsome blond haired feller, would he?'

'That's him,' agreed Smith.

'And that's *Mark* Counter,' Potts went on, then as if he thought more explanations might be needed. 'Dusty Fog's *amigo*.'

Now all the others were interested. Dusty Fog's name stood high amongst the real fast men in Texas.* Cousins and his bunch all knew the close ties of friendship and loyalty between Dusty Fog and the other members of the OD Connected crew, and Mark Counter belonged to that crew; more he belonged to the élite of the crew, the floating outfit, and his name had often been linked with Dusty Fog.

'Is either Dusty Fog or the Ysabel Kid with him?' asked the second man, Jacobs by name.

Not being a Cousins he did not have any particular stake in this game, he had no kin to avenge and came along merely in case there should be a chance to loot some place in town. He most certainly had not come along to tie into fuss with Dusty Fog, Mark Counter and the Ysabel Kid.

* *Dusty Fog's history is given in the author's floating outfit novels.*

'There's only Mark Counter in Tennyson right now,' Smith answered, then an inspiration struck him. 'He sent for the others, they're due here tomorrow.'

Cousins scowled at the others. He would have preferred to handle the matter of avenging his son with just his kin, but felt the need for a couple of extra guns to back him. He had planned to stay on out here for another couple of days to really give the folks time to stew on his threats. He had used the same system before when meaning to hit a town. The telegraph messages stirred things up, his blood-thirsty reputation did the rest. A couple more days of anxiety would see folks in Tennyson debating the futility of resistance, even with a good man to back them. Yet if Dusty Fog and the Ysabel Kid should arrive they would effectively stiffen the town in such a manner that no amount of threatening telegraph messages would worry them.

'We go in tonight,' he said, reaching the decision Smith hoped to get. 'Show me the layout of the town.'

Reaching into his pocket Smith produced a copy of the *Tennyson Herald* and passed it to Cousins. He stood watching the killer read the town council's orders to the population. At last Cousins crumpled the paper in his hands, then tossed it to the ground.

'Smart!' he snarled. 'Too damned smart for a bunch of hick yokels. This's Mark Counter's doing.'

'He had the town council in to see him yesterday,' Smith answered. 'They've appointed four special deputies who're on watch all the time day and night at the jail house. There's one thing though. The jail's only got one way out, straight on to the main street.'

The significance of the words did not escape Cousins. He scuffed his boot toe over the soil at his feet, making a clear level area to which he pointed.

'Show me how the town lays,' he ordered.

Taking a stick Smith squatted on his heels and started to make as good a map as he could manage under the conditions. He tried to show the full lay-out of the town, pointing out the salient points, such as the jail, the saloon and Doc Connel's house. Despite his lack of experience as a map-maker Smith gave Cousins a very clear idea of what he would run into when he reached Tennyson.

'How bad is Tune Counter hurt?' he asked.

'Pretty bad, by all accounts. And from what I heard Madam Bulldog tangled with Calamity Jane yesterday, They're both still in bed.'

'You mean they had a tooth 'n' claw brawl?' asked Tad Cousins.

'So the word has it. Only the saloon gals know for sure what happened. I was in there last night and the gals all talked about the fight, it was a real humdinger from what they say and I can well believe it.'

'You don't know for sure about it then?' Hank Cousins put in.

'Nope,' Smith replied. 'Calamity came in with Mark Counter and tied in with Madam Bulldog, got out-cussed, lost near on all she stood up in at poker, then got herself drunk under the table a couple of nights back. We all expected her to be back r'aring to go last night, but she never showed, so I reckon it's true what the gals said about being a fight.'

Cousins' usual scowl deepened as he looked Smith up and down. He did not know the man and wondered just what Smith expected to gain out of helping him. How far he could trust Smith, or even if he could trust Smith at all, Cousins did not know. He looked the man over with cold eyes and asked:

'Just what do you reckon to gain out of all this?'

'A saloon and good pickings. With Madam Bulldog and Tune Counter gone I'll get them both, provided your boys don't bust up the saloon too much. Which same's why I come out here, to see if you thought my help'd be worth not busting up the place.'

'You want us to kill Tune Counter and Madam Bulldog for you?' sneered Burt Cousins.

'You're going to kill him, and Madam Bulldog anyhow,' Smith replied. 'I reckoned that if I did you a favour you'd do me one in return.'

None of the men spoke for a long moment. Hank Cousins for one felt better about Smith now the matter had been put into terms he could understand. Smith stood to make money out of the deaths of two people and Cousins could see why the man would offer his help. He made his decision and prepared to tell the others his plan. He had one thing to attend to before he made any plans.

Looking at Smith, he pointed to the trees. 'Get going!' he said.

'What—!' yelped the startled man.

Coming forward fast Joe Cousins thrust the barrel of his rifle hard into the middle of Smith's back.

'You heard pappy?' he asked. 'Walk – or stay put permanent.'

'Don't gun him unless you have to!' Cousins barked, being under no delusions about Joe's regard for human life.

Not until Smith, protesting his friendship, departed, did Hank Cousins offer to tell his men his ideas for taking the town of Tennyson. He did not doubt that Smith had his interests at heart, especially as Smith stood to gain by those same interests. However, the less Smith knew the less he could tell should he be caught out and questioned. Smith did not strike Hank Cousins as being the most staunch of men and would crack under forceful treatment, so the less he knew about Cousins's plans the better the outlaw liked it.

'It could be a trap,' Potts said quietly.

'Reckon it is, Hank?' asked Jacobs.

'Nope, Smith wants that saloon bad and we're going to hand it to him. We're headed in tonight.'

'How?' asked Burt.

'Quiet and easy. I'll tend to Tune Counter myself. Joe and Tad take the saloon and hand Madam Bulldog her needings. Should be easy enough with her off her feet. Even if she's back on them likely she'll be too stiff 'n' sore to make any fast moves.'

All the others exchanged glances, for they'd heard what the wounded man who escaped the hold-up had to say on the subject of Madam Bulldog's way with a gun. Burt looked at his father.

'How about me, paw?'

'You, Potts and Jacob's be hid out opposite the jail, with your rifles. I'm counting on you to hold Mark Counter and the deputies inside if there's only the one door. To save us starting ahead of each other, Tad, don't you start shooting until nine o'clock, that's the time we'll be in town. By ten past nine we'll be riding out and both Tune Counter 'n' Madam Bulldog'll be dead.'

Calamity Jane stood in her hotel room and lifted her arms

over her head, standing so she could see herself in the mirror. Her body still looked mottled by the various bruises and abrasions but she flexed her arms and had no stiffness in them. It said much for Mrs. Kusin's skill as a masseuse that Calamity could move with such ease after the fight she had fought with Madam Bulldog. Three times Mrs. Kusin had come to Calamity's room and worked on her, probing, rubbing, slapping until the girl felt like she had been through the fight all over again. Now it was all over, the stiffness and aches no longer bothered Calamity and she felt the time had arrived when she must take up the cudgel and try conclusions with Madam Bulldog once more.

She took up the clothes Mark bought for her and dressed, grinning as she found the shirt to be a size larger than she usually wore. Once fully dressed she took up her old Navy Colt, checked that it still carried its loads, rested the butt on her knee and slipped percussion caps on to the nipples, set the hammer on the safety notch between two of the loaded chambers and thrust the gun into her waistband. She made sure of the set of the weapon, put her battered cavalry kepi on at a rakish angle and left her room whistling an old army tune.

A meal was Calamity's first requirement and she got this in the hotel's dining room. Then she left, walked out into the street and headed for the Bull's Head. The first thing she noticed on leaving was the deserted aspect of the town. Along the street only the Bull's Head saloon and the marshal's office carried lights to show they were open for business. Not a horse stood at any hitching rack and nobody walked the streets.

Knowing the west, Calamity could read the signs. Tennyson expected trouble. She could smell it in the air, feel it all around her. The citizens had closed their business premises and most likely stayed at home, loaded weapons ready to their hands as they had done in the old days when the Kiowa and Comanche Indians rode the plains.

Although she had thought of visiting Mark Counter and seeing if she could do anything to help him, Calamity overlooked one vital detail. The Bull's Head lay between the hotel and the marshal's office. At the saloon's hospitable doors she paused, then turned and entered.

Her foot barely touched the floor inside when she froze,

hands at her sides. The saloon contained only half a dozen townsmen for customers, but the full force of waiters, dealers and bartenders stood around and all of them wore guns. Guns towards which their hands dropped as she entered.

'Hi!' she greeted, unperturbed by the way the men watched her. 'Don't shoot until I've had me a drink.'

The hostile looks faded away and the men relaxed, although Viola and the few girls in the room threw scowls at the grinning Calamity as she headed for the bar. They might have shown their dislike in a more practical way, but Madam Bulldog had given definite orders which Viola passed on.

'You looking for trouble, Calam?' asked Sam, sliding a beer along the bar top towards the girl.

'*Me?*' she replied, looking innocent as a dove cooing in a peach tree. 'Why I never look for trouble. Where at's the boss?'

'Be down soon.'

Calamity caught the glass and raised it to her lips. 'First since the last,' she remarked, then looked around the room. 'You're sure slack tonight.'

'Yeah,' Sam replied and let it go at that, for he sure wanted to keep his eyes on the door.

Time passed and at ten to nine Calamity heard a sound at the head of the stairs. She looked up to see Madam Bulldog at the top and just starting to walk down, moving with her usual light footed, rubbery grace which told that Mrs. Kusin's handling had been just as successful as in Calamity's case. Only this night Madam did not wear her working dress. She wore a black two-piece ladies' suit with a frilly fronted white blouse. Calamity saw under the left side of the jacket as Madam Bulldog started to come downstairs. The saloon-keeper carried a revolver under her arm in a shoulder clip.

Before Madam reached the bottom, the batwing doors opened and two men stepped in, two men with drawn revolvers in their hands. They timed the move just right, for just at that moment all eyes had gone to Madam Bulldog.

'Sit tight, all of you!' snapped Tad Cousins.

'Do it, or we throw lead into the gals before you get us!' Joe Cousins went on. 'We're looking for Madam Bulldog.'

Their threat worked. The men might have taken a chance, but not to endanger Viola and the other girls' lives.

'I'm the one you want,' said Madam Bulldog, coming

slowly down the stairs and stepping forward to face the two men. 'The rest of them aren't in this.'

'You're her, huh?' grunted Joe and started to move his gun around.

At that moment Calamity Jane thrust herself from the bar, ignoring the gun Tad turned towards her. She pointed at Madam Bulldog and glared defiantly at the Cousins' brothers.

'Hold it!' she snapped. 'Listen, you pair, I don't know what's between you and her, but I got first claim on her. This fat old cow cold-decked me out of all I own at cards, hocussed my fire-water, then, when I come back the next morning for a reckoning, her and three of her calico cats jumped me and worked me over. So I've got me a gun and come looking for her. And I'm damned if I'll stand back to let a couple of ringtailed rippers come in and take her from me.'

'Reckon you can take her?' asked Joe.

'You reckon I can't?' Calamity spat back. Just stand back and leave me try.'

Joe threw a glance at the clock. By now his father would have the men staking out the jail house and be well on his way to Doc Connel's house. He flashed a glance at Tad who grinned and nodded. They did not object to committing a cold-blooded murder, but knew every man for hundreds of miles would be out after them if they killed a woman, especially a well-liked and respected woman like Madam Bulldog. If they let Calamity Jane do the killing it would serve their purpose and all blame fall on the girl. From the look of Calamity and Madam Bulldog they sure had tangled and as none of the girls showed signs of injury it looked like Calamity got licked fair and now made loser's music. If the girl tried and failed to kill Madam, then they could still cut in and finish the job.

'Get to it!' Tad ordered. 'Nobody else move.'

On receiving permission Calamity turned to face Madam. Her hand lifted to hover the butt of the Navy Colt. Madam moved around to stand squarely facing her, her eyes on the girl's face, the good one trying to read some sign of warning that Calamity was about to make her draw.

Behind the bar Sam threw a look at his ten gauge. He swore an oath to himself that, even if he died in doing it, he would cut Calamity in two pieces with a load of blue-whistlers should she throw down on and kill his boss.

'When you're ready, Madam,' Calamity said calmly.

Unaware of the developments around them, Mark Counter and his deputies sat around the desk and in a low stake, but highly enjoyable, poker game. Mark tossed his hand into the pot with an expression of disgust and rose from the desk.

'About time you lost one,' snorted old Corky. 'See now how you pay your deputies so good. You take it off 'em playing poker.'

Mark grinned and paced the room while waiting for the next pot. He knew he would have a fair wait, for Corky had become a long-winded card player given to much deliberation before making any move, even if the move be the simple act of folding and tossing into the deadwood in the table centre. So Mark strode the length of the room and turned. In doing so he chanced to glance out of the window.

That one glance told him the long awaited moments of action had come. It also warned Mark that he had made an error in tactics. He had one man in the rear cells, watching the back of the jail, but unless he was badly mistaken they were held prisoner inside the jail building.

What he had seen was two men standing in the alley between the two opposite buildings. More, he had seen one start to raise a rifle but be restrained by the other.

Mark did not panic. He knew he must think fast, for the Cousins bunch had at last reached Tennyson and even now would be moving. He crossed the room in the same relaxed and casual manner he had done several times before and threw a glance at the alley at the other end of the facing building. Sure enough another man stood at it, rifle in hand. That meant they were not just casual idlers even if the prevented raising of the rifle had not already told Mark as much.

He crossed to the desk and rested his hands on top, looking at the men. He stood with his back to the front windows so the men outside would not be able to guess what he aimed to do.

'Don't get up, or look,' he said. 'There's three men with rifles outside. They've got us bottled in.'

To give them credit, not one of the men at the table gave the slightest sign of surprise, or of being aware that the watchers had them pinned in with the only way out under easy range for a rifle.

'What're we going to do, Mark?' Cork asked. 'This means Cousins's in town.'

'I know,' Mark replied. 'We've got to get out.'

'Won't be easy,' growled Corky. 'Could try rushing 'em.'

'They'd cut us down as we went through the door,' Mark answered.

'I allus reckoned this place should have a back door,' growled one of the deputies.

Mark looked at his hands, then at the men. 'So do I. Keep on playing like we didn't know they were there.'

He passed back through the door into the cells section where Hoscroft sat in a cell and watched through the rear window. The banker, taking his turn like the rest at the most boring of all the jail duties, looked at Mark as the big Texan entered the cell.

'What's wrong?' he asked.

'Cousins's playing it smart. Got us bottled, three men out front. Just move to one side and leave me room to work.'

Taking up his shotgun Hoscroft watched Mark approach the window and take a firm hold of the bars, one in each hand. Then Mark lifted his right leg and pressed the sole of his foot against the wall.

'You'll never do it, man!' Hoscroft gasped when he saw Mark's intention.

Mark did not reply to this. His enormous muscles started to bulge and writhe as he strained with all his might against the strength of the stonework surrounding the bars. Never had Hoscroft seen such grim determination shown on a man's face and Mark applied all his might and power against the bars. Sweat poured down Mark's face but he kept up that steady, yet power packed pull on the iron. He felt as if his lungs must crack, yet still he held on and still his leg forced against the side of the cell.

'You can't do it,' Hoscroft began, 'No man c—!'

At that moment the words trailed off, for he became aware of a steady trickle of powder running from a thin crack at the side of the window. He realized what this powder must be. Concrete crushed up by the pressure. He stared and saw the very framework of the window begin to quiver.

'Warn the others!' Mark gasped, relaxing for an instant before a final effort.

Without needing other instructions Hoscroft left the cell. He entered the front office acting like a sentry relieved for a cup of coffee. While pouring his drink he told the others what Mark planned to do. They showed no sign of the tension all were under, but sat ready, though they doubted if even Mark could do it.

Inside the cell Mark drew in a deep breath and took a firm hold of the bars once more and put on the pressure. Slowly, so slowly that it appeared nothing would happen, the stone gave. With a rumble and clatter the bars and their framework were torn from their bed. Mark lowered the heavy frame to the ground and leaned against the wall breathing heavily.

Hoscroft came in fast, staring unbelievingly at the torn gash where the window had been. Mark rested against the wall for a moment then turned and said:

'Pass me the shotgun. I'll get around the side.'

Before the other men could make any objection Mark slipped out through the window. He took the shotgun Hoscroft passed through, drawing back both hammers and checking that the percussion caps sat ready for use.

'Get ready,' Mark ordered. 'I'll take the two, they're on the side nearest to the saloon and Doc's house. Once I start shooting get the windows bust and cut loose. There's no time to waste.'

He turned and headed around the corner of the building out of sight. Moving his feet carefully, feeling for anything against which he might kick and cause a clatter which would warn the watchers across the street, Mark kept to the shadows. Knowing there to be no door at the rear of the building, the men at the other side never suspected a thing until he almost reached the corner. Then one saw him and let out a yell, throwing his rifle up. Fast taken or not, his bullet kicked chips from the wall close to Mark's head. The big Texan did not hesitate, the ten gauge in Mark hands boomed out a reply to the rifle. He saw the man jerk back as buckshot ripped into him, stagger and hit his pard even as the second man tried to get his rifle up. Mark changed his aim slightly and emptied the other barrel. He heard the man scream, heard also the shattering glass and the roar of a rifle from the jail front and knew Hoscroft or one of the others must have been ready and waiting to cut in.

There was no time to waste. Mark dropped the empty shotgun, for he saw both his men lay on the ground. He did not know how badly hurt they might be, but he had to get to Connel's house as quickly as possible. Madam Bulldog had men to help her and the doctor stood alone.

One of the two men Mark cut down with the buckshot rolled clear of the other. It was Burt Cousins, and the outlaw, snarling with agony-filled rage, gripped and brought up his rifle, aiming on the big Texan as he sprang from the side of the jail and ran down the street. Even as Cousins took aim old Corky burst from the jail holding his old Dragoon, the gun roared like a cannon and Cousins lifted almost to his feet under the impact of the lead, then dropped, draping himself across the still body of Potts.

At the other end of the building Jacobs decided discretion to be the better part of valour, turned and ran for safety.

Calamity Jane's eyes locked Madam Bulldog's as the girl tried to pass a message. Calamity winked with her good eye, the eye on the side away from the Cousins brothers, but Madam gave no sign of knowing, or even seeing the wink.

'Take her, Calamity!' Cousins snarled. 'Or we will.'

At that same moment they all heard the thunder of shots from along the street. Joe and Tad Cousins threw quick glances at the wall clock, for it wanted five minutes to nine o'clock and they knew their father could not have reached Connel's house yet. More, the shots sounded from the wrong way. It seemed that Burt had run into trouble down at the jail. For an instant both men's guns wavered out of line.

'Now!' yelled Calamity.

She pivoted around, hand lashing to the butt of her Navy Colt. If Madam had not read her sign right she would damned soon know about it.

Madam Bulldog's right hand shot across, under her left jacket side, closed on the grip of the Cloverleaf and brought it out. A split second after Calamity's move, Madam also turned. She saw the brothers trying to bring their guns into line just as her gun barked – a flicker of a second before Calamity's Navy Colt spoke.

Too late the two outlaws tried to get their guns into line. Tad sent a wild shot into the bar between the two women, then Calamity's Navy bullet struck him. An instant ahead of Calamity's shot, Joe took a .41 ball in the chest and reeled back. He kept his feet and tried to line a gun. A ragged volley tore from the weapons held by Madam's male workers, drawn the moment they saw a chance. Joe hit the wall, almost torn to doll-rags by the lead.

Still on his feet Tad stumbled back through the batwing doors. He heard running feet approaching, pounding along the sidewalk towards him. Turning, he saw a big blond man wearing a marshal's star who came sprinting at him. Snarling in rage Tad tried to raise and use his gun.

Mark Counter saw Tad erupt from the saloon after hearing the shots. Saw also the gun Tad held and drew left handed, firing on the run. Twice his long barrelled Army Colt bellowed. Tad reeled back under the impact, hit the batwing doors and fell inside.

'It's Mark Counter coming by!'

The yell left Mark's throat as he holstered his Colt and landed on the board walk before the Bull's Head. He did not wish to get shot by someone inside under the mistaken impression he belonged to the Cousins gang.

'We got the other one!' came back an answering yell. Calamity Jane's voice or Mark missed his guess.

He did not stop, for the most dangerous of all the Cousins bunch was headed after his uncle.

Hank Cousins heard the shots even as he ran towards Connel's house, after making a round trip keeping well clear of the backs of the houses. He heard the rifle, then the boom of the shotgun. He heard other shots just as he started to mount the stairs leading to Connel's surgery. The meaning of the shots became clear to him. His plan had slipped somehow, failed and his boys were in trouble. Then he heard Mark's yell and caught the muffled reply. If Mark Counter had escaped from the jail his son Burt must be dead. This thought received stronger confirmation by the fact that no more shots sounded by the jail and Burt would die fighting.

Snarling in rage Cousins halted in his climb. His three sons had been killed and his own chances of getting Tune

Counter, and escaping after it, sank to lower than zero. He must get away, gather a big bunch around him and sweep down on Tennyson in a raid which would make Quantrill's attack on Lawrence, Kansas, look like a Sunday-school outing.

Cousins turned and started down the steps, his gun in his hand. He saw Mark burst into sight around the edge of the next house. With a snarl he brought up his gun to take a careful sight.

Against a lesser man it might have worked. Mark saw the shape against the white wall of Connel's house. Saw it and went down in a dive, fetching clear his right hand Colt (he had holstered the other to run the easier) even as he fell. He heard Cousins' bullet slap over his head, then he lit down and his left hand started to fan the hammer of the Colt. The shots thundered out like the roar of a Gatling gun. Splinters kicked from the bannister above Cousins, inched nearer for two more shots even as he aimed again. Just before Cousins touched off the shot Mark's next bullet caught him and caused his lead to fly harmlessly into the air. Twice more Cousins rocked under the impact of the lead, then slowly, almost reluctantly it seemed, his body crumpled forward and fell to the ground, his gun clattered down the steps away from him.

Coming to his feet Mark walked forward, holstering his empty right hand Colt and drawing the weapon from his left holster. He saw the door at the head of the stairs burst open. Connel and two men appeared, all holding weapons, they looked down at the body, then towards Mark, who hurriedly called out so they would recognize him and not throw lead.

The men closed in on Cousins' body, keeping their weapons ready for use but they did not need the precaution, for the outlaw would never rise again, not after being torn almost in two pieces by three bullets from Mark's Army Colt.

'Landsakes,' said Calamity Jane, looking at the circle of faces around the bar. 'I was like to pee my pants when I jumped them Cousins boys. I wasn't sure you get my meaning, Madam.'

'I wasn't sure I had either,' Madam replied. 'But I figured

to take at least one of them with me.'

The time was half past ten and Tennyson lay peaceful again, the bodies of the Cousins bunch on slabs at the undertaker's shop. Now a crowd of citizens gathered at the Bull's Head and Mark Counter stood with his 'deputies', Madam Bulldog and Calamity Jane, talking over the events of the evening.

'You mean you aimed to get one of the Cousins boys even if Calam cut you down?' Hoscroft asked.

'Sure, way I saw it Sam there was all set to settle Calam,' replied Madam Bulldog calmly.

'You can't trust nobody these days,' grinned Calamity, not at least worried by her narrow escape. 'Like to say one thing though. Madam licked me fair and square at everything, including shooting, way I saw it. One thing nobody's going to say is that lil ole Martha Jane Canary's a poor lo—'

Madam Bulldog's glass fell from her hand. She stared at Calamity's face for a moment after the girl announced her full name. Then Madam's hands shot out to grip Calamity by the shoulders.

'What did you say your name was?' she asked.

'Martha Jane Canary,' Calamity answered, lowering her fists which she had clenched ready to defend herself.

'Oh, my god!' gasped Madam Bulldog.

Her face lost its colour, her hands dropped from Calamity's shoulders and she went down in a limp heap on the floor. Mark bent and scooped the woman up while Viola dashed up and Sam came over the counter top in a bound.

'What happened?'

At least a dozen voices asked the same question. Calamity stared at Mark as he held the woman's limp body in his arms.

'She fainted!' croaked Calamity. 'Get her into her office, Mark.'

A pale faced Madam looked at Mark, Sam, Viola and Calamity in her office. She managed a wry smile.

'Sorry if I scared you. I'd like to see Calam alone for a few minutes, please. It'll be all right.'

The few minutes lasted for half an hour and when Calamity came out of the office she looked strangely subdued. She crossed to where Mark stood and wiped a hand across her brow.

'Sure she's all right,' Calamity replied to various inquiries. 'The evening's been a mite too much for her. Coming down to the hotel, Mark?'

'Yeah. I may as well.'

They walked along the street side by side and Calamity looked up at him as they passed the end of the Bull's Head Saloon.

'When you riding out, Mark?' she asked.

'In a couple of days. Old Corky can keep things under till Uncle Tune gets back on his feet and there's likely to be work waiting for me at the OD Connected.'

'I'm going in the morning.'

'Can let you have a couple of hundred to stake you until you get a start again,' Mark said.

'Thanks, *amigo*,' she replied. 'Only Madam's give me back all she won from me, so I don't need it.'

'A fine woman all round,' Mark drawled.

'Real fine. We talked for a fair piece. I'm going to tell you something, Mark, only it's something I don't want to get out.'

'You know me, old Clam Counter they call me.'

Calamity laughed, then she hooked her hand under his arm.

'I should have figured it when she out-cussed me, licked me at poker, drunk me under the table and then whipped me,' she said quietly, looking more subdued than Mark could ever remember seeing her look before.

'Guessed what?' he asked.

'There could only be one gal who's that much better than Calamity Jane. Madam Bulldog told me her name tonight. It's been so long that neither of us recognized each other.'

'What the hell are you on about?' Growled Mark.

'Madam Bulldog. Her real name's Charlotte Canary.'

Mark stopped in his tracks, turning the girl to face him. 'C – Canary?' he gasped.

'That's right as the Injun side of a hoss,' Calamity grinned. 'The only gal who could whup me the way she did would have to be my mother.'

PART TWO

THE GAMBLERS

DUSTY FOG, the Ysabel Kid and Waco had agreed unanimously that Mark Counter was the best man for the job although Mark objected most strenuously to getting it. They ruled out his objections on several counts. In the first place Mark's satorial elegance exceeded any of their own, which he could not truthfully deny. Secondly, Mark owned all the necessary items of clothing for such an occasion; so did both Dusty and the Kid, but they claimed Mark looked so much better in his. Waco said he did not own any such fancy low-necked clothes and hoped he never would, so that let him out of it. Thirdly, and perhaps most important, Dusty and the Kid had already sampled Brenton Humboldt's hospitality and thought Mark ought to take his fair turn.

'It looks to me like you've caught it then, Mark,' said Ole Devil Hardin when the members of his floating outfit stopped their talking. 'I'm sorry to land it on you and I never expected any of it when I put my money into Humboldt's meat-packing plant. I hoped that finished me with it, apart from drawing in my share of the profits and never thought he'd write and ask me to send my representative along to his daughter's wedding.'

'Maybe he wants backing in some other idea,' drawled the Kid who suffered no illusions about Brenton Humboldt's true nature.

'You be sure to apologize for Lon and me, Mark,' grinned Dusty. 'Tell Humboldt we're both suffering the miseries through having a touch of the grippe.'

'It'll be bad enough going there for you without telling your lies as well,' Mark answered. 'I'll pull out in the morning.'

'For a feller as doesn't want to go up there, *amigo,*' the

Kid put in dryly, 'you're sure in a tolerable hurry to get started.'

'Why sure,' agreed Mark. 'I could make it in maybe four days' hard riding. But I don't aim to try. I've been sent out on this chore against my will so I aim to travel easy and sleep under a roof every night as I go.'

The others laughed. They knew all too well that Mark hated sleeping out of doors. Even the fact that he spent much of his life using the ground for a mattress and the sky for a roof did not make him like it any the more. So he planned to make a leisurely journey of it and spend each night in a town, ranch house or line cabin. To do so would need careful arranging and involve swinging and swerving instead of riding in a near enough straight line.

At dawn the following morning Mark rode away from the OD Connected house. In his war-bag, packed neatly and rolled in the protection of his blanket's suggans and tarp, Mark carried his cutaway coat, white frilly bosomed shirt, town style trousers and shoes. If he must attend the wedding he intended to be dressed at his best.

Three days later, shortly after the sun went down, Mark hung his saddle on an inverted V-shaped wooden framework, known as a burro, in the stable of the Bella Union Hotel at Culver Creek. His big bloodbay stallion stood in a loose box and Mark glanced at the two fine looking harness horses standing in the adjacent stalls. He drew the Winchester Model '66 rifle from his saddleboot and threw a glance at the light two-horse carriage which stood at the side of the big stable building.

'Fine rig,' he said to the old-timer who slouched towards him, pitchfork on shoulder.

'Mighty fine picture it made coming in, too,' replied the man. 'With them two high-stepping bays hauling it and that right pretty looking woman driving. She sure could handle them.'

'She staying at the hotel?'

'Sure,' answered the man, waving a hand to the trunk lashed on the back, 'I don't know how long for though. Telled me to leave the trunk for today, so's she could see how she liked the look of the town. Me, I says, "Lady," I says, "happen you take time out to look at this here town you won't stay at all."'

'What'd she say?' Mark asked, knowing stable workers to be inveterate gossips who could lick barbers for passing on information or news.

'Just laughed and walked off with one fair sized bag. Sure don't know who she is or what she's doing out here, but I never heard an accent like she'd got afore.'

'She a saloon gal?'

'What, with a rig and team like that?' scoffed the man. 'Naw, she's maybe some rich eastern gal out west looking for a husband. There's a chance for you, happen you'd like a wife.'

'I wouldn't,' grinned Mark.

'Or me – trouble is I've got one.'

Carrying his bedroll and rifle, Mark walked away from the chuckling man. At the hotel's reception desk Mark booked a room for the night and took the key, then headed upstairs. He came to the passage with the hotel rooms on either side and saw from the numbers that he would be at the end of the passage, so he walked towards his room's door.

The door facing Mark's room opened just as he walked towards it and one of the most beautiful women Mark had ever seen stepped out. Mark was something of a connoisseur of female pulchritude and found nothing in the young woman's appearance to offend his predilections. She had hair as golden blonde as his own, not too long or too short and neatly combed and cared for. The fact was as near perfection as a man could ask for, holding an intelligent, calm and somewhat regal expression, the blue eyes meeting Mark's with neither shyness nor boldness, looking him over coolly. She wore a cloak which effectively hid whatever kind of dress lay under it, yet conveyed the idea that it would pay a man to unwrap the cloak and look.

Mark nodded a greeting. Carrying his rifle in one hand and bedroll in the other he could not remove his hat. She replied with a calm, grave 'Good evening', and carried on down the passage out of his sight. Mark watched her go before entering his room. It did not need a Comanche witch-woman's powers to guess this beautiful blonde woman must be the owner of the carriage and pair of horses he had seen. He had heard only two words and yet he could near enough swear she spoke in the accent of an upper-class

Britisher such as he had run across on a few occasions.

After washing and shaving in his room, and leaving his rifle by the bed, Mark headed downstairs to the hotel dining-room, hoping to see the woman again, perhaps even get to know her and satisfy his curiosity. In this he was disappointed, for the woman did not appear to be in the room. Mark asked the waiter and learned she left earlier bound on some business of her own.

So, after a good meal, Mark left the hotel and took his first look at Culver Creek. The first thing which struck him was the size of the town. Serving as a convenient fording spot of the Culver Creek of the Brazos River, the town found a lucrative source of income in trail herds headed north as well as being the centre of a thriving cattle area and having a large, well manned Army post within easy distance of it. All this gave Culver Creek a more pretentious atmosphere than might be expected in a Texas cowtown. Certainly the General Hood Saloon looked more in keeping with one of the better areas of Dodge City than a small town.

On entering the saloon Mark found himself surprised at the trade it drew, for there appeared to be a goodly crowd enjoying themselves in the big barroom, a mixed crowd of cowhands and soldiers. Both the army post and the local ranches appeared to have paid their men on the same day and the same men vied eagerly with each other to get rid of a good portion of their month's pay in one glorious night of fun and frolic.

Passing across the room, Mark came to a halt at the bar and a glass of beer slid along to his order. He took it up and spent a couple of minutes in looking around the room in the hope he might see someone he knew. However, the gambling tables, the groups of men gathered with the saloongirls in drinking, laughing and talking parties, failed to yield a friend, or even a casual acquaintance to his gaze and so Mark, who never liked drinking alone, decided he would finish the beer then head back to his room. He did not care for the atmosphere of the place. It seemed to carry all the money-grabbing intensity of a trail-end town joint making hay while the Texas trail hand sun shone, and bore none of the homely feeling of a small town saloon which also served as an informal social club for the cowhands.

'Howdy friend,' said a voice from behind Mark.

Turning to see who addressed him, Mark found himself being favoured with the attentions of somebody who must be either the owner, or floor manager, of the saloon. The man stood maybe two inches less than Mark, but looked like he would weigh a mite heavier, for although he had a spread to his shoulders he did not taper down to a lean waist. He wore expensive gambler style clothes, with just too much clashing colour to them for Mark's taste. His face was florid, jovial looking, yet there seemed to be a hardness under it, a kind of cold calculation as if the man would enjoy a good laugh only should it pay him to make it. To Mark's eyes the man looked like a hard-case who had gradually run to fat but who could still handle himself in a brawl.

'Howdy,' Mark replied. The man looked too much like a trail-end town joint owner for Mark to take to him, but he felt he would lose nothing by being sociable.

'You're new around here,' the man went on.

Even while he spoke the man's eyes studied Mark from head to foot, pricing his clothing and noting the matched guns in the hand-carved holsters of the gunbelt. Mark could almost guess what the man thought. That Mark was rich, a rancher's son maybe, possibly the owner of his own spread. A man who might have some influence or powerful backing, and a man who had it paid a saloonkeeper to know.

'I'm not old around anyplace,' drawled Mark.

The man bellowed out a real professional hand-shaker's gust of laughter, the kind which could be turned on even at a feeble witticism, should the maker of the joke be someone worth knowing.

'I'm Homer Trent,' boomed the man, clearly having decided Mark suitable material for cultivation. 'This's my place. Say, have a drink on the house.'

'Take another beer,' Mark replied. 'Did you ride under Hood in the War?'

'Huh? – Oh, the name of the place. Nope, I didn't ride with him. But folks in town here think high of him. You ranching out this way?'

'Nope, not yet.'

Before he spoke again Trent threw a look at the wall

clock. Then he grinned and dropped his voice in a confidential whisper:

'Say, if you feel like some real sport go sit in on the big faro table over there. It'll be worth it.'

'Will, huh?'

'Sure,' grinned Trent. 'I've got Poker Alice and Madam Moustache here and they both of them expect to be dealing the big table for me.'

Saying that Trent stood back a pace and grinned broadly, awaiting Mark's reaction to his words. The names did not pass over Mark's head, for he had heard them many times. Poker Alice and Madam Moustache had something of a name in western saloon circles. They were lady gamblers and almost unique. True there had been and probably still were saloongirls who handled a wheel-of-fortune, or maybe turned the cards at a vingt-un layout to draw in customers. But they offered only a come-on for the gullible and woman hungry male customers and remained no more than saloongirls throughout. Poker Alice and Madam Moustache were different. They did not work as saloongirls, but as professional dealers, highly skilled at their work and offered nothing more than a male gambler would under the same circumstances.

While Mark could see the reason for hiring such talent to deal faro, he could not see why Trent took on both women. Mark's eyes went to the big table at which Trent pointed. This would be the house's big game, the no-limit table where the high stake players gathered and as such be the place of honour in the professional dealer's eyes. Both Poker Alice and Madam Moustache had handled such a table before and could do so with ease, so Mark wondered which of them would receive the honour, or if there were two high stake tables. His glance around the room saw two other tiger decorated faro lay-outs, but each bore a stakes sign restricting the level of betting.

'Ah!' Trent said eagerly. 'Here comes Poker Alice.'

Mark turned to look in the direction which Trent stared. The man looked up at the stair which led to the upstairs balcony and rooms. The woman he had seen at the hotel came down the stairs slowly, drawing every eye to her. He could now see what she wore under her cloak and as he perceived that now discarded cloak concealed a figure well worth a second, third and as many other glances as a man could spare at it.

She wore a white dress which would not have been out of place at a high class New Orleans ball and which showed off her rich figure to perfection. Maybe Poker Alice stood just a little mite taller than most men would call ideal, but she was not skinny, her figure seemed to be just right.

Ignoring the envious glares of the saloongirls and the frank, pop-eyed staring of the customers, Poker Alice reached the foot of the stairs and swept majestically towards the faro table.

Excitedly Trent jabbed Mark hard in the ribs with his elbow and was lucky not to get tossed over the bar for doing it. If he noticed Mark's angry scowl he ignored it in his excitement as he pointed to the other side of the room and whispered. 'Look!'

Holding back his first instinct to remove Trent forcibly, Mark looked to where another woman also made her way across the room towards the main faro table. Mark studied her and decided that a man would be hard put to find two more beautiful women than the pair who converged on the dealer's seat. Yet they were as unalike as night and day. The other woman had none of Poker Alice's calm, regal detachment and cold aloofness. Her raven-black hair hung shoulder long and framed an olive skinned, beautiful face which radiated charm, vivacious love of life, merriment and a bold challenge. In height she stood maybe two inches shorter than the English woman, yet seemed much smaller. Her figure was ripe, richly curved, not quite plump but enough to give a man a good handful happen he took a chance and grabbed. Where Alice wore a sedate gown of white, cut in the latest eastern mode, the other girl had on a flame coloured dress which clung almost like a second skin to her and had a slit from hem to well above the knee through which a black stockinged, plump and inviting leg peaked and disappeared at each step.

One thing Mark noticed, neither woman had long nails, or wore rings. He knew why. Players who knew their business objected to joining a game where the dealer's nails were long enough to mark the cards during play, or who wore rings in which tiny 'shiner' mirrors might be concealed wherewith to see the value of each card dealt.

A second thing also struck Mark and he took his eyes from the two women to turn to Trent who stood watching in an expectant manner.

'Looks like they both figure to run the big table for you,' he said.

'That's right, they do.'

'That could mean trouble.'

Trent grinned a conspiring grin as if letting Mark be a party to his secret plans. He dropped his voice to a confidential whisper and said:

'If there ain't trouble we'll all be disappointed.'

'How do you mean?' growled Mark.

'Why'd you reckon I got 'em both here and started them on the same day, at the same time?' Trent replied. 'There should be a better brawl than the battle at Bearcat Annie's.'

It did not take Mark five seconds to see what Trent meant. The saloonkeeper had brought together the west's two foremost lady gamblers in the hope they would tangle in a hair-yanking brawl. He did not need both of them and would most likely let the winner stay on while the loser would have to leave town.

In this plan Trent showed a thorough working knowledge of the saloon business. Nothing could better bring a saloon to the notice of the public than a fight between persons of note. If two gunmen locked horns, especially two top name men, in a saloon, that saloon's reputation would be enhanced and people come to see the place where it happened. A remembered fight between two well-known females had the same effect. Bearcat Annie's saloon in Quiet Town, although under new management, still drew trade on the strength of the fight which had been fought in it and already customers made the pilgrimage to Tennyson to drink in Madam Bulldog's saloon where the girls recounted blow by blow descriptions of their boss' fight with Calamity Jane.

With this in mind Trent had set about building a legend about his place. He did not leave the meeting and fight to chance, but brought in the two lady gamblers, set them up and stood back hoping for the best, knowing full well that both had a lot of pride in their ability at handling a big stake faro game.

By now the women were almost at the table and Mark gave a low, angry growl. Trent looked at the big Texan and saw he did not give the hoped for reaction. With a shrewd knowledge of men, Trent could see that Mark did not approve of his idea and might even now spoil it, for Mark looked big enough to go against popular opinion and tough enough to back his actions. So Trent turned away and gave a sign which brought two of his bouncers to his side. He did not need to speak, a nod and a wink sent the two big, burly men to flank Mark, one on either side. If Mark noticed the arrival he did not connect it with anything to do with what Trent said, for his full attention stayed on the table and the two women. If he could prevent it he did not intend the fight to take place.

Not that Mark was a spoilsport in any way. He had the typical western sense of humour and liked the entertainment to be gamey and unrefined. If the two women tangled in the normal course of events Mark would not have objected and would have been quite willing to sit back and enjoy the fight, for he did not worry about the moral objections to letting a pair of women fight. What Mark did object to was that the women had been tricked into coming to Culver Creek for the sole purpose of causing trouble between them for the enrichment of the saloonkeeper. He aimed to walk across the room and stop the fight before it started.

Now would be the time to move, for already Poker Alice had reached the dealer's chair. Trent glanced at his bouncers and nodded. It cost him a considerable sum of money to bring the two women together and he did not intend allowing a chance passing stranger, even one who showed signs of being wealthy, to interfere.

'One moment, *mademoiselle*!' said a voice as Poker Alice was about to draw out the dealer's chair, a soft, provocative woman's voice which brought Alice's attention to the speaker.

She turned and faced the black haired beauty, looked her up and down, then replied, 'Well?'

'This is my table,' said Eleonore Dumont, better known as Madame Moustache, her accents those of a New Orleans French Creole of good birth and with a trace of an accent.

'I'm afraid it *was* your table,' Alice replied. 'I was brought in to take over the game.'

'You!' Eleonore gasped. 'Surely know that Madam

Moustache, which is me, always runs the big table in any house which hires me.'

'I'm afraid I've never heard of Madam Moustache,' sniffed Alice calmly. 'But I happen to be Poker Alice. Now trot along like a good little girl and I'm sure Mr. Trent will let you turn his wheel-of-fortune.'

Poker Alice had told a lie when she said she had never heard of Madam Moustache and Eleonore acted ignorant of who the blonde girl might be. They had their pride and were deadly rivals although they had never run across each other before. Neither was the type to become involved in unseemly brawls, but they also both knew how to take care of themselves when a quarrel was forced on to them by jealous girls. Also neither would back down, give way to her rival at the big-game table.

'Take your hand off the chair!' Alice ordered, seeing every eye on her and Eleonore, reading the expectancy in their gaze. She did not wish to be put into the indignity of fighting, but would not back down.

'Make me!' hissed Eleonore, who did not really want to fight but also would not give way.

With an annoyed frown Alice released the back of the chair. Instantly Eleonore moved. Her right arm swung around to land on Alice's cheek in a flat-handed slap which snapped the blonde's head across to her lashing left palm causing Alice to take a hurried pace to the rear. Alice rocked under the impact of the slaps and Eleonore waited, tense as an alley-cat. Usually such a savage and rapid attack resulted in the one receiving it bursting into tears and taking a hurried departure. Only this time Eleonore did not face a saloongirl.

After catching her balance Alice swung a fist, not a slap, in return. Her knuckles cracked against the side of Eleonore's cheek and the Creole beauty went backwards on her heels, arms flailing to prevent herself from falling.

She spat out a mouthful of rapid French curses then sprang forward like a wildcat. Alice attacked at the same instant and the two women seemed to meet in mid-air. Hands dug into hair, tugging and yanking, or flailed in wild slaps and punches while feet lashed and kicked just as wildly. Clinging to each other and swinging wildly the two women crashed to the floor and rolled over and over, Alice's pale skin making a contrast to the tan of the Creole girl.

As soon as the fight started almost everybody in the room either stood up and gathered around to get a better view, or climbed on chairs, tables, anywhere that offered them a vantage point over the heads of the standing crowd. The men yelled their encouragement but the saloongirls gathered in a sullen group and scowled at Alice and Eleonore, who they regarded as interlopers, for taking the centre of attraction away from them.

At the bar, as soon as the two women met, Mark felt hands clamp on both his arms, strong and powerful hands which knew their business.

'Let's go easy, *hombre*!' a growling voice whispered in his ear and the two bouncers started walking him towards the door. 'Just keep on going, boyo, and you won't get hurt.'

They took five steps forward. To one side the squeals, gasps and yelps of the two fighting women became almost drowned by the excited shouts of the crowd and the calls of the gamblers offering to take bets on the winner. Mark decided he had gone as far as he aimed to go.

Instantly the two men hustling him towards the door came to a halt as Mark dug his heels in. Up until that moment the bouncers had been fooled and lulled into a sense of false security by Mark's appearance. They regarded him as a rich dandy, which he was due to an aunt leaving her considerable fortune to him in her will, and easy meat, which he most certainly was not. So the sudden halt took them both by surprise for it felt as if they had run into a brick wall.

Before either man could make up his mind what to do, the one at the right felt himself lifted from the floor. It took him completely by surprise when he felt his two hundred and thirty pounds of bone and muscle hefted up into the air, which delayed his reactions.

With a sudden surge of power Mark flung the right hand bouncer from him like a hound-dog shaking off a fly. The startled bouncer let out a howl and went head first across the room to smash into a table on which stood several soldiers all eagerly watching the fighting girls. With a crash the table went over and half a dozen soldiers pitched all ways, bellowing out curses and landing on other spectators as they went down. Men cursed, yelled and tempers boiled, so it did not help matters that the bartender should be a man with a bad reputation amongst soldiers due to some rough handling he had handed out. Fists started flying and a general brawl developed rapidly.

At the same moment that he flung aside the first man Mark brought the other around with a jerk of his left arm. Before the bouncer could release his hold, Mark's right fist rammed into his stomach with a thud like a bass drum's stick striking the skin of the drum. The bouncer let out a startled and agonized gurgle, lost his hold on Mark's left arm and folded hands over his stomach as he doubled over. Mark shot down a hand, gripped the bouncer by the shirt collar and heaved, sending him shooting off after his pard into the tangle of spectators.

Next moment almost every man in the place became involved in the general brawl as the fight spread like stone-raised ripples crossing the surface of a pool. A waiter sprang at Mark, swinging up his heavy tray and launching a blow at the big Texan's head. Mark side-stepped, shot out his hands, gripped the tray, plucking it from the man's grasp and applying it with some force to its owner's head, sending him staggering dazedly off towards a group of fighting men. One of them turned on him and knocked him down. Mark heard Trent's enraged bellows and saw the saloonkeeper still stood at the bar. A chair hissed through the air and Trent ducked, allowing it to smash into the big mirror behind the bar. At that moment a cowhand flung himself at Mark who back-handed him aside then started towards the door. This proved to be a slow process, for the fight had now become general and not one between the various fractions in the saloon. It was now a case of attack the nearest person and hope not to get jumped by somebody else while doing it.

After thrashing over and over on the floor, Poker Alice and Madame Moustache made their feet, still holding hair with one hand and using the other to slap, push, punch and pull. They staggered clear of the fighting men and towards the foot of the stairs where the saloongirls stood screeching curses, yelling wild encouragement or watching; their retreat to the bedrooms remained open in case a hurried departure should become necessary.

One of the girls let out an angry yell and charged forward, making for the two fighting women. Why she decided to cut in even she probably could not say. It might have been excitement, a desire to get in on the act. It could even have been through annoyance; she had been on the verge of persuading a gullible young cowhand to give her money for a stageline ticket to visit her (non-existent) sick mother in Arkansas when the fight started and caused him to lose interest. Whatever the motive, she rushed foward, dug two hands into Eleonore's long, though now considerably ruffled and untidy, black hair and started to pull hard.

The attack from behind came as a complete surprise and Eleonore gave out a squeal like a tail-stomped cougar. She lost her hold of Alice and was dragged clear of the dishevelled blonde. Alice might have been grateful for the help, but did not get a chance to show it, for a second girl darted from the stairs, thrusting Eleonore and her attacker aside. She delivered a slap to Alice's face, hard enough to leave fingermarks on her cheek. With a squeal Alice staggered back a couple of paces. She caught her balance, shot out her left hand to the girl's shoulder, measuring her up. Then the right hand swung around, clenched into a hard little fist. The saloongirl walked into the punch and shot backwards amongst her friends as they advanced to lend a hand. They all went down in a pile and forgot about Alice and Eleonore as various feuds came to a head in wild fighting among themselves.

Twisting and squealing, Eleonore struggled to free herself from the girl behind her but could not. However, Alice, having dealt with her assailant, turned to renew hostilities with her business rival. She sprang forward and sportingly landed a punch on the saloongirl, sending her reeling and sprawling back into her friends, where she became involved in a fight of her own.

To show her gratitude Eleonore lowered her head and butted into Alice, ramming her backwards into the main brawl where they tangled and fought on amongst the flailing fists and flying chairs.

Mark heard a bellow of rage and from the corner of his eye saw the first bouncer he had tossed aside coming at him in a low crouching charge, arms widespread to clamp around Mark. Only at the last moment Mark side-stepped and his foot raised to drive behind the man's rump and send him hurtling into the side wall where he slid down and lay still. Another man sprang at Mark, lifting a chair, but Mark bent, stepped forward, caught his attacker around the knees, then straightened to pitch him on to a soldier who had been moving in for an attack from the rear.

'Get the marshal!' Trent howled. 'Get the shotgun from under the bar!'

Neither request had the slightest result, everybody in the room being far too busy defending themselves from a variety of assaults, even the bartenders, who might have handed over the shotgun from beneath the counter, had deserted the sober side of the bar to help out in the general tangle.

After howling out his request again Trent realized his position and started to lean over the counter. His hands almost closed on the butt of the shotgun when a hand grabbed his coat, hauled him off and sent him sprawling back into the fight where another fist smashed into the side of his jaw and knocked him further from the bar and his weapon.

By that time Mark had almost reached the doors, being driven aside so he now stood by the side wall. A pretty red-headed girl who had lost her frock and gained what looked like it would be a glorious mouse under her left eye emerged from the centre of a knot of fighting men in which she had been tangled. She held a bottle gripped by the neck and clearly meant to use it as a club against somebody. Her eyes settled on Mark first and she rushed at him. The bottle swung up and slapped her wrist into his palm. He hooked his other arm around her waist, pulled her to him and kissed her hard. The girl's free hand clawed wildly at Mark's shoulder, let loose, then tightened again. The fingers holding the bottle relaxed, allowing it to fall unheeded to the floor. He released the girl and she staggered back, glassy-eyed, to bump into a cowhand who turned and swung a fist which knocked the girl down even before he realized who he struck at. Mark flattened the cowhand as a matter of principle. He then looked around the room to try and locate Poker Alice and Madam Moustache, but among that seething, struggling crowd, he could not locate the two women.

For their part Alice and Eleonore went at it like a pair of Kilkenny cats. They had no fighting skill and their tactics were pure woman. They pushed, shoved, slapped and kicked at each other, climbing over, dodging behind or crawling between other fighters to get at each other. A man on his knees grabbed Alice around the waist. She felt her frock ripping but before she could escape or do anything about it Eleonore jumped in and launched a kick which a *savate* fighter might have envied. Her shoe caught the man under the jaw and landed hard enough to both make him release his hold and cause him to lose interest in the proceedings. Alice showed her appreciation for the help by landing a couple of explosive slaps across Eleonore's bare shoulders, then they closed with each other again. By now they were at the far side of the room but still going at it with all they had.

Trent was raging in fury as he saw his saloon being wrecked before his eyes. His careful plan for a bit of free advertisement had gone sadly astray. Instead of a cat-fight between the two women he had a brawl which saw his fixtures being shattered and his staff damaged.

A bunch of fighting men landed on the big-stake faro table which crumpled and collapsed under them. The wheel-of-fortune rocked from its place on the wall and broke on the floor. Trent saw this happen, then through a gap in the crowd, saw Alice and Eleonore. In his fury he blamed everything that was happening upon the two women and swore they would pay for every bit of the damage they caused.

He avoided a soldier's attack and smashed a blow at the side of the man's head, felling him. With a snarl Trent thrust himself forward and headed towards the two women, swinging a fist or a kick at anyone who crossed his path and without regard for sex or position in life. Coming on to the two women who he blamed for his troubles Trent let out a bellow of rage and stamped towards them, grabbing them by the arms.

It proved to be the wrong thing to do. With screeches which sounded like a pair of she-bobcats defending their young, the two women turned on Trent. His hair was yanked out in chunks, his shins hacked by wild lashing feet. Trent's enraged bellows changed to yells of pain. He grabbed the two women around their waists and tried to crush them to him as they all staggered backwards.

A flying chair just missed Trent and the girls, which proved to be fortunate for them as it shattered the big front window at which they headed. Tight and entwined as a king snake killing a diamondback rattler, the three went into the window frame and crashed through on to the street below, landing amongst the broken glass, luckily without cutting themselves. The force of the landing winded the two girls and they rolled from the dazed Trent's arms, laying on the sidewalk.

Trent rolled to his hands and knees, shaking his head and spitting out lurid curses. A large crowd had gathered before his place to see the fun, but the marshal had not made a show of himself yet. This did not surprise Trent who knew the marshal held his post by means of his lax law enforcement rather than by zeal and vigour in the line of duty. Having heard of the fight, Trent did not doubt that the marshal would be waiting for things to cool down before arriving and trying to do anything about breaking it up.

Forcing himself to his feet Trent looked down at the two exhausted women. His never amiable temper burst in full flood upon them, blaming them for everything which happened inside his place since their arrival.

'You lousy calico cats!' he screamed, no other word could describe the sounds he made. 'I'll teach you to have my place wrecked. I'll have the pair of you in jail and working for me until you've paid back every cent of the damage that's been done!'

At that moment the other front window smashed outwards as a table sailed through it. Thinking of the cost of those big windows, Trent bellowed in rage and drew back his foot meaning to sink it into Poker Alice's unprotected ribs.

Somebody landed a punch on Mark Counter's jaw and sent the big Texan sprawling through the batwing doors. Mark never did learn who hit him, all he knew was that whoever did it packed a real good punch. It propelled Mark through the batwing doors and into the hitching rail. Catching the upright support Mark stopped himself going flying into the street. He put a hand to his jaw and winced, that *hombre* inside landed a punch like his *amigo* Dusty Fog. For a moment Mark thought of going back and trying conclusions with the man who handled such a good punch. Then he saw something which drove all such thoughts from his head.

The shattering of the first window brought his attention to it so he saw Trent and the girl make their hurried departure through the broken frame. He also saw Trent rise and heard the threats uttered.

Not until Trent started to draw back his foot and kick Alice did Mark move. But when he moved – man he moved fast.

With long strides Mark shot along the sidewalk and reached Trent even before the saloonkeeper could draw back his foot. Mark's left hand shot out and caught Trent's arm. The saloonkeeper let out a low snarl and started to turn, throwing a punch. Faster than Trent moved, Mark deflected the blow over his head and then shot out a bunched fist which carried all his weight behind it. Trent's head snapped back and he reeled into the window, performed a neat somersault back over the low edge and disappeared from sight.

Mark looked down at the girls. He guessed from the fact that the town law had not arrived to help quell the disturbance what sort of marshal he could expect. The owner of a fine, or what had been a fine, saloon would undoubtedly exert some considerable pull over such a lawman and could arrange that Alice and Madam Moustache be jailed then fix such a heavy fine on them that they would virtually be his slaves until they paid it off.

This did not meet with Mark's ideas of the fitness of things. The two women came in all good faith to deal faro for Trent and under the agreement that each of them would run his big stake game. Either woman would have fulfilled her side of the bargain and brought in a good return for her cut in the game. Only Trent would not be content with that. He wanted to use the reputations of Poker Alice and Madam Moustache to glorify his place, by setting them at each other's throats. So Mark did not see why either of them should suffer.

He bent and scooped one girl up under each arm, holding them around the waist and letting head and feet dangle.

They hung there limp and unresisting as he headed around the side of the saloon. The watching crowd gave him a warm cheer of approval but none tried to interfere with him. In that they showed prudence, for Mark was in no mood to be trifled with. Before anybody could think of following Mark and discover what he aimed to do with the two girls, a bunch of screaming, fighting women burst through the saloon doors and drew the crowd's attention to them.

Carrying his limp bundles, Mark headed for the hotel's stable. He doubted if a night's rest would cool Trent's desire for revenge and so the only thing to do would be to get the two women out of town and away from his sphere of influence.

The stable looked deserted when Mark entered. However, as he dumped his load into the straw of an empty stall Mark heard a footstep and turned to find the old-timer he spoke with earlier had come from his office at the far end.

'Now that's what I call a couple of trophies,' he cackled, throwing a glance at the two girls.

'A man'd say you called it right,' agreed Mark, then pointed to Alice. 'This the one who brought that fancy rig in?'

'That's her. What happened?'

'Trent started a tangle between her and the other gal.'

The old man spat. 'That'd be his mark all right.'

'I've got to get them both out of town,' Mark went on, seeing the man did not appear to hold the saloonkeeper in very high esteem. 'The saloon got wrecked a lil mite.'

'Sounded that way.'

'Hitch the team while I go collect my gear from the hotel.'

'Why, sure, go right ahead.'

Mark threw a glance at the girls, seeing they had recovered enough to shove themselves up on their hands while still laying flopped out in the straw. Then he left the stable and headed to the hotel while the old man started to lead out the harness horses.

Clearly the hotel staff and guests had left to see the fight at the saloon, for he could see no sign of anybody. The reception desk was deserted and Mark looked at the register, hoping to locate Madam Moustache's room. He could neither find that name, nor one which sounded even remotely French, so concluded, correctly, she must be staying at some other hotel. There would be no time to try and find it and then collect Madam's belongings, so Mark decided he must abandon them until such time as they could be safely collected.

From his own room he gathered his bedroll and Winchester and, having taken her key as well as his own, Mark went across to Poker Alice's room and entered. He found that apart from one case she had brought little or nothing with her. With all the speed he could manage Mark stuffed Alice's belongings into the case, fastened it and left the room, locking the door.

By the time he reached the stables he found the hitching of the team to be going on. He also found that Poker Alice and Madam Moustache had recovered enough to be fighting with each other again. Muffled screams, squeals and scuffling noises came from the stall and the old-timer threw a look towards it.

'Yes, sir,' he said. 'A couple of real trophies. I sure admire you all for trying to take them on the hoof.'

Mark looked at the stall where four legs, each encased in a tattered black silk stocking and showing an expanse of white flesh slashed with black suspender above them, thrashed and waved as the struggling girls rolled over and over. The old man took a look also, for either pair of legs was neat enough to attract attention. He could not take much time to admire the view, for Mark wanted to leave town as soon as possible.

'Saddle your hoss, friend,' the old-timer suggested. 'Then if I need help you can give it to me.'

This struck Mark as being the best idea, so he followed the old man's instructions. By the time he had the blood-bay saddled and bridled, he saw the old man did not need his help. Mark lashed his bedroll into place and thrust the Winchester into the saddleboot. He secured the horse's reins to the rear of the carriage and turned to the business of separating the women without getting hand-scalped in the process.

At that moment they both reared up, then dragged themselves to their feet. Although on the last verge of exhaustion they still clung to each other. During the brawl in the straw Alice had lost her skirt. Now they rose and

Eleonore's dress at last gave up the uneven struggle and peeled from her, leaving her exposed in a set of the latest fashion, very brief, black lace underwear. Even this did nothing to make them break up their fight.

Without a thought, though with a good look, at how the two women were now attired, Mark stepped forward. He used a tactic a female deputy in Quiet Town demonstrated on several occasions as being best for such a situation. Shooting out his hands he gripped each woman by the scruff of her neck, drew them apart, then brought their heads together with a thud. Alice and Eleonore went limp and he let them fall into the straw. They would not be causing him any trouble for a spell.

'I sure likes to see a chivalrous southern gent,' grinned the old-timer who had finished hitching the team and was securing Alice's bag on top of the trunk.

'And me,' grinned Mark. 'Last one I saw who tried to split apart a pair of tangling females ended up as a bald-headed chivalrous southern gent and I'm too handsome to want to be bald.'

He handed the old man a twenty-dollar gold piece and then lifted first Alice and then Eleonore into the carriage, putting them in the rear covered seat and draping them over with the rug which had been curled on the seat. Swinging up on to the driving seat, Mark took up the reins and whip. He gave the old-timer a cheery salute and sent the horses out into the night, the bloodbay following on their heels.

On leaving Culver Creek behind him Mark gave thought to getting away from possible pursuit. He knew roughly the direction in which to head for Holbrock City and could most likely follow this trail to it. But then men who Trent would send after the girls could just as easily follow the road and make better time.

With this thought in mind Mark swung the team from the trail and headed out across the range. He headed at right angles to the trail for a mile, then turned the team in the direction he wished to go. Behind him he could hear gasps as the carriage bounced over the rough ground but kept his full attention on steering the team. He wanted to put as many miles as he could between himself and Culver City before finding a camp site for the night.

Not until Culver City lay a good six miles behind them did Mark draw rein. He located a small stream and followed its banks until he found a wood in which he could hide the wagon from chance passers. For the first time he looked around at his passengers. They were hanging on to each other's neck for all the world like two sleeping babies, although Mark could never remember seeing two babies at which he would rather look. Apparently they had been so exhausted that when they recovered from his pacifying methods they must have drifted off into sleep.

Poker Alice stirred, then opened her eyes. She stared at Mark for a moment and groaned, 'Where am I?'

'Sorry I had to bounce you about, ma'am,' Mark replied. 'It was that or stay on the trail and likely wind you both up back in the Culver City jail.'

For the first time Alice seemed to notice how she was dressed, for the rug had slipped down from them. She gave a gasp, bent and dragged the covering back up over herself, although only partially over Madam Moustache who groaned and opened her eyes.

'What is happening?' she asked. 'Where – wha—'

At that moment Alice turned and stared at her rival. Recognition was mutual and instantaneous. However, Alice made no move to resume hostilities with Eleonore. Her hand dropped under the rug and to the edge of the seat. From where it lay hidden, she drew a Remington Double Derringer and lined it on Mark.

'I think you owe us an explanation,' she said coolly. 'You'll find another Derringer at the edge of your seat, Madam, if you know how to use one.'

'I never needed one to deal with a man before,' Eleonore replied, then for the first time she appeared to become aware of the scanty nature of her attire. 'My dress!' she wailed.

'You left it in the stable back at Culver City,' Mark told her, then looked at the four .41 calibre barrels which lined on him, for Eleonore also produced a Derringer and handled it in a manner which showed she, like Alice, knew which end the bullet emerged.

He explained quickly what had happened, both Trent's plan for bringing them together and his threat at the end. They listened, but neither let their gun barrels waver any.

'I see,' Alice said when Mark finished speaking and she had thought over his statements. May I ask who you are?'

'The name's Mark Counter and I'd sure admire to see those guns pointed some other place. Happen I'd felt that way earlier I could have done what I wanted afore either of you knowed what was coming off.'

'You've a point there,' Eleonore replied. 'I think we can trust you.'

'I wouldn't want to accept your judgment on anything, darling,' Alice stated. 'But this time I believe you're right.'

They both tucked the Derringers out of sight once more and Mark waved a hand to the team.

'I'll tend to the horses,' he told them. 'Then I reckon I'd best throw some wood up and start a fire. I've some airtights in my war bag, if one of you ladies can do the cooking.'

'I think an improvement in dress is called for,' Alice remarked.

The words brought a wail from Eleonore. 'My clothes! I haven't anything here to put on.'

'That's deucedly awkward,' purred Alice. 'I took the precaution of leaving my trunk on my carriage. And our gallant rescuer appears to have brought my bag from the hotel too.'

'Sure,' Mark agreed, then looked at Eleonore. 'I'd've brought your gear, but I couldn't find if you had a room at the hotel.'

'I didn't. I was staying at the other hotel. I always leave my bag at the stage depot for the first two days, with word that if I have to leave town in a hurry they are to send it on to some other place.'

'Do you often have to leave town in a hurry?' Alice asked.

'Not often. I am a square gambler, as I have always heard you are,' Eleonore answered in an angry voice. 'But you know how the goody-goodies and do-gooders are in some towns. "A woman gambler? Tut, tut! How terrible. We can't have her besmirching the morals of our fair city." You know what I mean.'

Alice started to laugh. Whatever else she might be Eleonore could certainly make her voice sound just like a small town do-gooder denouncing the evils of a woman gambler, or any other kind of sin.

'I know,' she agreed. 'A few weeks ago I used to have a maid, but she married a cowhand. I've two of her uniforms at the bottom of my trunk. At least they'll serve until you can collect your belongings from wherever you sent them – if you can get into them, you are somewhat fatter than the girl.'

'FATTER!' squealed Eleonore, raising her fists and then bursting into a string of French Creole curses.

'Now hold it, girls!' Mark put in before either could make a move to resume physical hostilities. 'Was I you I'd leave off the hair-yanking until you get out of that carriage. Happen the team spooks and run, you'll be in bad...'

His words calmed the girls down enough to stop an immediate attack. Eleonore looked at Alice and saw the twinkle in the English girl's eyes. Her own volatile nature warmed immediately and she burst into a merry laugh.

'I've always found men prefer a woman with something they can get their hands on,' she stated. 'Of course you can't help being skinny. I suppose you never win enough gambling to afford a decent meal.'

'*Touché!*' smiled Alice.

'I'll make a fire,' Mark drawled. 'You can get into something warmer while I'm gathering the wood.'

When he returned from searching amongst the trees for dry wood Mark found Alice wearing a long housecoat while Eleonore had the carriage rug wrapped around her and looked in danger of losing it at any moment. Alice clearly thought an explanation for the lack of clothes to be in order, for she turned to Mark as he started to light the fire.

'We couldn't see to unpack the trunk, so we're doing the best we can.'

With the fire lit Mark went to take care of the horses. The two women came to lend a hand, but after she had lost the blanket twice Eleonore decided she would do better to attend to building the fire up. She left Mark and Alice to unhitch and hobble the team horses and raised a comforting blaze. Then while Alice opened her trunk, Mark cared for his big stallion, removing its saddle and bridle and letting it free to graze, knowing it would not stray far.

'It's no good,' Alice remarked. 'I've got my bedroll out, but I can't find our clothes. I suggest we turn in after a cup of coffee and I'll find the dresses in the morning.'

Clearly Alice had camped out at nights before, for she carried a coffeepot, skillet and the necessities of life in two sacks in her trunk, along with a western style bedroll.

For the first time, when they all gathered about the fire to drink the coffee, Mark found a chance of looking the girls over. Their hair looked tangled and untidy and their faces and shoulders were dirty, bruised, yet neither showed too much sign of the fight. Possibly Eleonore would have a black eye in the morning but nothing more, for the fight had been more hair yanking, slapping and pushing than fist swinging.

'I hope I don't look as big a mess as you do,' Alice remarked to Eleonore, reading Mark's thoughts from his glance.

'It is nothing that water and a comb will not cure,' Eleonore replied.

'Where are you ladies going to sleep?' Mark asked.

'I'll bed down under the carriage as I usually do,' Alice replied. 'Madam here can sleep on the back seat if we loan her some of our bedding.'

So it was arranged, Mark settled down after he had seen the two women rolled in the blankets. Time passed and the fire died down. A soft footfall woke Mark and he looked up to find Eleonore standing by his bed, the rug draped scantily about her.

'I couldn't sleep, Mark,' she said and sat down beside him.

'Thought you would be able to after that shindig back at the saloon,' he replied with a grin.

Throwing a glance at where Alice's shape could be seen under the carriage Eleonore gave a laugh.

'That is a tough girl, my Mark,' she sighed. 'What a brawl.'

'Sure was, Madam.'

She nestled closer to him and he felt that the rug had slipped from her body. Under the lace her body was warm and inviting.

'Don't call me Madam,' she said. 'I am Eleonore Dumont. Would you like to hear how I came by the Madam Moustache name?'

'Why sure.'

'It is chilly, can't we make ourselves more comfortable as we talk?'

'Anything you say,' Mark replied.

They stretched out side by side and he drew the blankets and suggans over them, then slipped an arm under her neck while her arms entwined with his.

Eleonore Dumont had been born to a middle class French Creole family but grew with the wanderlust in her feet. She left home to travel with a small show which presented plays like East Lynne to such backwood villages as they came across in their travels. One member of the show had been a retired Mississippi riverboat gambler and he taught the girl all he knew about the mysteries of gambling. She proved to be a willing learner and when the show finally broke up, as such shows always did, Eleonore found herself stranded in Wichita. There were few things a young woman might do to earn a living in the west, but none of them appealed to Eleonore. At last she decided to put her gambling knowledge to a test. Here she ran into her first snag. The saloons allowed women inside only as employees and a few gambling houses allowed women at all, none allowed them in the capacity of player.

In desperation Eleonore borrowed a man's suit from the belongings of the disbanded company of actors, also a false moustache. In this she entered Bailey's gambling house. Her luck stood fair and she brought her twenty dollar stake to two hundred on the faro layout, then joined a poker game. Once more the gods of chance smiled on their daughter and she cleaned out the players, winning over two thousand dollars. All this was possible only because Bailey did not believe in wasting money and had few lights except those fixed to illuminate the playing surface of his tables. In fact Eleonore might have taken her winnings and escaped undetected had not a sneeze blown her moustache on to the table.

At first Bailey had been furious when he found a woman not only entered his place but cleaned out a table. However, he saw the humorous side of it. He also saw the attraction Eleonore would offer to him. She started work two nights later, as a dealer at the faro layout. The story of how she came to get the job passed around and men crowded into see Madame Moustache, the lady gambler. From that day, five years before, Eleonore had never looked back. She travelled considerably and as Madame Moustache became well known.

That then was the story of Madam Moustache – but Mark

Counter did not hear it until the following day. After all the night was passing and it seemed foolish to waste time in talking.

At dawn Alice awoke to find Eleonore and Mark already up and about. Eleonore had already gathered wood and started a fire and now brewed coffee over it while Mark gathered in the horses

'Good morning,' Alice greeted. 'Sorry I over-slept.'

'A woman of your age needs her beauty sleep, darling,' replied Eleonore.

'Look,' sighed Alice. 'Let's call the whole thing off, shall we. I hate to have to start making catty answers before breakfast.'

She unpacked her travelling clothes and the older of her maid's costumes after they had eaten the food Eleonore cooked up. Handing the outfit to the dark-haired girl Alice suggested they went to the river, washed and changed.

Half an hour passed and the two women returned the maid's clothes fitted Eleonore a trifle loosely and she frowned in a threatening manner at Mark who looked her over with a grin.

'Don't you dare say anything, my Mark!' she warned.

'All right. Where do you gals aim to go now?'

'Where are you going?' Alice asked.

'Holbrock. It's a fair sized town up north of here.'

'That will do me, how about you, Madam?'

'I'll go along, we can chaperone each other,' Eleonore answered. 'I can telegraph Culver City and have them send my bags along.'

With their destination decided Mark helped the two women to prepare for the journey. They kept on the range until noon, then swung back towards where Mark guessed the stage route to be. It said much for his plainsman's instinct that they found the trail, nothing more than the well worn ruts left by stages, horses and wagons travelling northwards to Holbrock.

They spent the night on the shores of a small lake. The proprieties were observed by them all. The girls bathed in the lake while Mark hunted for and shot a couple of cottontails for food, then they buried themselves in preparing a meal and let him have a swim. The proprieties were observed later too, for Eleonore went to bed on the seat of the carriage and most certainly was back there when Alice awoke the following morning.

Rather than push their horses too hard they spent a third night out on the range within four miles of Holbrock. They had supper and went to their respective beds as usual.

Mark heard the stealthy footsteps and felt the warm body wriggle alongside him and rolled over.

'Did I tell you how I became known as Poker Alice?'

The voice sounded just as cool, calm and collected as ever. It also came as quite a surprise to Mark, who had been expecting Eleonore. He could almost swear he heard a low chuckle from the carriage.

'Why'd it take you so long to decide to tell me?' he asked.

'My dear chap, one should never rush into – er, telling one's life story.' Alice replied, slipping her hands around him and bringing her lips towards his face.

It appeared that Poker Alice had been born the only child to an eccentric younger son of a noble English house and that her mother died when she was just over a year old. Her father had been what she described as a bit of a masher, one of the men-about-town. Yet in his way he loved and cared for her and she grew up in an atmosphere of hunting, fishing, shooting as practised in England. She could ride a horse or handle a team and could use a shotgun very well. From one of her father's cronies, an earl whose family had lost its money in speculation which failed, she learned the secrets and arts of gambling.

On her father's death, riding to hounds (to disprove a doctor's theory that to do so with four broken ribs would prove dangerous), Alice took what she thought would be a trip around the world. In the United States she became fascinated with the gambling houses and with her calm assurance invaded the sacred domain of the male. Hoping to teach her a sharp lesson a group of poker players allowed her to sit in on their game. They taught her all right, to the tune of several thousand dollars of their money.

That night saw the birth of Poker Alice. She accepted the name they gave her and moved on. Seven years had passed and Alice's name was known over the west. Unlike Eleonore she rarely took the dealer's chair at a saloon faro layout, preferring to run her own poker game. She accepted

Trent's offer to come to Culver Creek more to see a new section of country than because she wished to work for the man, meaning only to stay on for a couple of weeks, then if the town looked like it could accommodate it, start her own game. Her stay had been shorter than she expected.

However, Mark did not hear her story that night. What he did learn was that beyond the cool, calm and regally carried exterior Alice was all woman and did not come second even to the warm, volatile and vibrant Eleonore.

All in all Mark would not have minded if the journey to Holbrock took another couple of days instead of finishing the following morning.

The carriage horses stepped out in a lively manner as if they knew they would be in a stall and getting grain fed when they reached the town. Mark rode his bloodbay alongside and listened to the story of Poker Alice's life, while Eleonore, with memories of telling her own life story still fresh in her memory, grinned broadly and winked at Mark.

Alice used the rest of the time until they came into sight of Holbrock to tell her life story. She stopped talking as the horses topped the last ridge and they saw the town at the foot of the slope.

From the look of things the town had grown considerably since the time, almost four years back. Dusty Fog and the Ysabel Kid paid it a brief but hectic visit.* Brenton Hunboldt's meat packing plant stood at the far side of the town, large and busy looking. The main street now looked more imposing and behind it ran other smaller streets leading to the houses of the workers at the plant and the subsidiary industries of the town.

On the side towards which Mark and his party now headed lay the homes of the richer members of the community, the influential citizens who controlled and ran the town. Showpiece of them all was Humboldt's house, a big, fine looking building of white stone and considerable elegance, with a large well cared for flower garden and lawns before it, a high iron railing fence around it, and a set of open wrought iron gates from which a gravel path swept in a curve to before the main entrance to the house.

Mark felt a little sad as he saw the gates ahead of him,

* Told in *The Half-Breed*.

soon he would be leaving the two girls to take on the boring task of being an honoured guest at the wedding of two people he had never met and did not know. The two women would carry on into town, put up at the best hotel and make their plans for the future, most likely he would not see them again. Neither woman would be likely to open her game in town and probably did not intend to stay on any longer than it took to book a ride on the stage, or rest the carriage team. He grinned as he wondered what Humboldt would say if he rolled up and introduced Poker Alice and Madam Moustache as his friends. It might be amusing to see Humboldt's dilemma as he tried to get rid of the girls without offending Ole Devil Hardin's representative. Only the fact that such an action might embarrass the girls prevented Mark from carrying out his idea.

For their first arrival into Holbrock, Eleonore had made her long hair up in a bun and hidden it under a maid's cap. The dress she wore, especially when she sat on the driving box by Alice, hid and effectively disguised her figure so she looked little or nothing like the vivacious and beautiful Madam Moustache. Alice, in her severe travelling clothes and with her hair taken back tightly under a hat, did not look like the coolly beautiful woman who dealt cards in high stake poker games.

Being aware of the vindictive nature of Trent's kind they quite expected him to pull strings and have a warrant out for the arrest of Alice and Eleonore, then cause their return to Culver Creek where he might force them to pay for the damage his greed brought to his saloon. So the two women decided to adopt the simple disguise on their arrival in Holbrock and to see how the land lay before making a move.

Suddenly Eleonore drew her breath in with a hiss as she stared at two riders who turned from a side street ahead of them, glanced their way and started to ride along the street towards the town centre. Mark studied the men and wondered what attracted Eleonore's attention to the men. To his eyes they, although wearing cowhand clothes, spelled hard-cases. They did not sit their horses or show that undefinable something which identified one cowhand to another. From the look of their low-hanging guns they were no more than a couple of toughs who would hire out fighting skill to the highest bidder. Yet Mark could almost swear he had seen some kind of a law badge on one's vest. Of course, their kind did find employment as deputies under a certain type of town marshal or county sheriff and Mark did not know what sort of law Holbrock might have.

'Those men!' Eleonore said, speaking quickly, but quietly. 'The one on the right worked for Trent. I saw them together on the day I arrived and learned the man was a hired tough, supposedly a deputy, but really on Trent's payroll.'

'You sure of that?' Mark asked, seeing the men talking together and taking surreptitious glances towards his party.

'Of course. I arrived in Culver Creek two days early, so as to look around and try to learn what sort of a place Trent ran. I saw that man and I rarely forget a face.'

Mark could guess what the men were doing. They had seen him and noted the two women. In a moment they would ride back to start asking questions. So far they were not close enough to recognize either woman and make-up concealed such marks of the fight as remained. Possibly the two men did not believe Poker Alice and Madam Moustache would be riding side by side in a carriage and on amiable terms, but they might turn and come up to check.

'In there!' Mark snapped, indicating the gates leading to Humboldt's home.

To give her credit Alice reacted fast. She swung the head of her team towards the gates and Mark followed. He threw a glance towards the two men, seeing they had started to bring their horses around towards him. Mark followed the carriage and caught up alongside as it approached the front of the house.

Just as Alice halted her carriage before the imposing main entrance, the doors were flung open and Brenton Humboldt emerged in something of a hurry. He came to a halt at the sight of his visitors and a frown puckered his brow, for he did not know any of them.

'Mr. Humboldt?' Mark asked, although the big, pompous looking man in the expensive broadcloth suit fitted Dusty's description so well that he could be none other than Mr. Brenton Humboldt himself.

'That's correct.'

Even as he made his reply Humboldt studied the party at

his doors with some interest. He noted the team horses and the stylish, though trail-marked, carriage, both of which cost good money. Then he looked up at Alice. In some way she contrived to look far different from Poker Alice, yet still retained her air of refinement and gentility. Humboldt noted her expensive, though travel-stained clothes of impeccable good taste and her calm, dignified demeanour. He glanced at the obvious lady's maid seated by Alice, then finally studied Mark.

'I'm Mark Counter, from the OD Connected,' Mark introduced. 'Dusty couldn't get here, or the Kid, so I came.'

A delighted beam crossed Humboldt's face, along with a flickering expression of relief, although Mark could not be sure whether this be caused by his arrival or the fact that the Ysabel Kid would not be on hand for the wedding.

Humboldt stepped forward with his hand extended. 'Pleased to see you, Mr. Counter, or may I call you Mark? We were despairing of seeing anybody from the OD Connected, the wedding is tomorrow at eleven. Get down. I'll have one of the servants take care of your horse.'

'I've got to take Lady Alice along to the hotel first,' Mark answered. 'She's travelling alone, except for her maid and I said I'd see her safe.'

'*Lady Alice?*'

'Why sure. This is Lady Alice Hatton-Green. I met them out on the range this morning.'

'I'm out here with pater,' Alice put in, guessing what Mark had in mind and going along with it. 'He's up-country on a big game hunt, but I decided I would come along and see one of your western towns.'

'Pater?' asked the puzzled Humboldt.

'My father, Lord Hatton-Green. I suppose there is a hotel in town?'

'Well, yes, there is,' agreed Humboldt. 'But I'm sure we could put your Ladyship up here for a few days.'

'I wouldn't wish to put you to any trouble,' Alice replied and lifted her hands to start the team forward.

She hoped that Mark knew what he was doing, for the two men sat their horses across the street and in front of the gate, ready to halt the carriage and ask all kinds of inconvenient questions.

Mark knew Humboldt to be a snob of the first water and

gambled on the man's willingness to be able to introduce a member of European nobility as a house guest when his friends came to his daughter's wedding. Mark knew Humboldt would never allow Poker Alice and Madam Moustache to enter his house, even to save them from trouble which was not of their making, so the big Texan used a trick. The lie had some slight truth in it. Alice did come from a noble British house but she could not claim to have Lady prefixed to her name.

'It will be no trouble,' Humboldt put in hurriedly, reacting just as Mark guessed he would.

'I couldn't really accept your hospitality,' Alice said and felt Eleonore dig a warning elbow into her ribs. However, Alice knew how to handle men of Brenton Humboldt's type and knew the more reluctant 'Lady Alice Hatton-Green' appeared to be, the more eager would be his efforts to persuade her to stay.

'But I insist. My wife would never forgive me if I let a Lad—you stay at the hotel. You must stay with us, we feel it is our duty to the good name of Texas to offer you our hospitality. Tell your maid to take your hand luggage to your room and I'll have your team attended to and your trunk brought up.'

'Very well, thank you for the offer,' Alice replied, giving in gracefully as if conferring a favour upon him. She looked towards Eleonore, 'Fifi, bring the bag.'

A hint of the red flush of annoyance crept to Eleonore's cheeks. Then she glanced at the gate and the two watching men. This was no time to object to a change of names.

'*Oui, oui,* your lady-*sheep*!' she answered, laying great emphasis on the last word although Humboldt thought it no more than a delightful French pronunciation.

Gallantly Humboldt helped Alice to alight from her carriage. He then turned and told the negro footman, who stood at the door watching everything with some pop-eyed amazement, to inform Mrs. Humboldt they had guests.

In the hall Mark and the girls watched with amusement as a rather annoyed-looking Mrs. Humboldt appeared from a room along the large hall which faced the main entrance. Humboldt bore down on her, leaving his guests, and began to whisper urgently. They could see the change in Mrs. Humboldt's attitude when she heard one of her guests was a

Lady and the other the son of a very rich Texas rancher and a trusted member of the OD Connected ranch crew. This latter meant much less to Mrs. Humboldt than the fact that she had a chance to introduce a real British Lady to her friends.

Mrs. Humboldt bore down on the party. 'James will show you to your room, Mr. Counter,' she said. 'And I will escort you, if I may, your ladyship. But I'm afraid that with the wedding tomorrow and everything we have no room to accommodate your maid. Perhaps she could stay at one of the hotels in town?'

'Hum!' Alice answered, seeing a chance to have some fun at Eleonore's expense. 'I think not. I lost my last maid by letting her go out, she ran away with a cowhand.'

'It's so difficult to get loyalty from the lower classes these days, isn't it?' agreed Mrs. Humboldt, throwing a glance at Eleonore who had to make an effort to stop landing her hostess a lusty kick in the bustle.

'Practically impossible,' said Alice. 'But I'll let Fifi stay in my room. Don't go to any trouble, just a few blankets will do and she can sleep on the floor. She's used to roughing it.'

Only with an even greater effort did Eleonore restrain herself from planting a kick firmly on Alice's rear at the words. For the past few days she had tried to explain to Mark and Alice how she loved her creature comforts. Sleeping on a hard wooden floor did not come under the heading of creature comfort where she was concerned. However, through the still open front doors, she could see the two men sitting their horses and so kept a grip on Alice's bag and promised herself revenge at a later and more convenient date.

Not until alone with Alice in her room did Eleonore give vent to her feelings.

'Fifi!' she gasped. 'She will be happy to sleep on the floor. I ought to—!'

'My good girl, that's no way for a maid to address her mistress,' said Alice, trying hard to keep a straight face.

'Why you—!'

Not even Alice's years of gambling training could help her now and she began to smile, then laugh. For a moment Eleonore glared at Alice and contemplated all kinds of violence, then she, too, saw the funny side of things and also began to laugh.

'We're safe in here,' Alice remarked. 'That pair of hard-cases are still out front, but they'll hear that Lady Alice Hatton-Green— I wonder where Mark dug that name up from, is a guest of Brenton Humboldt. They might be suspicious, but nobody in Holbrock's going to ask their leading citizen questions about his guest.'

'They might, thinking to gain his approval by exposing us.'

'Not if they know Humboldt. He'd rather have us stay here as Lady Alice and her maid than have it known he couldn't tell a real member of the aristocracy from a notorious gambling woman.'

Thinking on it Eleonore agreed with Alice's judgment of Humboldt's character. One thing was certain. Humboldt would not thank the man who showed him up as a fool.

At that moment a knock came at the door and Eleonore opened it and proceeded to give her impression of how a French maid should act. Luckily the men gained their ideas of French maids from the same source as Eleonore, the theatre, so they expected her saucy winks and behaviour.

'Breeng eet een here, *mon cherie*,' she said to the burly man in the lead. 'And be ver' careful or ze Lady Alice weel be mo' angry wiz me.'

With that she ushered the two men into the room, chattering in the most atrocious broken English Alice could ever remember hearing as she had the trunk set down just where her mistress would like it.

After the men left, Alice turned to Eleonore and grinned broadly. 'Where did you pick up that accent?' she asked.

'My mother was French,' Eleonore answered, also grinning. 'Don't you think I'd make a good maid?'

'To be frank, no.'

'Or me. Look, I'd like to go into town and send a telegraph message to the Wells Fargo agent in Culver City and have him ship my trunk to me.'

Alice frowned. 'That could be risky if Trent is still looking for us. But I suppose you'll do it anyhow. It might not be safe for you to go alone though. I'll ask Mark to walk in with you.'

Mark agreed to escort Eleonore into town and a few

moments later walked down the main stairs to the hall with the girl at his side. Eleonore seemed determined to keep up her part as the French maid and carried on a chattering conversation in the same atrocious accent. She had cleared all traces of make-up from her face, except just enough to hide the traces of her black eye and, with her hair tucked up under the maid's cap would have been all but unrecognizable as the famous Madam Moustache.

Just as they reached the bottom of the stairs, the sturdy door opened and Humboldt stepped out. He beamed at Mark, the kind of look he reserved for important and influential people.

'Mark!' he boomed. 'Come on in and meet my future son-in-law.'

'Sure,' Mark replied. 'Wait here, Fifi.' At the door he jerked his head towards the girl. 'Lady Alice asked me to take her maid into town to do some shopping. So I said I would.'

'I'll arrange for the buggy to be brought around for you, if you wish.'

'Thanks,' Mark replied sincerely, for he was a cowhand and never walked if he could avoid doing so.

'Come in then,' said Humboldt and beckoned to his footman to give the orders. 'I trust Lady Alice is comfortable.'

'Why sure. She'll likely be down soon.'

In the study Mark met Iris Humboldt and her fiancé. The girl stood about as tall as Eleonore and had much the same build, although not the same beautiful features, or slimming down at the waist. She looked pleasant enough, not too bright, although well educated. This showed in the short conversation Mark had with her and Gavin Stout, her fiancé. Maybe she was not bright, but she must have had something, for Stout looked like a good catch. He stood six foot tall, with good shoulders and tapering to a slim waist. His head and eyebrows were blond, while his face looked to have been shaven only a few minutes before and sported neither moustache nor side whiskers although these were fashionable back east. His clothes fitted him well and followed the latest eastern trend. His hand, when Mark took it, felt soft as if it had never done any work.

'Pleased to meet you, Mark,' he said, giving the big Texan a searching glance.

'Have you been out west for long?' Mark asked, making conversation.

'This's my first trip,' Stout replied, slipping an arm around Iris and squeezing her gently. 'But we aim to make our home out here, don't we, darling?'

They talked on for a few moments. Stout had a ringing voice with a strong upper-class eastern accent and he seemed friendly enough. He started to tell Mark about the honeymoon trip they planned after the wedding, but the destination of which they meant to keep a secret.

'No sense in having everybody know where to find us, is there?' he chuckled.

At that moment he glanced through the door and saw Eleonore standing in the hall. Filled with female curiosity she had stepped into view to see what kind of a man met with Mrs. Humboldt's approval enough to be allowed to marry her daughter. She stood for a moment, looking hard at Stout.

A frown creased Stout's brow and an expression of fear almost flickered on his handsome face for a moment.

'I didn't know you had a new maid, darling,' he said to Iris.

'We don't?'

'Then who—?'

'That's Lady Alice's maid,' Mark put in.

He did not fail to notice the expression of relief flicker across the man's face, any more than he failed to see the fear which showed for a brief instant when Stout first saw Eleonore.

Before any more could be said, Humboldt returned with news that the buggy waited outside. Mark nodded to Stout and the girl, then left the room. Stout watched Eleonore pass out of sight, then turned back to talk with his fiancé once more.

Neither Mark nor Eleonore spoke as they left the grounds of Humboldt's residence. The two hard-cases were not in sight and nothing out of the way happened as they drove along the rutted road making for the main business area of the town, towards the Wells Fargo office and the jail.

'Who was the handsome man you talked with?' she asked.

'Me,' Mark modestly replied.

'I meant the other one.'

'That's the bridegroom-to-be,' grinned Mark. 'You handed him a shock coming out like that.'

'His voice gave me one. I thought I should know it. In fact I'm sure I ought to know that man, but I can't place him.'

Mark thought of that. He did not know why Stout should looked surprised, almost scared at seeing Eleonore. His thoughts on the subject were broken by Eleonore's hide searing comments on a friend who used trickery to make her sleep on the floor while the friend had a large and comfortable bed. The tirade lasted until they passed the Long Glass saloon.

'Say,' Mark drawled. 'You sure make a real fetching maid, though.'

'Alice thinks so. With her "fetch me this" and "fetch me that",' groaned Eleonore. 'Oooh! Why didn't you say I was an eccentric lady who liked to have her maid dressed up. Then I would have shown Alice a few things.'

They were approaching the Wells Fargo office and Mark remembered something. 'Say, if you need any money I can manage a stake until things go better for you.'

'I have enough for my needs, thank you, *mon ami*,' she replied. 'I didn't lose everything at Culver Creek.'

'But how did you carry it?' Mark asked, thinking back to the first night out of Culver Creek, when she came to tell him her life story.

'Zat is my beesiness, *m'sieur*,' Eleonore answered with a saucy grin and a wink, reverting to her assumed French accent for the benefit of the loafers who stood before the office.

'And real nice business, too,' Mark replied, jumping from his seat to help her down. 'I'll collect you after I've seen the town marshal – Fifi.'

She smiled, curtsied and entered the office. Mark climbed back into the buggy and drove along the street to halt before the marshal's office. He left his buggy at the hitching rack and walked into the office. One look at the man behind the desk told Mark which of his stories he could tell. The man wore a town suit, just good enough in quality for him to be honest and even if Mark had not recognized him, he would have told the truth of the happenings in Culver Creek. He knew George Abbot well enough to expect a fair hearing and understanding of why he brought the two girls out of Trent's reach.

'Howdy, George,' Mark said.

The old-timer's leathery face creased in a broad grin. 'Howdy, Mark.'

'Never thought to see you in a town like this.'

In the old days George Abbott ran the law in bad, wide open towns. Before the war and for a couple of years after it, his name went out far as a straight and brave lawman. However, his age began to tell and he gave up handling the wild ones to look for safer employment. He drifted to Holbrock and took on the badge, finding a growing town which but rarely saw the wild horse-play of cowhands.

'Shucks, it's a living,' George went on after explaining his reasons for ending in Holbrock. 'Better'n getting shot down by a wild bunch of wild yahoos on a spree. What brings you here, you ain't just come along to see poor famous old George Abbott, now have you?'

Before Mark could reply the office door burst open and the two hard-cases came to a halt, the one with the deputy's badge pointing to Mark.

'That's him!' he yelled.

'Who, Brown?' asked Abbott calmly, though his eyes took on a frosty glint at the intrusion.

'The big jasper who come in with those two gals.'

Mark swung to face the two men, not liking the look of either. He heard the marshal's chair scrape back and guessed Abbott had stood up ready to take cards. The marshal came around the side of his desk and halted by Mark.

'Where'd you come from, Mark?' he asked.

'The OD Connected,' replied Mark, which was true – as far as it went.

'That'd mean you was a hell of a way off your line, happen you went to Culver Creek.'

'I tell you he was with two women!' Brown, the deputy snapped.

'Knowing Mark here, that don't surprise me,' drawled Abbott. 'Who are they, boy?'

'Guests up at Humboldt's place. An English lady and her maid,' Mark replied, which again, as far as it went, was the truth.

From the suspicious gleam in Brown's eyes he did not entirely believe Mark's story. He threw a glance at Abbott and waited for the marshal to make some reply to the big Texan's words.

'Look,' Brown finally growled, when Abbott made no comment. 'A big cowhand, fitting this jasper's description, and those two gals bust up the boss – Trent's place in Culver Creek and I—'

'Thought in the fust place you said the gals took to fighting over who was to boss the big table,' Abbott interrupted. 'Don't sound likely that they'd be riding into town all friendly and sat on a wagon together, or however they come in.'

Brown scowled. 'Yeah, well the boss wants them gals finding and send—'

'Your boss don't run this town, office, or me!' Abbott barked.

'I'll soon get the truth out of him!' Brown snarled.

He took a step towards Mark, coming in his most threatening manner and dropping his hand towards his hip. Mark did not bother to clench his fist. He swung his right hand around in a flat-palm slap which caught Brown across the cheek and sprawled him clear across the office. Brown's pard gave an angry grunt and dropped his hand, then froze, for Mark's left hand dipped even as he slapped the deputy down. The long barrelled Army Colt came clear of leather and lined on the man, ending any moves he might be planning.

'All right,' Mark said quietly, yet in a voice the other man would never forget. 'I'm saying this just once, so both of you listen good to me. I came up here from the OD Connected and I didn't start any saloon brawl. If I see either of you in town comes nightfall I'll spit in your faces. You hear me?'

'I hear you,' replied the second man, for Brown lay on the floor wondering what hit him.

'Then get your pard on his feet and out of here,' Mark ordered.

The man helped Brown to his feet and steered him from the door. Abbott followed them out on to the sidewalk and spoke words of wisdom.

'You saddle up and ride. I'm not having you getting killed

in my town and that would sure happen should you go up against Mark Counter in a fair fight. And, just happen you're fool enough to reckon on taking him any other way, me and his pappy were old pards, so I'll be standing 'side of him. And even if I weren't I sure wouldn't want to be the man who bushwhacked Mark Counter when Dusty Fog and the Ysabel Kid caught up with them. You go tell your boss there's no sign of the folks he wants here.'

He stood and watched the men. In his time as a lawman Abbott learned much about handling hard-cases. He knew how they looked when they aimed to yell 'calf-rope' before a better man. Brown and the other would not be staying on to trouble Mark, or Abbott would be surprised. He watched them slouch away and knew they would be out of Holbrock long before nightfall.

'Who are those pair at Humboldt's?' Abbott asked, when he returned to his office.

'Poker Alice and Madam Moustache.'

'And Humboldt took them in?'

'He reckons they're Lady Alice Hatton-Green and her maid. Tell you one thing though, I called in at Culver Creek. That's where I met them.'

'Did, huh?'

'Sure. I'll tell you how it all happened.'

At the end of Mark's story, Abbott gave a low grunt. His expressed views on Trent as man and saloonkeeper came pungent and obscene. Nor did he for a minute doubt but that Mark told the full truth of what happened. He agreed that the two women were in no way to blame for what happened. Trent brought them together for the resulting fight and should have no cause to complain. Abbott chuckled immoderately as he heard how come the girls were now house guests at the Humboldt place.

'If he knew he'd throw a whingding,' the marshal stated. 'I'm looking forward to meeting Poker Alice at that fancy dinner tonight. Sure, I'm invited.' He paused, studying Mark. 'You seen the future son-in-law yet?'

'Why sure.'

'What do you reckon to him?'

'I only saw him for a few minutes,' Mark answered in a non-committal tone.

'Know what you mean. Why'd a handsome cuss like him,

with money of his own, way he flashes it about, take a plain gal like young Iris?'

'They allow beauty's only skin deep,' grinned Mark.

'Sure, especially when it's got a ten thousand dollar dowry skin and maybe another ten thousand in jewellery to go along.'

Mark let out a whistle of surprise. 'As much as that?'

'Yep. Give old Brenton credit, he sure dotes on that gal of his'n. She gets it all to make a start with. Taking most of it along with 'em on their honeymoon.'

'You got a suspicious mind,' grinned Mark.

'That's what keeps me alive,' Abbott replied. 'Whyn't you take a walk. I've got some important work to do.'

'Sure, I'll pick Lady Alice's maid up from the Wells Fargo office. See you tonight – and don't snore too loud, the tax payers might hear you.'

Leaving Abbott spluttering and trying to make an adequate reply, Mark stepped from the office and decided to walk along to the front of the Wells Fargo building as the local stage had just come into sight and the usual sort of crowd gathered to see it arrive. He could see no sign of Eleonore and this surprised him, for he expected her to be waiting for him.

The coach came to a rocking halt before the stage office and Mark strolled down the sidewalk towards the rear of the crowd. He saw a drummer leap down and hold open the door in a manner which showed, by his gallantry, that ladies of some kind must be aboard. He offered his hand to assist a flashily dressed blonde woman from the coach and an equally flashily dressed young redhead came to the open door standing waiting to be helped down. Her eyes went around the crowd with some interest, starting on the side away from where Mark stood.

A man turned hurriedly at the rear of the crowd and bumped full into Mark as he started to walk away. With a muttered apology the man stepped around Mark and strode off along the street at a good speed. Mark turned to watch him go, for as they came together he had felt the hard shape of a short-barrelled revolver under his coat.

Normally a man *not* carrying a gun would be an object of interest in Texas. For a man to carry one, even concealed under his coat, was completely ordinary – except that the man who bumped into Mark wore a black suit, round topped black hat, a black stock and white reversed collar. In fact the man who bumped into Mark wore the street clothes of a preacher belonging to a certain religious sect and Mark had never seen one who went armed about his work.

After watching the remarkable sight of a armed preacher swing away out of sight between two buildings, Mark turned once more to try and see Eleonore. He saw nothing of her, only the two new arrivals, clearly saloongirls in town to start working, headed along the sidewalk away from him. With the departure of the girls, the crowd broke up and went about their business, but still with no sign of Eleonore. Mark headed for the office, meaning to ask if the girl had left for he thought Brown and his pard might have seen her and taken a chance to grab her for return to Culver Creek.

Just as he reached the door of the office, Mark saw Eleonore come around the corner in a furtive manner, peering towards him first, then back to the chattering, laughing saloongirls and their escort who passed along behind her.

'Whew!' gasped Eleonore, coming to Mark. 'That was a close one.'

'How do you mean?'

'First I come out of the office and almost walk into the Parson, I turn, take cover until I think he has gone away. Then come out and almost run into Ginger Lil. So I have to get back out of sight again quickly.'

'They know you, huh?'

'Sure they know me. I caught the Parson trying to doctor a deck in a poker game and he was bounced around a little by the house muscle. So he sent his girl friend, Ginger Lil, after me and we tangled. My Mark, I don't think she has forgotten Madam Moustache yet, although her injuries have healed.'

'Say, that Parson *hombre* wouldn't stand about five foot nine, have a thin, sharp face that looks like he's been drinking alkaline water for the first time?' asked Mark.

'He does.'

'And he's real friendly with the red headed gal?'

'I did hear they quarrelled and split up,' Eleonore answered. 'He left her behind while she was recovering from the fight I had with her.'

'That figgers. He took off like the devil after a yearling

when he saw her come off the stage. You'd best tell me some about the Parson.'

'I don't know too much. He travels the circuit working various confidence tricks, posing as a parson most of the time. I don't know why he is here.'

Apart from deciding to warn Abbott of the man's presence in town Mark did nothing about the Parson. He took Eleonore back to the Humboldt house and left her while he went to make his preparations for the evening dinner and social gathering.

Later that evening the town and county's most influential people gathered at Humboldt's to be introduced to the guests of honour, Mark Counter and Lady Alice. It gave Mark much innocent amusement to watch the way Alice carried herself amongst the guests and he knew none of them doubted her or imagined her to be other than Lady Alice Hatton-Green. Much to Mark's surprise, Eleonore made her appearance clad in the best maid's dress, with a neat starched white hat and apron, tripping around the room, helping out Humboldt's over-worked staff and never putting a foot wrong, although her French-English accent did sound just a little too broad.

Mark saw that Gavin Stout paid a lot of attention to the girl when she made her first appearance, then seemed to decide she was harmless and joined the group of men who surrounded Lady Alice.

'Would you care for ze ponch, m'sieur?' asked Eleonore, carrying a small tray to where Mark stood by the door. She dropped her voice and a merry twinkle came to her eyes. 'Old Ma Humboldt doesn't cotton to her future son-in-law getting friendly with Alice.'

Mark glanced across the room to where Mrs. Humbolt entertained some of her friends. The woman kept throwing looks to where Alice held court and her fan flicked in angry jerks as she watched Stout laughing at something Alice said. To one side of the room Iris also stood watching, pouting a little as she saw her fiancé behaving in a manner he never used when in her presence.

Taking a glass of punch from Eleonore's tray. Mark strolled across the room to where he saw Abbott entering the room. He meant to warn the marshal about the mysterious gentleman known as the Parson. Before he reached

Abbott, Mark caught a snatch of conversation between Humboldt and the local preacher as they sat at the edge of the room.

'He's a splendid fellow,' the preacher remarked, carrying on with something started before Mark came within hearing distance. 'Staying with us. We couldn't allow a brother of the cloth to put up at the hotel.'

'You should have brought him along with you,' Humboldt replied.

'I thought of it. But he came from taking a stroll just before we came here and said he had a headache. He retired to his room to rest.'

'You could go around later and see if he feels up to making an appearance. Ah, Mark – you haven't met the Reverend Pooley yet, have you?'

So, what with being introduced to Pooley, then various other people. Mark did not get a chance to speak with the marshal. They were headed towards him when the butler came to Abbott's side, whispered in his ear and nodded to the door. Finishing his glass of punch, Abott turned and left the room and the butler came to Humboldt.

'Mr. Abbott sends his apologies, sir,' he said. 'He has been called away to investigate a murder.'

'M—murder?' Humboldt gulped. 'Who was killed?'

'I couldn't say, sir,' answered the butler and faded away.

Before Humboldt could say any more on the subject, he found the local preacher at his side and pointing to the door. Mark glanced in the direction of the door and saw the man Eleonore called the Parson walking towards Humboldt.

'Oh, oh!' said a voice at his elbow and he turned to find Eleonore at his side, holding a tray of drinks and looking towards the Parson. 'If he recognizes me, he—'

'He can't expose you without giving himself away,' Mark replied calmly. 'But he'd best not see you. Go tell Alice you feel sick and want to get some air. I reckon she'll know.'

Curtsying as if she had been offering Mark a drink, Eleonore turned and went to where Alice sat amongst a gathering of men. It took Alice one quick glance to know something was wrong and she came forward, passing through the men as if they did not exist.

'What is it, Fifi?' she asked.

To give her credit, Eleonore presented a masterly display

of a woman about to be overcome by what polite folks termed the vapours. Instantly Alice expressed her concern, took the girl's tray and placed it on a small table, then escorted Eleonore from the room. Mrs. Humboldt saw this and followed, to come back and explain to the others how Lady Alice's maid had taken ill and the lady insisted on seeing her safely to her room. The incident did a lot of good for Alice's prestige and, on seeing this, Mrs. Humboldt's suspicions dulled, even though her future son-in-law appeared to be showing a great deal of interest in the beautiful English woman.

The gathering broke up fairly early, for the wedding would be held at eleven o'clock the following morning and Mrs. Humboldt wished to have her guests arrive on time, not to roll up at all hours, bleary eyed from a night's revelry.

Mark sat on his bed, removing his town shoes and wondering why men wore such things by choice. He heard the knock on his door and wondered who might be coming to see him, for he had been one of the last to retire, having been talking with Humboldt and a couple of local ranchers until the rest of the guests departed.

He rose, crossed the room and opened the door. Alice and Eleonore, both wearing their housecoats, entered quickly. He closed the door behind them and looked each girl up and down for a moment.

'No life stories tonight, gals,' he grinned.

'This's more serious than that,' Alice replied.

'Alice's right,' agreed Eleonore. 'Mark, Ginger Lil has been killed.'

'Where?' Mark asked.

'It was she they fetched the marshal to see,' Alice replied. 'They found her in a livery barn, a knife in her back.'

None of them spoke for a time, all busy with their own thoughts. Then Eleonore snapped her fingers.

'I have it. I remember where I saw Gavin Stout before!'

'Where?' Alice asked.

'In Newton. He married a rich storekeeper's daughter. They went on their honeymoon and he left her in Kansas City, but he did not leave the dowry, nor the jewellery she brought on her honeymoon. I remember just now. I also remember, he had dark hair and a moustache then. Of course, I look different also, so he does not remember me.'

'Are you sure of this?' Mark asked.

'Very sure,' replied Eleonore. 'All the time since I first saw him I have been thinking, where did I last see this man, I studied him as I take the drink tray and at last I remember.'

'If you're right—' began Mark.

'I am.'

'That means the dear little Iris will have a rather short married life,' Alice put in. 'I wouldn't wish that even on her.'

'There's one thing I don't get though,' drawled Mark. 'Why didn't the law get after him?'

'I don't know,' Eleonore replied. 'The storekeeper sold up in Newton and left soon after. What can we do, Mark?'

'Could try telling the Humboldts.'

'And have Mrs. Humboldt suspect a trick to grab Gavin from her darling child,' Alice put in. 'She has been watching me most suspiciously all night. I thought he did it a bit brown myself, the way he hung around. Possibly he is thinking that Lady Alice Hatton-Green might be a better catch than little Miss Humboldt.'

'Or his next catch after he gets rid of little Iris,' Eleonore suggested. 'We must do something, though. Do you think the Parson is connected with Stout?'

'Maybe, maybe not,' Mark answered. 'I'll drop a word in George Abbott's lil ear comes morning. I reckon the Parson might know something about that gal though. There's nothing we can do, except sleep on it.'

Eleonore rose from where she had been sitting in a comfortable chair. 'I can take a hint,' she said. 'Coming, Lady Alice?'

'Er, in a few minutes,' Alice replied. 'I've a few theories I want to discuss with Mark. No, you needn't stay, I can manage.'

On entering their room, Eleonore laughed, removed the housecoat, put out the light and climbed into the comfortable bed, ignoring the mattress on the floor. Knowing what deep thinkers Mark and Alice were, she doubted if she would be disturbed until early morning.

'I trust you slept well, Lady Alice,' said Mrs. Humboldt as she entered the dining-room and found Alice and Mark just finishing their breakfasts.

'Very well, thank you,' Alice replied, neither blushing nor

even glancing at Mark, for she knew the woman meant nothing more than polite conversation.

Before any more could be said, the butler entered and came straight to Mrs. Humboldt, followed by the Parson, whose face bore a look of sorrow.

'I'm afraid I have bad news for you, my dear Mrs. Humboldt,' he said. 'The Reverend Pooley has taken ill during the night. Nothing serious, but sufficient to keep him in bed all day. I thought I should bring you word of it so as to give you time to make other arrangements.'

Mrs. Humboldt's face showed horror. 'But – but, he can't be ill. The wedding is this morning and there isn't another preacher within – but you are a man of the church. Would you take the wedding ceremony?'

She turned her eyes to the Parson, who appeared to have been on the verge of leaving. He halted and faced her once more and held out a hand.

'If you wish, dear lady. I will attempt in my humble way to fill the Reverend Pooley's shoes.'

Even as she opened her mouth to speak, Alice felt Mark's foot come down on her toe. She closed her mouth quickly, with a barely concealed wince, watching his face and seeing the almost imperceptible shake of his head. She did not know what to make of this development and aimed to learn about it quickly.

'Excuse me, please,' she said. 'Are you coming, Mark?'

Her tone meant, 'Either come and explain or I spill all I know and chance the consequences.'

Mark rose, nodded to the Parson and followed Alice from the dining-room and up to enter her room. Eleonore still lay in the bed and she grinned, then lost her grin and sat up.

'What is it?' she asked.

After Mark told her of the latest development Eleonore snapped, 'Why didn't you speak?'

'Because it's your word against his,' Mark replied. 'And happen he spooks and runs from here he's left free to pull the same game in some other place. Even if Stout gets lost in the deal he can easy find another good looking feller to take on. Then some more innocent gals'll suffer.'

'But he killed Ginger Lil!'

Mark studied the dark-haired girl for a moment. 'You see him do it?'

'Of course I didn't.'

'Then you can't prove that either. Sure it looks likely he did. He knew her and happen she recognized him she might want paying too much to keep her mouth shut. Or she might be after his scalp for running out on her and wouldn't take pay. So he quietened her. But we can't prove it.'

All this time Alice had been pacing up and down the room. She came to a halt and faced the other two.

'I've an idea that might work.'

She told her idea and the other two exchanged glances. It looked like a real risky game, but happen it worked would save Iris from a terrible mistake. Mark gave his approval of it and Eleonore shrugged, then agreed to take her part.

'Get to it, gals,' Mark drawled. 'I've just time to see George Abbott before the marrying starts.'

Mark learned little from Abbott. The old marshal knew his business, but admitted frankly to being puzzled. From Ginger Lil's blonde friend he learned that the girl came to Holbrock looking for work and the blonde travelled along, being tired of her last place. Lil never mentioned knowing anybody in Holbrock and the girl could think of nobody in their last town who might have hated Lil enough to kill her. They left their rooming house to walk to the saloon just as it grew dark but halfway to the Long Glass Lil said she had forgotten her bag and would go to collect it. The blonde went on to start work and had been in the Long Glass in full view of the customers all night, also a couple of loafers had seen the girls part, so Lil had been alive when the blonde last saw her, which let the blonde out as a suspect.

'Why all the interest, Mark?' asked Abbott.

'Let's just say I'm curious.'

'Yeah? Waal, was you a mite smaller I'd say let's just say you're lying.'

'All right then. Set fast and listen,' drawled Mark.

On hearing Mark's story Abbott's first inclination was to rush out and arrest both Stout and the Parson. However, it took him a bare ten seconds to see how little chance he would having of making any charge stick, so he settled down to hear the plan Mark, Alice and Eleonore formed. At the end he gave a low grunt which might have meant anything and agreed to let Mark play the game his way.

Mrs. Humboldt had worries. Never a good organizer, she

managed to get herself in quite a state before the ceremony. She wanted to see to the seating of the guests and also wished to help her daughter dress. So she felt relieved when Alice came with the offer of helping Iris to get ready, allowing Mrs. Humboldt freedom to attend to her other affairs.

After Mrs. Humboldt left the room Eleonore closed and locked the door, an action which went unnoticed by Iris who had worked herself into a state of near panic waiting for someone to help her dress. Alice eased the girl into a chair and looked down at her.

'We want to tell you something first,' she said.

Quietly and without showing any emotion. Alice told of Gavin Stout's previous marriage, of the fake preacher who would officiate at this wedding. When she finished she saw at a glance that she could have saved her time and put the other idea into practice, for Iris made the reply she expected.

'I don't believe a word of it. I saw you making up to Gavin last night. You want him for yourself.'

'My dear girl,' Alice replied. 'I assure you I've no interest in Gavin Stout other than preventing him from hurting you.'

'It's a lie!' Iris gasped. 'It's all lies. Papa got in touch with Gavin's bankers in Hartford and they told us about him.'

'And who told you how to find Gavin's bankers?' Eleonore asked.

'Gavin did. He had nothing to hide,' answered the girl, her voice rising higher. 'Now get out of my house. I'll tell—'

She thrust herself to her feet, shoving between the two women. Eleonore gave a shrug, caught her by the arm and turned her.

'Doesn't she look beautiful?' sniffed Mrs. Humboldt, watching the white clad shape come along the aisle on her husband's arm.

The guests all looked. Mark Counter, on the front row, watched everything and wondered which of their plans had been put in operation. He studied the veiled face for a moment, but could see nothing of the features below that which might help him know. Alice had appeared shortly before the notes of the Wedding March rose from the harmonium at the side of the room. She nodded to Mark as she took her seat, but could say nothing.

Looking severe and very holy, the Parson conducted the ceremony. He must have learned his subject well, for he made no mistakes through the entire business of marrying Gavin Stout to the veiled girl. At last the ring slipped on to a plump finger and the Parson said:

'You may now kiss the bride.'

With a well simulated self-conscious smile Stout lifted the veil as the girl turned towards him. He gave a sudden horrified gasp and staggered back, his face suddenly ashy and ugly. The watching guests let out a cross between a gasp, cry and moan. Mrs. Humboldt screeched, half rose from her chair and then collapsed in a faint.

'Hello, Parson,' said the bridal-clad Eleonore calmly. 'Remember me?'

With a snarled out curse the Parson took a hurried pace back, staring at the white clad figure before him. Then his hand shot under his coat towards the butt of the five shot Colt House Pistol hidden beneath it.

'Hold it!'

Mark Counter had come to his feet as the veil raised, guessing what must be happening, that Eleonore, not Iris, stood before the Parson. His well tailored cutaway jacket would have shown a bulge if he tried to carry one or both of his big Army Colts, but a Remington Double Derringer took up little room and could easily lie concealed without attracting attention.

Whirling around, the Parson saw his danger. He tried to swing the Colt towards Mark but the big Texan reacted with the speed his name might have become famous for had he not lived under the shadow of the Rio Hondo gun wizard Dusty Fog. Twice the Remington belched flame and cracked out before the Parson's gun came full around. Mark shot in the manner of a trained lawman, shot the only way he dare under the circumstances, for an instant kill. He threw two bullets into the Parson, secure in the knowledge that the light charge and small barrels of the Double Derringer did not raise sufficient power to send the bullets clean through his man. Twice the Parson rocked as lead hit him. His gun fell from his fingers and he went down in a limp pile on the floor.

Even before the Parson made his desperate play, while the other man's gun came clear, Stout turned and dashed down the aisle. Most of the watching crowd were still too stunned to think clearly but George Abbott sprang forward. He did not wear a gun, but leapt at Stout and was knocked aside. A moment later Stout felled the amazed butler, having heard shots and guessing his partner would not be following. He raced to the front doors, through them, turning to grab the key, saw Mark Counter coming after him and closed, then locked the doors on the outside. That would slow down the pursuit for a few moments and a buggy with a fast horse stood waiting in case a hurried departure became necessary. Without a thought for his partner, not caring whether the Parson lived or died, Stout leapt into the buggy and untangled the reins, then reached for the whip.

After shooting the Parson, Mark dropped his empty weapon and raced down the aisle in pursuit of Stout. Luckily for them none of the guests got in the way, for Mark intended to get the man. Men shouted, women screamed, Abbott cursed and tried to untangle himself but Mark ignored any of it. He saw the departure and heard the click of the lock. Mark did not even slacken his pace or break his stride. At the last moment he ducked one shoulder and hurled himself with all his strength into the stout doors, bursting them open as if they had been made of matchwood. He saw the buggy, saw Stout in it and lunged forward.

The whip in Stout's hands lashed out at Mark, only once, for Mark reached the buggy, his hands clamped on the spokes of the wheel and with a tremendous surging heave he threw it over on to its side. Stout howled as he shot out and lit down on the ground.

He came up fast but Mark was on him before he could even think of defence or flight. In his time Stout had been in more than one rough-house brawl and thought he knew how to defend himself. He stood no chance at all against a cold, grim, angry Mark filled with a decent man's hate of all Stout stood for. With all his anger Mark lost none of his skill and Stout suffered the more because of it. Iron hard fists, powered by giant muscles, ripped into Stout's face and body. He felt his nose crushed and spread over his face, his level white teeth break and his body take smashing blows.

Then he went down and all became black and still.

'You got a real mean streak in you, boy,' Abbott remarked, coming from the door of the house. 'Happen you hadn't stopped in ten – fifteen minutes I reckoned on stopping you. He'll never look pretty again, that's for sure.'

'Take him to jail, George,' Mark replied. 'I'd best go inside again.'

In the big room the wedding guests stood chattering, pointing and talking. Mark entered and the talk died down, the guests waited to hear an explanation of what they had seen.

'It worked, Mr. Humboldt,' Alice said suddenly, in a loud and carrying voice even before Mark could speak. 'Thanks to you we caught him.'

She had watched Humboldt ever since Eleonore revealed herself. The man's face showed sickness and hurt as he guessed what must be happening. Alice guessed at the feelings of the pompous man who prided himself on his judgment of character, who had his friends believing in his omnipotence and found himself shown as a fool who allowed a confidence trickster to fool him. He could hardly stand the humiliation, the expectancy of jeers to come. Alice took pity on him, she thought fast, came up with a possible way out, used it and hoped Mark and Eleonore would go along with her in its use.

'My fellow operative and I,' she said, indicating Eleonore who had removed the bridal veil and was helping revive Mrs. Humboldt, 'have been after the Parson and Stout for some time. We trailed them here and told Mr. Humboldt of their activities, hoping he would stop the wedding. With a courage I can only describe as magnificent, Mr. Humboldt insisted we let the marriage carry on so as to trap them both red-handed and prevent some other girl being victimized by them. We all apologize for bringing you here, but you will all understand that it was necessary and I'm sure none of you can object to helping remove a couple of dangerous and heartless men, probably saving heartache and distress to other young, innocent girls.'

Alice hit at the crowd in a manner they could not pass over. They might not like the idea of being tricked, but who would dare to say so in public when word of the reason for their being invited came out. Alice knew human nature, knew the kind of people who might object would also be the kind to see how their social standing would be enhanced by having it known that they helped trap two men who preyed on innocent girls.

Looking across the room Alice met Humboldt's eyes and she would never forget the look of gratitude in them. At the same moment she remembered Iris still remained upstairs, bound with her own stockings and gagged.

'Who are you?' asked one of the guests.

'We operatives aren't allowed to disclose our true identity.'

'Pinkertons!' whispered a man, reaching the conclusion Alice hoped he would.

That evening a small group gathered in Humboldt's study. Mark, Humboldt, the two lady gamblers and Abbott sat around discussing the happenings of the day. In more ways than one Humboldt had cause to be grateful for the arrival of Poker Alice and Madam Moustache. Not the least reason was the way Alice talked with his daughter and finally persuaded Iris everything happened for the best. The girl would be sent east to forget and time would heal the ache she felt.

'Stout talked plenty, when he come around,' Abbott remarked. 'Seem like him and the Parson run this game five times already. Always use the same address in Hartford, there's a feller at it answers the letters for them, when the father wrote to check on Stout. The Parson slipped something in Pooley's coffee last night, nothing serious, just enough to keep him off his feet until after the ceremony.'

'But why did they do that?' Humboldt asked.

'Look at it this way. Your gal gets married by a real preacher, that's legal and only a divorce in the courts can bust it. Which attracts attention to what's happened, might bring the law in. So they figure that after Stout dumps the gal they let her father know the wedding was a fake. So he now has an unmarried daughter and most likely'll let it go rather than admit that he's been made a fool of. In time, when it's all blown over, or maybe because he's moved to another place where he's not known, he can get the gal married again and not risk divorce, or bigamy. It's happened each time they played it.'

'Who killed Ginger Lil?' Eleonore asked.

'Stout lays it on the Parson and I believe him,' Abbott

replied. 'She'd traced the Parson here and wanted half of the take. Stout reckons the Parson got him to one side last night and told him that he'd closed Lil's mouth for good.'

Soon after the meeting broke up, with Humbolt showering his thanks on all concerned for their help. In a few weeks' time he would most likely have forgotten that they helped and be sure that his own astute nature brought about the successful conclusion of the affair.

Mark walked with Alice and Eleonore in the garden shortly after dark. He slipped an arm around each girl's waist and they stood by the gate looking towards the lights of the town.

'You did the right thing, Alice,' he said. 'Telling the story the way you did, clearing Humboldt.'

'They could call you "Lady" Alice all the time,' Eleonore agreed. 'I am proud to know you, Alice.'

'And I'm proud to know you, Eleonore,' Alice smiled. 'But don't you ever try to take my table from me again.'

'Your table!' Eleonore squealed. 'Why you—'

Holding them apart Mark laughed, then they laughed. He leaned forward and brought their heads together, whispering something in their ears. Two startled faces looked at him.

'Both of us?' Alice gasped.

'What a man!' sighed Eleonore.

All in all Mark was not sorry to ride back towards the OD Connected at dawn. He left Alice and Eleonore preparing to travel from Holbrock and hoped he might run across one or both again in the future. Right now he was headed home and did not care – it sure took it out of a man to tell his life story to two gals, especially two gals like Poker Alice and Madam Moustache, in one night.

Rangeland Hercules

For Brian Babani, even though he never published my Rockabye County stories.

CHAPTER ONE

THE DANGER OF BEING AN INNOCENT BYSTANDER

THE wagon lumbered slowly along Hood Street in Austin, capital city of the State of Texas, carrying a pyramid of three huge wine barrels to some saloon or other destination. On its box sat a bulky, bearded driver looking half-asleep in the warmth of the late-afternoon sun. Plodding leisurely ahead, the two powerful draught-horses appeared to be fully aware of their delivery point, for the driver only rarely found the need to guide them.

Being something in the nature of a business and entertainment section of the city, Hood Street's sidewalks attracted a mixed collection of people. Cowhands fresh off the range rubbed shoulders with town dwellers and ogled the passing women in admiration. Blue-clad soldiers, not quite so hated since the end of Reconstruction as practised by Davis' corrupt and inefficient government, mingled unopposed with supporters of the late Confederate States. A few buffalo hunters strolled along, their grease- and blood-smeared buckskins giving off an unmistakable odour to anybody unfortunate enough to pass close to them. Hanging on the arm of her mac, a pretty, garishly dressed lobby-lizzy paraded her wares to anybody who might be in search of female company; and ignored the obvious disapproval of such 'good' women who drew aside to let her go by.

Although young, the lobby-lizzy had been selling her body for long enough to know the genuine customer from the merely curious. Studying the male members of the crowd as the wagon approached, she noted a couple of potential clients and a man she felt she might be only too pleased to offer her services to free of charge.

The man who so attracted the young prostitute's attention would catch the eye in any crowd. Six foot three in height, his head topped most of the crowd around him. On his head rode a costly white J. B. Stetson hat with a silver-concha decorated band, moulded into the shape which marked a Texan to knowing eyes. Clearly he had been making use of a near-by barber's shop's facilities, for his curly, golden blond hair showed signs of recent attention. So did his tanned, almost classically handsome face, its cheeks as smooth as only a very good barber

7

could shave them. It was a strong face, with intelligence and humour in its lines. His tan shirt looked freshly pressed and had clearly been made, like his levis pants, to fit his frame. That great spread of shoulders, lean waist and long powerful pair of legs could not be clothed so well from the shelves of a general store. Around his waist hung a fine-quality gunbelt. Matched ivory handled 1860 Army Colts, with the Best Citizen's Finish to their metal work, rode in the contoured holsters just right to permit ease and speed of withdrawal.

Everything about the blond giant hinted at wealth. Yet anybody who took him for a dressed-up dude stood a better than fair chance of being rapidly and painfully corrected. He walked with a long, easy stride, light on his feet despite his size, and those matched Colts flared their butts out just right for a reaching hand to grip them with the minimum of movement.

Not that anybody but a stranger to Austin would have made such a foolish mistake as to play Mark Counter for a dude. He had been in the State capital long enough to establish his identity among the citizens. Any member of the great OD Connected ranch ranked high in the matter of salty toughness, and Mark Counter belonged to the elite of the crew, its almost legendary floating outfit.

Born the third son of a wealthy Texas rancher, Mark became rich in his own right when a maiden aunt died and left him all her considerable fortune. He could, if he so desired, have bought his own spread and possessed the ability to make it pay. However, he preferred to remain at the OD Connected, siding the man who saved his life in Mexico shortly after the war.* As Dusty Fog's right bower, Mark stood high in the ranch's hierarchy. Many who knew them both claimed that Mark's knowledge of the cattle industry exceeded that of Dusty Fog, despite the other being segundo of the ranch. A dandy dresser, Mark's taste in clothing dictated what the well-dressed Texas cowhand wore; just as during the War he had set the trend in uniforms among the bloods of the Confederate States Army.

Since the meeting at the Appomattox Courthouse brought, if not peace, a cessation of military hostilities, Mark built up a reputation approaching legendary dimensions as a cowhand second to none. Men spoke of his giant strength, told awe-filled tales of his ability in a rough-house brawl. Yet, skilled as he was, few spoke of him as a gunfighter. In other fields he stood almost alone; there were very few could equal his muscular prowess. When using his matched Colts he was in the shadow of the fastest, most accurate of all, the Rio Hondo gun-wizard

* Told in *The Ysabel Kid*.

Dusty Fog. Yet the select few in a position to know stated he came a close second in speed and accuracy to his friend.

Normally Mark rode accompanied by Dusty Fog and the Ysabel Kid, a combination hard to beat in the fighting line; and also a factor that prevented his full expertise from showing. Circumstances caused a temporary separation of the floating outfit's leading lights. After helping to bring off a successful peace treaty with the majority of the war-like Comanche nation*, the Ysabel Kid stayed at Fort Sherrard to attend to final details and see his grandfather's *Pehnane* band housed on their reservation. On their return to the OD Connected, Mark hoped to accompany Dusty to the wedding of an old army companion. Receiving a message that his uncle, Tune Counter, needed help against a family of vengeance-seeking outlaws, Mark put off all thoughts of weddings, rode fast to Tennyson and became involved in the affairs of Town Marshal Counter, Calmaity Jane and the woman known as Madam Bulldog.†'

With the affair brought to a satisfactory conclusion, Mark began his return journey to the OD Connected at a more leisurely pace. His way lay through Austin, and no prominent Texas gentleman could pass his State's capital without paying its sights a courtesy call. Although he found a telegraph message from his employer waiting at the Houston Hotel, he was not surprised. Ole Devil Hardin knew the blond giant's tastes well enough to assume Mark would put up at the city's best hotel. The message told him to stay in Austin for a few days in case Dusty Fog should need further help in untangling the threat to the newly-wedded couple's life in their new home.‡

Never one to object to orders, Mark settled down at the hotel and then went out to see what Austin might have to offer a gentleman of taste and discernment. As he strolled along Hood Street, he wondered how his two companions in many a wild celebration handled their chores.

Despite being the State's capital, Austin retained much of the traditional Texas cattle town. The site of the city had been selected in 1836 by a commission appointed from the Republic of Texas' ministers to find the most attractive area in their territory on which to erect the seat of government. After some deliberation they decided on the bluffs over the Colorado River below Lake Travis. The Governor's mansion, perched on a hill overlooking the city, the home built for France's minister to the Republic and the homes of various civic dignitaries were as fine examples of Southern-colonial architecture as could be

* Told in *Sidewinder*.
† Told in *The Wildcats*.
‡ Told in *McGraw's Inheritance*.

9

found anywhere in the country. To the east of those imposing structures rose the home of lesser citizens, their business premises and places of entertainment. Of the latter, Hood Street ranked as the site of many of the better-class saloons, a dance-hall, a theatre, on whose boards trod some of the great names of the day, and gambling houses. No fine colonial dwellings here, only the false fronts and wooden walls to be seen in any other town above the adobe belt.

Suddenly the doors of a saloon across the street from Mark burst open and a scared-looking townsman appeared. Hotly pursued by a screeching saloon girl, the man bounded from the sidewalk on to the street. Realising that she could not hope to catch him, the girl halted and raised her right hand, which gripped a Remington Double Derringer.

'You lousy, no-good piker!' she squealed. 'I'll teach you to go making eyes at that damned Sally-Mae!'

With that she jerked the trigger and cut loose a shot. Even in the hand of a skilled man the stubby Derringer lacked accuracy. Used by a woman who did not spend time at target practice, and was also wild with indignation-fired excitement, it became less so. Missing its intended mark by some feet, the .41 bullet punched a neat hole through the ear of the nearside horse of the wine wagon and brought a scream from the injured horse. It reared, forelegs in the air, and swung to crash into its partner. Equally startled by the unexpected assault, the off-side horse slammed into its breast harness with some force and swung away from its hurt team-mate. Taken by surprise as the wagon swung violently, the driver pitched off his seat and ploughed a furrow in the dirt of the trail.

Dragged forward by the plunging horses, the wagon's wheels scraped on the edge of the sidewalk. Rain running from the edge of the sidewalk porch had eaten away at the edge of the trail and formed a hollow under the planks at the foot path. Usually wagons missed the weakened area, but as this one scraped along so its off wheels crushed through the crumbling earth and sank down. Doing so brought the wagon to an abrupt halt and caused it to tilt over. Although secured by ropes, the pyramid of big wine barrels began to move dangerously. Nor was their security helped by the rearing and lunging of the two horses, the knots of the holding ropes started to slip. The upper barrel immediately began to sink, forcing the other two apart.

When the wagon raked into the sidewalk the man saw its danger. Thrusting the girl from his arm, he sent her staggering into the wall of the nearest building and bounded along until clear of any possible chance of being caught by the slipping barrels. Shock twisted at the lobby-lizzie's pretty face as she stared at the enormous barrels. Not an intelligent girl, she could still guess what would happen when the ropes parted. She wanted to run, but her legs seemed to refuse the frantic dictates of her mind. Horrified, she watched the ropes moving inexorably towards the point where the knots must cease to function. When that happened all three barrels, weighing well over two hundred pounds each, would come down upon her.

Mark read the situation even more rapidly and took steps to avert it. Leaping forward, he ran by the horses. Long before they could be brought under control, the knots would part. Nor did he think there was time to lift and carry the girl to safety. Even as he reached that conclusion the first rope flew free, fortunately at the centre of the barrels, although that would merely speed the disintegration of the other knots.

Halting with his back to the girl, Mark placed both hands against the centre of the bottom barrel. The forward knot came free, its end whipping into the air and a moment later the last fastening parted. Instantly Mark felt the barrel begin to move. Gritting his teeth, he braced himself against the weight. His shirt leapt and writhed as the muscles of his shoulders took the strain. Though ample, the cloth of his shirt sleeves drew tight under the expansion of his deltoid and biceps muscles. The boots he wore had been made by the El Paso leather-worker Joe Gaylin, designed so that their high heels would spike into the earth and hold firm against the pull of a wild horse or longhorn bull when roping on the ground. Often Gaylin claimed that nothing short of a miracle could rip the heels from any boots he made and, not for the first time, Mark concluded the old timer spoke nothing but the truth. While they had not been made to grip on wood, the heels caught and held at a time when to slip would have been fatal.

Attracted by the sound of the shot, people gathered quickly about the wagon. Seeing what confusion her shot had caused, the saloon girl put aside thoughts of extracting revenge on the fleeing man and disappeared hurriedly into her place of employment. Although a good-sized crowd formed, at first nobody made a move to help Mark. Amazement at the feat of strength they were witnessing held men and women alike immobile. At first it seemed impossible for even so large and powerful a man as Mark to hold the barrels, but he did so, despite the jerks caused by the two horses tugging at their harness.

Then help came. Thrusting himself through the crowd, a tall, middle-aged man in range clothes took in the scene and acted fast. From his hat down to the high-heeled boots on his feet his clothes spelled Texas cowhand, lean as a steer raised in the greasewood country. His tanned, moustached face bore an expression of authority. Certainly he gave orders like a man long used to doing so.

'Grab those hosses' heads and hold 'em still, one of you!' he barked. 'And let's have some help down there.'

Given the stout guidance and leadership of the cowhand, a man leapt to lay hold of the horses' reins. Swiftly he brought the animals under control, even calming down the injured one. However, the cowhand found difficulty in persuading other members of the crowd to follow him. If the barrels rolled from the wagon's bed, anyone who got in their way stood a better than fair chance of being spread like a flap-jack over the sidewalk.

Only the barrels did not roll off. Exerting all of his giant strength, Mark not only held them but started them back into their original place. Slowly, almost imperceptibly, the top barrel started to inch its way upwards under the pressure of Mark's push. Sweat poured from a face that bore mute signs of the tremendous effort he made.

'Come on, blast you!' yelled the lean cowhand, walking swiftly along the boards until he reached Mark. 'Hold her steady, boy, I'm coming by.'

Carefully avoiding touching Mark, the cowhand stepped by him and ordered a couple of men following him to watch how they moved. Clearly a man of decisions and action, the cowhand snapped rapid orders which received immediate obedience. Two men on each side of Mark got their hands to the barrel and, adding their strength to his, forced the bottom barrel back to its original place while the cowhand grabbed hold of the first rope.

'Just keep her steady, boys,' he said and started to fasten it to the side of the wagon. 'Hold it while I get the other end.'

Passing behind the men, the cowhand knotted the second rope into place. He then crept under the barrel holders and secured the central fastening. Checking on the security of the knots, he backed out and nodded in satisfaction.

'Ease off slow and easy until we see if they'll ride,' he suggested.

Carefully the men relaxed their hold on the barrels, ready to stop them should there be any sign of movement. None came and they stepped clear, grinning in the pleasure of achievement. Pushing herself from the wall, the lobby-lizzie ran to Mark's side and steadied him as he staggered slightly. For a moment he struggled to catch his breath, then rubbed a hand across his brow.

'You saved me!' the girl gasped, clutching at his arm. 'I thought I was a goner for sure.'

'Now that'd be a real waste,' Mark replied, having recovered enough to take an interest in the object of his rescue. 'I'm——'

At that moment his eyes located a member of the crowd who made him forget whatever he had meant to say. While the lobby-lizzie was real pretty, she could not compare with the girl who caught and held Mark's attention. Topped by a stylish little hat, flaming red hair framed a truly beautiful, almost regal face. Nor did the figure below detract from the beauty of the features. The elegant dark dress of the latest Eastern cut emphasised the rich curves of a magnificently proportioned female body. Expensive jewellery, in perfect taste, flickered on the girl, just enough of it to add to her charms. Standing at the side of a man Mark knew to be the president of the Land & Trust Bank, the beautiful young woman's face lost its expression of concern and took on one of blank lack of recognition.

'She'll hold if they pull her out, easy, Mark,' said the cowhand whose timely arrival had jolted the crowd into assisting the blond giant.

'Huh?' Mark grunted, jerking his eyes from the gorgeous red head to the speaker. 'Hey there, Tule, long time no see.'

'That's for sure,' grinned the cowhand. 'You could've got hurt just now.'

'Somebody had to do something.'

'And you was fool enough to do it. All you Counters're the same.'

Having been with Mark's father ever since Big Ranse Counter had come into Texas and helped to build the great R over C ranch, Tule Bragg could speak with some authority on that subject. From his birth until riding off to join Bushrod Sheldon's Confederate cavalry during the Civil War, Mark had known and respected Bragg as second only to his father. From Bragg came much of Mark's knowledge of cattle work, the foreman being an acknowledged master in that field.

Although the lobby-lizzie showed willingness to stay by her rescuer she received no inducement to do so. Knowing better than force her attentions too closely, she joined her man and proceeded to tell him at length what she thought of his desertion. He took it, deciding that a man who risked an unpleasant death to save a girl would be just as likely to take her side if he saw her being abused. Besides, time was passing and Austin offered too many alternative sources in the girl's trade for them to waste time. Taking her arm, he steered her off along the sidewalk and through the crowd. In passing, the lobby-lizzie darted a curious glance at the beautiful red head and wondered if it had been her who had attracted the blond

13

giant's attention.

Having recovered from his involuntary dismount, the wagon's driver swung back on to the box. Carefully he guided the horses forward and eased the wagon away from the sidewalk. When he was sure that there was no danger of a further tipping, he continued on his way.

'What's brought you up this ways, Tule?' Mark asked after they had seen the wagon safely on its way.

'We're running a herd of Mexican cattle up to Newton,' Bragg replied. 'Your pappy bought 'em below the border and reckoned to sell off the steers to cover it.'

'Pappy coming in?' Mark inquired hopefully.

'Nope. He sent me to handle some business and figures to let Sailor Sam fill up the chuck wagon here.'

'When'll Sam be here?'

'Late tomorrow or the next day, depending on how the herd moves.'

A grin came to Mark's face at the prospect of meeting his father's cook again. At some time in his youth Sailor Sam had followed the sea as a career and had also picked up a sound, thorough knowledge of fist-fighting. It had been the cook who'd taught Mark most of what he knew about defending himself with his bare-hands. Nor did Sailor Sam belong to the stand-up-and-slug school of pugilist thought. Instead he'd learned Mark to block punches, dodge, weave and hit accurately in a way which disconcerted opponents trained in the old slugging school. So Mark looked forward to seeing his old teacher. With any amount of luck a city the size of Austin ought to hold somebody desiring to prove he, or they, could fight. If that was the case, Mark and Sailor would be only too willing to oblige and the blond giant could show how well he'd learned his lessons.

'I don't want Sailor getting all stove up in no fist fight,' warned Bragg, following the blond giant's train of thought like a bluetick hound laying after a raccoon.

'Yah!' Mark replied. 'You're beginning to sound like that schoolmarm you was sparking back home.'

'Blast it, boy!' bristled Bragg. 'I never sparked no schoolmarm. You danged Counters figure everybody's like you, always a-chasing some poor unfortunate gal. Tell you, I figured you'd take off that pretty bachelor's wife you done rescued and give her a fate they reckon's worse'n death.'

'That's a real offensive remark to make to the boss' son,' Mark grinned.

'Your pappy'd fire me for it, only he figures that everybody'd say he done it 'cause he can't lick me at poker,' Bragg answered

14

calmly. 'To show you that I didn't mean it, I'll let you buy me a meal.'

'Damned if I see why I should buy you the meal,' Mark said. 'But it'll save arguing if I do. Let's go eat.'

Saying it, he looked to where the beautiful redhead walked by on the arm of the banker. She did not look the blond giant's way, and he did not offer to speak. Following the direction of Mark's gaze, Bragg grinned.

'What's that jasper got that you haven't?'

'A fancy dude suit, a paunch, a gold watch chain and a bank,' Mark replied.

'Don't worry none,' Bragg consoled him. 'Maybe you'll have the suit, gold watch chain and bank one day. You've already got the paunch.'

'That being the case, maybe we'd best not eat,' Mark drawled.

'I said you'd got it, not me,' Bragg replied. 'So you're not getting out of buying me a meal that ways.'

CHAPTER TWO

A QUESTION OF OWNERSHIP

AFTER a hearty, if leisurely, meal at the Bon Ton Eating House, Tule Bragg looked at Mark with a broad grin.

'Now what do we do, boy? This here big city's got to have some mighty evil temptations for us country boys to avoid.'

'Let's go take a look for them then,' Mark replied, shoving back his chair. 'Like Pappy allus says, a man doesn't know which kind of temptations to avoid unless he tries them.'

After paying for their meal, Mark led the way out of the building. Night had come and lights glowed invitingly from various places of entertainment. Already the sounds of revelry reached their ears. Pianos, growing tinnier and more discordant the farther east they originated along Hood Street, rattled out a variety of tunes. As the quality of saloon improved, so did the music offered grow in volume and number of available instruments. After studying the bill for the theatre, Mark and Bragg decided that it offered nothing they wished to see. So they continued strolling in the direction of the Bigfoot Saloon, the largest, most expensive place in the area if not the whole town.

'Hey, look up there!' Bragg said, catching Mark's arm and pointing into the sky to where a streak of light flickered through the blackness.

'It's nothing but a shooting-star,' Mark replied.

'It's nothing but a sign, boy,' corrected the foreman. 'Why every time I see one my luck's running high and can't be beat.'

Which meant, as Mark knew full well, that their night's entertainment and study of temptations would not go far beyond some gambling game. In addition to being a tophand with cattle, Bragg was also an inveterate gambler. Let him once see what he felt to be a sign of any kind and he headed for the nearest game of chance on the run.

Leading the way into the Bigfoot Saloon, Bragg paused and looked around him. Not that he had eyes for the fancy fittings, the display of choice types of drinks behind the long mahogany bar, nor the attractive gaily dressed girls all hot and eager to join any customer who wished for company. Instead Bragg glanced around the various ways in which the management allowed their clientele to wager money. Ignoring the black jack and chuk-a-luck layouts, for he knew no man could hope to beat the house's percentage at either, Bragg searched for a poker game and did not find one of the kind he wanted; playing straight, with no wild cards, fancy hands or limit. Failing a chance to match his wits in a top-class poker game, his eyes went to where a sign with a painting of a tiger hung over a big table.

'Let's go buck the tiger for a spell,' he suggested. 'The signs tell me I'm set to howl tonight.'

'The last time they did that you lost a month's pay,' Mark reminded him.

'That was 'cause I mixed the signs up,' replied Bragg. 'I'm older and some slicker now.'

Nobody knew who first used the sign of a tiger to advertise that faro was the game played, but the two had become synonymous. Being conservative by nature in their hatred of change, gamblers also demanded that the table's layout remained the same. So, whether thirteen real cards were used, the symbols chalked on rough planks, scratched in dirt or tastefully stained upon green baize cloth, players insisted that spades be used. Laid out in two rows of six cards, from ace to king, with the seven on its own at the left centre of the rows, the layout varied only in the nature of its making.

Already eight players sat at the table, but the game had not yet begun. Facing them across the table, the dealer riffled a deck of cards with practised skill. Before him stood the dealing box, open at the top so that only one card at a time would be available. However, the cards could not be removed from the top during play, but had to be slid through a narrow slit on the side facing the players. A small spring in the bottom of the box held the remaining cards firmly against the top of the frame.

While the dealer sold stacks of chips from the rack placed at his right hand, to his left the case-keeper prepared to play his important part in the game. Looking something like an abacus, the case-board carried pictures of the thirteen spade cards instead of numbers and four wooden balls rested on each symbol's wire. As the case-keeper pushed all the balls to the left side of the frame, the lookout mounted his high stool; from which he watched the entire action, ensured that bets were paid off correctly and prevented any chance of cheating.

'I'll take a stack of them fancy yeller chips, friend,' Bragg announced.

Mark had already studied the chips and seen the small marker stamped with the numerals 200. That meant the twenty chips in the stack cost two hundred dollars, or ten dollars each.

'Same for you, mister?' asked the dealer, looking at Mark.

'Nope. I'll just watch a spell,' the blond giant replied and guessed it would be some time before Bragg pulled out of the game.

After a thorough riffling of the cards the dealer offered them to be cut. Everything seemed to be fair enough to Mark, and he doubted if a place like the Bigfoot would resort to cheating. The dealer's box had an open top, a sign of honesty. 'Sand Tell' cards, specially treated for cheating at faro, could be used only from a special box with a closed top and small hole left to thrust out the cards. The big stake table in a saloon of the Bigfoot's quality attracted professional gamblers capable of detecting any cheating device and men of sufficient social standing to make things very awkward for a saloonkeeper who crossed them. So Mark figured nothing but luck would separate Tule Bragg from his savings during the game.

Luck alone won at faro, especially during the early stages, which was one of the reasons Mark did not play it. When he gambled he wanted to use some skill and to be able to play the cards himself.

'Lay on your bets, gents,' said the dealer after the cut had been made and the cards placed into the box.

'I'm betting the seven to win,' Bragg told Mark, placing a chip in the centre of the appropriate card on the layout. Then he moved between the two and three, but placed a hexagonal black marker on it. 'And coppering the deuce and trey seeing's they both owe me some loser's money.'

All the other players set down their bets, following the various methods of indicating whether they wagered on one card or a combination of two, three or four. Carefully the lookout watched every bet, memorising them so as to act as mediator in case of disputes. For that reason lookout men needed to be intelligent, cool and tough enough to back their decisions against objecting players. One player set down a red chip on the table level with the represented deuce and in front of the dealer to indicate that he bet the winning card each time would be an even number.

'All bets down?' the dealer inquired and received a chorus of agreement. 'Here we go then, gents.'

With that he slipped the first card out of the box. Known as the 'soda', it was dead and could not be used in the play. Placing the soda alongside the rack of chips, he drew out the next exposed card and put it down at the right of the box.

'Deuce loses,' he told the players and indicated the seven of hearts at the top of the box. 'Seven's a winner.'

Which meant that Bragg collected on two of his bets during that 'turn' of two cards from the box. Sliding out the winning seven, the dealer placed it on the 'soda'. Already the case-keeper had run along one of the jack's buttons to touch the opposite side of the frame and show that one of the four had been taken out of play as the 'soda'. Next he moved the first deuce marker clear across the frame to signify it lost. The winning seven was shown by its button on its wire being halted half an inch from the edge. In a well-conducted game the 'case' offered a visible and accurate record of every card played and what its result might be.

Once again the dealer drew out the exposed card and placed it on the loser pile at the right of the box, showing the winner card underneath. While faro interested its players, Mark found being a spectator boring. He knew that Bragg would object to being disturbed, so turned and walked across to the bar. A group of well-dressed men stood there, and Mark recognised one of Shangai Pierce, a prosperous rancher and friend. Letting out a cowhand whoop, Pierce extended a powerful hand to Mark and introduced the blond giant to the rest of the party. Next Pierce demanded to be told how the treaty council went, something in which every man at the bar had an interest. So Mark told them what had happened, making lurid oaths as he mentioned the attempts by both white and Indian elements to prevent the affair being brought to a successful conclusion.

'Look who's just come in,' Pierce growled, nodding towards the main entrance. 'Know 'em, Mark?'

Turning, Mark looked the new arrivals over. In front strode a big, heavily built man. A battered high hat sat on a mop of shaggy greying hair, the face under it lined and seamed until it disappeared into the mat of beard. He wore a wolf-skin jacket, tartan shirt, levis pants tucked into calf-high Indian moccasins. Around his waist hung a gunbelt with a Dragoon Colt butt forward at his right side and tomahawk in slings on his left. All in all, he looked a mean, hard customer who would make a bad enemy.

Behind him came three younger men, all showing a certain family resemblance. They wore range clothes, yet Mark did not take them for cowhands. At the bearded man's right side stood a tall, handsome jasper. Dandy-dressed, he sported a gunbelt with its holster fitted to it by a rivet-swivel, the tip of the Colt's long barrel poked through the bottom and not by accident. At the dandy's left and behind the big man was a gangling bean-pole in his early thirties, untidy in appearance but wearing a brace of Cooper Navy revolvers in low hanging holsters. The last of the quartet had a medium-height stocky built frame, red hair and belted two Freeman Army revolvers butt forward in low cavalry twist-hand holsters.

While the quartet gave the impression of salty toughness, they did not particularly worry Mark. Not could he see them causing the burly rancher at his side any great concern. In addition to owning a big Texas ranch, Shangai Pierce bore a well-deserved name for handling salty toughs no matter how they came.

'Can't say I do,' Mark admitted. 'Who are they?'

'Big jasper's Churn Wycliffe, runs a trading post and hoss ranch up the top end of Lake Buchanan,' explained Pierce. 'The flashy-dresser's his nephew, Billy Wycliffe, and claims to be fast with that fancy half-breed holster. T'other two're kin. The beanpole's Loney Sandel, and the last one's Evan Shever.'

After looking around the room Churn Wycliffe spoke to his companions. Billy grinned and made some reply, indicating the bar, only to have the big man snarl back at him. Then Wycliffe stamped across the room to where a tall, thin, bearded man in a top hat, frock coat, dirty collarless shirt and patched pants sat nursing a glass of beer at a table. Nodding a greeting, Wycliffe sat with the man and signalled to a waiter. His companions stood undecided for a moment and then trooped across to the high-stake faro table. Billy took the last chair and the other two jostled a space for themselves, Evan Shever sitting on the edge of the table and grinning at the dealer in a challenging manner. However, the trio knew better than make too much of a nuisance, for the Bigfoot Saloon's bouncers could be mighty persuasive in such cases.

'Trade must be good,' Mark remarked, turning back to the bar.

'Likely,' Pierce replied. 'Only I wouldn't want to guess at where they get the stuff they sell—or how.'

'It's not off Jake Jacobs there, that's for sure,' another rancher in the group stated. 'He's a pedlar but he don't often have anything of value to sell.'

'Are they wanted?' asked the youngest man present, a touch eagerly.

'Nope,' admitted Pierce. 'More 'cause nothing's been proved on them than for any other reason.' Clearly, thinking of the Wycliffe clan's possible criminal tendencies brought something more to the rancher's mind for he went on, 'Say, the Bad Bunch've pulled another one.'

'What's it this time?' asked a prominent businessman.

'The Wells Fargo office in Fort Worth while the Governor was handing out prizes at the County Fair there. Knifed the agent and nobody saw a thing.'

'I wonder who they are?' breathed the youngest man; he worked for the local newspaper and longed to be in on a big story that would bring him national acclaim, or at least the

20

chance of being hired by one of the Eastern daily papers.

'Dick Dublin and the Kimble County boys,' guessed one of the crowd.

'Not them!' snorted the second rancher. 'It's the Marlows.'

'When Alf Marlow or any of his kin get brains, you'll maybe convince me they're the Bad Bunch,' snorted a man from the Fort Ewall country, full of civic pride and extending it to cover the leading light of his area's criminal element. 'It's Jim Moon and his bunch.'

A comment which aroused considerable derision among the other members of the crowd, all of whom appeared to favour some different outlaw as leader of the mysterious gang called, for want of more information, the Bad Bunch. In fact, the discussion began to grow heated, and Mark felt that he ought to put a damper on it in the interests of peace and quiet.

'I reckon it's time we had another drink and talked about women,' he declared, as an otherwise peaceable pillar of East Texas society demanded instant recognition of Cullen Baker as brains, leader and organiser of the Bad Bunch. 'Which same it'd be one helluva note if some of you gents were thrown in the pokey for brawling over which owlhoot's the best.'

A point that the others readily accepted, especially a well-known lawyer from South Texas who had been vehemently insisting that Bill Brooken—later sentenced to *one hundred and twenty-seven* years in prison—alone possessed sufficient savvy to run the elusive gang.

At that time Mark had no interest in the identity of the Bad Bunch. Soon circumstances would bring him into contact with them, and they proved to be more than the cream of the floating outfit could handle.*

Wishing to change the subject, he told of his last meeting with Calamity Jane and gave details of her defeat at the hands of Madam Bulldog, while omitting to mention the surprising fact which emerged concerning the woman who out-cursed, -drank, -fought and -shot Calamity.

'Last I heard she was up Utah way, driving a stage,' Pierce remarked. 'Calamity, I mean. Helped U.S. Marshal Cole to bring in a gang of owlhoots.'

'Cole?' repeated the lawyer from South Texas. 'I knew a Cole used to ride in Captain Jack Cureton's Rangers in the War. Is that the same jasper?'

'Sure is. He's my cousin,' Mark agreed and wondered how Solly Cole had got on with the volatile Miss Martha Jane Canary.†

* Told in *The Bad Bunch*.
† Told in *Calamity Spells Trouble*.

The subject changed to less provoking subjects than the identity of the Bad Bunch. After some of the Calamity Jane stories had been passed around, the men turned once more to Texas' major industry and talking point, cattle. After a short time Mark remembered Tule Bragg and decided to take the foreman a drink. So he ordered four fingers of Old Scalp Lifter and carried the glass across the room.

'Five's the loser,' announced the dealer. 'Pay the coppered bet on it.'

'That's mine,' Billy Wycliffe stated.

'The red chip may be,' Bragg put in quietly. 'But that yellow with the copper on it's mine.'

Silence dropped on the table and the other players began to draw away from the speakers. Under cover of the movement, Sandel eased around to halt on the opposite side of Bragg to his cousins. Mark found no difficulty in reaching the table due to a sudden and hurried withdrawal of standing players and kibitzers. In Texas a question of ownership around a card table could result in some fast, deadly and convincing arguments being used.

Slowly Billy began to swing on his chair seat in Bragg's direction. At the same time his hand moved towards the Colt's butt. Using a swivel-mounted holster, he did not need to draw the gun but could turn it still in the leather and fire through the bottom. Mark did not know whether Bragg had noticed how young Wycliffe wore the Colt and felt disinclined to wait and see. Not wishing to spill the drink in his left hand, the blond giant held it out to the side. Bending, he gripped the right rear leg of Wycliffe's chair in his free hand and jerked it from under the dandy.

Letting out a yell of surprise, which turned into a yelp of pain, Billy lit down rump-first on the floor. In their own area, the Wycliffe clan packed considerable weight and authority. Few men around San Saba would cross them, and so they expected the same to apply wherever they found themselves. Unfortunately for their peace of mind, Mark Counter cared little for reputations and showed respect only to those who warranted it.

From the corner of his eye, Mark saw Shever drop from the table and reach for his gun. Bringing up the chair in a backhand swing, Mark crashed it straight into the stocky redhead's face. Bright lights seemed to burst before Shever's eyes and he reeled backwards, tripped then sat down hard. After which he flopped on to his back, losing all interest in the proceedings.

Like Shever, Sandel did not expect such a prompt, devastating disrespect to be shown for the clan Wycliffe. However, he considered it necessary to assert the family superiority, in the interests of maintaining their reputation of having never been curried below the knees. So he snaked a hand towards the off-side Cooper's butt. The move was fast, although not exceptionally so, and might have been capably performed had he been permitted to finish it.

When settling down to play, Bragg had removed his hat and hung its storm-strap on the back of the chair. He invariably kept his hair cropped short, which turned his head into a mighty effective weapon as Sandel discovered. Leaving his seat with surprising speed, Bragg butted the gangling Sandel in the belly. There was not even a growth of hair to cushion the impact, so Sandel felt like he had been struck in the stomach by either a cannon-ball or a charging bighorn ram. Pitching backwards, his hands folded on the injured area and he doubled over to collapse in a retching, twitching pile in the sawdust.

Across the room Churn Wycliffe threw over his chair, rose and started to reach for his Colt. Figuring that the man ought to be taking a hand at about that time, Mark had already swung to face him. The chair dropped as Mark's right hand flashed down. Fingers curled around the smooth ivory handle of the right side Colt and slid it from leather. As it came out, Mark's thumb eased back the hammer; but his forefinger remained straight along the triggerguard until the eight-inch barrel slanted away from him. In slightly over three-quarters of a second a cocked, lined Colt pointed in Churn Wycliffe's direction with a finger around its trigger all set to turn lead loose.

That was the kind of smooth, practised speed and ability which set the top gun apart from a man who was merely fast. Churn Wycliffe could read the signs and recognise Mark's true potential as easily as a schoolteacher going through a child's first addition papers. Such speed only rarely came without an equal skill at placing the bullets in any desired area. Nothing about Mark led Wycliffe to believe he faced an inaccurate exception. So the burly man spread his hands away from his sides in clear proof of his pacific intentions.

'Take it easy, friend,' he said in a voice deep as the growl of a Texas grizzly chewing cow meat. 'And you-all, Billy, you stop that right now.'

Spluttering curses, Billy swung around still seated on the floor and reached towards his Colt. At his uncle's bawled-out command, he removed his hand. Or it could be that he heard the cocking click of Bragg's Dance Bros. Army revolver as the foreman threw down on him.

'The boy shows some sense, mister,' Bragg drawled as Wycliffe walked up. 'Only not at a card table.'

'Mind telling me what's up?' Wycliffe inquired with surprising mildness, or so it would seem to anybody who knew him.

'I coppered a bet on the five, he didn't and the card came out a loser,' Bragg explained. 'So he tried to claim my bet.'

'That true, boy?' demanded Wycliffe as Billy climbed sullenly erect.

'It's my——' Billy began.

'Don't lie to me!' bawled Wycliffe. 'You didn't have enough to buy yellow chips at this table. How about it, lookout?'

'That was the gent there's bet, the coppered yellow,' the man in the lookout chair replied, indicating Bragg.

CHAPTER THREE

A VISITOR FOR MR. COUNTER

FOR a moment Billy Wycliffe stood glaring at the lookout as if he could not believe his ears. Nobody up around San Saba would have dared to go against the wishes of a Wycliffe. What Billy failed to recognise, but his uncle saw all too clearly, was that they had passed out of their sphere of influence. While they could claim to be real big fish in their own small pond, the same did not apply in Austin. Not only did the blond giant dress well and handle a gun like a master, but he had been in some mighty important company. Any man on such amiable terms with Shangai Pierce, to say nothing of the other dignitaries at the bar, could not be shoved around like some small town cow-nurse.

That fact alone weighed heavily, but Wycliffe had another point to take into consideration. Jake Jacobs might not have a high-class range of wares to peddle, but he supplied top-grade information on a number of subjects if the price be right. What the pedlar passed on to Wycliffe made the burly man decline to become involved in trouble; especially against so obviously capable a man as the blond giant. Jacobs' information called for the services of all the men Wycliffe could lay hands on. He stood a good chance of losing, permanently or temporarily, at least a portion of his help should they push the matter further.

'You hear the man, boy?' he growled at Billy. 'Now just tell the gents that you're sorry for the mistake.'

'Like——' Billy started to say.

A big hand clamped hold of his shirt front, bunching it up and shaking him like a terrier with a rat. Looking at his uncle's face, Billy felt scared.

'You do it, boy!' ordered Wycliffe. 'You hear me now!'

Set back on his feet, Billy glared his hatred at Mark and Bragg. For all that, he spat out. 'All right, so I made a mistake.'

'Now get the hell out of here!' Wycliffe ordered. 'And take Cousin Evan with you.'

Muttering under his breath, Billy helped the moaning Shever up. With his cousin's arm around his neck, feet dragging along, Wycliffe started for the door. Wycliffe stepped to Sandel's side and hoisted him on to his feet. Snarling a curse, he slapped the

25

beanpole's hands away from the Coopers and shoved him after his two cousins.

'Damned fool kids these days,' Wycliffe said, watching the trio leave. 'I don't know what the hell they're coming to. No hard feelings, gents?'

'There's none on my part,' Bragg assured him.

'Or mine,' Wycliffe declared.

'You'd maybe best watch them, mister,' Mark put in. 'They could get hurt if they come fussing around me again.'

'I'll see they don't,' Wycliffe promised and nodded to the glass Mark held. 'You've got a mighty steady hand, friend, never spilled a drop.'

Which was the truth. All through the hectic few seconds of his intervention Mark neither dropped nor spilled any of Bragg's drink. Twirling away his Colt, he corrected the lapse by tossing the contents of the glass down his own throat.

'I did now,' he said. 'You'll watch them three, mister?'

'We're just now pulling out and won't be back,' Wycliffe replied. 'No hard feelings on either side I hope, gents.'

With that he turned and walked out of the room. Some of the crowd looked disappointed that the affair ended so tamely. Others showed their relief at not being too close to a gun battle where stray bullets might start flying. Naturally such an event could not pass without discussion and comment.

'That's the first time I've seen the Wycliffes back off,' said one of the players at the chuck-a-luck table. 'They don't go that easy most times.'

'Most times they're not up against one of Ole Devil's floating outfit,' the man handling the dice cage replied.

'Is he Dusty Fog?' inquired another player.

'Nope. Mark Counter.'

'Man. If Dusty Fog's faster than him, that's real rapid.'

'You expecting a war, Shangai?' asked Mark, returning to the bar for a replacement drink.

With a grin, Pierce slid his Colt back into leather. 'It's not every day you see Churn Wycliffe sing low that ways. Not that I blame him, mind.'

Which, coming from a man who made more than one allegedly tough Kansas trail town marshal hunt for his hole, was quite a tribute to Mark's ability and toughness. The general feeling in the place seemed to be that Mark acted in the best possible manner and showed considerable tolerance in not taking more severe measures against the trio. So the house manager raised no objections to the blond giant's continued presence; although he told the bouncers to make sure that none of the departed Wycliffes returned. While a gunfight brought publicity and an increase in trade, it could also come a mite expensive to the fittings and furnishings.

Mark had intended to leave after buying Bragg the drink, but changed his mind. Not a man to back away from any trouble forced on him, he did not go out of his way looking for it. If Churn Wycliffe wanted to take his nephews out of town and so avoid further friction, Mark had no desire to prevent him from doing it. To walk outside while they gathered their horses could be interpreted as an open challenge.

'You figure they'll leave, Shangai?' he asked.

'If Churn says for them to, they will,' the rancher stated. 'Those three, and all the clan're real scared of him. What're you fixing to do now?'

'Have another drink and go,' Mark replied. 'Way Tule's stacking up the chips, it'll be a fair piece afore he's ready to leave. So I'll be on my way.'

'There wouldn't be a gal around, would there?' grinned one of the party.

'Would you believe me if I said "no"?' Mark asked.

'Oh, sure,' grinned the man in a tone which meant he would not. 'We *all* believe you, now don't we, boys?'

'As much as we believe that all Banker Snodgrass's interested in's that red-headed gal's paintings,' grinned the second rancher.

'Is *that* what he told you?' inquired the South Texas lawyer. 'The last one was his niece from Boston.'

'Not this one,' said the man who started the conversation on its present line. 'Or if she is, she's the first Boston gal I ever heard that sounded like a Georgia peach-blossom.'

'She must be real rich, way Snodgrass took to her,' grinned the rancher.

'Likely she won't stay that way when he's through,' put in the youngest member of the group.

'There's times you talk too much,' warned the lawyer. 'Saying things like that out loud could wind you up getting called out with a gun, or hauled into a legal court.'

'She sure is a real good-looking gal though,' Pierce commented, watching Mark all through the conversation.

'Real god-looking,' the blond giant said in a non-committal tone. 'Well, I reckon I'll be pulling out.'

'Not me,' Pierce drawled. 'Who's for a few hands of poker?'

'Did somebody say poker?' called Bragg from the faro table 'Cash me in, friend, I hear sweet music.'

If there was little chance of getting the foreman away from the faro table, Mark knew none at all would separate him from the kind of poker game Pierce meant to start. Still, Mark de-

27

clined to play.

'I reckon I'll go to bed,' he said. 'You wanting to use my room, Tule?'

'At the Houston?' yelped Bragg. 'That's not my kind of range. I'll see you sometime tomorrow.'

Walking from the saloon, Mark put aside all thoughts of the red-headed girl and Banker Snodgrass. Maybe Wycliffe told the truth; but if he did not and planned to avenge the insult on his family, walking the streets day-dreaming would be a good way to wind up lying in the dirt and looking like a horse tromped you.

Mark's caution proved unnecessary, which did not mean he regretted showing it. From the lack of incidents he concluded that Wycliffe had carried out his promise to lead the trio out of town. Entering the imposing Houston Hotel, Mark went to the reception desk and rang the bell for the night clerk. Unlike the smaller hotels of the range country, one could not reach over and take a room key from the rack. So Mark leaned on the desk and waited. His eyes went to a large book lying closed by the ink-well. Following the growing trend in the East, and to show that Austin had risen above the status of a rough, uncurried range town, the Houston maintained a register of its guests; something likely to be regarded as showing an unnecessary inquisitiveness in most places west of the Mississippi River.

Two men entered the building and walked across to the desk Turning the register, one of them flipped it open. Although no snob, Mark did not regard the pair as being potential Houston guests. One of them stood almost Mark's height, although without a corresponding heft, wore a derby hat, town suit shirt, tie and boots. His face bore a tough, mocking sneer as if he felt that he did Texas a favour by being there. Studying the man, Mark noticed that the right side jacket pocket sagged as if carrying a heavy weight. Not a gun, for the bulge made was the wrong shape and he carried a light calibre Colt butt forward at his left side.

Something in the second man's attitude attracted Mark's attention. Tall, lean, dressed in range clothes, his moustached tanned face was not that of a city dweller. Hanging in a fast draw holster, an Army Colt showed signs of much use. The man looked Mark over from head to foot, with particular emphasis to his features. In a way it reminded the blond giant of a rancher examining a stud horse or bull and estimating its marketable value.

Another man once looked at Mark in such a manner. Remembering the circumstances, an uneasy feeling crept over him. Before he could decide what action to take, Mark saw the night clerk appear from a door behind the desk. Indignation showed on the clerk's face as he stepped hurriedly forward, spun the register back to its original position and closed it with a bang.

'Was there something?' he demanded with studied politeness.

'We want a room,' the city man replied.

'Sorry. We've no vacancies.'

'Maybe this'll ch——' the city man began, reaching into his jacket's inside pocket.

'Let it ride, Quigg,' growled the other man, darting a glance in Mark's direction. 'There's other places we can try.'

For a moment Quigg seemed inclined to dispute the point, then followed the other's gaze. 'Sure, Burbage, there's other places. Let's go find one.'

'You want your key, Mr. Counter?' the clerk asked after the two men left.

'Why sure,' Mark agreed. 'Any messages?'

'None, sir. Do you want a call in the morning?'

'Not unless a telegraph message comes. Good night.'

'Good night, sir.'

Taking his key, Mark crossed to the stairs. Before going up, he glanced at the door and saw the two men standing outside. Neither looked back, or showed any sign of entering the building, so Mark walked upstairs and along the corridor of the first floor. Reaching room number twelve, he slipped the key into the lock and opened the door.

Instantly Mark felt something to be wrong. The room was in darkness and usually a place like the Houston left a lamp lit for its guests' benefit. Stepping forward cautiously, Mark caught a sweet aroma which most certainly had not been present when he left earlier.

The door closed of its own volition—or did it? From behind it came a soft rustling sound. While almost sure what was happening, Mark took no chances and turned towards the sound with his right hand dropping gun-wards. Then two arms went around his neck, a firm, yet undoubtedly feminine body pressed against him and warm lips crushed on to his mouth, kissing hard and passionately. Certain that he did not need to fear his visitor, Mark put his arms to a better use than drawing weapons and kissed back.

Freed at last from his unseen caller's grasp, he asked, 'Is it all right for me to light the lamp?'

'Go to it,' replied a gentle, cultured female voice.

For the first time Mark realised that more than normal night darkness caused the pitch-black condition of the room. The

Houston ensured its guests' privacy by fitting thick drapes to the windows. However, the management allowed each guest to decide whether to make use of the facility. Although Mark had not drawn them before he left, they appeared to be pulled together now. Taking a match from his pocket, Mark rasped it on the seat of his pants. He found the lamp and applied the flame to its wick. Not until the lamp's light bathed the room did he offer to turn around and face his visitor.

Like all the Houston's first floor rooms, number twelve offered more luxury than usual in Texas hotels. Facing the rear of the building, the room had a large, comfortable bed, dressing-table with drawers, wash-stand that sported a clean white towel, and a large wardrobe.

In the centre of the room stood the beautiful red-headed girl who had drawn his attention on Hood Street that afternoon. A warm, inviting smile added charm to her features as she came towards him with arms out-stretched. Once more she pressed her mouth against his. Never averse to such treatment at the hands of a beautiful girl, Mark gave her an adequate reply.

'They told me this was the safest place in Austin,' he remarked on releasing her and moving her back to arms' length.

'The lock's an ordinary lever and fitted for a master key,' she replied. 'I could have opened it with a bobby-pin.'

'I just bet you could. Say, Belle honey, I thought you'd got too high-toned to speak to old friends back there on Hood Street.'

'You put me in one hell of a spot, Mark,' she answered in her attractive Southern drawl. 'If that feller had stepped in a couple of seconds later I'd've already started getting you some help.'

'Would that've been bad?' Mark asked.

'Not for you, maybe,' the girl admitted. 'But it would for me. Snodgrass thinks I'm a shy, unassuming lil Georgia gal with money to invest and he might've changed his mind if he heard me cussing like a trail hand hauling cows out of a mud-hole.'

'So you're working on Snodgrass,' Mark said a touch coldly.

'Nobody else but.'

'Why?'

'Because he can afford it and I figure he's asked to be trimmed for a fair piece now.'

'Damn it all, Belle!' Mark began.

'Don't you go all high-toned on me, Mark Counter!' she snapped back. 'I'm a thief, but I've been one ever since you met me and never pretended to be anything else but one to you.'

'A nice gal like you doesn't have to be one,' he growled.

'No,' the girl agreed. 'I could go back home and marry off to

30

some rancher. Grow old before my time raising kids and watching him sweat out his guts to make a decent spread from a strip of beat-up range. See every red cent he makes go into the bank to pay off interest on a mortgage and then, just when it looks like he's going to make it, have the bank foreclose and run him off.'

'That's what happened to your folks, huh?' Mark said gently.

'Sure. Paw struggled to keep the place going through the War. Sold cattle to the Army—only they paid him in Confederate money. Then after it ended—well, you saw what happened.'

'I was luckier than most, pappy kept his money in gold not paper.'

'So did my paw, what he had, put it into a real safe place too. A bank. Only the bank failed. The new feller who took it on sounded real helpful, lending us and our neighbours money to keep going. Only he stopped being helpful before we could pay him back.'

'The law didn't help?'

'What law? Davis' lousy State Police? It was them who ran us off our spread. I swore I'd make that banker sweat and did.'

'His name's not Snodgrass,' Mark pointed out.

'They're so alike you'd think the same father spawned them,' Belle snorted. 'I'm no saint, Mark. And I'm not the James boys making out that I rob the rich to give to the poor. But I've never yet robbed a man who didn't ask for it.'

Coming to a halt, with her heated tirade, the girl stared half-defiantly at the blond giant. Looking back, a smile played on Mark's lips, but he felt a little sad too. Ever since their meeting the previous year he had felt a strong attraction for the beautiful lady outlaw, Belle Starr.* A spirited, gay girl, she had a zest for life which set her apart from any other woman he had ever met. The only one who came close being Calamity Jane, and Mark regarded her in a very different manner. Where he thought of Calamity almost in the light of a tomboy sister, he regarded Belle as a woman—and what a woman.

'It's your life,' he told the girl.

'Thanks for not preaching at me,' she replied. 'There's no sound so sweet to me as the screech of a banker when he's been plucked. I tell you, Mark, there's nothing I like better than making one screech.'

'*Nothing?*' Mark repeated.

'In the way of business, I mean,' Belle answered and looked pointedly across the room. 'You never did finish teaching me to

* Told in *Troubled Range*.

31

play poker.'

For the first time, following the direction of the girl's gaze, Mark noticed a boxed deck of cards lying on the bed's covers. Crossing the room, he sat on one side of the bed. After unbuckling his gunbelt and placing it on the dressing-table, he took up the cards. Thumbing open the box, he slid out the pasteboards and then raised his eyes to Belle's smiling face as she sat at the other side.

'Come to think of it,' he said. 'I never did at that. The first thing we have to do is shuffle the deck.'

'Is it?' asked the girl innocently.

'Sure is.'

'But it might take all night for us to—finish the game.'

'Darned if I'd've thought of that,' Mark grinned. 'Only according to Hoyle——'

'A feller I know says that Hoyle never played poker in his whole life,' Belle objected. 'Anyway, what right's some limey got to tell us red-blooded Americans how we should play cards?'

'You've convinced me,' Mark grinned and dealt out two hands.

'I'll open with a pair of shoes,' Belle remarked, without picking up her cards.

Half an hour later, after an instructive period of betting and raising, the lesson had ended. Darkness once more filled the room.

'Why'd you rescue that lobby-lizzie on Hood Street?' asked Belle's voice. 'You could've got hurt and then I'd never have learned how to play poker.'

'It seemed like a good idea at the time,' Mark replied.

'She looked like she'd've liked nothing better than walk off on your arm.'

'I was a mite disappointed when she didn't,' grinned Mark.

'What'd she got that I haven't?' demanded Belle.

'Nothing,' admitted Mark. 'And a whole heap less of it.'

'Flattery will get you a long way, young man,' purred the lady outlaw. 'As long as you don't spend all night talking about it.'

'I always figured to be a man of action, not words,' Mark told her.

'Then act.' Belle replied.

CHAPTER FOUR

A LADY OUTLAW IN DISTRESS

MARK stirred in the bed as he heard a pounding on his door. While the room remained dark, he could see daylight through a small gap in the curtains. Sitting up, he called, 'Who is it?'

'You're expecting maybe Robert E. Lee?' Tule Bragg's rasping voice answered. 'Rise up, boy and let a tired ole man inside.'

Which, in view of how Mark had spent the night, could prove a might embarrassing. Then he realised that he had the room to himself. Reaching out his left hand, he touched only the sheets and he made out the empty shape of the pillow, sunk-in by a head's pressure, at his side. Swinging his feet to the ground, Mark sat up and reached for his pants, looked around and found no trace of his visitor of the previous night.

'She sure moves soft and easy,' he mused, drawing on the pants, 'in more ways than one.'

Suddenly he remembered that he did not mention the two men to Belle. Yet he wondered if their business might be connected with her. On the first time he met Belle, a bounty hunter called Framant had been after her. When Framant came on Mark in the Elkhorn livery barn, he looked the Texan over in the same way that Burbage had; calculatingly, trying to see if his face struck a note from a wanted poster. Hunting wanted men for the price on their heads had been the way Framant made his living. Burbage too, or Mark missed his guess.

Deciding that he would give Belle a warning at the earliest opportunity, Mark walked across to the door and unlocked it. He knew something of the girl's skill at opening locked doors and felt no surprise to find it secured as it had been before they finished their game of poker.

Bragg leaned against the door-jamb, unshaven and yet showing no sign of having missed a night's sleep.

'Afternoon,' he greeted laconically, although the time was no more than half past nine in the morning.

'How'd it go?' Mark growled inhospitably, allowing the foreman to enter.

'Could've been worse. I come out a lil mite ahead.'

'Which means you've won a bundle and won't stop bragging about it all week.'

'You boys at the OD Connected sure live well, happen this's

the time of day you get up,' drawled Bragg, crossing the room and pulling open the curtains. 'And I never got to boasting about my winnings. Say though, talking about that, there was this time down in Amarillo back in '58——'

'There I sat, two lil deuces showing and nothing in the hole,' Mark interrupted. 'And him with two pairs kings riding high.'

'Have I told you about it afore?' inquired Bragg in a surprised tone.

'Not more'n twenty-thirty times, I'd say,' Mark replied and scowled as the foreman began to sniff the air. 'Now what's wrong?'

Wrinkling his nose in an expression of disgust, Bragg crossed the room. He drew apart the curtains, unfastened and raised the bottom part of the window.

'Figure to clear the air a mite,' he explained. 'Way this room smells, the cleaning gal might get the wrong idea, or the right one; and I'm damned if I know which'd be worse.'

'To each his own,' drawled Mark tolerantly. 'You like gambling and I don't.'

'Neither did I when I was your age,' grunted Bragg. 'I'm hungry.'

'We'll get a shave in the barber shop downstairs and then have some breakfast,' Mark suggested as he dressed.

'Damned if I'd pay the sort of prices they ask for a room and let 'em make me shave afore I eat,' the foreman drawled. 'Anyways, in a fancy place like this, I thought they'd make you have a shave afore they let you into the barber shop.'

All through his shave and while eating breakfast, Mark tried to decide what he should do about Belle Starr's presence in town. To some people the answer would have been clear, warn the banker. Mark did not see it that way. All too well he remembered the conditions during Reconstruction when 'liberal' bigots sought to smash down those who dared oppose their lofty ideals and carpetbagger scum used official positions to loot and rob. Many an otherwise honest Texan had been driven into a life of crime at that time. Maybe Mark would have been under different circumstances. There were personal loyalties involved too. A man like Mark Counter did not easily turn his back on a friend.

Refusing Bragg's offer to go along and help with his father's business, Mark walked the streets of the city and tried to solve his problem. From the comments made by the young man at the Bighorn the previous night, Snodgrass might deserve plucking. Reaching a decision, Mark turned his steps towards the office of a prominent lawyer. As the lawyer was also his uncle, Mark gained admission with no difficulty. After talking over

34

different subjects, Mark brought up the subject of Snodgrass' character. Always a forthright man, his uncle left him in no doubt that the young man's views had been correct. The lawyer refrained from asking any questions as to Mark's reason for making the inquiry and the meeting ended as amiably as it had begun.

By the time Mark reached the street, he decided to let things ride. When he suggested she forget the whole deal, during the previous night, Belle insisted that other people were too deeply involved for her to back out and leave them. One thing Mark felt sure of. With Belle planning and organising things there would be no violence involved. He also felt willing to bet that she'd arranged things to ensure no innocent person would suffer through the robbery.

Having made his decision, Mark gave thought to his horse. He knew that Belle rented a room on his floor at the hotel, although on the other side of the passage, but did not intend to go to see her. While intending to remain impassive in the affair, he also felt that any further contact between them must come in some other town. So he went to the livery barn where he left his huge blood-bay stallion on arrival in Austin. Everything necessary for the horse's well-being was attended to by the time Mark arrived and he knew the rest would do it good. On checking, he found one of the blood bay's shoes needed replacing and went to attend to the matter.

With his horse reshod, Mark returned to the hotel. He found a message from Bragg warning that the business would take longer than expected, but no word from Ole Devil. Dining alone in the hotel, he felt bored and decided he would head for San Garcia after seeing Sailor Sam. Maybe Dusty did not need help, but anything beat hanging around Austin unless he had his friends with him.

Like most men who often spent long periods with little sleep, Mark had developed the habit of grabbing some when the opportunity arose. Going to his room, he removed hat, boots and gunbelt, lay on the bed and drifted almost immediately to a deep sleep.

Night had fallen when Mark woke. Sitting on the bed, he looked around the room and then came to his feet. Crossing the room, he opened the door with the intention of looking for one of the hotel staff to ask for water. Then he heard voices on the stairs.

'It's room seven, gentlemen,' came the fruity tones of the night clerk. 'I can't say that I approve——'

Mark drew the door until it was nearly closed at the words. Standing in the darkness, he peered through the slit and

35

listened to a conversation he knew to be private. Number seven room across and along the passage was rented by Belle Starr, under the name 'Magnolia Beauregard'.

'You're not paid to approve or disapprove,' said a hard, clipped New England accent. 'That letter I showed you said for you to give us every co-operation.'

'Is she up there now?' asked a second Eastern voice as the night clerk appeared in Mark's range of vision.

'She hasn't handed in her key if she's gone out,' replied the hotel man.

The other two speakers came into sight. One of them Mark recognised as the dude who showed such an interest in the hotel register the previous night. At his side walked another obvious dude. Not quite so tall, but with a powerful build, he dressed in better taste than his companion. Much the same kind of gunbelt hung under the man's city jacket, a pearl-handled Smith & Wesson No. 2 revolver in its cross draw holster. At .32 calibre, despite its manufacturers calling it an 'Army' revolver, the gun did not impress Mark. He had been reared in the Texas tradition that even .36 was a touch light in calibre when one's life depended on it. Handsome but hard as nails was the way the man struck Mark, studying him through the crack in the doorway.

Moving around cautiously, Mark watched the three men halt before the door marked '7'. Either the two dudes did not regard Belle as dangerous, or they lacked training in certain basic peace officer matters. Flanking the clerk as he knocked on the door, they would have been in the line of fire should the room's occupant start throwing lead. That did not happen, nor did the door open. After a moment the second dude looked at the clerk.

'Use your pass-key.'

'It's on your head if anything goes wrong,' warned the clerk as he obeyed.

Once again Mark marvelled at men whom he imagined to be peace officers, acting in such a suicidal manner. Neither of them took the precaution of drawing a gun as they entered the room. Then they walked out again, alone.

'She's not there,' Quigg growled.

'Our guests occasionally take their keys with them when they leave,' the clerk pointed out. 'The cleaning staff have pass-keys——'

'I've got the bank covered,' interrupted the other dude. 'In case she comes back, I'll wait in the hall. You'd best stay here, Quigg.'

'Sure, Mr. Shafto. You want for me to wait in the passage?'

'In her room, damnit! If you hang around in the hall, some-body'll see you and start yelling for the manager.'

'I'm not sure that——' began the clerk.

'You don't have to be sure of anything!' Shafto barked. 'I'll handle any complaints. Go on in, Quigg.'

Mark felt as if a cold hand touched him as he watched Quigg enter Belle's room. While he did not know what kind of law-man Shafto might be, he felt that he could hazard a pretty fair guess. Certainly he was no Western-trained peace officer, that showed in the lack of precautions taken at the door to Belle's room. In the early 1870s there was no national law enforce-ment office, it all being managed at State level. Even the U.S. Secret Service concerned itself only with forgers and counter-feiters. As Belle only operated in the West, she could not have fallen foul of Eastern lawmen; except for one kind. It could even be debated that the men involved had no official standing, if the point arose.

After retiring from the command of the U.S. Secret Service at the end of the Civil War, Allan Pinkerton had organised his own private detective agency. Using the methods employed with varying success against the South's efficient spy networks, Pinkerton worked for banks, railroads and other big business combines to stamp out the enormous crime-wave which rose with the uneasy peace. Unless Mark missed badly in his guess, Shafto, Quigg and Burbage belonged to the Pinkerton Agency; the former pair being regular operatives and the latter hired for local knowledge.

If the men had belonged to an official law enforcement agency, Mark would have been faced with the serious problem of his future actions. He felt no such responsibility where Pinkerton's men were concerned. Like most Southerners, Mark disliked Allan Pinkerton and regarded his agency with sus-picion. Not for another eighteen or more months would come the 'bomb incident', when Pinkerton agents threw either a bomb or a harmless 'Grecian-fire' flare into the home of Jesse James' parents to kill the outlaw's eight year old half-brother and blow his mother's right arm off; but every man who served the Confederacy remembered ugly rumours of Southern prisoners-of-war being tortured by the Yankee Secret Service under the flimsy pretence of extracting information. So Mark felt no compunctions about helping Belle to avoid falling into Shafto's clutches. From the little Mark saw of the man, he guessed any prisoner with information would be worked on to be induced to part with it.

Crossing to his bed, Mark dressed quickly. As he reached the door, he remembered that the window, opened by Bragg that morning, was not closed. Although the room overlooked a wide alley and the rear of a line of business premises, he doubted if anybody could reach its window without the aid of a ladder. Even if they did, there was little could be stolen. When heading for Tennyson, he'd travelled light and had only taken a change of clothes in addition to spare ammunition. The big wardrobe held only a few garments unlikely to fit the average sneak-thief, and his rifle. He had left his heavy low-horned, double girthed saddle hanging on a burro in the locked room at the livery barn. So Mark left the window open, stepped into the passage and locked the door. He could hear Shafto and the clerk talking as he walked down the stairs.

'I can't hardly believe it,' the clerk wailed. 'Miss Beauregard's been——'

'You don't have to believe anything,' Shafto put in. 'And don't let out a peep to anybody about what we're doing here. I'll stay in the lobby here until she comes back. Is there another way in?'

'Only through the rear door and up the service stairs at the back.'

'You go and watch there, Burbage,' ordered Shafto and darted a glance to where Mark stepped into view at the bottom of the stairs.

'Good evening, Mr. Counter,' greeted the clerk. 'Do you wish to hand your key in?'

'Sure,' Mark replied, doing so. 'No word from Ole Devil yet?'

'None. Where will you be if it comes?'

'It's likely to be anyplace. I couldn't make a start tonight anyway.'

With that Mark turned and walked out of the front door. As he went, he could feel the men's eyes on him. Crossing the street, he stood for a moment and tried to decide how he might best find Belle to give a warning of her danger. From what he heard, the men appeared to expect her attempt to be made that night. So he made his way through the town until reaching the street on which Snodgrass' bank was situated. Fortunately enough people used the street for Mark to stroll along in a reasonable crowd. Having worked as a lawman both in a tough Montana gold town and on the Rio Hondo ranges, Mark could guess what kind of arrangements Shafto had made. As he walked along, his eyes darted constantly around. He saw three obvious members of Shafto's defending force, looking just too casual propping up walls to a trained eye. There would be more at the rear of the bank. Much as he hated to admit it, Mark saw that Shafto had been thorough. Any attempt to rob the bank that night was doomed to failure.

For a time Mark waited in a small saloon, watching the bank. Then he decided to return to the hotel. If he located the waiting Pinkerton men, Belle would be no less successful. So she would either postpone or call off her robbery.

While walking along the street towards the Houston, Mark saw a shape emerge from a side alley in front of him. Although a hooded cloak effectively concealed the shape's face and figure, Mark felt sure enough of her identity to stride forward in her direction.

'Belle!' he said.

Turning, the lady outlaw reached her right hand into the top of her reticule. Then she brought it out empty, although Mark guessed that her Manhattan Navy revolver rode in the special holster which prevented its presence being detected.

'Hi, Mark,' she greeted.

'Let's get off the street,' he growled, taking her arm and steering her back into the alley.

'What's wrong?' she asked, suddenly realising that he called her by her name instead of using her alias.

'There're Pinkertons waiting at the hotel and watching the bank.'

If Mark expected to create a sensation with his words, he failed. Not that he expected the girl to show too much emotion, but he felt the news ought to have come as something of a surprise. Instead, all she did was nod her head gravely.

'I figured they'd be covering the bank,' she admitted. 'But not the hotel. Are you sure it's me they're after?'

'They asked for your room and there's one of them in it right now.'

'Damnation!' Belle snorted. 'If I thought that——'

'What?' prompted Mark. 'Do you reckon somebody snitched on you?'

'Somebody must have,' agreed Belle.

'Me?'

Gently she took his powerful hands in her own, raised herself on to tiptoes and kissed him lightly on the lips. 'You'd be the last one I'd think it of. No Mark, I've an idea who sold me.'

'You'd best get out of town,' Mark told her.

'Sure. But there're a few things I must get from the hotel. A change of clothes, things like that.'

'One of them's in your room, like I said,' warned Mark.

'If I sneak in the back way——' the girl began.

'Nary a chance, gal. There's a hard-eyed jasper called Burbage watching the back door and another in the front lobby.'

'That sounds like Dick Shafto's work. He's thorough and one

39

man I wouldn't want to have laying hands on me. But I have to get into my room. I can't get away dressed like this.'

'That's for sure,' Mark said, catching a glimpse of a decollete silk dress under her cloak. 'How'd you plan to leave happen everything went all right?'

'By stage,' Belle explained. 'But I've a good horse waiting in case I had to break for the tall timber. That means wearing something a whole heap more suitable than this frock.'

'You can walk on in through either the front or back door and I'll be right behind to see you're not stopped,' Mark told her.

'And after you've done it?' she asked.

'Let me worry about after.'

Slowly Belle shook her head and squeezed his hands. 'No, Mark. You're not breaking the law to help me.'

'We'd be together.'

'When we get together, it won't be so we have to watch our back-trail and run every time a stranger looks sideways at us.'

A plan began to form in Mark's head, one which could work. If it did, Belle would have the chance to collect her property. While the plan had more than a little risk, with the chance of him ending up on the run from the law, Mark decided to put it into practice.

'I reckon I can get you into the hotel without being seen,' he said. 'After that——'

'I'll play the hand out my own way,' Belle stated. 'Don't argue, Mark. It's the only way I'll go along with you.'

'You're a determined woman, Miss Starr,' he said and kissed her. 'Now let's get the hell from here.'

With that Mark took the girl's arm and led her to the rear of the alley. Keeping to the back streets, they reached the Houston. Not on the street at the front, but in the darkened area behind the building. Watching how Mark looked up at the first floor windows, Belle guessed partly at what he meant to do. For all that, she felt a touch surprised when he came to a halt below his room. Placing his back to the wall, he bowed his legs slightly, cupped his hands together and held them before him.

'You're figuring to hoist me up *there*?' she asked. 'So I can go through the window into your room.'

'If it's not my room, there's likely to be some screaming,' Mark replied. 'I left the window open and it's the only one that is.'

Stepping forward, Belle raised her right foot and placed it in his hands. She threw the cloak back over her shoulders and nodded. 'Ready!' she said, then smiled. 'No peeking mind.'

'Why'd I need to peek?' grinned Mark. 'Get set. Shove up!'

Obediently Belle forced down with her left leg and felt herself rising into the air under the thrust of Mark's arms. Higher she rose until her feet reached the level of his chest.

'I'll have to go up still more!' she warned.

Mark guessed that and changed his hold. Carefully he eased his hands apart, one under each of Belle's shoes. Sucking in a breath, he continued to raise her upwards. Resting her hands on the wall, Belle stretched above her head. She felt the window ledge and her fingers closed over it.

'I'm almost there!' she hissed. 'Just a little higher.'

At which point a man came from the shadows of the next building and walked towards them.

CHAPTER FIVE

A MISTAKE ANYBODY COULD MAKE

NEVER had Mark felt so completely at a disadvantage as he did when he saw the shape walking towards him from the blackness of the next building. The surrounding darkness prevented him from doing more than identify the approaching figure as being male, he could see nothing to tell him who the other might be. Nor could he think of any acceptable reason for his actions when the newcomer started to ask the obvious questions. Supporting the girl above him at arms' length, Mark could not draw a weapon. If he removed one hand, always assuming he could hold Belle's weight on the other, it was doubtful if she would be able to keep her balance.

Drawing a gun was no answer, and Mark knew it. While he wished to help the girl escape, he would not do so at the cost of another man's life. Even if the newcomer proved to be a Pinkerton man reporting to Shafto, Mark doubted whether he could kill the other. Besides which, the sound of the shot would bring Burbage out to investigate.

Before any solution presented itself to Mark, or Belle—and, to give her credit, her first instinct was to warn him not to shoot the new arrival—the man spoke.

'You-all should use the kind of hotel I do, boy,' came Bragg's drawling voice. 'Then you wouldn't have to sneak the gal in.'

Relief flooded over Mark at the sound of his old friend's tones. 'Damn you, Tule,' he growled. 'Kind of place you stop in, they'd not expect you to sneak anything but a pig inside.'

'Not even that,' said Bragg cheerfully. 'You should hear 'em grunting in the room next to mine. You all right up there, ma'am?'

'Apart from being scared white-haired, I'm fine!' Belle gritted, realising that she did not need to worry about the man below betraying her. 'Hold firm just a mite longer, Mark.'

With that she started to shove up the window section as high as it would go. Cursing the dress and cloak, although she knew that Snodgrass would never have accepted her as a *bona fide* rich, naive Southern belle had she visited him dressed in the kind of clothing the present situation called for, she began to pull herself into Mark's room. Cloth ripped, shapely legs waved wildly and a number of unladylike comments broke from Belle before she slid through the window. She landed in an undignified roll learned when coming off a horse's back involuntarily during her rearing-years on the ranch. Rising, she looked out of the window at the two men and waved a cheery hand.

'I'm all right.'

'Wait until I come up there,' Mark replied in as low a voice as he could manage with the hope of the girl hearing him but not the waiting man in the hotel. 'Do it, gal. I've got a jim-dandy idea for getting your gear. And without needing to shoot up any of that Pinkerton bunch.'

'Dang it, and I figured you to be eloping,' Bragg said as the girl ducked back into the room. 'Or have her folks set the Pink-eyes on your trail?'

'Something like that,' Mark agreed, turning to walk towards the corner of the building. 'You game to help me bust the law a mite, Tule?'

'I'm game. Figured there was something wrong when I saw you haul the gal into the alley back there. Got to thinking and remembered how you looked at her back on Hood Street yesterday. I'd've sworn then you recognised her and thought she'd speak. That's mighty sweet-smelling perfume she uses, boy, if it does linger just a lil mite. So I tagged along just in case.'

'You allow I'd fallen for the old badger game, or something?'

'I don't know what I reckoned, but I allowed to be on hand should you need some help.'

'Which same I need,' Mark admitted.

'That figures,' Bragg replied.

'The gal's Belle Starr and the Pink-eyes are waiting to grab her.'

'Boy, I wronged you for sure when I thought you might be heading for trouble,' the foreman stated soberly. 'Yes sirree, bub, I was sure wrong.'

'Was, huh?' grunted Mark unsympathetically.

'Yep. You're not in trouble. It's just that the water's up over the willows and your swimming hoss died,' drawled the fore-man, mentioning one of the hazards a cowhand on a trail herd met in the form of a river running in full flood. 'Let's go get her out. Damned stinking Yankee Pink-eyes!'

'We'll do that,' Mark promised as they reached the street and turned along the front of the hotel. 'Only we do it this way.'

With that he quickly explained the new version of his plan. Bragg's presence allowed Mark more scope and made his idea more practical than before. Although the foreman snorted and

43

growled a curse when hearing of the Pinkerton agent in Belle's room, he admitted that Mark's plan ought to work given just a smidgin of Texas good fortune.

'Anyways, you'll have a mighty good reason for jumping him,' Bragg continued cheerfully.

'Things could go wrong,' Mark pointed out. 'If they do, we'll have trouble.'

'Day I start worrying about trouble, I'm going to quit working for you fool Counters and go live with my sister back East,' Bragg answered. 'The hell with the Pink-eyes. Who the hell do they reckon they are, coming to Texas and abusing honest folks this ways?'

While a moralist might have pointed out that Belle Starr did not come under the category of 'honest folks', Mark let the matter ride. Comforted by the knowledge that he had a loyal friend at his side, the blond giant led the way into the hotel. Seated to one side of the front entrance, Shafto lowered the newspaper he pretended to be reading for long enough to look at Mark and Bragg. Then he raised it once again and gave the impression of being engrossed in the latest Austin happenings. Discussing the likelihood of Sailor Sam arriving the following morning, Mark and the foreman crossed the lobby and halted at the desk. After collecting his key and asking for any messages, Mark led Bragg upstairs.

On entering his room, Mark found that Belle had not wasted her time. While she still wore the cloak, her dress lay in a neatly folded pile on the bed. Guessing what the cloak concealed, Mark almost wished that Bragg was not on his heels. Belle looked calm and unruffled despite having climbed through the window and undressed quickly. Smiling from Mark to Bragg, she looked expectantly back at the big blond.

'You see, I waited,' she said.

'If you hadn't, I'd've caught you and paddled your hide,' Mark replied. 'I put a heap of thinking into getting you out of here.'

'Thinking don't come easy to them Counters, ma'am,' Bragg went on. 'I'm Tule Bragg, his pappy's foreman.'

'Mark's told me about you,' smiled Belle.

'It's lies, every danged word of it!' Bragg insisted, then became sober. 'You ready, boy?'

'Passage's clear, let's give it a whirl,' Mark replied. 'We're going to haul that jasper out of your room, Belle gal.'

'No——!' she began.

'Boy's got a real tricky lil idea worked out, ma'am,' Bragg put in.

'Has he told you who you're helping and why?'

'Yep. Not that he needed to tell me, there's only one Belle Starr.'

'You'll be making me blush next,' she said and turned to Mark. 'How do you plan to do it?'

Mark told her and she nodded in agreement. Not only did the plan stand a good chance of working, but it offered Mark and Bragg a passable excuse for their actions. Certainly the new scheme sounded safer than Mark's original idea. So any objections she might have felt died away. Her chief concern had been for Mark's fate after she made her escape, knowing the vindictive nature of her hunters. If everything went smoothly, the worst light Mark could be regarded in was for acting a touch hastily.

'Go to it,' she said.

'We're on our way,' Mark replied.

For all that, only Bragg walked along the deserted corridor towards Belle's room. Mark remained at the door of number twelve and Belle stood out of sight behind the door. While waiting for the men to join her, she had drawn the curtains to prevent any chance of being seen from outside. Everything depended on how the man in her room acted.

Coming to number seven, Bragg drew close to the door and turned its handle. He heard a scuffling sound from inside and pressed his ear against the panel. For a short time nothing happened, then he detected stealthy foot-steps approaching inside the room. Swiftly and silently the foreman glided along the passage and around a corner out of sight of Belle's door.

Slowly the door to Belle's room opened and Quigg's head emerged. He looked towards the corner around which Bragg disappeared. Acting as if he had just arrived and was letting himself into his quarters, Mark coughed. Just as Mark hoped would happen, Quigg swung to look his way and then ducked back into the room. To a casual observer the man's actions would have appeared highly suspicious, one of the things Mark counted on happening.

Darting along the passage, Mark dropped his shoulder and charged the door. The Houston had been built to last, its rooms far more sound-proof than those of most hotels in Texas and its doors stoutly constructed. Struck by two hundred pounds of driving muscle and sinew, the door still burst open. Standing just behind it, Quigg saw his danger too late. The door swung inwards, catching him and sending him sprawling across the room. He hit the wardrobe, which halted his progress and saw the blond giant enter.

Once again Quigg acted as Mark wanted him to do. Spluttering a curse, the dude stabbed his right hand into the sagging pocket. While most western men would have reached for their gun, Mark figured that Quigg went for a weapon he understood better than a firearm. Anyway, Quigg's action gave Mark the excuse he wanted.

Bounding across the room even as a wicked leather-wrapped, lead-loaded billy whipped from Quigg's pocket, Mark ripped a punch into the man's belly. The billy fell from Quigg's hand as he grabbed at his middle and doubled over. Up came Mark's other hand in a driving blow that caught the dude's offered chin with smooth precision. Lifted erect by the blow, Quigg smashed into the wardrobe again. His legs buckled under him and he collapsed as if he had been suddenly boned.

'Neat,' said Bragg at the door. 'Nobody's showing themselves.'

'Get Belle here *pronto*,' Mark replied, kneeling by Quigg and making sure he could not hear or see anything.

Not until Bragg left to obey the order did Mark find time to look around the room. It seemed that Quigg had spent his time searching Belle's property, for every drawer had been turned out and her clothes lay in a pile on the floor of the wardrobe. Hearing the rapid patter of feet, Mark turned and saw the girl enter. Annoyance flashed on her face as she studied the condition of her belongings, then she gave a chuckle.

'Much good that did him,' she said.

'Is anything missing?' Mark asked.

'There was nothing for him to steal,' she replied. 'And he didn't look in the right place for the things that matter.'

Going to the bed, she drew away the covers until she exposed the mattress. Like all the other Houston fixtures, it offered the guest plenty of comfort; being thick and well packed. Collecting a pair of scissors from the work-basket Quigg upended in his search for evidence, Belle cut open the stitching at the bottom of the mattress. Reaching into the slit she made, the girl drew out a man's shirt and levis pants. She then carefully closed the gap and rapidly remade the bed. All the time she worked, Mark stood guard over the unconscious Pinkerton agent and Bragg remained at the door, watching the passage.

'Move it, Belle,' Mark said. 'He won't be out much longer and I don't want to have to hit him again.'

'All right,' she replied, darting to the wardrobe and taking out a pair of riding boots. 'This's all I need. My gunbelt, saddle and hat're with friends.'

'How about the rest of your stuff?' asked Bragg, indicating a velvet-lined box which stood open on the dressing table and showing several items of apparently costly jewellery.

'That can stay here,' Belle answered. 'It's not real and the

46

clothes were bought for this job. If I leave them, it will give me a start.'

'They'll not know you've been back,' Bragg admitted.

A low moan from Quigg warned them of the need for movement. Holding the clothes and boots, Belle left the room and headed towards Mark's quarters. Waiting until the girl entered and closed the door, the two men hoisted Quigg up between them and hauled him out, then along towards the stairs.

Throwing off her cloak, Belle stood clad in a brief set of underclothes which would have aroused Banker Snodgrass' suspicions had he been privileged to see them. Not that he would have found anything to complain at in the way she filled the flimsy silk. Kicking off her shoes, she retained the black stockings which showed her magnificent legs to their best advantage and donned the trousers. Next she drew on the shirt, tucking it into the pants and buttoning it up. The riding boots came next. Belle drew them on, snuggling her feet into the comforting touch of the stout leather. Then she thrust the Manhattan revolver from her reticule into the waistband of her pants. With a sigh of content, she knew that she could now make good her escape.

A coiled rope hung on a peg fixed to the side of the wardrobe. Modern in many ways, the Houston still retained the traditional Western style of fire precautions. Taking the rope, Belle doused the lamp and went to the window. She drew back the curtains and looked out. Satisfied that nobody watched the rear of the building, she slipped the honda of the rope over the hook stoutly fastened to the wall and tossed the other end out. Then she gathered her property, wrapping the cloak around her dress and shoes. At the window, she let the bundle fall and waited to see if its soft thud attracted any attention. When it did not, she climbed from the window and slid rapidly to the ground.

'Thanks for everything, big feller,' she breathed, looking up at the window. 'I'll never forget this.'

Her chance to repay Mark would come much sooner than she imagined.

Hearing the thud of feet on the stairs, Shafto started to lower his newspaper to take a surreptitious glance. When he saw Mark and Bragg hauling Quigg down between them, he lost his casual air. Crumpling the paper, he threw it aside and came to his feet. Behind the reception desk, the clerk stared with bug-out eyes and a mouth that hung wide open.

'Get the marshal here,' Mark ordered in a loud voice as he and Bragg let their groaning burden drop un-gently to the floor.

'We caught this jasper robbing a lady's room.'

'But—but he's a——!' spluttered the clerk.

'Go fetch the marshal, son,' Bragg told a gaping bell-hop who came loping up. 'They do say this town's so plumb law-abiding that a feller has to ask real polite afore he shoots a thieving son-of-a-bitch.'

'There's no call to do that,' Shafto growled, coming to the desk.

'You wouldn't say that had you seen the sneaky way this *hombre* ducked back inside the lady's room when he saw us coming,' Bragg replied, stirring the moaning Quigg with his toe. Then suspicion glowed on the foreman's face and he took on the attitude of a country-bumpkin in the big city for the first time. 'Maybe you're in it with him, feller.'

'I am, in a manner of speaking,' Shafto agreed and started to reach for his inside breast pocket.

He stopped, frozen immobile by the barrel of Bragg's big Dance ramming into his favourite belly.

'Don't you-all try it!' the foreman warned. 'I've allus heard you city jaspers are mighty tricky.'

'Damn it!' Shafto yelled at the clerk. 'Tell them who I am!'

'This's Mr. Shafto of the Pinkerton Detective Agency,' the clerk announced, trying to sound as if it was not his fault. 'That's one of his men.'

'You should try paying your help better, mister,' Mark said as Bragg thrust away the Dance.

'Huh?' grunted the startled Shafto.

'We found him in that pretty young lady's room and from the way her gear was thrown around, he'd been robbing her.'

'He was waiting there to arrest her!' Shafto snarled, kneeling at Quigg's side. 'Did you have to rough-handle him this bad?'

'I'd say "yes" to that,' Mark replied calmly. 'When I got to her door, I didn't knock polite and shout, "Hey, are you-all in there robbing the lady." I went in fast.'

'And when that Jasper started reaching for his pocket, ole Mark didn't reckon he was looking for his wipe,' Bragg went on. 'Which same that *hombre* can reckon he come off lucky. There's some who would've shot him first and apologised when they found that all he wanted was his handkerchief.'

Shafto looked at the two men in cold anger, yet he thought only that pure accident caused the disruption of his plans. Any man born in the range country, where gun-handling was taught as a matter of simple self-preservation, would have acted in the same way under the circumstances. Only, as Bragg had said, many would not have restricted themselves to merely knocking Quigg unconscious when he had tried to produce the wicked billy Shafto knew he carried.

Before any more could be said, the front door burst open and a dishevelled, red-faced Banker Snodgrass charged in. Mark could never remember seeing a man look so all-fired, out-and-out furious as Snodgrass did as he bore down on the Pinkerton agent. An expression of almost sick realisation began to creep over Shafto's features, as if he could guess what was coming.

'Shafto!' Snodgrass howled. 'Just what kind of fool game are you playing?'

'What's happened?' countered the detective.

'Damnit, I pay your Agency a retainer to be protected and I expect value for my money, sir!'

'But what——'

'You come to see me with the tale that my bank's going to be robbed. So I allow you every facility, let you bring in men that I'll have to pay for—and what, I say *what* happens?'

'Maybe you'd best tell me,' Shafto growled.

'I've every intention of telling you, sir!' screeched the banker. 'While all this high-priced help that I don't aim to pay for are sitting watching my bank, my house is robbed.'

'Your house?' gulped Shafto.

'My house, sir. MY HOME!' Snodgrass went on. 'As I returned to discover.'

Shafto's mouth dropped open, then clamped home in a tight line. Watching the Pinkerton agent, Mark could see him making an almost visible attempt to rally under the shock. Despite the blond giant's antipathy, he could not help admiring the manner in which Shafto regained control of himself. Standing at the desk, the detective glared down at the moaning, writhing Quigg, then looked at the clerk.

'Get Burbage from the back!' Shafto ordered. 'I'll go with you in a minute, Mr. Snodgrass.'

'Go to it,' the clerk said and the bell hop took a reluctant departure.

'What's up?' asked Burbage, coming from the rear of the building. Then he skidded to a halt and stared at Quigg. 'Who——'

'I'll explain later,' interrupted Shafto. 'Go up to her room and wait in case she comes back.'

'Sure. What happened to Quigg?'

'Forget him, damnit. And make sure that *you* stop in the room so nobody sees you.'

Then Burbage guessed what had happened and a broad grin creased his face. Hired temporarily for his local knowledge, he had so far found the smug, big-city condescension shown him by his employers annoying. It seemed that they were not so smart after all. Quigg must have been seen looking out of the girl's room and was jumped by the two cowhands who took him for a thief.

It was a mistake anybody could make. Yet Burbage began to get an uneasy feeling that something went wrong in it. Realising that he would have to stay on the alert while dealing with a smart, range-bred girl like Belle Starr, Burbage put out of his head the nagging, all but forgotten something which pricked at him.

After Burbage went to take over his new lookout post, Quigg had been taken into the clerk's office and Shafto accompanied Snodgrass to the scene of the crime, Mark went back to his room with Bragg.

'The lil devil,' the foreman said with an admiring grin as he pulled in and coiled the rope. 'She pulled the damned job after all—and in a way that only Snodgrass could get hurt.'

'Him and Pinkerton's bunch,' corrected Mark. 'They won't forget it, Tule.'

CHAPTER SIX

THE DEATH OF A FRIEND

NEXT morning all Austin buzzed with talk of the robbery. Although almost every outlaw band in the State received credit for looting Snodgrass' safe, the Pinkerton agents did not announce Belle's part in it. That did not surprise Mark. Most people in Texas knew that the girl only robbed people who deserved, by their treatment of others, to be trimmed. Probably Snodgrass demanded that the identity of his robber be held back. He had suffered a heavy personal loss, and his ego badly bruised, but felt things could be far worse. If folks learned that Belle Starr had robbed him, they might easily fight shy of depositing or leaving their money in his care. Maybe Shafto might not have been so compliant but had he not objected to people knowing that a woman had out-smarted him.

When the girl apparently did not return to collect her property, Shafto gathered his men and went out of town looking for her. The sheriff of Travis County offered to lend the services of his posse, but Shafto declined. So two groups of men rode from the State capital to scour the surrounding district in search of some sign of Belle's passing.

Mark spent a quiet morning, although he could not help wondering how soon it would be before Shafto heard of the slit-open mattress in Belle's room and began to get suspicious.

After attending to his horse, Mark paid a delayed courtesy call to the Governor. In addition to being the man appointed to clear up the mess left by Davis' corrupt administration, Stanton Howard was a friend of both Mark's father and Ole Devil Hardin. So he would have regarded Mark's non-arrival as a slight. Explaining that he figured Howard had enough on hand without entertaining every drifting cowhand, Mark excused himself for not appearing sooner, or attending a formal visit at the Governor's mansion. They discussed state affairs, including the organisation of more Ranger companies to fight the criminal element, talked of cattle and general matters. At last the Governor saw Mark out, apologising for not being able to offer the same standard of hospitality and sport received when he had visited the OD Connected shortly before taking office.

At lunch Mark met Bragg and a number of the men who had shared his first night in the Bigfoot Saloon. After the meal they went to the rear of the livery barn housing both Mark and Bragg's horses to pitch horseshoes.

The game had been going for some time when an interruption came. Riding tired horses, the sheriff's posse came from off the range. At the lead rode Sheriff Jules Murat, a tall, slim, handsome man who wore range clothes, yet managed to give the appearance of being dressed in some fancy European Hussar's uniform and that he should wear a cavalry sabre instead of the two matched Army Colts holstered at his sides. A successful rancher, he had accepted the post of county sheriff —soon to be followed by appointment to captain of a Texas Ranger's company—to do a job of work and not as an office-filler mainly concerned with politics or lining his pockets. One of Mark's chief concerns for Belle's safety had been the knowledge that Jules Murat would be hunting for her.

Urging his mount at a faster pace, Murat cut ahead of the rest of the posse and drew rein before the horseshoe pitchers. His eyes went straight to Mark and Bragg, worry in them as he started to speak.

'Mark, Tule, there's bad trouble.'

Looking past Murat, Mark and Bragg saw a tarp-wrapped figure draped across the back of a harness horse. Before Mark could start to think that Belle had been shot and told of their part in her escape, Bragg let out a low curse and headed towards the posse. Then Mark noticed that three more members of the sheriff's party led harness horses, although without the sinister loads of the first. Next Mark realised that the shape wrapped in a tarpaulin sheet would be too big for Belle. Suddenly, with shocking impact, he understood what made Bragg act in such a manner. Murat dropped from his saddle at Mark's side.

'Is it——?' Mark began.

'It's Sailor Sam,' agreed the sheriff quietly.

'An accident?'

'No, Mark,' Murat replied.

'Then what——?' Mark demanded.

'We'd been out since morning and nary a sign of whoever robbed Snodgrass could we find. Coming back in we saw where a wagon'd been driven off the trail. It had maybe six riders with it, so we followed the line. Found it in a clearing down close to the Colorado——'

'And?'

'Don't ask me what'd happened. All the gear'd been turned out of the wagon, opened up. There were signs of a helluva fight and Sam'd been shot in the back of the head.'

'So you brought his body in,' Mark said.

'We'd tired horses under us, Mark,' Murat replied. 'It'd been afore noon that they shot Sam and left soon after. With a start like that, we needed fresh mounts to catch up.'

'Sure you did, Jules,' Mark admitted and walked to where Bragg stood cursing in a low, savage voice. 'Let's get our rifles and the hosses, Tule.'

While the other players seethed with questions they wished to ask Murat, all remained silent as they realised the gravity of the situation. Hearing what Mark said, one of them stepped forward.

'Do you need any help, *amigo*?' he asked and it was a genuine offer, not made out of a morbid desire to take part in a man-hunt.

'No thanks,' Mark gritted. 'Tule and me'll tend to all that needs doing.'

'Let me go get a fresh horse and I'll ride with you,' Murat put in.

Without any hesitation Mark gave his agreement. Murat might be sheriff of the county which housed the State's capital, but he was also a mighty efficient practical peace officer. Shrewd, capable, honest, he fought crime hard and, where necessary, trod on toes without a thought of their owner's social standing. Such a man would do to ride the river with and be of the greatest help in the grim work ahead of them.

'Do you have anybody who can read sign, Jules?' Mark asked.

'Tejas Tom there,' the sheriff replied, indicating a tall young Indian wearing a town suit, collarless shirt and derby hat. 'Don't let his duds fool you, he'd run the Ysabel Kid a close second in reading sign.'

'We'll see to Sam for you, Mark,' one of the horseshoe pitchers promised. 'You go fetch what you'll need, I reckon we can saddle your hosses.'

'Thanks,' Mark replied. 'I'll pay for the burying so see he gets the best.'

Half an hour later Mark rode out of Austin with Bragg, Murat and Tejas Tom, the last two on fresh mounts. During the ride, Murat went into greater detail of what they saw and deduced from the Indian's reading of the sign.

'I'd say those fellers laid for him, hiding just off the trail,' Murat told Mark and Bragg. 'Made him drive down there where they couldn't be seen. Then it looked like he lit into them.'

'Plenty big fight,' confirmed the Indian. 'That feller put two-three down at least afore they shoot him.'

That figured to anybody who knew the fist-fighting ability of Sailor Sam. The knowledge that his old tutor went down fighting made Mark feel a little better, although it did nothing to

53

lessen his determination that Sam's killers would pay.

Two miles out of town Murat brought his horse to a halt and pointed to a clump of scrub oak trees close by it. 'This's where it happened. They hid up in the trees and rode out peaceable like. Then they took him off towards the river.'

Following the direction Murat indicated, Mark saw the tracks left by Sailor Sam's killers. While he did not put himself in the same category as the Ysabel Kid when it came to reading sign, Mark could tell that the men had ridden from their cover at a leisurely pace. Most likely Sailor Sam took them for a bunch of cowhands heading into Austin and looking to pass the time of day with him. By the time he realised the danger, it was too late to escape. So he behaved sensibly, going along with the gun-backed orders while watching for a chance to turn the tables on his captors. At the other side of the trail he saw where the wagon left escorted by the cook's killers. Starting his horse moving, Mark followed the tracks.

None of the party spoke as they rode through the wooded country in the direction of the Colorado River. Then at the foot of the slope, well-hidden from the trail, they came into sight of the wagon. Apart from unhitching the team and taking the cook's body along, nothing had been moved. Boxes and barrels lay on the ground, their tops opened and a few contents scattered.

At Murat's suggestion they left the horses well clear of the wagon and went forward on foot. Tejas Tom took the lead and as he drew near the foot of the slope began to describe the men who made the different sign.

'One was big feller, plenty hefty, ride bay mare. Two of 'em tall, lean, got dun and blue roan. 'Nother middle height, heavy with it, ride bay man-hoss. Other two maybe five foot ten, one lean, other heavy, got a black and iron grey hoss.'

Having seen the Ysabel Kid in action, Mark knew just how accurate a well-trained visual tracker could be. He did not doubt that when they finally caught up to the gang, the descriptions would prove correct. Going on, Tejas told how Sailor Sam fought and finally went down, shot by the tallest of the slim men. The Indian took Mark and Bragg to where a small rock rose from the springy grass. There they saw the marks made by a man falling down hard, but the Indian showed them something more important.

'See um?' he asked, pointing to a black mark on the side of the rock. 'Him shoot from ground after him knocked down.'

Igniting black powder threw out an awesome muzzle-blast as Mark well knew, but only in a forward direction. Which meant that the man must have held his gun barely out of the holster to shoot. Then Mark remembered the Wycliffe clan. The men he met in the Bigfoot Saloon fitted the description of part of the gang. More than that, Billy Wycliffe carried his gun in a swivel holster and did not need to draw the weapon to shoot. Fired from the leather, his Colt's barrel would have been low and close enough to leave the powder burns on the rock.

At which point the Indian dropped another bombshell. 'Was girl with wagon.'

For a moment the words did not sink into Mark's furiously-thinking head. Then he stared from Tejas to Bragg and said, 'A girl?'

'Not from the herd, that's for sure,' Bragg stated.

'Sign show she jump off box and run. Feller go after her and drag her back. They take her with 'em when they go.'

'Sam must've picked her up on the way in,' Murat guessed. 'Maybe from one of them nester spreads down that ways.'

'I reckon I know who killed Sam,' Mark said quietly.

'Who?' asked the sheriff.

'Billy Wycliffe.'

'Why him?'

'We had a run-in with 'em last night,' Mark explained. 'Billy was wearing his gun in a half-breed holster.'

Having seen the powder blackening on the rock, Murat knew what Mark meant. However he did not take the other's suggestion at blind face value.

'And you figure they jumped Sam to get even?' he asked.

'No,' admitted Mark. 'I don't reckon they'd go a round-about way like that to get even with anybody.'

'Weren't but four of 'em we saw,' Bragg reminded Mark.

'Way the fellers at the Bigfoot talked, there're plenty more,' Mark replied.

'That's for sure,' Murat agreed. 'Only you can't be sure it was them, Mark.'

'Everything points that way,' Mark replied, his big hands working in the unspoken, deadly rage which filled him. 'We'll know for sure when we find them.'

'Likely,' answered the sheriff.

'It's a heap more than likely!' Mark snapped. 'Sam fought back. That means all of them are carrying marks he gave them.'

'Let's go get 'em!' growled Bragg.

'We haven't more than a couple of hours afore dark,' objected Murat.

'We'll have a start for morning,' Mark put in. 'Maybe you'd best leave it to Tule and me, Jules.'

'To run them down and nail their hides to the wall?'

'Something like that.'

'Is that the way Hondo and Dusty Fog taught you to handle the law?'

'Damn it to hell, Jules!' Mark snapped. 'You knew Sailor Sam. He was a good-hearted cuss who never did harm to anybody who wasn't asking for it. He worked for pappy near as long as Tule here——'

'Which shouldn't stop you thinking and acting right,' Murat said quietly. 'Sailor Sam was your friend, Mark. Only if you start thinking on that instead of on proving who killed him, you could make a mistake.'

'Maybe,' Mark replied.

'There's no maybe about it and you know it!' Murat snapped. 'Sure everything points to the Wycliffe bunch. Only that's a mighty small description Tejas gave us and it could fit plenty of men. I can tell you three fellers in Austin alone who use a half-breed holster, two of them would fit the description of the one who shot Sam if it comes to that.'

'You figure one of them two did it?' growled Bragg.

'Nope. One of 'em's a Wells Fargo messenger and the other works for me as a deputy. I just mentioned them to show you that it could be somebody else,' Murat replied. 'Not that I reckon the Wycliffes wouldn't pull something like this—— But they'd want a reason for doing it.'

'Maybe figured to rob Sam,' Bragg guessed. 'Figured he'd have money to pay for whatever supplies he bought in town.'

'Not if it's the Wycliffes,' Murat answered. 'I wouldn't put robbing a blind man's begging-cup past the young'uns, but Churn's not that cheap. So if he was along, they came after more than the chance of picking up a few hundred dollars. And I went through Sam's pockets; whoever killed him hadn't.'

Which ruled out robbery as the motive for the killing. In such a secluded spot, a well-armed gang meaning to steal not be deterred by having murdered their victim. With robbery apparently ruled out, the question of motive rose once more. It seemed unlikely that the Wycliffes would take their revenge on Sailor Sam, or even that they knew his connection with Mark and Bragg.

'Who's on the trail behind you, Tule?' Mark asked.

'Nobody that we know of.'

Occasionally the trail crew following another herd would take steps to slow down and pass it so as to reach the rail-head market first. So every trail boss kept a wary eye on his rear, ready to counter such moves. While killing the cook would have at least nuisance value, Mark doubted if that had been the reason for Sam's murder. Yet it was a possibility, slim maybe, but Mark knew one could not afford to overlook the most slender chance. Murder, very sensibly, carried the death penalty, so a man like Mark Counter knew better than make the mistake of picking the wrong suspect when hunting for a killer.

Murat's warning had worked. With the first flush of his anger worn off, Mark remembered the training he received in peace officer work from two of the most enlightened lawmen in Texas. Although grief nagged at him, the blond giant forced himself to face the issue with an open mind. While almost certain that the Wycliffe clan were behind Sailor Sam's death, he was prepared to search for other possibilities.

'Let's make a start,' he said. 'We'll see which direction they're headed if nothing more.'

Satisfied that they could learn no more at the scene of the crime, Murat gave his agreement to Mark's suggestion and told Tejas to cut for sign. Quickly the Indian collected his horse and led the way along the tracks left by the departing killers. From the leisurely way the tracks had been made, fear of discovery did not cause them to leave before looting their victim. Nor did they go far. Swinging off through the trees, the tracks halted in cover near the trail. Once again the horses had been left tied to trees or bushes—it had been hair rubbed from their coats along with traces of urine which told the Indian each horse's colour and the fact that one was a mare—while their riders went on foot to watch the trail.

'Stopped here for a spell,' Tejas told the others. 'Maybe hour.'

'Looks like they were fixing to grab off and rob anybody who come along,' Bragg growled.

'Or they waited for somebody special,' Mark went on. 'Maybe they weren't after Sam at all.'

'Whoever it was, they didn't find him,' Murat stated. 'They fetched their horses and rode off.'

'Go up that way,' Tejas said, pointing.

'There's a nester's place maybe two mile along the trail,' Murat commented. 'Let's go ask if he's seen anybody go by.'

'He should notice six men and a gal passing,' Mark said as they started to ride in the direction indicated by Tejas Tom. 'If they've still got the gal along.'

'They took her,' the Indian replied. 'Leave her fastened to a tree while wait at side of trail. Then come back for her and hosses.'

While riding along, Tejas Tom had the others help him keep watch for sign of the other party leaving the trail. However there were several places at which Sailor Sam's killers could have swung off without leaving any tracks, due to the nature

57

of the ground. Certainly they did not take their horses off at any point where sign would show.

The nester showed some surprise at seeing the sheriff's party ride up to his cabin. However Murat possessed a reputation for fair dealing and was made welcome. Accepting the offer of a cup of coffee, the men dismounted and entered the small cabin. Mark and the others sat around the table while several children hovered in the background and stared wide-eyed at them. When asked if he had seen Sailor Sam's wagon go by, the nester nodded.

'Sure did. He stopped here and had a cup of java, seemed a right friendly sort of a jasper and talked real pleasant.'

'Not any more,' Bragg put in bluntly. 'He's dead.'

'The hell you say! And the gal that was with him?'

'They took the gal along with them,' Mark told the man.

'I'm not at all surprised!' snorted the woman of the house. 'She looked——'

'Hush now, Martha!' the nester said.

'You knew her, ma'am?' asked Murat.

'No. She's not from these parts, I'd swear. Looked like some fancy woman, headed for Austin to work in a saloon.'

'She didn't dress like one,' objected the nester.

'Or like a decent woman, in her shirt and pants, or with all that paint and powder on her face!' his wife answered.

'She didn't come back this way with maybe six fellers on horses then?' Murat inquired.

'Nope. I've been outside here working all afternoon and nobody come by,' the nester replied.

Studying the man, Mark felt sure that he spoke the truth and had not been paid by Sam's killers to remain silent. Which meant that the gang must have left the trail at one of the points where their tracks did not show. Only an extensive search, or some luck, would find the tracks where they left the hard ground. Mark knew that making it at such a late hour of the day would be futile.

'Do you get many wagons coming by here?' he asked, thinking of the gang's actions after leaving Sam's body.

'Some, mostly neighbours or cooks from trail herds going through,' the nester replied.

'Don't forget that trader who comes through maybe once a month,' his wife put in. 'It's near on time he was coming by.'

'Trade, ma'am?' Mark repeated.

'Hell yes!' ejaculated the nester. 'Him. Why sure. Say, he's a feller with a beard and used a four hoss wagon just like that the cook this morning drove.'

CHAPTER SEVEN

MORE VISITORS FOR MR. COUNTER

THE nester's comment brought Mark and Murat's eyes to him, then they looked at each other. Both saw the implications of the man's words. An entirely new field of conjecture opened for them.

'Do you know him, this trader, Jules?'

'I can't say I do, Mark. They come and go. Unless they break the law, or I had dealings with them before I took on this sheriff's chore, I wouldn't likely get to know any trader.'

'But he looked something like Sam,' Mark said. 'Maybe not much alike, but enough for those jaspers to've made a mistake. They stopped Sam and made him drive off the trail—— Why'd they do that?'

'So's they could rob him without being seen,' Bragg suggested. 'Most folks in Texas take a mighty poor view of robbing going on in plain daylight.'

'Then why take him down there and start searching?' asked Mark. 'Why didn't they just up and drive off with the whole wagon-load?'

'Could be they wanted to know something from the feller they thought Sam to be,' guessed Murat. 'Took him down by the river to start asking. Only Sam jumped them and got his-self shot before they had chance to start.'

'That fits,' Mark agreed. 'When he'd been shot, they searched the wagon and must've guessed they'd picked the wrong man. So they went back to the trail and waited again.'

'Then maybe saw my posse in the distance and lit out,' Murat finished. 'We came on to the trail between where they watched the first and second times, so we missed finding the place where they waited for the feller they wanted.'

'As soon as the burying's done tomorrow, we'll start looking,' Mark said.

'I'll have Tejas out at dawn to see what he can find,' Murat promised.

'How about Banker Snodgrass?' asked Mark.

'How about him?' countered the sheriff.

'He'll expect you to be hunting for whoever robbed him.'

'Likely. Only I rate murder and the abduction of a girl a whole heap more pressing and serious than the theft of money.

59

Besides, he's got all that high-priced Pinkerton help to do his hunting.'

'You couldn't be a mite jealous, now could you, Jules?' Mark grinned.

'Nope,' Murat answered with a smile twisting at his lips. 'But I figure any man who hires private law shouldn't expect the local peace officers to bust a gut helping him when he gets robbed. Say, I hear that you had a mishap with one of the Pink-eyes, Mark.'

'It was all their fool fault!' Bragg snorted.

'So I heard,' Murat said complacently. 'Only, was I you, I'd watch them, Mark. They won't forget what you did to their man.'

'I'll watch,' Mark promised. 'Let's get moving, shall we?'

'Sure,' agreed Murat. 'Thanks for the java, ma'am.'

While riding back in the direction of Austin, Mark turned to the sheriff. 'I wonder if they've still got the gal with them, Jules?'

'Likely. They'll not kill her unless they have to.'

'That's for sure,' Mark admitted.

Killing a woman, even one not regarded as socially-accept-able, ranked among the most heinous crimes out West. Any man who did so could expect to be hunted down without mercy. Every hand would be against him, even other outlaws declined to accept a woman-killer in their midst. So Sailor Sam's killers would keep the girl alive as long as possible.

'If she is a saloon gal, they might talk her round to forgetting what she's seen,' Murat remarked.

'And she'll make a dandy hostage should the law start crowding them, or get them pinned down someplace,' Mark went on. 'Should we catch up to them, we'll have to handle things careful to keep her alive.'

'What happens if we can't find their tracks?' Bragg demanded.

'I'll telegraph every town and stage relay station in the area, ask them to watch for half-a-dozen riders and a girl, some of the fellers looking like they've been in a fist-fight,' Murat replied.

'And if nothing comes of it?' insisted the foreman.

'I'll get word to Dusty and the Kid,' Mark stated. 'Then we'll drift up San Saba way and look in on the Wycliffes.'

'You're still set on it being them, Mark?' asked the sheriff.

'Sure enough, Jules,' Mark answered. 'Only I figure there's more chance of me learning something happen I take a couple of friends along to watch my back when I start asking.'

On their return to town, Mark and Bragg put up their horses

at the livery barn. Its owner, an old and trusted friend, complained with salty bitterness at their lack of success and heaped curses on the heads of Sam's killers. Then he offered to hold the two men's rifles with the saddles that night ready for use in the morning. After attending to their mounts and locking the rifles away, the owner pointed to a bunch of lathered horses which his help cleaned up after hard use.

'Damned Pink-eye sneaks!' he grunted with all the contempt of a Texan for men who neglected their horses. 'They've been out all day trying to find whoever robbed Snodgrass and come back in all pot-boiling mad 'cause they couldn't pick up a track.'

'It won't do them city jaspers any harm to get out and breath good Texas air,' Bragg grinned.

'Sure won't,' agreed the owner. 'Only this bunch aren't appreciating it.'

'They can allus go back where they come from,' the foreman commented.

'Say, Mark,' the owner said. 'You killed a bounty hunter called Framant last year, didn't you?'

'I figured it was the best thing to do at the time,' Mark answered, 'seeing how he was fixing to shoot me.'

'That Burbage jasper was telling three of the Pink-eyes about it just afore they left here. Sounded real interested.'

'He maybe reckons Mark might've got the taste for gunning bounty hunters,' suggested Bragg dryly.

'Could be,' cackled the old owner.

'Now they know about you and Framant,' Bragg said as he and Mark walked out of the barn.

'Word about that kind of thing gets around,' Mark answered.

'Reckon they can tie you in with Belle from it?'

'I don't know. The marshal up to Elkhorn never let on to anybody that she was mixed in the game. Only me, him, Belle and Calamity Jane knew the truth.'

'Calamity had no cause to like Belle, from what I heard,' Bragg commented. 'They had one helluva fight, way you told it.'

The previous night Mark had told Bragg about the happenings in Elkhorn when he first met both Belle Starr and Calamity Jane. Knowing he could rely on the foreman's discretion, Mark gave almost the full details of the affair.

'They laid into each other until they both got tuckered out,' Mark admitted with a grin. 'But after it Calam helped me smuggle Belle out of town and risked getting shot to save her. Nope, Calam wouldn't talk out of turn.'

'I know I'd never heard who the other gal was, 'cepting a

blackjack dealer in a saloon,' Bragg said. 'But if they should know you stopped Framant laying hands on her, they could get all suspicious and fancy notions about you jumping that yahoo in the hotel.'

'We'll just have to worry about that when it comes,' Mark stated. 'Let's go down to the sheriff's office and see if Jules knows anything.'

At the office they waited until Murat returned from sending out telegraph messages to peace officers in the surrounding towns, although both realised that no answer could be expected until much later. When Murat came in, he told them what he had done so far and discussed their line of action the following day. With that attended to, Mark and Bragg left. They visited the undertaker's shop to which Sailor Sam's body had been taken and satisfied themselves that everything would be as the cook wanted in the matter of the burial.

'We'll have to let pappy know about Sam,' Mark said as they left the building. 'You wouldn't go tell him, I reckon.'

'You reckon right!' snorted Bragg. 'Write him about it and we'll get some cowhand to take the letter out.'

'Come on then, we'll do it at the hotel,' Mark said. 'After we've got it off, we'll go down to see Jules in case he's heard anything. They do say he plays a mean game of checkers.'

'That'll be something,' sniffed Bragg.

On their arrival at the Houston Hotel, the reception clerk held out a message form. 'This just came for you, Mr. Counter.'

'It's from Ole Devil,' Mark told Bragg after reading the message. 'He says Dusty won't need help and for me to come on home.'

'What'll you do?' asked the foreman.

'Telegraph to tell him what's happened and say I'm going after Sam's killer,' Mark replied.

'Reckon he'll object?'

'Nope. He'll likely send Dusty and the Kid out to help me. Let's get that letter to pappy written.'

Taking his key from the clerk, Mark led the way upstairs and to his room. After unlocking the door, he shoved it open and let Bragg go in first. As the foreman started to enter, removing his hat, an arm holding a wicked leather-wrapped billy lashed at his head from inside the room. No man grew up in the wild frontier country of Texas without developing fast reflexes. Hearing the faint hissing sound, Bragg jerked his hat back on to his head so that the billy struck its crown. While that broke the full force of the blow, it still arrived with enough power to drop him unconscious to the floor.

Like a flash Mark lunged forward, hands reaching for the

62

arm which struck down his friend. Even as his fingers closed on their objective, Mark heard a sound from the other side of the door and saw it start to swing close. The lamp had been lit and turned down to a faint glow. By its light he saw a tall man in range clothing by the wardrobe and a second, a slightly shorter dude, at the window.

All that registered in his mind as he laid hold of the arm of Bragg's attacker. Before any of the men in the room realised just how wrong their plan had gone, Mark gave a swinging heave at the trapped arm. A startled, agony-filled yelp rose as the billy slipped from limp fingers. Then Quigg, the Pinkerton agent, swung into sight. His feet struck against Bragg's body and he tripped to crash his head into the door.

Bracing himself, Mark kicked hard at the door, slamming it back into the man behind it and hearing a pain-filled curse in a western voice. Then he heaved Quigg back again, twisting the man around to slam into the wall. As Quigg struck, Mark released him and he collapsed forward limply.

Bounding over Bragg's body, Mark saw the other two men rushing at him. He clenched his fists and whipped them both up and out in back-hand swings that drove hard knuckles into his attackers' faces. Each man shot away, spun around by the force of the blows.

Blood running from his nose, Burbage sprang from behind the door. Mark heard him coming and turned. Going under the blow Burbage lashed at him, Mark hit the man in the stomach. Before he could follow up his advantage, the man in range clothes reached him. Mark felt the other's fist catch him at the side of the face and staggered. Driven sideways by the force of the blow, Mark brought himself to a halt. His attacker sprang after him and the second dude rushed forward holding a billy like Quigg used. Out shot Mark's hands, grabbing the westerner by the shirt front. Then Mark pivoted around, swinging the man. Too late the dude saw what Mark intended. Already the billy rose and hissed through the air in a blow aimed at Mark's head, but the blond giant moved backwards. With a dull thud, the billy landed on the western man's head and the force of his being turned had caused his hat to fly off. So he lacked the protection Bragg's Stetson afforded when Quigg made the treacherous attack.

Feeling the man he held go limp, Mark hurled him at the billy-armed dude. Struck by the flying body, the dude reeled backwards. He and the unconscious westerner went down with a crash by the wardrobe. The force of their arrival caused its door to commence opening. Then, in an inexplicable manner, the door reversed direction. It slid back until almost closed, remaining still maybe an inch from its shut position.

Burbage caught Mark's arm, turned him and hit him in the face. Across whipped the man's other fist, snapping Mark's head the other way. Closing in, Burbage felt hands like steel traps clamp on his vest. To his amazement he felt himself lifted and hurled over Bragg's body through the door. Landing on his feet, Burbage could not prevent himself continuing backwards and his progress was halted by colliding with the door of the room facing Mark's.

Spluttering curses, the dude rolled his limp companion from him and sat up. His billy lay halfway across the room where he dropped it when struck by his companion's body, but he made no attempt to reach it. Instead he drew the Smith & Wesson No. 2 revolver from its holster. A puny weapon to most range-dwellers' way of thinking, the .32 bullet would still kill or wound at close range given the chance. As Mark had his back to the other man, it seemed that the chance was being presented. Up lifted the revolver, for the man did not intend to miss if he could help it. So engrossed was he in taking aim that he did not see the wardrobe door open, or notice the arm which came from inside. Down drove the arm, clothed in a dark shirt's sleeve and hand gripping around the frame of what at first sight looked like a Navy Colt. The butt of the weapon landed with some force on top of the dude's head and he collapsed as if he had been boned, the Smith & Wesson dropping unfired at his side. Instantly the arm disappeared into the wardrobe and the door closed completely to.

Mark heard the sound behind him, so turned ready to deal with whatever fresh menace might arise. Before he faced into the room, the wardrobe door had shut and he stared wonderingly at the sprawled out shape of the dude. Time to think over what caused the dude's condition was not granted to the blond giant. Three of his attackers might be rendered *hors de combat* —although he could not think how one of them came to be so—yet a fourth and maybe the most dangerous remained active. Just how active Mark rapidly discovered.

After hitting the door facing Mark's room, Burbage bounced forward a step before digging in his heels and bringing himself to a halt. While determined to take revenge for his rough treatment at the blond giant's hands, Burbage had no desire to continue fighting with fists. Twice he had received samples of Mark's great strength and seen enough to warn him that further fist-fighting was out. Seeing the big blond's back towards him, Burbage grabbed for his gun. The door into which he collided opened and an indignant-looking man glared out. Seeing Burbage reaching for a gun, taken with the sight of

64

Bragg sprawled in the doorway opposite, the man's indignation became rapidly tinted with caution. His angry demand to be told what the hell somebody thought by damned nigh knocking the door off its hinges died with barely four words said. Retreating hurriedly, he slammed the door closed and twisted himself with some rapidity around until he stood with the wall and not the door's flimsy panelling between himself and any stray flying bullets.

Hearing the sound behind him, Burbage tried to do two things at once. The Houston catered for a good class of customer and there was a possibility that whoever opened the door might be Mark Counter's friend. In which case Burbage knew a warning would be given at least; or possibly a bullet driven into him to stop his attempt on the blond giant's life. No Texas jury would convict a man who used a gun to prevent somebody shooting another in the back. So Burbage looked over his shoulder, but did not prevent his hand drawing the gun. Such were the trained reflexes a man like Burbage possessed that he completed his draw and fired while still looking away. A man shooting for pleasure or practice might have felt highly satisfied by the result, for the bullet sent Mark's hat spinning from his head and punctured a hole in the top of its crown. Not bad shooting under the circumstances—if Burbage shot for pleasure or practice.

Only he did not. His bullet had been intended to cripple Mark and, in missing, achieved nothing more than to warn him of his danger. As the big blond whirled around, his right hand dropped down to and drew the off-side Colt. Already angry at the treacherous attack, Mark did not hesitate in his actions. He did not know that Burbage merely meant to wound him, nor would the knowledge have made him feel any more inclined to leniency. All he knew was that a man tried to shoot him and stood holding a revolver capable of being used for another attempt. So Mark countered the threat as fast and completely as he could manage.

Flame tore from the barrel of Mark's Colt. Like Burbage, he shot from waist high and by instinctive alignment. Only he looked towards his target and had nothing to distract his attention. The .44 bullet drove into Burbage's shoulder, spinning him around and causing him to drop his gun. Striking the wall instead of the door, he slid down to the floor. Pain tore through him and his right arm felt numb, refusing to obey the dictates of his mind. Through the haze that misted his eyes he saw the revolver and reached towards it with his left hand.

After shooting, Mark lunged through the door. He cocked the long-barrelled Colt on its recoil, ready to shoot again. Nor would he have hesitated to do so if the man showed any sign of fight. Stepping across the passage, Mark kicked the revolver from Burbage's reach. Foiled in his attempt, the man gave a low moan and went limp, flopping forward on to his face.

Voices raised in the lobby and feet thudded to, then up the stairs. Doors along the passage opened, people looking out cautiously. Seeing that there did not appear to be any chance of further shooting, the guests left their rooms. Most of them knew Mark and put the shooting down to his having disturbed a thief in his room, or about to enter it.

Ignoring the guests who converged on him and the clerk appearing at the head of the stairs, Mark returned to Bragg's side. Holstering his Colt, Mark knelt by the foreman. An expression of relief came to the blond giant's face as he saw Bragg start to force himself up. A glance into his room told Mark that there would be no further trouble from that direction. Then he looked at Bragg who had reached hands and knees, staying there while shaking his head to clear it.

'Whooee!' Bragg groaned as Mark helped him to rise. 'What happened? Who in hell done it to me?'

'What's happening here?' demanded the clerk, forcing his way through the guests and speaking before Mark could answer Bragg's question.

'How'd you feel, Tule!' Mark asked.

'Lousy. What happened?'

'The Pink-eyes jumped us.'

Despite being dazed by the blow and dizzy from it, Bragg did not make any incautious or incriminating statement. Putting his shoulder against the door jamb, he looked first at Burbage and then into the room.

'Did I get any of 'em?' he asked.

'None, you just lay down and slept through it all,' Mark replied and turned to glare at the desk clerk. 'Just what kind of a place do you reckon to run? Last night I see a feller in a gal's room and figure he's robbing it. Now I come here and get jumped by a bunch of yahoos.'

Figuring that the best defence was a good strong attack, Mark launched it immediately. He did not know how much the Pinkerton agents told the desk clerk, or what excuse they made to obtain entrance to his room, but decided to arouse doubts in the man's mind before any of his assailants could contradict it.

Surprise showed on the clerk's face as he stared first at Burbage and then into the room. 'I assure you, Mr. Counter, that I had no idea they were even in the hotel!' he squeaked with such sincerity that Mark believed him.

66

Before he could say any more, Mark saw the bell hop and two deputy marshals appear at the head of the stairs. Thrusting through the crowd, the peace officers holstered the revolvers they drew when climbing the stairs.

'Howdy, Mark,' said the taller of the pair. 'What happened?'

'This bunch jumped me,' Mark replied.

'Hey!' yipped the second deputy. 'That's Burbage, he's been working with them Pinkerton sneaks——'

'You'll find three more in the room there,' Mark told him.

'You shoot 'em too?'

'We only heard one shot, Buck,' the taller deputy reminded.

'There were two fired,' Mark said. 'That feller put a hole in my hat.'

'Tried to shoot this gent in the back, too,' put in the man from the room opposite and whose actions saved Mark from injury.

'What set 'em on to you, Mark?' asked the taller deputy.

'I rough-handled one of them last night——'

'So I heard. Looks like they figured to jump you and get even. They lay for you in your room?'

'Sure,' Mark agreed. 'Only being a gentleman I let my guest walk in first.'

'Gentleman nothing!' snorted Bragg, holding his hat in one hand while he delicately rang a finger-tip across his skull. 'I reckon he knowed they was there and sent me in first to get whomped on the head.'

'You'd maybe best make sure they didn't steal anything, Mark,' the taller deputy suggested. 'We'll tend to their needings.'

Entering the room, the two deputies hauled the westerner and dude towards the door. While they did so, Mark crossed to the wardrobe. He doubted if the Pinkerton men would have searched his property, but noticed that the wardrobe key was no longer in the lock. Yet it had been when he left the room. So he walked to the door and tugged at its handle.

Fortunately the deputies had their backs to him and none of the people in the passage could see by his powerful frame. The wardrobe's door began to open and Mark became aware that it held something not there when he last looked inside. Only with an effort did he prevent an exclamation of surprise from slipping out and he closed the door before the deputies could learn what lay behind it.

'They didn't take a thing,' he said and hoped that his voice sounded natural.

67

CHAPTER EIGHT

A DEBT REPAID

THE taller of the deputies proved to be a man of action. A doctor staying at the hotel had already attended to the wounded Burbage. After dispersing the remainder of the crowd, the deputy gave thought to disposing of the rest of Mark's attackers. He looked at the groaning men, then turned to the big blond.

'Do you want for me to haul them down to the pokey, Mark?'

'You'd best until their boss allows that they'll steer clear of me,' Mark replied. 'The next time I might not go so easy on them.'

'I'll see he gets to know,' the deputy promised, walking to where Quigg sat by the door. 'All right, *hombre*, on your feet.'

Realising the futility of argument, Quigg rose and helped the other dude lift the still unconscious westerner. Then the two deputies escorted the men from the room. Mark followed them and prepared to defend his position to the desk clerk.

'I can't tell you how sorry I am, Mr. Counter,' the man said before Mark could start. 'But I didn't know they had come into the hotel, or were in your room.'

'It's not your fault,' Mark replied. 'I'm sorry it happened.'

Leaving the removal of Burbage and the other men to the deputies, Mark entered his room. After doing what he could to save Burbage's life, the doctor went to check whether any of the others suffered damage. With the passage clear, Mark returned to his room. Watched by a surprised-looking Bragg, he locked the door and then drew the curtains before turning up the lamp.

'What the——?' Bragg began.

'You can come out now,' Mark said in the direction of the wardrobe.

Bragg had taken a seat on the edge of the bed, but he bounced to his feet as if the cover was red hot. With bugged-out eyes he stared at the wardrobe door, which opened apparently of its own volition.

At another time Mark might have found the sight of Bragg's show of emotion to be amusing. Under normal conditions he would have been pleased to see a beautiful young woman—

even if she also be an outlaw—stepping from his wardrobe. Neither sight particularly attracted him at that moment.

Dressed in the same clothing she wore when they last saw her, Belle walked across the room. She read disapproval on Mark's face and hurried to explain her conduct.

'I had to come back, Mark. I know who killed Sailor Sam—and why.'

'So that's why you risked your fool neck,' Mark growled.

'Why else?' smiled the girl. 'You took a big chance for me, both here and in Elkhorn.'

'It was a pleasure both times,' Mark assured her. 'Only I don't——'

A knock at the door chopped his words off. Swiftly Belle darted across the room and disappeared into the wardrobe, closing the door behind her. Bragg resumed his seat and adopted an attitude of studious innocence. Walking to the door, Mark unlocked and opened it. He found the doctor and desk clerk standing outside.

'Your friend was hurt, Mr. Counter,' said the latter. 'So I asked the doctor if he would come up and examine him—at the hotel's expense of course.'

For a moment Mark hesitated, then decided that having witnesses to the fact that apparently only he and Bragg were in the room might be advantageous. So he thanked the clerk for showing such consideration and allowed the doctor to enter. Despite being eager to hear what Belle had to say about the murder of Sailor Sam, Mark forced himself to stand and wait while the examination of Bragg's head took place. After what seemed a long time, although it was not, the doctor straightened up and grinned.

'You'll do,' he told Bragg. 'It raised one hell of a knob, but hasn't done any damage or broke the skin. Those leather-wrapped billies don't cut as a rule.'

'How about the feller I shot?' asked Mark.

'He'll live, but won't be getting around for a spell. Should think himself lucky for all that. I don't reckon you picked that particular spot to hit him.'

'That's for sure,' Mark admitted and glanced at his bullet-holed Stetson. 'I just pulled and cut loose to stop him improving his aim. Thanks, doctor. If this worthless ole goat——'

'He means me,' Bragg put in.

'Who else?' demanded Mark. 'If this worthless ole goat lives——'

'You mean you reckon you can kill a cowhand by whomping him on the head?' grinned the doctor. 'That's not what he works with. I wonder how much the hotel'll go for?'

After the doctor left, Belle came once more from the wardrobe. She walked to the bed and sat on its edge, crossing one shapely trouser-clad leg over the other and looking at the expectant faces of the men.

'I got clear of the hotel with no trouble and went to hide out with friends in town,' she explained. 'Figured on staying with them until things quietened down a mite. Only when I heard about Sam, I decided to help you.'

'How?' asked Mark.

'You remember that I said somebody had sold me to the Pinkeyes?'

'Sure.'

'And that I thought I knew who it might be?'

'Yep,' agreed Mark.

'Well, I had my friends get the feller and fetch him to see me. They had masks on and blindfolded him so that he doesn't know where he is. I questioned him about the killing——'

'Who is he?' growled Bragg.

'That's not why I came here,' the girl answered. 'He bought his life by telling me everything about Sailor Sam—and it was plenty.'

'Such as?' asked Mark.

'Firstly, Sam was killed by mistake; which makes it a damned sight worse. Churn Wycliffe's bunch were waiting for a trader who ought to have come into town along that trail. Their descriptions tallied, so Wycliffe thought Sam was the man he wanted.'

'Was this feller there when it happened?' demanded Bragg.

'No. He told me about the Wycliffes waiting for the wagon and described the driver. So I guessed what had happened.'

'It was Billy Wycliffe who shot Sam,' Mark told Belle. 'We read that from the sign out there. Where are they now?'

'I don't know, nor does the man who told me about it,' Belle admitted. 'But I may be able to help you find them. You know Runcorne of the Lone Rider Saloon?'

'Not to speak to, but I've heard about him and've seen his place.'

'Well he's been trading whisky, guns and other stuff to the Kaddo Indians for silver. Not silver money, but mined bars of it. I think it comes from some deserted and lost Spanish diggings the Kaddos found.'

'This feller told you about it?' Mark inquired.

'He told me,' Belle agreed. 'And he makes most of his living by picking up information. It seems that he sold the news to Wycliffe who planned to learn where the silver came from by forcing the trader to talk.'

'So that's why they took Sam off the trail,' Mark said. 'Only he jumped the whole damned bunch of them and Billy shot him.'

'I bet Churn nearly killed Billy for doing it,' Belle replied.

'When I get hold of Billy, he'll wish he had,' Mark promised. 'You wouldn't like to tell me who the man is who told you all this, Belle?'

'No. Like I said, he bought his life with the information.'

'I could guess, but I won't,' the blond giant drawled, thinking of the meeting between Wycliffe and the pedlar that he witnessed at the Bigfoot Saloon. 'Only I don't see why he told you all this.'

'Not because he suspects about you and me,' Belle assured him. 'He wanted to buy his life, figuring I might aim to kill him for selling me out to the Pink-eyes. His idea was that I and my "gang" went after Wycliffe's bunch, then took the silver from them after they found it.'

A faint smile flickered across Belle's face at the thought. Her 'gang' had only two other members; an elderly man of sombre, if commanding appearance and a mild-natured young feller with considerable skill at opening locked safe doors. Neither of the men who brought the informer to her had been involved in the robbery and Belle had nothing that might by any but the widest stretch of the imagination be called a gang. However the informer knew nothing of that; believing, like many other people, that Belle commanded a large, well-organised gang willing to carry out her orders.

'Then Wycliffe's likely to be watching the trail,' Mark said, guessing at Belle's thoughts.

'Unless he's already met the trader and learned what he needs to know,' the girl agreed. 'If he has, he'll be headed for the place.'

'Your feller didn't say where that'd be?' asked Bragg.

'He swears he doesn't know and I think he's scared enough not to lie,' Belle replied. 'If he had known, Wycliffe wouldn't've needed to grab off the trader and ask about it.'

'That figures,' Mark went on. 'But I'd like to know where to go in case Wycliffe's already met the feller and learned how to find the silver.'

'You could try asking Runcorne,' Belle suggested. 'He knows.'

'Reckon he'd tell us?' asked Bragg.

'If we ask him real polite,' Mark answered and looked at the girl. 'What do you aim to do about this talkative jasper now, Belle?'

'Turn him clear and steer well clear of him in the future. And if he's one ounce of good sense, he'll do the same with me.'

71

'You maybe better find some way to tell him to ride a wide circle around me from now on,' Mark said. 'I'd as soon not see him again, seeing as how he helped get Sam killed.'

'I don't think you need worry about that,' the girl replied. 'And don't look worried, I'm not planning to kill him. But one day somebody will, the way he tries to run with the fox and hunt with the hounds.'

Belle wondered how Mark came to tie the pedlar Jacobs in with Wycliffe, for he had not mentioned seeing the men talking in the Bigfoot Saloon. Less than a year later her prediction came true. After selling information to Murat about the leader of a gang of cow thieves, Jacobs made the mistake of falling into the person he sold's hands and paid the penalty.*

'Let's go see Runcorne, Tule,' Mark ordered. 'What're you going to do, Belle, wait here for me?'

'I think not,' she smiled. 'Maybe Shafto'll start putting things together when he hears why his men came after you. So I'd better be away from here before he puts a watch on the place.'

'It'd likely be best,' Mark admitted. 'I'll see you around.'

'That's for sure,' she replied. 'I'm sorry about what happened to Sam.'

'So'll the Wycliffes be when we catch up to 'em,' promised Bragg.

'There's one other thing,' the girl said as the men prepared to leave the room. 'Runcorne keeps the silver and a stock of trade goods hidden in the wine barrels in his saloon's cellar. The feller told me that and suggested we raided them.'

'We'll mind it,' Mark said and put his hands on her shoulders. Gently he kissed her and then went on, 'You ride careful, Belle honey. Or have you decided to take up that feller's offer?'

'I told him my mammy didn't raise any idiot children.'

'She raised a mighty smart one,' complimented Bragg.

'Only half-smart, pulling a fool game like this tonight,' Mark replied.

'You helped me out twice,' she pointed out. 'I like to repay my debts.'

'Maybe you'd best stay here, Tule,' Mark said. 'That was a nasty crack you got on your pumpkin head.'

'I'm over it now,' snorted the foreman. 'And anyways, you'll likely need somebody to watch your back at Runcorne's place.'

'*Loco* as a fool-hen,' grinned Mark. 'And afore you say it, that figures working for pappy.'

'It's getting so a feller can't speak around here,' sniffed Bragg. 'Let's go put some custom Mr. Runcorne's way. It couldn't

* Told in *The Cow Thieves*.

72

happen to a nicer son-of-a-bitch from what I've heard about him.'

While walking through the streets towards the Lone Rider Saloon, Mark and Bragg discussed Belle's information. They also thought up a scheme by which they could gain entrance to the saloon's cellar. If Belle's informant spoke the truth, neither man expected Runcorne to permit an inspection of his underground storeroom. However, given one little piece of Texas luck, Mark reckoned they could get into the cellar and learn enough to put its owner in a talkative mood.

Although the Lone Rider was as big as the Bigfoot, it catered for a different class of trade. While the Bigfoot drew most of its custom from the higher income bracket, the Lone Rider attracted men of lesser means. So its furnishing and fittings looked cheaply garish, like a dancehall girl's imitation diamonds. Not that the clientele objected, for the place offered them everything they asked for in the way of entertainment and at a lower rate than the more elegant Bigfoot.

Looking around the room on making his entrance, Mark noticed a number of cowhands present. Any man with Mark's practical experience of workers in the major industry of Texas could read the signs. So he guessed that the three groups of cowhands each consisted of a different ranch's crew. While the conversation of the previous night at the Bigfoot made no mention of trouble between the local spreads, something certain to be discussed if it existed, Mark felt his scheme would work. Loyalty to the brand he worked for made a cowhand touchy on the subject. He believed his outfit to be the best and was willing to rear back and prove it should any doubts be raised. If necessary Mark intended to make use of that loyalty as an aid to checking on the truth of Belle Starr's story.

In addition to the brawny bouncers hovering at strategic points about the room, the waiters also seemed to be selected for muscular development rather than ability at serving drinks. Such men would be able to prevent even the blond giant from gaining unpermitted entrance to the cellar unless diverted.

Which raised another point, locating the cellar's door. Standing just inside the building, as if waiting for somebody or searching the crowd for friends, Mark and Bragg studied the room. A wide staircase led up to a balcony and the saloon's upper floor. That did not interest either man, for what they wanted was a cellar. In addition to the main entrance, customers could come in through smaller doors at the left or right. Again Mark and Bragg ignored the sight, concentrating on three possibilities; none of which struck them as being attractively situated for their purpose.

The three doors studied by Mark were in the wall behind the big bar. Of the three Mark liked the central one least of all. No matter how well his diversion worked, there would be no chance of getting behind the bar undetected. Not that the other two doors offered much greater chances, being set one at each end of the bar.

Even as Mark watched, the door behind the bar opened and a bartender went in. He left the door open, allowing Mark an uninterrupted view of the room beyond. It seemed to be an ordinary small store, shelves holding bottles around the walls.

'That's not it, unless there's a trapdoor in the floor, ' Mark told Bragg.

'From the way those two jaspers went through the door at the left of the bar, I'd say that wasn't it either,' Bragg answered.

Mark had also noticed a townsman and cowhand pass through the door Bragg mentioned and concluded that it led to a men's room at the rear of the building. So only one possibility remained. And then Mark remembered that most saloon owners had an office on the premises and mostly on the ground floor.

'Where's the boss?' he asked a passing waiter.

Reluctantly the man came to a halt. He eyed the blond giant, first taking in the expensive clothing. Any idea that Mark might be no more than a rich, soft-living dandy affecting cowhand dress died swiftly. Not only did those well-used matched Colts hang just right but under the costly clothes lay muscles equal, if not superior to those of any man in the room. So the waiter held down his angry comment about having work to do and no time to answer fool questions.

'You want to see him?' he inquired with what passed for politeness.

'Likely,' Mark replied.

'That's his office at the right of the bar. Just go up and knock. If he's in, he'll maybe see you.'

'Do you-all have snake-fights here, feller?' asked Bragg.

'Huh?' grunted the waiter, scowling at Bragg.

Once again belligerence became tinted with caution. While not as imposing a physical specimen as his companion, Bragg did not strike the waiter as easy meat or even a man to be pushed around. There was a leathery toughness about the foreman which hinted that anybody pushing him would be pushed back, even harder.

'Snake-fights, friend, that's having two snakes fighting each other in a pit. They have 'em in plenty places down south.'

'Sure do,' Mark agreed. 'In the cellar of the Casa Moreno at San Antonio.' He looked at the waiter. 'You hold 'em in your

74

cellar, friend?'

Surprise showed on the waiter's face and he darted a glance in the direction of the stairs. 'Naw. We don't have 'em.'

'Let's go someplace where they do then,' Mark said to Bragg. 'I'll just have me a drink here first,' the foreman replied and the waiter walked away before an order could be given. 'What do you reckon, boy?'

Looking towards the stairs, Mark saw a door let into the wall beneath them. He had seen it before, but overlooked it as a possibility. From the waiter's involuntary action, Mark concluded that more than a simple broom closet lay behind the door under the stairs.

'I reckon we've found it,' Mark replied. 'Go do your part.'

While Bragg headed for the bar, Mark walked across the room and halted near the cellar door. He ignored the interested glances of a couple of girls and leaned by the door, apparently waiting for his companion to bring a drink.

Like Mark, Bragg knew cowhands. So the foreman saw his task would be much easier than he expected as he approached the bar. At that hour of the night any cowhand in town could be relied upon to be carrying a fair amount of Old Scalp Lifter and in the state of intoxication where one felt on top of the world and ready to prove it against anybody.

Joining a bunch of the cowhands, Bragg offered to set up drinks. He soon learned they belonged to the Bench M, the finest dod-blasted cow outfit ever sired.

'Well then,' Bragg said, lifting his glass. 'Here's to the Bench M, the best spread in Texas.'

'In the United States!' corrected one of the cowhands.

'In the whole danged wide world!' declared another.

Along the bar, one of a second group of cowhands let out a laugh, staring pointedly at the Bench M crew.

'Sounds like somebody don't believe you,' Bragg remarked.

'Don't it though,' agreed the spokesman for the Bench M. 'Anyways, them Bradded A bunch wouldn't know a good cow outfit if it rode all over 'em.'

Thrusting himself from his place at the bar, the Bradded A contingent advanced towards Bragg's party. 'What'd you say?' he demanded.

'You heard me, your ears're big enough.'

'Well you just take it back right now!'

'Make me!'

Before the bartender could signal to the bouncers, the Bradded A's leader threw a punch at the spokesman for the Bench M. Next minute both parties charged at each other with fists flying. Cursing bouncers and waiters began to converge on the spot. Just as Bragg and Mark anticipated, the employees of the saloon were heartily disliked by most of the customers. So the third group of cowhands pitched in to prevent interference with the fight. In a very short time a full-scale battle began to rage. Screaming girls fled from the room and one of them started to blow on a whistle. The short, blocky shape of Runcorne appeared at his office's door and started to howl curses at the fighters, interspersed with orders that his men most probably could not hear.

Nimbly slipping around the edge of the fight, Bragg joined Mark at the cellar door. Already Mark had tried the door and found it locked, which they both expected. However, everybody else either watched or took part in the fight. Mark had created his diversion. Everything now depended on whether he could force an entrance and gain admittance to the cellar.

'We won't have long,' the foreman stated. 'You'd best go to it.'

CHAPTER NINE

THE SECRET OF THE BARRELS

WHILE Bragg kept watch on the crowd, Mark swung to face the door. The blond giant measured the distance as he flexed his left knee, raised his right leg and drove its boot at the door. Following the method taught to him by Dusty Fog, Mark crashed his foot into the door just below its lock. He did not try to burst open the door, but to spring the lock. Provided that the door did not also have bolts on its inside, he felt he should be able to do so. As his boot collided with the door, his full weight and power went behind it. Immediately the lock cracked and the door flew inwards. While the action took only a few seconds, it could not have been performed in full view of the crowd without attracting attention. Engrossed in the fight, nobody saw Mark make his move.

Stepping through the door, Mark found himself at the head of a flight of stairs. Possibly Runcorne expected the arrival of another consignment of silver. Whatever the reason, lamps lit the stairs and cellar. On the surface everything seemed normal enough. Across from the stairs, a chute ran down from the outside entrance. While Mark knew it was used for carrying barrels and other items from the side alley into the cellar, he could not make his entrance by it. On reaching the saloon, he and Bragg looked down the alley and saw a pair of armed men standing guard over the cellar door. That fact gave added credence to Belle's story for it seemed unlikely Runcorne would trouble to hire guards over an ordinary cellar's contents.

Cases of whisky, gin and rum bottles were stacked against the walls along with barrels and kegs of beer. Incongruous, considering the type of clientele the Lone Rider attracted, three huge wine barrels rested on racks by the goods chute. According to Belle's informant, the silver and merchandise to be traded to the Indians ought to be inside those big barrels. With such proof Mark figured he could learn all he needed from the saloonkeeper as the price of his silence. Not that Mark intended to allow the trafficking in whisky and arms to the Indians to continue. A hint in the right place would see Jules Murat starting an investigation that ought to put an end to the evil business.

At the foot of the stairs Mark and Bragg started to walk in

the direction of the wine barrels.

'Hey, you there!' yelled a voice from behind them.

Turning, they saw a pair of bouncers at the door. One of the burly men started down the stairs but his companion turned to call something in the direction of the bar room. Although he turned to follow his companions, the other had already reached the foot of the stairs.

'Get set, boy!' ordered Bragg and lunged towards the bouncer.

While tough and capable, Bragg was no fool. He knew that he stood no chance should the bouncer lay hands on him. So he planned his move fast. Stout wooden pillars rose from the cellar to support the floor above. Before the bouncer could lay hands on him, Bragg caught hold of the nearest pillar and used it to swing himself clear of the danger. Nor did he allow the matter to end there. Continuing his swing, he came up at the man's rear. Still using his momentum, Bragg brought up both feet and drove them into the man's back. Taken by surprise, the bouncer went shooting forward to where Mark waited. Around lashed the blond giant's fist in a smooth punch to the side of the bouncer's jaw. The blow caused an involuntary and hurried change of direction. Unable to help himself, he went sprawling across the cellar and crashed into a pile of empty crates.

Bouncing down the stairs, the second man flung himself at Bragg. Before the big hands clamped hold of him, Bragg side-stepped. He snapped up his right foot with all the ease of a French-Creole *savate* fighter, sending the toe of his boot into the bouncer's belly. A croak of agony burst from the man and he doubled over as he blundered by Bragg. Pivoting around, the foreman placed his boot against the other's rump and shoved hard. Shooting forward, the man rushed towards Mark. Down came Mark's hand, catching the bouncer by the scruff of the neck and heaving to send him flying after his companion. Colliding with the wall, the man crumpled and collapsed limply.

'Let's get to those barrels, *pronto*!' Mark suggested.

'Hold it right there!' ordered a voice from the head of the stairs.

Followed by two of his men, Runcorne started down into the cellar. He came with a face showing fury and a gun in his hand. Glancing at Bragg, Mark saw he did not need to pass any warning. The foreman realised the danger just as well as Mark and did not plan to make any wrong moves.

'Howdy,' Bragg greeted politely.

'What're you doing in here?' Runcorne demanded.

'Looking for the way out,' answered Bragg.

'That door was locked———!'

'Could be we'd heard how good a wine you sell and figured to try some,' Mark interrupted.

Emotions flickered across the man's face as he drew closer. Anger, a hint of fear and some curiosity warred with each other. Yet Runcorne retained sufficient control of himself not to make the mistake of coming too close to Mark or Bragg. Unless Mark missed his guess, the saloonkeeper knew more than a little about gun-handling. Enough to make taking fool chances a mighty dangerous proposition.

'Maybe I'll get some answers when my boys start asking the questions,' Runcorne hissed.

'Two of them already tried,' Mark pointed out, nodding to the first pair of bouncers as they lay groaning at the sides of the room.

'These two have an advantage,' Runcorne replied, making a small but significant gesture with his revolver. 'I'm on hand to slow you two down a mite.' He paused to let the words sink in. 'All right, what're you doing down here?'

'That's a real good question,' came Murat's voice from the head of the stairs and he stepped into view. 'Put up the gun, Runcorne.'

'Damn it, sheriff, I caught this pair down here———'

'Like we-all told the gent, when the fussing started upstairs we just natural-like come down here out of harm's way,' Bragg drawled. 'Us being such peaceable souls and all.'

'I can see *that*,' Murat said dryly, having examined the door and noted the signs of forced entry. 'Put up that pint-sized hawg-leg, Mr. Runcorne—as a special favour to me.'

Slowly and reluctantly Runcorne slid the Colt Police Pistol across into its holster under the left side of his jacket. Even if he did not know that Murat distrusted him, the use of the word 'mister' would have served as a warning. A Texan only said that word when he disliked an acquaintance. So Runcorne obeyed the order and awaited developments.

A shrewd peace officer, Murat suspected Runcorne of being involved in illegal activities of various kinds but lacked proof. Coming to help the town marshal's deputies break up the fight, he saw Runcorne leading two bouncers into the cellar. The sight aroused Murat's interest and sent him across the room to investigate. He wanted to learn why the saloonkeeper had considered the cellar's contents so valuable that he'd ignored the damage to the bar room. More than that, the saloonkeeper had taken along his two toughest bouncers when they could hardly be spared from their work in quelling the brawl. Finding that the door had been kicked open added to Murat's desire to learn more. On seeing Mark and Bragg in the cellar he felt that at last there might be a chance to nail Runcorne's hide to the wall.

Watching Murat come down the stairs, Runcorne scowled. The mention of the wine's quality rang a warning bell for him. If the intruders knew something about the barrels' contents— and their presence hinted that they might—he did not want the matter brought up in Murat's hearing.

'They could be telling the truth, sheriff,' he said. 'Anyways, there's no harm been done.'

'Except for the way the door was opened,' Murat answered. 'It takes a strong man to do it, and one trained as a peace officer. All right, Mark, what brought you pair down here?'

'Maybe Tule told you the truth.'

'And maybe he didn't. You pair wouldn't run out on the chance of a fight without good reason.'

'We thought we'd got it,' Mark admitted. 'A feller passed word to me that Runcorne'd been trading guns and whisky for silver with the Kaddos and that it tied into Sam's death, so we came along to see if the story was true.'

'*Me* trading with the Indians?' yelped Runcorne in a tone oozing with contemptuous indignation. 'That's likely, isn't it?'

'The proof's in the whisky barrels,' Mark said.

'Is it, Mr. Runcorne?' asked Murat.

'There's only one way to find out,' the saloonkeeper answered and walked across to the barrels. Taking a wooden dipper from the top of the first, he held it under and turned on the tap. Liquid trickled down into the dipper and he offered it to the sheriff. 'Taste the "proof".'

'It's wine all right,' Murat said, after obeying, and he sounded a mite disappointed. 'How about the other two?'

Watching the saloonkeeper's face, Mark noticed a glint of self-satisfied amusement creep across it. Certainly Runcorne exhibited no concern as he went to the next keg, turned on its tap and filled the dipper with more of the red fluid. After allowing Mark and Murat to taste the contents, Runcorne walked across to the last keg. Once again a flow of wine filled the dipper and the mocking expression grew broader on the saloonkeeper's features.

'It looks like you heard wrong, Mark,' Murat stated after sampling the wine from the last barrel.

'It sure looks that way,' agreed Mark. 'I wouldn't've thought you'd sell much wine, Mr. Runcorne.'

In general the Texas cowhand stuck to whisky and beer, leaving the drinking of wine to Mexicans, town dwellers and others with educated thirsts.

'I ship it East, or to the coast,' Runcorne answered cheerfully. 'Are you satisfied that I'm not peddling fire-water and guns to the Indians now?'

Everything about Runcorne's attitude struck Mark as being wrong. Every instinct he possessed told him that Belle's information had been correct. A man in fear of death, desperately trying to buy his life, would not lie. Nor would Belle have risked capture by returning to the hotel unless she believed that Jacobs told her the truth. In addition, the saloon-keeper acted just a mite too sure of himself. Runcorne had the air of a man who brought off a mighty slick bluff at poker. Yet he showed concern at first hearing Mark mention the wine barrels. If they were, as now seemed obvious, filled with wine he did not need to worry.

'How about it, Mark?' demanded Murat, cutting into the blond giant's flow of thought.

'Who told you that wild story, friend?' asked Runcorne.

'Yeah, Mark, who told you?' Murat went on.

'A reliable source, most times,' Mark answered.

'Reliable!' snorted Runcorne. 'You tell us his name——'

'A smart feller like you should know better than ask that,' Mark replied. 'Let's get going, Jules.'

'I reckon I ought to be told who started this pack of lies about me, sheriff!' Runcorne insisted. 'If it's one of my business rivals I've a right to protect myself, don't I?'

'Like I said,' Mark drawled. 'A feller who can be relied on, most times.'

With that he walked slowly and casually to where several small kegs of whisky were stacked against the wall. Reaching down, he raised one of the top kegs in his two hands.

A mocking sneer crossed Runcorne's face. 'You don't reckon I've got that stuff hid in those kegs, do y——?' he began.

The words chopped off as Mark turned, swung up the keg and hurled it at the front of the right-side wine barrel. Wood cracked and splintered under the impact and whisky spurted from the stove-in surface of the keg—but no wine gushed out the barrel. Instead its front sank inwards.

An explosive grunt left Murat's lips at the sight. As the upper part of the front tilted into the barrel, its lower edge automatically came out. Fitted to the inside of the front and connected to its tap was a one-gallon keg of wine. The rest of the space held nothing but a number of stone whisky jugs. The sight so surprised Murat that for once he forgot caution. Without taking time to look at Runcorne's party, he started to walk in the direction of the barrel.

Probably Runcorne had no intention of making trouble. The

81

mere possession of the whisky and other items in the remaining barrels was not, in itself, proof of illegal trading with the Indians. It was unlikely that a court would convict him just on that. At the worst he would be told to sell up his place and get out of Austin. So what happened stemmed from one of his men failing to grasp the situation correctly.

Letting out a snarl of rage, the bouncer grabbed out his gun. Bragg flung himself forward, cannoning into the sheriff's back and staggering him aside even as the bouncer's gun cracked. The bullet aimed at Murat's back missed its mark and instead raked a furrow across Bragg's shoulders.

While Runcorne would have cheerfully strangled the bouncer for acting in such a way, he realised what must be done. Knowing that Murat and the two intruders would assume his employee had acted under his orders, he did the only thing left for him to do. Across lashed his hand to where the Colt Police Pistol rode in its butt-forward holster.

Just as Mark guessed, Runcorne was very fast. Not that Mark wasted time in self-congratulation over his shrewd judgement of character. Instead he flung himself backwards in the opposite direction to which Bragg had thrust Murat and, in going, sent his hands diving towards the butts of his Colts. Fast though Mark might be, other things stood in Runcorne's favour. The Colt Police Pistol had been designed as a weapon for peace officers to carry concealed; .36 in calibre, it had only a three-and-a-half-inch barrel which meant four-and-a-half inches less to clear the holster lip than had Mark's Army Colt. So the saloonkeeper's gun left leather even as Mark's fingers closed on the ivory handles of his Colts.

Out whisked Runcorne's revolver but he made the fatal mistake of hesitating. While taken by surprise, Murat still started to draw while staggering from Bragg's push. Despite his wound, the foreman also reached for a weapon, grabbing down at the Dance's worn butt with commendable speed. Small wonder that the saloonkeeper showed indecision in the face of three possible threats to his life. Against a man of Mark's ability such vicillation was fatal.

Flame ripped from the barrel of Mark's right-hand Colt as it lined on the saloonkeeper. An instant before Runcorne decided to concentrate first on Mark, the blond giant's bullet caught him between the eyes. Mark shot the only way he dare under the circumstances. Against a man of Runcorne's ability there could be no hesitation in placing the bullet where it would kill instantly. Even so, despite being thrown backwards by the impact, Runcorne got off a shot which narrowly missed Mark's head.

Landing on the floor, Murat cut loose on the bouncer who'd started the gunplay. Caught in the chest by a bullet, the man spun around, let his revolver drop, collided with his companion and then slid to the floor. Finding himself covered by Bragg's old Dance, the second bouncer hastily raised his hands and yelled that he was not making any fuss.

The rear entrance's door jerked upwards and one of the guards looked in. Seeing what had happened, he started to raise his gun. Rolling over to face the door, Mark made sure that it offered a fresh menace to his friends' well-being and then took steps to counter the threat. The sight of the lined gun and lack of a badge told him that Runcorne's guard and not one of the deputies looked in, so he threw a shot which struck the edge of the door and sent up a cloud of splinters. The man jerked back, letting the door fall down into place. However, he had seen the sheriff and noticed his boss sprawled on the floor. So he called off further attempts at hostilities.

'Close,' Murat said, coming to his feet as two deputy marshals appeared at the head of the stairs. 'Thanks, Tule.'

'That was a fool trick you pulled,' Bragg answered and winced as a movement caused his wound to throb. 'Damn it, I'm shot.'

Thrusting away his Colt, Mark sprang to Bragg's side and knelt by him. However the foreman let out an explosive snort and pointed. 'See if Runcorne can talk. I'll last a mite longer.'

'How is it upstairs?' Murat asked the deputies and, on learning the fight had been brought under control, ordered them to attend to the wounded men. Then he turned to Mark. 'Let's take a look at the barrels.'

Seeing that the deputy seemed competent to care for Bragg until the doctor arrived, Mark accompanied Murat to the wine barrels. They examined the neat way in which Runcorne gave the impression that the barrels held wine.

'It's a pity that Runcorne can't do any talking,' the sheriff remarked as he kicked at the front of the centre barrel. 'Not that I blame you for stopping him, Mark. He was a good man with a gun.'

'Sure,' Mark answered. 'Maybe some of his men can give us the answer.'

Before questioning Runcorne's staff, Mark and Murat opened the other two barrels. In one they found a number of Winchester rifles and ammunition, while the other held sacks containing raw silver.

'It's been stored a long time from the way it looks,' Murat remarked as he opened one sack.

'So I heard,' Mark replied. 'The feller allowed it came from some old Spanish mine the Kaddo found.'

'You'd best tell me as much as you can,' Murat suggested, knowing that only in the most exceptional circumstances would a man like Mark divulge the name of an informant who gave confidential information.

'There's not much to tell. Like I said, word came to me that Runcorne was trading with the Kaddo and that it tied in to Sam's killing. The Wycliffes were waiting for Runcorne's man, who fitted Sam's description enough for them to make a mistake. So I allowed to see if it was true. Reckoned to make Runcorne talk, tell me where the gold came from. That way I'd have a start at finding the Wycliffes should we miss picking up their tracks.'

'It was mighty lucky, that fight starting when it did,' Murat commented. 'You'd never've kicked open the door if all Runcorne's men hadn't been busy with it. Yes sir, Mark, mighty lucky.'

'Sure was,' agreed Mark. 'And to show how grateful I am for being so lucky, I'll pay any fines the gents up there might get.'

'It'd be best,' said the sheriff judiciously. 'What's up with you?'

The last came as the unwounded bouncer moved closer, darted a glance at the first pair, his wounded companion, winked at Murat and nodded in the direction of the stairs. At the sheriff's words, the bouncer showed some agitation and again gazed hurriedly at the other saloon employees. Relief showed on his face as he realised the others did not notice his actions.

'Can we talk?' the bouncer asked in a low tone.

'Go to it,' Murat answered.

'Not here, someplace where I'll not be seen doing it,' the bouncer said.

'All right,' Murat replied in a loud voice. 'Show us Runcorne's office.'

'Sure, sheriff,' agreed the bouncer, trying to sound reluctant. 'Come this way.'

On arrival at Runcorne's office and with the door safely closed, the reason for the bouncer's agitation became obvious. He wished to betray certain of his late boss's secrets, but not in the presence of the other members of the staff. While Runcorne was undoubtedly dead, the man wanted to continue working in saloons and had no desire to become known as one who told tales to the law.

Not that the man knew much beyond the fact that his employer had traded, through a man called Pegler, with the Kaddo

84

Indians. Pegler would collect the trade goods at night in exchange for sacks of silver, beyond that the bouncer knew nothing. However he bought his freedom to leave Austin, along with Murat's demand that the departure be immediate, with his information. The sheriff showed no sign of it, but he knew something of Pegler.

'He runs a small trading post out on the headwaters of the Pedernales,' Murat told Mark after a relieved bouncer left the office.

'That'll be a good place to start happen the trail peters out,' Mark replied.

'For you, maybe. But it's well beyond the county line and I've no jurisdiction out there,' Murat pointed out. 'I'll come along if you need me.'

'Thanks, Jules,' Mark said. 'But you're needed here. Reckon Tejas'll go with me?'

'I reckon he might, but that's the fringe of the Kaddo country.'

'I'm still going,' Mark stated. 'I aim to have the bastards who killed Sailor Sam—even if I have to fight the whole damned Kaddo nation to get them.'

CHAPTER TEN

THE COMING OF THE YSABEL KID

THE white stallion made a magnificent sight. At least a full sixteen hands in height, yet so perfectly proportioned that it moved with swift and easy grace. It might have been a wild creature, despite the bridle and low-horned, double-girthed saddle it bore, for it moved with an air of constant alertness. Not the tense watchfulness, ready to flee at the first hint of hostile sound or scent, a whitetail deer or broomtail mare showed, but the constant readiness of a master animal willing to fight for its right to survive.

Nor did the man sitting the saddle distract in any way from the stallion's untamed appearance. Six foot tall, his lean frame gave an impression of whipcord strength and whang leather toughness. He had a handsome face almost babyishly young and innocent in feature, if one discounted the wild red-hazel eyes and an Indian-dark tan. At first glance one might take him to be in his early teens. Closer inspection warned that his looks were deceptive; or if he was in his early teens, they had been very hard years. A black Stetson hat of Texas style sat on his raven-dark head of hair. The black motif ran through his entire outfit, bandana, shirt, pants, boots and gunbelt all being of that sombre hue. Only the brown walnut grips of the old Dragoon Colt holstered butt forward at his right side and the ivory hilt of the James Black bowie knife sheathed on his left hip relieved the blackness. The butt of a Winchester Model 1866 rifle showed from his saddleboot and his armament did not end there.

In his right hand, augmenting the Indian air he gave in appearance and the way he rode, was a Comanche war lance. Its seven-foot-long handle of *bois d'arc* wood supported a thirty-inch head of finely tempered steel. Painted with medicine symbols and decorated by a cluster of eagle feathers, the lance looked what it was; a deadly efficient fighting weapon.

Man and horse made a good pair. Between them they exhibited an aura of wolf-cautious alertness; the kind of air a full grown grizzly bear showed when crossing its selected territory.

All the time as he rode, the young-looking man watched the range around him with eyes that missed little. He saw the distant rump-flashing of a startled pronghorn start off other flickering signals from its kind. Near at hand a prairie falcon rose from the body of a jack rabbit and winged clear of the approaching man. Then he slowed the horse, reared up in the stirrups and looked ahead. Most men could have seen only a patch of brown on the rolling green of the range, but the rider knew he looked at a very important segment of Texas' major industry; a trail herd bedded down for the night. On riding closer he made out the chuck and bed wagons halted in an advantageous position and the smaller mass of the remuda which supplied fresh mounts for the men who worked the cattle.

Feeling that he might like to spend the night in human company, the rider pointed his stallion towards the distant herd and allowed it to make better time in the new direction. All the time he rode, he studied the night camp. There were a few Texas outfits who would not make him welcome and he did not wish to force his company on any man. Before he covered half the distance, he knew that he rode towards friends.

Gathered about the fire while waiting for the cook to start serving the inevitable beef stew and beans, the trail crew watched the approaching rider. One of them, a brash youngster making his first drive north, grinned broadly as he studied the newcomer's armament and gave particular attention to the war lance.

'Damnit!' he grinned to the grizzled veteran at his side. 'A war-whoop's done jumped the reservation.'

'Was I you, I wouldn't say it so's he could hear you,' counselled the other.

'Why not?' demanded the youngster truculently.

'Because that feller's a particular good friend of Big Ranse for one thing,' the oldster explained. 'And iffen that's not enough, he's also the Ysabel Kid.'

Maybe mere loyalty to his employer might not have prevented the youngster making further comment, but the name spoken by the old timer and what went unspoken about it caused him to keep silent. New to the trail, a touch wild and reckless on occasion, the young cowhand possessed sufficient good common-sense not to play games with that babyishly innocent looking rider.

Many knowledgeable people claimed the Ysabel Kid to be the most dangerous member of Ole Devil Hardin's floating outfit. True he could not equal either Dusty Fog or Mark Counter's speed on the draw, although he performed passably well with his old Dragoon Colt in time of necessity. His talent in the skilled use of the bowie knife made up for any close-range deficiencies with a hand-gun and his marksmanship when using the rifle almost passed belief. Yet those attributes alone did not make him one to be feared.

Born of an Irish–Kentuckian father and French Creole-Comanche mother, the Kid spent his rearing years among the *Pehnane* band of his mother's tribe. From his maternal grandfather, Chief Long Walker, he learned those things a Comanche warrior needed to know.* He could ride any horse ever foaled, follow tracks where lesser men might see nothing, move in silence through any kind of country, hide and locate hidden enemies and knew the ways of the great Texas plains. Less of a cowhand than his two companions, he acted as scout in time of danger. So the talents taught to make him a brave-heart warrior found many uses among the white men.

After seeing his grandfather's people settled on their new home and satisfying himself that the White Father in Washington's word would be kept to the *Pehnane*, the Kid began his journey to the OD Connected. On his way he had to deliver the war lance to the Governor of Texas, being both a tribute to the man who made the peace possible and a sign that the Wasps, Raiders, Quick Stingers—those names being the nearest white equivalent to *Pehnane*—rode no more to war. Cheerfully he rode towards the trail drive's camp, knowing he could expect hospitality from Big Ranse Counter's crew.

Mark's father equalled him in size and muscular development, although age had put thickness to Big Ranse's middle. Dressed like a working cowhand, with an Army Colt hanging at his side, the rancher swung away from the bed wagon and raised his hand in greeting to the newcomer.

'Howdy, Kid. This wouldn't be some of your Comanche witch-craft, would it?'

'How's that?' asked the Kid.

'You've sure showed up at the right time.'

'For what?'

'Mark's likely to need help.'

'Where and for what?'

Forgotten was the visit to Austin and presentation of the war lance to the Governor. The Kid's face showed little, but interest glinted in his red-hazel eyes as he listened to Ranse Counter's story of the happenings in the capital. Just a hint of worry began to show on the Indian-dark features as Ranse told how the Wycliffe gang's tracks had been lost but that Mark went on with the search.

'Just him and Tejas Tom went on,' the rancher concluded. 'They're headed up the Pedernales River towards Pegler's place.'

'That's on the edge of the Kaddo country,' the Kid breathed,

* Told in *Comanche*.

88

thinking of a story going the rounds of the *Pehnane* camp before he left it.

'And he'll not stop there if the Wycliffes've gone on,' Ranse continued. 'I'm fixing to go after him.'

'How about your herd?' asked the Kid.

'That's just what I've been asking the old goat'l!' yelled a peevish voice from the bed wagon and Bragg thrust his head into sight. 'I've got all shot 'n' can't ride trail boss. There's fifteen hundred head of our stuff and another thousand for two other spreads bedded down back there that he has to get to market.'

With beef prices at the Kansas rail head standing high, that amounted to a tolerable sum of money. Far too much to be tossed aside without real good reason. Not that the financial considerations worried Ranse Counter with his son in danger, but the Kid guessed that the other two spreads relied upon the rancher to take the herd through. So the Kid reached his decision fast, knowing that Ole Devil Hardin would expect him to act in such a manner.

'Let me go after him,' the Kid suggested. 'I can travel faster than you, and faster alone than if you come with me.'

For a long moment Ranse Counter hesitated and digested the Kid's words. All too well he knew the close ties which bound the floating outfit's members, so realised that every effort would be made to reach Mark in time and back his play no matter how great the odds. The Kid's timely arrival presented the best possible answer to Ranse's problem. While the rancher had fully intended to ride to his son's aid, he knew the penalty for doing so. He could survive the loss of the herd, but two neighbours depended on him to deliver and sell their cattle, providing them with badly needed money to carry them through until the next year.

Knowing the Kid's reputation, Ranse had no doubt in the other's ability to find Mark. Also the Kid spoke the simple truth when he stated that he could travel faster alone.

'Go to it, Lon,' the rancher ordered. 'Is there anything you want?'

'Reckon I've everything I need,' the Kid replied. 'Can you send my war bag into Austin, I'll be travelling light.'

'I'll see to it for you,' Ranse promised.

Dawn found the Kid in the saddle, although his bed roll no longer rode on the cantle. All he carried besides his clothing were bullets for the rifle, a powder horn and twenty ready-moulded balls to be used in the Dragoon, his knife and the war lance. To his way of thinking the latter did not form added weight, but was his passport into the Kaddo camp should one

89

be needed.

Being a white man, Ranse Counter would have ridden down river from his camp at the junction of the Llando and Colorado, followed the edge of Lake Travis to where the Pedernales flowed into it and up the latter stream. Not so the Kid. Using his inborn sense of direction, he proposed to ride across country at an angle that would bring him to the headwaters of the Pedernales. Doing so would save time and, he hoped, bring him to the vicinity of the Pegler trading post ready to back up Mark on the blond giant's arrival.

The route taken by the Kid took him through country not yet occupied by rancher or town dweller. For all that he lived well, relying on his rifle to supply meat and augmenting it with fruits or nuts and the tuberous roots of the Indian potato. Despite the urgency of the situation, he ensured that both he and the horse ate well. He knew that he travelled faster than Mark could while following tracks and on a route that he hoped would converge with the other's before arrival at the trading post.

For two days the Kid rode over the rolling Texas range without the sight or trace of another human being. He had covered over forty miles the first day and figured to be coming close to his destination. However, search the horizon as he might, he saw no smoke rising from the trading post's chimney nor distant glint of the sun reflected from the building's windows.

The rapid drumming of hooves came to the Kid's ears from beyond the rim up which he rode. At the same moment the wind, coming from the direction of the sound, carried a scent to the white stallion's nostrils, setting it fiddle-footing nervously and snorting as if to blow away the offending odour. Reading the signs correctly, despite the lack of confirmatory noise, the Kid started his horse moving up to the head of the rim. While he knew roughly what to expect, the sight before him brought a deep-throated exclamation bursting from his lips and caused him to bring the stallion to an abrupt halt.

Anywhere west of the Mississippi River, especially on the open ranges of Texas, the sight of a saddled, riderless horse gave rise to concern. Yet not even the sight of eight wolves loping after the fleeing horse at the foot of the valley beyond the rim added to the shock received by the Kid. That wolves hunted so large an animal did not surprise him. He knew they would take after any creature offering the possibility of a meal when hunger gnawed at them. What caused the Kid to sit back and take notice was the fact that he recognised the fleeing horse.

There might be other huge blood-bay stallions in Texas, probably most of them would carry a similar style of saddle—

the low-horned, double-girthed rig being much favoured by sons of the Lone Star State—but the Kid suffered from no doubts. He knew the horse to be Mark's favourite mount and could have picked it out from a big remuda.

Although the sight of Mark's riderless horse handed the Kid one hell of a shock, it did not freeze him into panic-filled immobility. Letting the lance fall from his right hand, he tossed his right leg across the front of the saddle and dropped to the ground. In passing he slid the rifle from its boot and his eyes measured the distance separating him from the horse. The rifle carried a slide rear sight graduated from one hundred to nine hundred yards. Loyal supporter of Oliver F. Winchester's product though he might be, the Kid admitted the upper graduations on the sight's scale were no more than wishful thinking. Twenty-eight grains of even the best powder could not propel the two hundred grain bullet nine hundred yards with any hope of hitting its intended target. However the horse and wolves came along the valley bottom in his direction and at much less than a quarter of a mile.

Even as he sank to his left knee and rested his left elbow on the bent right leg, the Kid knew he had no time to spare if he hoped to save the horse. As if sensing the danger of an intervention between it and the pack's prey, the big dog wolf in the lead increased its speed. Like most of the other species of its kind, the medium-sized, dark grey coloured, comparatively thin-coated Texas grey wolf could lope along at a speed of ten to twelve miles an hour for long periods. At a spurt, it might touch more than twice that speed. The dog wolf put on such a spurt, closing on the racing blood bay with the intention of chopping at the tendons of the lower leg. A bite there would ham-string the horse, bring it to a halt and leave it at the mercy of the pack.

The Kid did not take time to raise and adjust the leaf sight. At such a short range he could use the ordinary V notch sight and allow for deviations of distance. Swiftly he sighted, right forefinger curled around the trigger and starting to take the pressure. Even as the wolf gathered itself for the final leap, the Winchester cracked. Drilled through the chest, the wolf uttered a shrill yelp and somersaulted over. Down and up blurred the rifle's lever, throwing out the empty cartridge case and replacing it with a loaded bullet. The Kid changed aim and sent his next bullet through the shoulders of the second wolf, tumbling it under the feet of the remainder of the pack. Again he fired, sending lead into the wolves as they halted, snarling and tearing at their fallen companions.

Even in an area far from human habitation, the wolves knew

what the sound of a rifle meant. So they did not stick around to face more of the Kid's lead. Pulling away from the shot animal at which they mauled, the five unwounded wolves raced off at such speed that trying to shoot them would have been a waste of lead.

Booting his rifle, the Kid darted around his horse. The big white had stood like a statue, ignoring the crack of the rifle, smell of burning powder and scent of the wolves. Nor did it make a move until after the Kid, scooping up the lance in passing, bounded afork the saddle. Urged forward by its master, the white started down the slope in the direction of the fleeing blood bay.

Ridden by a man trained from his earliest days in the business of staying astride a horse, the white went down the slope at a good speed. Once on the level floor of the valley bottom, it really stretched out and showed how it could run. Crouching lightly in the saddle, the Kid used all his considerable skill to help the white. All too well he knew the speed at which Mark's blood bay could travel. While the white could run faster, it carried more weight than the blood bay and so needed every aid its rider offered.

Fear kept the blood bay running, but it had been pushed hard and long by the wolves. For all that, a quarter of a mile fell behind them before the Kid's white caught up. Grunting out a curse, the Kid thrust the lance under his left leg to leave his hands free. Slowly the white drew level with the other horse. Looking across, he saw the reins looped around the saddlehorn. Like the Kid, Mark could rely on his horse to stand without tying for a short time. Something must have spooked the blood bay and set it running after Mark left it. The Kid wanted to learn what the something had been.

Leaning across, the Kid gripped the blood bay's reins. A knee signal caused his white to slow down and between them they brought the other horse to a halt. The Kid retained his hold as he dropped from the saddle. On landing, he set to work to calm the blood bay so that he could examine it closer.

'Easy, big feller,' he said gently. 'Easy there.'

The Kid's familiar scent, mingled with his voice and firm, capable handling swiftly brought the horse under control. Although badly blown and heavily lathered by the wolves' long chase, the blood bay yielded no immediate sign of damage. After making sure that another flight would not be the result of letting go of the reins, the Kid examined its right side. Alert for any sign of restlessness, he passed around the horse's rump. Then he saw the reddish tint of the lather on the left hip and went closer to investigate.

Gently the Kid placed a finger on the discoloured patch, meaning to clean away the lather. He felt the horse quiver and spoke softly to calm it before continuing. Underneath the coating of lather he found a shallow graze in the skin. Bending closer and wiping off more of the froth sweated out during the chase, he saw that the hair had been burned away at the start of the groove. One did not need the powers of a Comanche witch woman to guess at the cause. Somebody had cut loose with a revolver at close range, the muzzle-blast singed the blood bay and the bullet sliced a nick in its flank. Pain started it running and somewhere in its flight it attracted the attention of the wolves. Luckily the wound had been only superficial or the pack would have pulled the blood bay down long before it came into the Kid's sight.

Glancing towards the horse's head, the Kid's eyes came to a halt at the saddle. He saw a dark stain on the leather and, hoping against hope, he moved closer to check the evidence of his eyes. Shock and anxiety twisted at his usually unemotional face as he looked at the stain. All too well he knew what the dark mark was, human blood. Far worse, he identified the greyish lumps which clung to the leather among the bloodstain. Blood and human brains had been smeared down the saddle. The Kid looked back in the direction from which the blood bay came and tried not to think that the hideous stain might originate from Mark Counter's shattered-open skull.

CHAPTER ELEVEN

SANDEL'S GRATITUDE

CAREFUL searching had located the tracks of the Wycliffe gang and Murat's small posse had followed until they had reached the border of Travis County. By that time they had reached the shores of Lake Travis and found that the gang had crossed the Pedernales River to turn upstream along the northern bank. When Mark had stated his intention of continuing the hunt, Murat had offered to accompany him; although the sheriff's jurisdiction ended at the county line. While Mark and Murat discussed the matter, a rider from Austin galloped up with news. It seemed that the Dick Dublin gang had been seen at Williamson and rode out of that town in the direction of Austin. The town marshal of Williamson believed Dublin planned a robbery in the State capital. Even if he did not, Dublin's name appeared on sufficient wanted posters to make his capture a matter of some importance. As county sheriff, senior law enforcement officer of the area, Murat would be needed. Knowing the reputation of the Dublin gang, Murat did not want to face them with casual help and required the services of all his deputies. That left just Mark and Tejas Tom to follow Wycliffe's party.

The young Indian came from a tribe long noted for its friendship to the white man. As Murat said, his clothing meant little for underneath lay the primitive instincts and knowledge of the red warrior. Throughout the trailing of the gang Mark had studied Tejas and knew him to be capable and skilled at his work.

Once again refusing to take men Murat might need to handle the Dublin gang, Mark turned his blood-bay stallion across the river. Tejas, cradling a tack-decorated Spencer carbine across his arm, followed and then led the way on the tracks of Wycliffe's bunch.

After a time Mark concluded that the bouncer at the Lone Rider had told the truth. Wycliffe's gang had swung away from the river only to avoid contact with the occasional settler's home. Once past the dwelling, the gang had returned to the river trail.

During the afternoon Tejas pointed out where a further six riders had joined the Wycliffe party.

'That makes maybe twelve of 'em.' Mark said, glancing at the Indian.

'More than we figure on,' Tejas answered.

'You want to go back?'

'Are you going on?'

'Sure,' admitted Mark.

'I took on to find 'em for you,' Tejas pointed out. 'Not done it yet.'

'Let's go then,' Mark drawled.

They started their horses moving once more, finding no difficulty in following the other party even though Wycliffe had stuck to the trail most of the time. Two miles farther upstream the trail petered out, having grown narrower and less used after each settler's buildings. Still the gang had stuck close to the river, until they had made camp for the night.

'They split up here this morning,' Tejas explained after circling the camp and reading tracks in the light of the setting sun. 'Look like they spread out, four bunches of them.'

That figured, thinking of the Army map Mark had studied before leaving Austin. Discounting the usual twists and bends, the Pedernales River formed a rough crescent from its source in what would one day form the eastern edge of Kimble County and where it entered Lake Travis. If Pegler knew the country, he might avoid the extra miles caused by following the windings of the river and take a direction line from the headwaters to Austin. So Wycliffe split up his party, spreading them out across the range in the hope that one group might see the trader.

Which left Mark with a problem.

'Who do we follow?' he asked.

'These three took girl with 'em,' Tejas answered, indicating the set of tracks which pointed along the bank of the river.

'Was Billy with them?' Mark asked.

'His hoss tracks go with 'em,' Tejas agreed.

'Then they're for us,' the blond giant growled. 'I'll be satisfied if I can nail his hide to the wall.'

'They not make such fast time with girl along,' commented Tejas. 'Not try hide their tracks either. Maybe so we catch 'em tomorrow.'

'Let's push on as far as we can today,' Mark suggested.

That proved to be another mile, by which time the sun had set and night came blackly to the land. Much as Mark liked his creature comforts—his habit of including a comfortable pillow in his bed roll when on the trail had been the cause of amused comment—he accepted that the conditions called for making a very primitive camp that night. They settled the horses on good grazing but limited themselves to drinking river water and eating the cold food brought from Austin, not even troubling to make a fire. Then Mark settled down to sleep, using his saddle for a pillow, the earth forming a hard, unsatisfactory mattress and the sky a roof.

Just how long Mark had been asleep he did not know. At the first gentle shake Tejas gave his arm, he came immediately and silently awake.

'I heard something,' the Indian said. 'Listen!'

Sitting up, Mark strained his ears. At first he heard nothing but the normal night sounds. Then it came, the scream of a terrified woman mingled with whoops, laughter and voices.

'Not white men!' Tejas breathed, reaching the same conclusion as Mark.

'Let's go take a look,' the blond giant replied.

Even as he spoke a further scream rose, to be chopped off as if a hand clamped over the woman's mouth. Taking up their rifles, Mark and Tejas moved swiftly through the trees in the direction of the sounds. The country bordering that part of the Pedernales River lay in thickly wooded rolling folds. It was an area not well suited to the raising of cattle, one of the reasons for the sparse population, also the U.S. Cavalry did not maintain regular patrols through the district. So Mark and Tejas did not discount the possibility of finding hostile Indians responsible for the screams. Not until they topped the second ridge from their camp did either man see any sign of other human beings.

Shapes moved about a large fire in a clearing down close to the river. Even from where they stood Mark and Tejas could make out sufficient details to tell them that they must intervene—and also enough to warn them that doing so would involve some risk.

Swiftly Mark counted the Indian ponies he could see standing at the far side of the clearing on the edge of the firelight. He made the score ten, not taking in the four horses of better breeding than the small, wiry broomtails. Ten corresponded with the braves around the fire. Six of that number helped themselves to liberal doses from a brace of stone whisky jugs. The remaining quartet appeared to be engrossed in preparations for entertaining their companions, with the unwilling aid of at least one of their prisoners.

Close to the horses, bound to a tree and with a stick forced into her mouth as a gag, was a blonde-haired girl clad in a man's shirt which had lost one sleeve and levis pants. Just as securely fastened, although not gagged, the lanky form of a man in range clothes lay by the fire. Mark needed only one glance to identify the prisoner as Loney Sandel, one of Wycliffe's companions from the saloon.

After studying the camp, Mark turned his attention back to the quartet of industrious braves. All the party wore a mixture of traditional and white man's clothing, while three sported gunbelts and revolvers. Three of the quartet appeared to be laying a second fire, for they piled dried leaves and small branches on the ground beneath a tall old white oak tree. Taking up a rope, the fourth buck flipped its noose end over a branch directly above where his companions built the new fire. Mark could guess what the quartet had in mind.

Whooping their delight, the three braves left their work and crossed to where Sandel lay. Like Mark, the lanky man knew what the Indians planned and began to throw his body from side to side in a vain attempt to free his arms. He achieved nothing other than to bring whoops and laughter from the watching braves. Grabbing him by his bound ankles, the trio of braves hauled him bodily to the oak tree. The fourth buck, with Sandel's gunbelt and Cooper Navy revolvers slung about his waist, deftly flipped the noose over the prisoner's feet and drew it tight about his ankles. Watched by the remainder of the party, the three braves sprang to the other end of the rope and began hauling at it. Laughter and shouted advice rose from the watching warriors as Sandel's body started to rise feet first into the air.

'Young Kaddo bucks!' Tejas whispered as he and Mark advanced down the slope.

'Looks that way,' Mark agreed. 'We'll have to jump them fast or they'll kill the girl.'

'Noise they're making, they'll not hear us come,' Tejas guessed.

Certainly none of the braves showed any hint of knowing, or caring, that they had been discovered. They laughed, whooped, yelled comments to each other. Hauling on the rope, the trio drew it up and over the branch until they suspended Sandel head downwards over the mound of inflammable material. Then the fourth buck darted to the fire and dragged out a blazing branch. Waving it over his head, he started back across the clearing.

While Mark would have preferred to be much closer before cutting in, he did not dare wait any longer. Sandel might be one of the crowd who helped kill Sailor Sam but the blond giant could not stand by and watch him tortured. In addition to his revulsion at the thought of a man being hung head down over a fire, Mark wanted to question Sandel and learn if Billy Wycliffe owned one of the riderless horses standing with the

Indian ponies. If Billy had died at the hands of the braves, Mark would be willing to call off his hunt. Yet Mark doubted if Billy had fallen victim to the Kaddo braves. None of them wore a gunbelt with a swivel holster.

Skidding to a halt, Mark swung the Winchester rifle to his shoulder and took aim at the brave with the blazing branch. When sure of his aim, the blond giant squeezed the trigger. Flame lanced through the darkness and the bullet ripped into the brave's head. Spinning around, he flung the torch aside and tumbled to the ground.

So engrossed in the forthcoming torture were the rest that the shot came as a complete surprise. Nor did their whisky-slowed minds take in what the sound meant with any kind of speed. On the heels of Mark's shot, Tejas' Spencer bellowed to crumple over one of the men holding the rope. Sandel's weight dragged the other two braves forward and he had sense enough to curl his body forward as it sank down. In that way he saved himself from injury, landing on the unlit pile of branches and then flopping to the ground.

After ending the immediate threat to Sandel's life, Mark concentrated his efforts on preventing the remaining bucks from recovering from their surprise and organising a defence. While the Winchester's mechanism enabled a skilled man to get off two shots a second, no amount of practice could teach him to change his point of aim at that speed. So Mark concentrated on sending lead fast and in the general direction of the braves; all the time making the woods ring with bawled-out cowhand yells.

At Mark's side, Tejas showed a remarkably good grasp of the situation and of his companion's intentions. Long before they could render all the braves harmless, the initial shock would have worn off. Maybe the Kaddo did not rank with the Comanche as fighting men, but they could handle their end in a fracas and were not to be despised. Given a brief time to regain control of their startled wits, any of the party left alive would at least kill the two prisoners before being settled. However the need to thumb-cock the hammer between shots prevented the Spencer from equalling the Winchester's speed of discharge. So Tejas used the extra time to take aim. He might not be able to put down such a volume of fire as Mark, but made at least as much vocal disturbance.

Another buck went down, thrown across the fire by the shocking impact of a .52 calibre Spencer bullet. By that time the Kaddos milled about the clearing and Mark did no more than catch a brave high in the shoulder, giving him a bad graze but nothing worse.

Then the rest of the Indians broke. Like many of the Indian tribes, the Kaddo did not care to fight at night. They believed that the Great Spirit might fail to find a dead warrior in the darkness, preventing him from being guided to the Land of Good Hunting. So they raced for their horses, wanting only to escape from their unseen attackers. One of the braves had to pass the girl and snatched the tomahawk from his belt as he approached her. Seeing her danger, Mark swung the barrel of his Winchester and sighted. Rifle and carbine cracked at the same moment. Caught in the head by a .44 calibre bullet and raked through the body by a .52 ball, the Kaddo was a tolerable dead Indian even before his body crashed down at the girl's side.

Showing the kind of skill one expected of horse-Indians, the remainder of the band mounted their ponies. Even the wounded brave hit his mount's back with commendable speed. Nor did they intend to leave such valuable loot as horses in the hands of their attackers. Their own ponies stood with no more than a hackamore tossed across the branch of a bush. Only the captured white men's horses needed fastening and the braves succeeded in cutting free all but one. Lead whistled around their heads, coming close enough to prevent any great effort to sever the fine-looking dun's reins. While that horse was the best of the looted quartet, none of the braves felt like giving his life to free it. Taking all but the dun, the braves fled into the darkness and could be heard crashing off through the trees at speed.

Cautiously Mark and Tejas advanced into the firelight and moved forward to ensure they did not need to worry about the braves lying about the clearing. They held their weapons ready and did not regret the precaution even after it proved to be needless.

'Cut that jasper free, Tejas,' Mark ordered. 'Then go fetch up our horses. We'd best get the hell out of here.'

Although the Kaddo did not fight in the night, the departed bucks might be tempted to return in an effort to retrieve their abandoned property. The discarded whisky jugs alone would form a mighty strong inducement. If the braves returned, they would come in silence and follow their attackers' tactics of cutting loose out of the darkness. There might be more Indians in the vicinity, in which case Mark's party might find themselves faced with greater odds than they could handle. All his and Tejas' spare ammunition had been left with their saddles and Mark wanted a reserve on hand should an attack come.

Even without going into details, Tejas followed Mark's line of thought. Taking a Green River knife from its sheath beneath his jacket, the Indian knelt at Sandel's side. As he started to free

99

the man, Tejas watched his face and the manner in which his eyes followed Mark.

Crossing the clearing, Mark rested his rifle against the tree trunk, took a jack-knife from his pocket. First he removed the cruel gag from the girl's mouth. In normal times she would have been a pretty girl, with a freckled face, snub nose and smiling lips. The ordeal she had gone through left marks of terror and exhaustion on her features.

Working fast, Mark cut the girl free and she collapsed sobbing into his arms. Gently he held her, feeling the sobs which tore at her and the uncontrollable trembling of her body against his.

'Easy now,' he said quietly. 'Just take it easy. It's all over now.'

After cutting Sandel's bonds, Tejas turned and faded off into the darkness. Sitting up, Sandel rubbed at the inside of his wrists and cursed the pain restored circulation shot through him. Then his eyes returned once more to Mark and verified the identification already made. Most men would have been filled with gratitude for an escape from agonising death, but Sandel thought only of his future. That future did not look any too bright in view of the identity of the man who had rescued him.

Despite his apologies and professions of good feelings, Churn Wycliffe had taken time to learn the name of his family's assailant before leaving Austin. The Wycliffe clan relied too much on their name for salty toughness to mildly accept the kind of treatment handed to them before witnesses in the Bigfoot Saloon. Any plans for extracting retribution had been put off until finishing the business that had brought them to the State capital. More than that, Churn Wycliffe hesitated before making trouble for a member of Ole Devil's floating outfit unless he could select the time and place.

So Wycliffe had led his party out of Austin in search of Trader Pegler. Too late they discovered the mistake they had made when grabbing that bearded jasper and girl. A search of the man's body and his wagon informed them of his name and that he worked as cook for the R over C ranch; owned by Big Ranse Counter, father of the man who had rough-handled three prime members of the Wycliffe bunch.

Which meant that Sandel owed his life to Mark Counter. Maybe Sandel was not bright, but he could guess what brought the blond giant out along the Pedernales River. Even if it be no more than chance, the girl knew everything. She would tell how Billy Wycliffe shot Sailor Sam and mention Sandel's part in the affair. Even if Mark did no more than take Sandel in for trial, the girl's evidence would be damning. Most Texas juries held every member of a gang present to be responsible for the actions of the others. Sandel knew that family influence could not save him if Mark Counter handed him over to the law.

Darting a glance around him, Sandel could see no sign of Tejas and concluded that the Indian had gone to obey Mark's orders. Then his eyes went to the dun horse which still stood tied to a bush. With the horse between his knees Sandel figured he could make good his escape and either join up with the rest of the gang or head for the safety of the San Saba country. Added salvation lay not far from him, in the shape of the brave who had taken his gunbelt when he fell into their hands. The butt of the right-side Cooper revolver stuck up like a signpost directing Sandel to escape from his perilous position.

Slowly and cautiously Sandel inched his way to the Kaddo's body. Mark still stood with his back to the man, comforting the girl and oblivious of his danger. It never occurred to the blond giant that Sandel knew him, or understood his presence in connection with the murder of Sailor Sam. There would be time to deal with Sandel after they put some miles between themselves and the clearing—or so Mark believed. First he must get the girl in a condition where she could stand a hard, fast ride through the night.

Sliding free the Cooper, Sandel used the Kaddo's body as a rest. After being tied for so long, his right hand lacked the strength to control the gun adequately. He knew the penalty of missing, so gripped his right hand in the left and propped them on the immobile flesh of the dead Indian. Running the tip of his tongue across lips which felt suddenly dry, Sandel lined his gun on Mark's back.

While resembling the Navy Colt in a number of external details, including being the same general shape, the Cooper differed from its more famous rival in one major aspect. Being single action, the Colt must be hand-cocked for each shot. The Cooper offered its user the advantage of operating 'double'-action; pressure on its trigger serving to carry the hammer back to full cock and then snap down on to the percussion cap. Sandel only rarely made use of the double-action, preferring to thumb back the hammer. Lining his gun on Mark's back, he squeezed the trigger. To manually cock the hammer gave off an audible click which might reach the blond giant's ears. One could not give chances to a man like Mark Counter without the danger of him taking them with fatal results to the giver.

The shot roared out loud in the stillness of the night. Whirling around, Mark sent his right hand down to its Colt and used the left to grip the girl and thrust her to safety behind the tree should it be necessary. He saw Sandel rear up, let the Cooper fall from limp hands and pitch forward to lie face down across the Kaddo's body.

Smoke curled up lazily from the barrel of Tejas' Spencer as he walked from the trees.

'That one had a bad heart, *amigo*,' the Indian said, nodding to Sandel. 'I see it in his eyes. Wait among trees and watch him. He tried to kill you.'

'*Gracias*,' Mark replied. 'I should have figured on it. It's a pity, I'd questions I wanted to ask him.'

'He not answer you now,' Tejas stated, looking at the ruin his bullet made of Sandel's skull. 'Bring girl, *amigo*. This is not a good place for us to stay.'

CHAPTER TWELVE

THE REMAINS OF PEGLER'S TRADING POST

TEJAS insisted Mark checked the saddle of the dun. Then, while the Indian appropriated Sandel's gunbelt and Cooper revolvers for his own use, Mark helped the girl on to the horse. Much as he wanted to question her as to the fate of Sandel's companions, one glance told him doing so at that time would be fruitless. Shock and strain rendered the girl incoherent. So, even without the urgent necessity to leave the area, he wanted to take her from the clearing and give her a chance to recover.

Leading the dun, Mark followed Tejas through the trees to their camp. After helping the girl down, the big blond saddled his blood bay. No less swiftly Tejas prepared to leave and led the way through the woodland away from the river. Already satisfied with Tejas' abilities, Mark found the Indian worthy of ranking with the Ysabel Kid in the matter of moving through the darkness. So Mark left the guiding of the party in Tejas' hands, staying by the girl's side to encourage and support her through a four-mile ride.

After falling behind for a time, so as to listen for sounds of pursuit, Tejas caught up with Mark and the girl. He told Mark that they had travelled far enough, but he wished to find a secluded spot in which they could spend the rest of the night. Ranging ahead, Tejas selected a draw with steep walls and a stream flowing along its centre.

'This what we want,' he told Mark in satisfaction, leading the way between the walls.

By that time the girl seemed on the verge of collapse. She slid limply from her horse as Mark swung out of the blood bay's saddle. Turning, he caught her and set her down on the springy grass.

'Reckon we can chance a fire, Tejas?' he asked. 'She's cold, tuckered out and could likely stand some food in her belly.'

'Nobody followed us that I could hear,' the Indian answered. 'Down here we make small fire and not be seen. Have it out before daylight then they not see any smoke. I make-um, you watch girl.'

However, the girl seemed over the worst of the shock, so Mark left her and went to tend to the horses. She shuddered, but could think well enough to realise. they might need the animals when daylight came. Neglecting their mounts at that moment could easily cost them their lives later, so she made no objections. Sitting on the ground, she hugged her arms about her knees and shuddered at the thought of what the past two days had brought her.

Soon a small fire blazed close to the girl, and her rescuers joined her after removing saddles and seeing to the horses' welfare. While Mark looked after the girl at the clearing, Tejas had taken time to gather various things discarded by the Kaddo which his party could use. It seemed that the Indians hunted with some success and travelled intending to feed well. They had left behind a cooked hindquarter of prime whitetail buck meat, a parfleche-covered slab of pemmican and a cleaned-out buffalo paunch filled with honey. Bringing the food along, Tejas presented his companions with the means of making a good meal. Despite the ordeal she had passed through, the girl ate well and at the end, although tired, seemed to be recovering from the shock.

'Now you just settle down,' Mark told her when she finished eating. 'We've made up a bed for you and comes morning we'll see about taking you back home.'

'Home!' she gasped. 'Lordy lord, I never thought I'd want to go back there.'

'We'll see you get there, don't worry on that score,' Mark assured her. 'So just lie down and get some sleep.'

The girl shuddered, but obeyed. 'After what's happened to me and what I've seen these last couple of days, I doubt if I'll ever sleep again,' she groaned as she drew one of Mark's blankets over her.

'Talk then,' he suggested. 'It'll maybe help you to go to sleep and I'd like to hear how you came to be out here and all.'

Slowly the girl's story came out. Her name was Winnie Odville and her folks ran a small place down on the Cibolo River. After hearing travelling men talk about the gay, exciting life in the cities, Winnie had decided to see some of it for herself. Borrowing an older brother's clothes, she took one of the family's plough mules and set out for Austin. On the way to the capital a black bear had spooked her mule and set her a-foot. Catching up to her on the trail, Sailor Sam had offered her a ride. He accepted her story that she lived in Austin and had been visiting kin when the mule threw her.

Mark listened patiently to the girl as she began to tell him about her family. While life had been boring and occasionally hard, she no longer wanted to put her home behind her. Instead she wished that she had never left and would be only too pleased to return, even if Paw did whale the tar out of her for losing the mule.

Then she returned to telling him what he wanted to know. He let her tell the story in her own way, knowing that way would give him more than if he pressed questions on her.

Much of what Winnie next told him did no more than confirm Tejas' reading of the sign. Wycliffe's men had rode up to the wagon, acting in a friendly manner until close. Then they had drawn guns and ordered Sailor Sam to leave the trail. Down by the river he had attacked his captors in an attempt to let Winnie escape. Billy Wycliffe had shot the cook in his rage at having been knocked down.

'That big feller they call Churn went near crazy wild with Billy,' Winnie went on. 'I think he'd've whupped him right there and then only one of the others said he thought they'd got the wrong man. And they had. They thought Sam was a trader called Pegler.'

'What happened then?' Mark prompted gently.

'They just left Sam where he lay. I thought they'd kill me as well, but the big feller said for them to take me with them—so they took me, went back and watched the trail—Sheriff came, they saw him and a posse in the distance.'

While talking, her eyes fought to stay open. Then the exhaustion which filled her took over and she sank into a deep sleep.

'Girl not tell much,' Tejas commented.

'Only what we knew,' Mark replied. 'Likely we'll get more out of her after she's rested.'

The two men settled down once more and spent the remainder of the night undisturbed. Waking before daylight broke. Tejas doused the fire and made sure that no smoke rose from it. The girl slept on for some time and they let her. While Mark stayed in the draw to guard her, Tejas slipped off to scout the surrounding country for signs of the Kaddo. He returned before the girl awoke and brought disturbing news. Although the braves from the clearing did not appear to be on their trail, Tejas saw a bunch of maybe a dozen more passing in a down-river direction.

As the men sat discussing the news, Winnie stirred and sat up rubbing her eyes. Then she seemed to remember where she was and stared at her rescuers for a few moments in panic before realising who they might be.

'There's only water to drink, but we've still food left,' Mark told her.

'Food cold,' Tejas went on. 'We can't have fire.'

Cold venison without salt might be unpalatable, but pemmican, 'Indian bread', generously coated with honey rated as a delicacy and more than made up for the deficiencies of the meat. After eating, Mark prompted the girl to start telling her story again. Shaking her head sadly, Winnie cursed the Wycliffes in general and Billy in particular.

'He's a mean one, that,' she told the two men. 'Why, he just shot old Sam down like I'd swat a fly. And he figured to bad-use me, only his uncle wouldn't let him. That was in camp the night they killed Sam. Next day they got me on a hoss, it was a spare that Sandel feller had along, and made me ride with them. Churn said they daren't wait around with the sheriff on the prowl and they'd go look for Pegler. So they brought me up to that river, crossed it and started going upstream. Then they met another six of his men. All the time Billy kept eyeing me and mauling me. I tell you I was one scared gal until his uncle told him to keep his hands off.'

Shuddering, Winnie stopped talking for a short time. Then she regained control of herself and went on with the story. There had been some argument about the best course of action among the men. At last Churn Wycliffe had stated they would split into four parties of three men each. He had also stamped on Billy's suggestion of being the one who escorted Winnie, putting her in the care of Sandel. During the night Sandel won Billy's dun horse in a poker game, although Churn insisted he loaned the youngster his own mount. The Kaddo braves had ambushed Winnie's party, killing two of the men. Thrown when the dun reared, Sandel had been captured alive along with the girl. After riding a time, the braves made camp for the night. At first they had ignored their prisoners, but decided to have some fun following a drinking session. When she realised the braves' intentions, Winnie screamed and was gagged. The rest Mark knew without her telling.

'What'd Wycliffe tell the others before they split up?' he asked.

'To spread across the range and watch for Pegler and they'd meet up again at the trading post,' Winnie replied. 'Say, how'd you come to be out this way?'

'I'm looking for the Wycliffes. Sailor Sam worked for my pappy and was a good friend.'

'It was Billy killed him——'

'I figure to see Billy about it.'

'That big feller, Churn, he didn't want it to happen and he stopped Billy abusing me.'

Possibly Wycliffe had acted in a chivalrous manner, but Mark doubted it. More probably the burly man had kept Winnie alive and unharmed for less noble reasons. He could not be sure how soon the law might come after him and did not want the rape or death of a girl added to his crimes. So he kept Billy at bay. Sending Winnie with Sandel showed more cunning than trust in the man. If a posse should be on his party's trail, they would probably follow the group with the girl. Wycliffe did not want to be in her company should the law catch up with him.

'I never got 'round to telling you my name,' Mark drawled, not mentioning his thoughts to Winnie. 'It's Mark Counter——'

'Them Wycliffes talked about you,' Winnie answered. 'Billy claimed when they found out they'd made a mistake and who Sam was that shooting him helped them get evens for what you did to them in some saloon. Is that why Loney Sandel tried to kill you after you saved him?'

'Some of it,' Mark replied. 'When I saw the dun, I thought maybe the Kaddo got Billy.'

'He wasn't with us,' the girl said. 'Are you after Billy now?'

'After we've put you someplace safe,' Mark agreed.

'Don't you bother none about *that*!' Winnie hissed. 'You take me along so's I can see that damned Billy get his. He's the worse of them all.'

'Maybe as safe to take her on as try to go back,' Tejas put in. 'Kaddo're behind us.'

'How far's this Pegler place?' Mark inquired.

'Not know,' admitted Tejas. 'But river getting smaller. What you want to do, *amigo*?'

'We may as well keep going. At least, if the worst comes to the worst we can fort up at the trading post.'

When agreeing to Mark's going after the Wycliffes, Murat had stated his intention of gathering a strong posse and following should the blond giant not return by the end of the week. If the Kaddo did corner Mark's party at the trading post, they ought to be able to hold out until help arrived.

Receiving the girl's assurance that she could stand up to the journey, Mark and Tejas made preparations to leave. The Indian went ahead as scout and selected a route which kept them from being seen on a sky-line, or offered cover in which they might hide to make a fight should the need arise. While they saw no raiding parties, Tejas found tracks which told of considerable Indian movement.

'Hunting parties, maybe,' Mark suggested when given the news.

'Indian only hunt buffalo in bunches of ten or more,' Tejas replied. 'Too many braves make noise, scare off deer. This not buffalo country.'

'On the war path then.'

'Maybe so. Not have women with them. Could be raiding.'

'Is there any difference?' Winnie inquired.

'Some,' Mark answered. 'A war path means just that, they're looking for a fight. When they're raiding, they're out for loot. Sure they'll fight if they have to, but they'd sooner not take chances. Let's get going, Tejas.'

Under such conditions travel must be slow, for they had to pick their way carefully. Nor did they stick to the river, but followed a line parallel to it at a distance of a mile. Once they hid among a clump of white oak and chestnut trees for almost an hour while a band of Kaddo braves ate a meal and rested their horses on a slope a quarter of a mile from them. Night came without Mark's party reaching the trading post, or even seeing anything to tell them how close they might be. So they made camp, waiting until after dark before lighting a fire, and finishing off their food.

Dawn came and they rode on again. Before they had covered more than a few hundred yards, Tejas found tracks of six shod horses going their direction the previous afternoon. Riding on again, the Indian soon came to a stop. The tracks went up a slope and Tejas signalled his companions to halt while he advanced on foot. After peering cautiously over the slope, he turned and waved.

'Get down, we'll walk up there,' Mark ordered, noticing that Tejas remained in cover.

'Trading post over ridge,' the Indian announced, slipping back down the slope to meet the others. 'What's left of it.'

Carefully keeping to cover, Mark joined the Indian and looked down a bush dotted slope to an open valley floor. Only one building remained standing, the other two log cabins having been reduced to burned-out ruins. Even the corrals and wood-pile had been destroyed, but Mark could see no sign of the wagon. The six tracks led down to the remains of Pegler's trading post, yet he failed to locate the horses which had made them.

'We'd best go down and take a look,' Mark said.

'Could be trap,' Tejas warned.

'Stay here with Winnie and cover me then,' ordered Mark. 'I'll ride in like I don't expect any trouble.'

Leaving the girl and Indian, Mark started down the slope. While he rode as if completely unaware of the possibility of danger, he stayed alert and watched the small cabin's front. Lying at the rear of the burned-out buildings, the cabin had one door and window in the front. At its rear, some thirty feet behind, rose the other side of the valley in a sheer wall.

Every instinct Mark possessed warned him that somebody

other than his two companions watched him. Try as he might, he could not locate the watchers. Knowing he could trust the stallion, he fastened his reins to the saddlehorn and let them hang. That left his hands free and he used knee pressure to guide the horse while taking out his makings to roll a smoke.

The door of the cabin opened as Mark reached the foot of the slope. He brought the horse to a halt some thirty yards from the building and studied the two men who came out. They wore range clothes, looked a couple of hard-cases, but he did not recognise either of them. Noting the wolf-cautious manner in which they darted glances at the valley sides, he guessed they might have had Indian trouble.

'Howdy,' greeted the taller of the pair. 'You alone?'

'You could say that,' Mark agreed. 'What's up?'

'Injuns run off our hosses last night,' the shorter man replied. 'You seen anything of 'em?'

'Nary a sign,' Mark drawled. 'I've come down from Brady way. It's been a mighty lonesome ride.'

'Come ahead and rest your saddle,' offered the taller hard-case.

Something in the man's attitude rang a warning alarm for Mark. It may have been the way he eyed the big stallion, or the fact that he did not look the sort to offer hospitality without expecting to see a return for his generosity. Left a-foot, faced with the possibility of more trouble with the Kaddos, a fast horse would be mighty tempting. However, Mark continued to act as before and gave no hint of his suspicions. He wanted to get closer before making a move.

Then Mark saw the rifle's barrel poking through the loophole in the cabin's wall. Almost imperceptibly he steered the horse so as to put the two men between him and the rifle. He doubted if the man in the cabin would cut loose until the other two were close enough to grab the stallion.

Suddenly the taller man jerked up his head and stared past Mark at the slope down which the blond giant rode.

'Mark!' yelled Winnie's voice. 'They're two of the Wycliffe bunch!'

While the girl acted in good faith, she put Mark in one hell of a spot. On seeing him ride towards the men, she thought that he failed to grasp the danger of the situation. Before Tejas could stop her, she rose and ran into view of the two hard-cases and shouted her warning.

At the first word Mark thrust himself sideways out of the saddle. Snarling a curse, the taller man grabbed for his gun and his companion followed his lead. Flame ripped from the rifle in

109

the cabin and Mark heard the bullet split the air where his body had been an instant before. While falling, he fetched out his matched guns. Having been in a similar situation, the blood bay started to swing away from its master and loped off to one side.

When Mark struck the ground, he held a cocked Colt in each hand. The right-hand gun spat once, driving its bullet into the body of the taller hard-case an instant before he cleared leather. At almost the same moment Tejas intervened from up the slope. Dirt flew between the shot man and his companion. Realising that Mark had lied when claiming to be alone, the second man turned and sprinted for the cabin.

Close to where Mark landed, a bush offered concealment and some protection from the rifle in the cabin. He cut loose with a shot from either hand, driving the bullets at the loophole. Fast though he moved, his aim proved good. Splinters flew from the edge of the hole and the rifle jerked at the moment its user squeezed the trigger. Instead of coming at Mark, the bullet flew harmlessly into the air. Before the man could reload, Mark rolled behind the bush and wriggled to more satisfactory shelter at the rear of a rock.

Already the rifle slanted down into line again. Glass shattered and a Winchester appeared through the ruined window. Carefully Mark searched the front of the building and could see no other weapons. Then he turned to see what had happened to his companions. He found that Tejas had pulled the girl back into cover and lay behind a tree lining the Spencer at the cabin.

Satisfied that the other two were in no immediate danger, Mark gave thought to the problem of what to do next. He did not know which of the Wycliffe gang used the cabin, or how many of them, but aimed to find out. Another important point arose; all day they had seen signs of Indians and one of the parties might be within hearing distance. The sound of shooting would bring them like iron filings to a magnet. When that happened, Mark wanted to have the girl inside the cabin. Out in the open they stood no chance. Yet he knew the men in the building would not allow his party to enter.

Once again Mark studied the cabin and surrounding area. They would have to force an entrance and he sought for the means to do so without taking lead in the process. Twisting around, he signalled his intentions to Tejas and the Indian showed that he understood.

Mark's horse stood some distance away, having come to a halt in a hollow and partially hidden from the men in the cabin. Wanting the horse, the Wycliffe men were unlikely to shoot it. However it stopped some distance from Mark's position and to reach it meant crossing open ground. So he put aside thoughts of collecting the stallion and went into action on foot.

CHAPTER THIRTEEN

A STUDENT OF A HIGHLAND PASTIME

RISING swiftly, Mark darted away from his horse in the direction of the next piece of cover. His move took the two men at the front of the cabin by surprise and the bullet which came from the window missed him by several feet. Up the slope Tejas' Spencer cracked a reply, although he achieved nothing. Then Mark made another dash and landed safely behind a large rock. From there he progressed in dives, by running or crawling along on his belly, until he reached a point where neither rifle at the front of the building could line on him.

Unfortunately his intention of approaching from the windowless side of the cabin came to nothing. Before making the attempt, he studied the wall and noted it carried loopholes. At one hole a slight but significant movement caught his eye. Unless he missed his guess, a man waited there ready to throw down on him at his first unwary movement. That ruled out any chance of getting close to the building from his present position.

Thrusting himself from cover, Mark raced towards the rear slope. Confirmation of his suspicions came as a rifle's muzzle stabbed through the loophole. Before its user could take aim, Mark dived once more into shelter. He landed where he could study the rear of the cabin. Some thirty feet separated it from the sheer slope and with nothing behind which even a jack-rabbit might hide to give cover during an attack on the rear.

'Pegler's done that on purpose,' Mark told himself bitterly. 'Maybe I'll have better luck on the other side.'

With that he went up the slope, which, at that point rose at a gentler angle than behind the cabin. At the top he found that the thick wood-land started again, although Pegler had been doing some timber cutting recently. Along the top, level with where the roof of the cabin showed, a tree trunk rested on two sawing-horses. Branches and roots had been cut off, leaving a straight log almost twenty foot long suspended between the two X-shaped frames.

Although Mark glanced at the log, he gave it no thought and moved along the edge of the cliff. Then he saw something black against the roof timbers. Alert for danger, his senses screamed a warning which caused him to leap backwards. Not a second too soon either. Flame spurted from the hole and a bullet sang through the air where his body had been a moment before.

'Damn him, that Pegler was one smart *hombre*,' Mark growled. 'That loophole in the roof's a mighty sneaky ace-in-the-hole.'

It seemed that the cabin offered good all round defence, yet the urgency of entering grew greater by the second. Swinging around, Mark studied the country behind him. He noted that it offered ideal cover for any hostile Kaddo bucks who might want to sneak up on him. So far he saw no hint of danger from that angle. True the woods seemed strangely quiet, but the shooting could account for that.

To study the woods Mark had to look across the sawing-horses and their burden. Then his eyes dropped to the log. It would be too short by almost ten feet to be pushed across to the cabin, even if doing so would achieve any purpose. However another possibility sprang to mind.

Back in the War, when he rode in Bushrod Sheldon's cavalry, Mark's company commander had been a Scottish major. Angus Farquharson, younger son of a noble house, retained his love of Scotland and introduced the men under him to a number of traditional Highland pastimes. Even then Mark had been very powerful and under Farquharson's guidance became adept at one particular strength sport. Since joining the floating outfit he kept his hand in and won many a bet for the ranch with his skill at tossing the caber.

Walking across to the thicker end of the log, Mark tentatively lifted it and estimated the weight. Unless he missed his guess, the log weighed over two hundred pounds; heavier than he had yet tossed. Kicking the sawing-horse aside, he set the butt of the log on the ground. He then went to the other end and raised it until it stood on its end. Resting the weight on his shoulder, he bent down until he could get his hands underneath the butt. After making sure of the balance, he began to straighten up. The old knack had not deserted him. Taking the strain, he thrust himself forward in the wind-up run for the throw.

On the other slope Tejas and the girl watched without understanding just what use Mark hoped to make of the log. Then they saw, although neither could barely credit the evidence of their eyes. Sighting his Spencer, Tejas fired at the cabin. He guessed at the loophole in the roof and wanted to distract the occupants if possible.

Forward strode Mark, powerful legs driving his body and the burden it bore on. Then he gave a surging heave and propelled the log up into the air. It was a sight which would have gladdened Major Farquharson's Scottish heart, the way the log turned over in the air. Out it sailed, over the edge of the slope to land on the roof of the cabin. While stoutly made, the roof had not been erected to stand up against the impact of some two hundred and twenty pounds of timber crashing down on it. Realising his danger, Mark threw himself flat after making the magnificent caber toss. He could not see the result of his throw, but heard the creak of breaking wood as the ridge-pole snapped and the roof caved in, followed by the scream of a man in pain.

A moment before, inside the cabin Evan Shever, fourth member of Wycliffe's party in the Bigfoot Saloon, had turned from his place at the front. He looked to where the second hard-case stood on a cupboard after firing at Mark. The cabin was of only one room and bare of furnishings, probably one of the reasons the Indians did not burn it when they had attacked and wiped out Pegler's assistants: Shever had seen the charred bodies in the burned-out buildings on his arrival.

'You get him?' Shever had asked.

'I don't know. That big jasper's fast.'

'Dib's cashed out there. Damn Cousin Churn, why'd he have to leave us three here while he went out again?'

'Like he said, he figured to round up the other boys and see if we could find where Pegler went for the silver,' the hard-case had answered. 'If they hear the shooting, they'll come running.'

Silence had fallen for a time and the hard-case had watched the top of the slope. He had not seen Mark and had failed to notice the erection of the log. Suddenly a bullet had come through the window and sunk into the dirt floor. Wondering if the man on the slope could see him, the hard-case had twisted around.

'What's he doing?'

'I don't kn——!' Shever had begun.

At that point a terrific crash had sounded above them and the roof had caved in. The hard-case had seen his danger a moment too late. Down came the roof timbers and log, pinning and crushing him under them. Letting out a scream of agony, he stared wildly across the cabin at Shever.

No help came from that source. Panic filled Shever as he saw the wreck of the roof and realised that he no longer had the backing of his two companions. Thoughts ripped through his head, working at a way to save himself. After the muscular effort required to hurl the log on to the cabin, Mark Counter ought to be so exhausted that he would be temporarily out of the game. That left the other man, armed with a Spencer carbine—not the most accurate weapon—unless Shever missed his guess. At that range Shever figured he could chance running the gauntlet of the other's fire in an attempt to reach Mark's blood bay.

Dropping the rifle, and ignoring his companion's moans for help, Shever jerked open the cabin door. He sprang out, drawing his right hand Freeman revolver, and ran towards the horse. The Spencer boomed out and its bullet whapped through the air close to him but he never broke stride or bothered to shoot back.

Growling a cowhand curse, Tejas lay down his carbine. He had just fired his seventh shot and saw there would not be time to reload. Nor could he hope to make a hit at that range with his newly-acquired Cooper revolvers. Telling the girl to keep down, he thrust himself out of cover and bounded forward.

Shever saw the Indian coming but still made no attempt to use his gun. Instead he concentrated on running as fast as he could to the horse. Holding the cocked revolver, he started down into the shallow hollow where the stallion stood. It showed no great concern at the man's approach and he felt sure escape lay close at hand.

From along to the right of the valley a rifle crashed. Caught in the head by a bullet, Shever pitched forward. His revolver went off, its muzzle-blast singeing the horse's hair and the lead slicing a graze on its rump. Even as the stallion screamed with pain and reared, Shever's body collided with it. Blood and brains smeared the saddle as he slid to the ground and the stallion started running.

Bounding down the slope, Tejas heard the shot and twisted around. Two Kaddo braves knelt in sight behind bushes and three more came into view from various points of concealment. Smoke rose from the Springfield rifle cradled against one of the pair's shoulder. The other lined a Sharps carbine at Tejas. Before the young Indian could make a move to save himself, flame licked from the Sharp's barrel. He felt the shocking impact of the heavy bullet, spun around and fell to the ground. Badly wounded, he still tried to raise his revolver as the braves ran towards him. Halting, a buck whipped up and drew back his bow. The arrow flashed forward and completed the work the bullet began.

Up on the slope Winnie saw Tejas die and the Kaddo braves leaping towards him. So intent on counting coup and collecting loot were they that none gave the girl a thought. Unlike when she gave her warning to Mark, Winnie remained in hiding. She realised that showing herself would be asking for a painful death.

While young, poorly educated and filled with romantic

notions, Winnie possessed a fair share of good Texas common sense. Being unarmed, she could do nothing for her companions. Instinctively she knew what Mark would want her to do. So she put aside any thoughts of staying around and slipped back. When sure that the braves could not see her, she rose and ran to the waiting horses. Unfastening the dun, she swung astride it and started it running.

At first the girl rode with the fear of pursuit filling her. Then the feeling left her and good sense caused her to draw rein. During the time she rode with Mark and Tejas, Winnie learned some lessons. So she found a place where she and the horse could hide before halting. Studying her back trail, she concluded that nobody followed her. Then she gave thought to what she should do for the best.

'We come up river,' she told herself. 'So if I can find it and ride down, I ought to reach some settler's place—if the Injuns don't get me first.'

With that the girl started the dun moving. She rode at a trot, scanning the country ahead of her regularly and often turning to look back along her tracks. Seeing birds rising from the trees ahead of her, she decided to take cover until finding what had alarmed them. Hiding among some bushes, she retained sufficient presence of mind to keep the dun quiet. That proved fortunate for a party of Kaddo braves rode by, heading towards the trading post. Watching them go, she saw puffs of smoke rise into the air. However she lacked the skill to know that the smoke signals originated from some place beyond the post.

Although the Indians rode straight by, Winnie did not offer to leave her hiding place for almost an hour. Deciding at last that she could ride on in safety, she started the dun moving in what she hoped would be the right direction. Time passed, although she had no way of judging it in hours and minutes, until an uneasy feeling came to her. Slowly she began to wonder if she had picked the right direction, she wondered if the Pedernales River did lie ahead of her.

Coming to a small stream, she halted the horse and allowed it to drink. As she slipped from the saddle, her eyes went to the water. For a moment the significance of what she saw did not sink in. Then she realized that the steam flowed in the opposite direction to which she had been riding. Her instincts told her that the stream join the Pedernales and she must retrace her route. By following the stream, she would find the river.

By that time the sun hung low in the western sky. No child, even a girl, grew up on a small spread in frontier-Texas without learning how to live off the country. So the desire to survive forced Winnie to look for food. She gathered edible fruit and nuts while looking for a safe place to spend the night. They would fill her stomach and keep her going until she could find more appetising food.

Finding a small valley close to the stream, she prepared to spend the night in it. First she cared for the horse, off-saddling it and making sure that she fastened it securely to a small tree. The dun offered her only small chance of survival and she did not dare take the chance of being left a-foot. Although the Kaddos had taken Sandel's bed roll as part of their loot, Mark had fastened the blanket Winnie used to the dun's saddle. So she could make use of it to give some protection and warmth during the night.

After the dreary, restless hours of darkness dragged away, Winnie rose cold and stiff in the light of the early morning. In one respect she could thank the Kaddo; their roaming bands scared off most of the larger wild life, including bears, cougar or wolves, all of which possessed a taste for horse flesh. Saddling the dun took time and she did not dare ride at any speed. Nor could she if she hoped to following the windings of the small stream. She decided against leaving the water for fear of again losing her direction.

Noon came and went without a sight of the river. Just as despair began to fill the girl, she saw water glinting through the trees ahead. More water than ran in the little stream. Feeling almost like crying with relief, she came on to the bank of the Pedernales River. Once again she decided to ride by the water, taking her chance on running into more Indians rather than risk losing her way.

Holding her horse to a steady trot, which slowed to a walk as the sun rose towards its noon height, Winnie followed the flow of the river. She saw no sign of human beings of any kind and slowly started to lose her fear. An animal track led through sassafrass bushes and she rode along it with more confidence than she had felt since beginning her flight at Pegler's trading post.

Suddenly a man lunged up from among the bushes, catching hold of the dun's reigns and bringing it to a halt. Even as Winnie opened her mouth to scream, she realised that he was no Indian. Tall, well-built, young looking despite a beard, clad in range clothes and belting two Army Colts, she recognised him as one of Wycliffe's men. More than that, he had been the one Churn Wycliffe treated as an equal—and accompanied Billy when the party split up.

'Just look who's here, will you,' said Billy's voice from the other side of the trail. 'It looks like she done snuck off from Loney, and with my hoss.'

'There's more to it than that, from the look of her,' replied the bearded man as his companions came into sight. 'Where's Loney and the boys, gal?'

'Got killed by the Injuns,' Winnie answered.

'How'd you get away?' Billy demanded, slouching up with a stocky hard-case on his heels.

'Mark Counter and an Indian called Tejas saved me.'

'Where're they now?' the bearded man, Augie by name, snapped.

'At Pegler's trading post. There were more Injuns there,' Winnie replied.

'Any of our boys there?' Augie wanted to know, although the other two showed more interest in the girl's back trail than for their companions' welfare.

'Th—Three of them,' the girl told him.

'Uncle Churn?'

'Not that I know of. It was the other one——'

'Cousin Evan,' Billy growled. 'They get him?'

'They got all of them, Mark, the Indian—I got to my hoss and ran.'

'When was this, gal?' Augie inquired gently.

'Yesterday. I've been riding and hiding ever since.'

'See any Injuns?'

'Only one bunch. They went riding towards the trading post.'

'That bunch we saw were headed up-river,' commented the hard-case.

'Sure did, Rags,' Augie agreed. 'Took with the smoke we saw going up, it could be their chiefs're calling them in to the camp.'

'What're we going to do?' Rags inquired and it was significant that he turned to Augie for advice.

'Go to the trading post and see if Churn's made it there,' Augie answered.

'I say we head back down the river,' Billy put in.

'How about Churn and the other boys?' Augie growled.

'The gal said they're all cashed——'

'Only Loney and Evan's bunches,' Augie pointed out. 'If Churn's alive, he's likely headed for the post. Six guns stand a better chance than three.'

'I've thought all along this was a damned fool game!' Billy spat out. 'Now I say we get the hell back towards Lake Travis and head for home.'

'Nobody's stopping you going, Billy boy,' Augie replied. 'Just turn your hoss and ride.'

'How about you, Rags?' Billy asked.

'I'm with Augie.'

'It's your scalp. Me 'n' the gal——'

'The gal stays with us,' interrupted Augie. 'You do what you want.'

Only for a moment did anger show on Billy's face. Then he made an effort and regained control of himself. Although his uncle gave him nominal command of the trio, Augie had taken over as their leader almost from leaving the rest of the band. Nor had Billy objected for the bearded man's guidance had kept them safe despite the fact that they saw plenty of Indian sign. Billy figured himself to be good with a gun, but knew Augie to be better. So he accepted the other's quiet-spoken order with as good grace as he could manage.

'All right, already,' he said. 'I'll go along with you.'

'Take the point, Rags,' Augie ordered. 'Ride careful and if you see anything at all get back here *pronto*.'

'Sure, Augie,' Rags replied and disappeared into the bushes.

'You ride ahead of me and the girl, Billy,' the bearded man went on.

'Yeah!' grunted the young man.

Collecting their horses, the three men started to put Augie's orders into operation. Tired, frightened, hungry, Winnie kept her horse at the bearded man's side and prayed that they might meet up with Churn Wycliffe's party before reaching the trading post.

'Rag's coming!' Billy hissed, twisting around in his saddle.

Galloping up, Rags slid his horse to a halt before reaching the others. He signalled and Augie told the girl to dismount. Then he left Billy to watch her and joined the other man. Whatever news Rags brought, he clearly did not want the girl to hear it. Dropping his voice to a whisper, he passed on his information to Augie.

'Are you sure?' the bearded man snapped.

'I didn't stick around long, but I'm sure enough.'

'What's up?' Billy called worriedly.

'Get your rifle and bring mine,' Augie answered. 'Rags, stick by the gal and keep her quiet.'

CHAPTER FOURTEEN

A PRIMITIVE PIECE OF MINING EQUIPMENT

AFTER the exertion of making the tremendous throw with the log, Mark had stayed on the ground. He wanted a few seconds to recover from his great effort, knowing the need to be fully alert before tangling in a gun fight. Hearing the shooting, he thrust himself erect in time to see Shever killed and his horse go racing off out of the valley. Even as the situation sank home and he started forward, sounds behind him gave a grim warning. Before he could turn to investigate, something hissed through the air. The loop of a hair rope dropped over his head, tightened about his upper arms, then jerked him backwards.

With an effort Mark caught his balance and twisted around, his arms forcing against the constriction of the rope. Several Kaddo bucks rushed at him and, to his surprise, they came without weapons in their hands. A brawny buck gripped the rope which trapped Mark's arms, leaning back in his attempt to maintain the loop's grip. Mark threw his weight backwards, jerking the rope-wielder towards him. In the background stood a war bonnet chief with a Winchester rifle cradled across his arm. He yelled something to the braves, but made no attempt to use the weapon.

Having gained some slack on the loop, Mark stabbed his hands towards the Colt's butts. Deftly the brave holding the rope halted his forward progress, flexing and snapping back with his arms. Just as Mark's hands closed on the ivory handles, the rope's loop tightened. While loose it slipped lower and gripped just below the elbows, effectively preventing him from drawing the Colts. Showing a skill equal to any cowhand, the Kaddo flicked the rope to send a coil snaking along it. Although Mark knew what the brave intended, he could not counter the move. Twirling over his head, the coil tightened about his upper arms and added to the grip of the loop.

Screeching in triumph, the rest of the braves descended on Mark. They flung themselves at the blond giant and bore him to the ground. Hands closed upon his body, others wrenched the Colts from their holsters. Knowing the penalty for being taken alive by hostile Indians, Mark put up a tremendous struggle. Two braves went flying, thrown through the air by his powerful legs, but not even the big Texan's strength could prevail against such odds. With his arms free he might have done more, but the two turns of rope held fast. At last sheer weight of numbers wore him down. The Kaddo worked fast, securing his ankles and wrists with knots that would not slip.

Bound and helpless, Mark watched the Kaddo chief walk in his direction. The braves drew back and their leader gave orders to them. Some of the party turned and faded off into the woods from which they had stalked to capture him.

'Will you ride, big one, or be thrown across the back of a horse?' asked the chief in Spanish.

'I'll ride,' Mark answered.

Sat astride a horse there might be a slight chance of escape. Certainly riding offered a greater opportunity than being taken along slung bodily over a saddle. Mark wondered a little at the cause of the offer, also why the Indians went to the trouble of taking him alive. He could guess what happened. Most probably the Kaddo left scouts to watch the cabin, with the main body waiting close by ready to strike at the most favourable moment. Seeing Mark's arrival, the scouts alerted their chief and he gave orders which sent braves moving in silence to grab any advantage offered to them.

After checking on the ropes holding his arms, the braves freed Mark's ankles and helped him to his feet. Turning, he looked across the valley to learn what had happened to his friends. Already scalping knives had done their work and loot from the bodies had been gathered. A brave, carrying Tejas' Spencer and the Cooper-loaded gunbelt, came up the slope and approached the chief. Although unable to follow the conversation, Mark guessed from various gestures at its meaning. He decided that the brave mentioned Winnie and asked what they should do about her. Looking at the top of the other slope, Mark saw two braves appear leading Tejas' horse. From all signs the girl must have fled and the brave wanted to know whether they should take out after her. With something like relief Mark watched the chief shake his head, rattle out a few words and point to the west.

'Your woman has run away, big one,' the chief told Mark.

'Are you fixing to follow her?' asked Mark.

'No. By the time my men bring horses she will be far away. There are more of our warriors down the river. If they do not find her, she will die in the woods.'

'And what of me?'

'You are coming to our place of medicine.'

Which left a whole heap unexplained and gave Mark food for conjecture. He could guess at the reason for taking him with them now they had him prisoner, but still felt puzzled at their actions. Like all Indians, the Kaddo tortured prisoners but Mark had never heard of them going out of their way to capture men to do it. Just about the only consolation left was that Winnie appeared to have made good her escape. Given just one mite of luck the girl ought to reach the Pedernales River and follow it down to safety.

A faint grin creased Mark's face as he saw the mount selected to carry him. Although it carried a saddle, the boney scrub possessed none of the qualities he normally expected in a riding horse. With that sorry bang-tail between his knees he could not hope to out-ride his captors; which, as he well knew, was why they put him on it. Being a smart fighting man, Mark understood when he must sit back and do nothing. As long as life remained, there was hope. He did not doubt that the Kaddos would kill him if he made trouble for them.

Pushing their horses hard, the Indians led Mark to the west. They passed through wooded land and along rocky valleys, winding their way along with complete assurance through what seemed almost like a maze to their prisoner. At last they turned into the mouth of a canyon. Passing around a corner Mark found they had arrived at their destination.

Tepees scattered in an untidy circle across the floor of the canyon, which appeared to be blind, having its further end closed by a rock wall. Although a few young women appeared from the tepees, Mark saw most of the camp's occupants were men of warrior age.

'Get down,' ordered the chief, halting the party before one of the largest tepees and looking at Mark.

A man stepped from inside the tepee. Although he wore the dress of a Kaddo chief, he had a white man's face; especially about the cheeks and lips. While the chief spoke in rapid Kaddo, Mark studied the white man and a suspicion arose. Mark could guess that he was the subject of the conversation for both chief and white man directed long glances in his direction. It seemed that the chief told of how Mark threw the log on to the cabin, for he went through the motions of bending, raising and heaving something heavy and used his hands to indicate the bulk of the object.

'Bear Killer here tells me you're a real mighty man, feller,' the white man finally remarked, turning to Mark.

'You could say that, Mr. Pegler,' the blond giant answered, putting his theory to the test.

Surprise etched itself on the man's face and Mark knew that his guess at the other's identity proved correct.

'You're smarter than the other one,' Pegler growled. 'Him and me've played poker in the same game a couple of times and he didn't recognise me. Only I don't even remember ever meeting you afore.'

'You never did,' Mark admitted. 'I heard you wore a bushy beard. Your face hasn't tanned since you shaved it off.'

'Smart thinking. Is that why Churn Wycliffe brought you along?'

'Nope.'

'You're working with ole Churn to find my silver mine though, aren't you?'

'Nope,' repeated Mark. 'I came after him and his bunch.'

'Now why'd anybody want to come after a mean bunch like them?' Pegler asked; for the word 'after' used in such a manner meant only one thing, hunting down the other party for some serious purpose. 'Light down from that saddle and rest your butt end. I'd say you're used to something better in hoss-flesh than that crow-bait they gave you.'

'You never said a truer word,' Mark replied sincerely, tossing his right leg across the saddle and dropping to the ground. 'I wouldn't wish even a Kansas fighting-pimp* to have to ride that horse.'

'You fixing to tell me what brought you after the Wycliffes?' Pegler asked.

'Billy killed an old pard of mine and I figured on asking why. Only I didn't count on running into Indian fuss like this.'

'Just one man and you figured to take on the Wycliffe bunch?'

'There were two of us, your bucks killed the other at the trading post.'

Before any more could be said, the chief spoke and pointed along the canyon. Following the other men's gaze, Mark saw a strange sight. A wide ledge around eight feet high ran the length of the end wall, with a set of steps carved up from the ground at one end. Roughly in the centre of the ledge a slot maybe four feet wide and three deep had been cut—it formed too perfect a rectangle to be entirely natural—into the rock. Above the slot stood what looked like an exceptionally strong and powerful windlass for a well, with handles on either end of the spindle. The rope around the spindle was of greater strength than ever seen on a well; and needed to be, for its end appeared to be connected to the top of a block of rock which stood on the ledge and had been shaped to pass up and down the slot.

'You find it interesting?' Pegler asked.

'I might if I knew what the hell it was,' Mark replied.

* Fighting-pimp: Texans' derogatory name for Kansas peace officers.

'It's a primitive piece of mining equipment. I'd bet you've never seen its like before.'

'You'd win.'

'Few people would know its purpose,' Pegler grinned and his voice took on the tone of an educated man. 'In fact it wasn't until I saw the raw silver Bear Killer brought in to trade that I realised what it was.'

'Feel like telling me?' Mark asked.

'It's a press for crushing the ore-bearing rock. I rigged it up again in the hope of—— Say, you know me, but I don't know you.'

'Matt—Smith,' Mark answered.

'Is that your summer name?'

'It does well enough any time.'

'Come on into my tepee, you look like you could take a meal.'

'Won't the Injuns object?' Mark asked.

'Not as long as you don't try any fool stunts,' Pegler replied and spoke to the chief. At first Bear Killer seemed inclined to object, but finally grunted and walked away. Pegler grinned at Mark, 'Go on inside.'

'How about cutting me free?'

'Sure. Only don't try anything stupid like making a run for it. I've got an offer for you if you're interested.'

'I'm interested in anything that'll keep me alive,' Mark admitted frankly.

'Play along with me and you'll not only be kept alive, I'll make you rich too,' Pegler promised, taking the knife from his belt sheath and cutting the ropes which bound the blond giant's arms.

Mark looked at Pegler with interest as the ropes fell away. Clearly the man had some hold over the Indians, for none raised any objections to his actions. Further proof came with the arrival of bowls of hot, nourishing stew. While Mark ate, Pegler left the tepee to return carrying the blond giant's gun-belt with its Colts in the holsters. However, Pegler placed them at the far side of the tepee.

'They've no caps on and the loads've been drawn,' the trader warned. 'Later I'll see you're given powder and shot.'

'How're you going to make me rich?' Mark asked. 'And why?'

'Why's easy. I'm going to need a good man backing me in the future.'

'And I'm a good man?'

'Anybody who goes hunting the Wycliffes for evens is either *loco*, or tough and real good with a gun. You're not *loco*. From what I've heard, you're strong and tough. That gunbelt tells me you're good with a gun.'

'I can take 'em out fast enough when I have to,' Mark admitted. 'And hit what I aim at as long as it's not too far off. You want for me to show you?'

'Later maybe,' grinned Pegler. 'When I'm sure I can trust you. I reckon I'll have a better chance of doing that when I've told you some about me.'

'Go right ahead and tell me,' offered Mark. 'I've nothing but time right now.'

Although Pegler did not go into details, he hinted that he came to Texas on the run from the law. A trained engineer, he did not dare to chance following his profession even in frontier Texas. However he possessed enough money to set up as a trader. Seeking an area where he would not come into too great contact with other white men, he settled on the head waters of the Pedernales. At that time the Kaddos maintained an uneasy peace with the white brother and his business grew steadily.

Then Bear Killer brought in some raw silver to trade—and knew something of its value. The chief refused to take anything but a repeating rifle and ammunition for the silver and hinted that he could bring in more to buy other weapons. However he declined to disclose the source of the silver and warned against any attempts to find it.

'Most folks'd've gone ahead and looked, either getting killed or turning the Injuns against them,' Pegler stated smugly. 'But not me. No sir. I traded guns for silver and added a few jugs of whisky when asked. Guns and bullets were the main thing. I didn't want the Kaddos getting liquored up and starting a scalphunt—at least until I was ready for it.'

'You wanted to have time to light out before they began?' Mark suggested.

'Something like that.'

From the mocking grin on Pegler's face, Mark guessed a deeper motive was involved. As Pegler clearly wanted to tell the story in his own way, Mark refrained from asking questions. He eyed the trader up and down. Something over middle height, brawny, he would still be no more than child's play for the blond giant to handle when a chance arose. Until then Mark aimed to learn all he could and keep Pegler believing in his support for whatever the trader planned.

Continuing his story, Pegler told how he gained the chief's confidence and became accepted by the tribe. With the aid of chloroform and other scientific wonders the Indians had never seen, backed by predictions of carefully arranged accidents, he won the reputation of a medicine man. Backed by his new-found position, he demanded to be shown where the silver originated. Unwilling to go against popular opinion, Bear Killer brought Pegler to the canyon and showed him the hidden entrance of a cave. Inside Pegler found many sacks holding the raw silver and a sizeable stack of rocks bearing veins of the precious material. Seeing and recognising the primitive press, he rebuilt the windlass and prepared to start mining operations.

At which point he discovered that the original miners—Spanish explorers from the days before Texas gained her independence—suffered a cave-in which fetched down all their workings.

'There's a fortune in silver to be brought out,' Pegler informed Mark. 'But the Kaddo won't let me mine it. This's a medicine place, they wiped out the greaser miners for digging here. It was all I could do to get them to let me work the rock from the cave. One thing they won't do is give me permission to bring in the modern equipment to get the mine working again.'

'There went my fortune,' Mark said dryly.

'Maybe not,' Pegler replied. 'I still plan to mine that silver.'

'With me holding off the Kaddo while you do it?' Mark scoffed. 'Mister, are you sure you didn't reckon I was crazy enough, not tough or fast enough to go after the Wycliffes?'

'Nope. When we come here to start mining, there won't be any trouble from the Kaddos.'

'Just how do you figure that out?'

'The U.S. Army'll have tended to them for us.'

'Why should they?' Mark demanded. 'The Kaddo're reasonably peaceable and nobody wants this neck of the woods bad enough to come after it.'

'I've spent time priming the Kaddos for trouble,' Pegler said quietly. 'One of the reasons they kept the peace was because they wanted guns before starting to make war. Another was that they figured no white folks wanted their land. Now they've got the guns—and figure somebody's after the land.'

'Meaning Wycliffe and his bunch?'

'Meaning Wycliffe and his bunch. One of my men brought me word that they'd learned about the silver and were coming after it. A stinking pedlar found out and sold the news to Churn Wycliffe. My man stayed long enough to learn what Wycliffe planned and then high-tailed it to me with the word. So I reckoned the time had finally come for me to kill off Joe Pegler.'

'You burned your own place down?' Mark said.

'What better way to make sure that nobody could identify

126

the bodies?' the trader asked. 'I had a couple of half-breed helpers and a pair of white trash. Between them they'd been robbing me blind for years. So I figured I might as well make them pay for it and be more use to me dead than they ever were alive. I couldn't leave them alive and talking; and they'd've been nothing but trouble if I fetched them along.'

Hooves drummed outside and the two men rose to look through the door. A party of braves rode into the camp area, heading for the chief's tepee.

'Who're they?' Mark asked.

'Scouting parties. Bear Killer must've called them in.'

'Why'd your men be trouble had you brought them here?'

'One of their pards, a breed, used to come with me, but he laid hands on a Kaddo girl. I thought I was a goner then. The chief figured to hand the breed head down over a fire, only I showed him a better way. It was just after we'd rebuilt the windlass. I put the breed in the slot and we lowered that big block of granite down on to him. He held it off for nearly a minute before it got him. The sight satisfied the braves and kept them off me.'

'So you figure to start the Kaddo on the war path, then the cavalry'll be sent to wipe them out, or shove them on to a reservation?'

'Sure. Then we'll come here, having already taken out the mineral rights to this area. I'm not good with a gun, that's why I want somebody like you backing me.'

Fury rose inside Mark as he looked at the trader. Even as he tensed to hurl himself at Pegler and finish the man with his bare hands, Mark heard a considerable commotion outside the tepee. Once again they went to the door, seeing Bear Killer and an elderly man approaching. From the excellent quality of his clothing, the designs on it and the buffalo skull head dress worn by the chief's companion, Mark decided he must be a senior medicine man of the tribe. A moment later Pegler confirmed the conclusion.

'Damn it!' the trader snorted. 'That's Moon Watcher. He was their boss medicine man afore I took over and hates my guts. What in hell does he want here?'

Coming to a halt, Bear Killer spoke to Pegler and Mark could see that the words did not please the trader.

'What's up?' Mark inquired.

'Seems that some bucks were killed last night and they figure to take the war path,' Pegler answered. 'Only that old bastard, Moon Watcher wants a sign that the Great Spirit favours war.'

At that moment a group of braves appeared from a tepee dragging Churn Wycliffe between them. He looked in poor shape, half naked, hair and beard matted with blood, one arm crudely bandaged and a raw gash showed through a tear in his right trouser leg. Making nothing of Wycliffe's feeble attempts to strugle, the braves draged him to the end wall and thrust him into the slot. Looking at the windlass, Mark saw four braves stood at the handles and the block of granite hung over the slot's mouth.

'What the hell?' Mark growled.

'Moon Watcher asked for a sign, we're going to give him one,' Pegler replied. 'When we put a feller under that block one time I told the Kaddos that they'd crush the white men like the rock crushed him. Bear Killer allows that Wycliffe's a real strong feller and he's putting him to the test. They'll lower the block down easy. If Wycliffe can save himself, they'll call off the war—— Fact being, that's why Bear Killer had you took alive, figured you'd give his boys some more sport. I warned him that you just might spoil his medicine, so he handed you over to me to soften up for later. Come on, this's always worth watching.'

CHAPTER FIFTEEN

A SLENDER CHANCE TO KEEP THE PEACE

MARK and Pegler walked forward, mingling with the Indians who stood before the canyon wall. Already the block started to sink down, the braves at the windlass strained against the drag it imposed upon the spindle. Crouched in the slot, Wycliffe suddenly became aware of the interest showed by the crowd. Looking up, he saw the block. A low moan of terror broke from his lips and he tried to move out of the slot. Standing ready to deal with such an action, two braves used their lances' points to drive him back again.

Sucking in a deep breath, Mark thought of things the Ysabel Kid told him about Indians. One thing all the fighting tribes had in common was their belief in good and bad medicine. When making ready for war they consulted the medicine men and asked for guidance, preferably a sign that the Great Spirit favoured their line of action. Let anything happen to spoil their chosen medicine and they would not go out to fight.

All too well Mark knew the horrors of an Indian war. Sure the U.S. Army possessed the weapons to whip the Kaddo, but first many white folk would die. After the Kaddo being so long at peace, the settlers around their country were unlikely to expect trouble. Unless something could be done to stop it, there would be murder, arson and looting—and a tribe of Indians, poor dupes of an evil white man, most likely wiped off the face of the earth.

Only one thing could stop it happening, for the Kaddo's medicine to be broken. Mark knew the only way that could be done and aimed to make a try at doing it.

Before Pegler realised what he planned, Mark lunged forward. He went through the crowd like it did not exist, sprang forward to brush aside the lance-armed guards and went towards the slot. Shooting out his right hand, Mark caught Wycliffe by the neck and heaved him from beneath the rock. A low rumble of anger rolled from the crowd, then died as they realised that Mark did not merely save the other white man from being crushed.

Turning, Mark backed into the slot. He bent his legs slightly, bowed his head forward and let the weight settle on his shoulders. Slowly and carefully he moved up his hands, placing the flat of his palms against the rough bottom of the block then bracing himself. The meal and rest in Pegler's tepee had given him a chance to regain his full power and he knew that he was going to need every ounce of strength in the minutes ahead.

Excited comments rose from the watching crowd. The braves at the windlass left the handles and moved to the edge of the ledge to see what happened. Giving a low snarl of rage, Pegler started to move forward. He guessed what Mark planned and fury filled him at what he regarded as the blond giant's treachery. A powerful hand closed on the trader's arm and halted him. Turning, Pegler looked into the cold eyes of the chief.

'Leave him, Hair Face!' Bear Killer ordered. 'If your medicine is good, it cannot fail.'

Something told Pegler that he had better not force the issue. Then he gave a shrug. Although he did not mention the fact to Mark, the block had been used to crush men more than once. After the first demonstration the Kaddo used it on their own law-breakers or other Indians who fell into their hands. No man ever survived the crushing weight of the block. With the big man dead, the Kaddo would take to the war path and Pegler ought to be able to slip away in the confusion. Skilled fighting men had never been in such short supply in Texas that he could not hire other help to push through his plans.

After stopping the rock's downward movement, Mark studied the situation and made a shocking discovery. It had been his intention to tip the rock forward from the slot and found it to be impossible. The old Spanish miners knew their work. To prevent accidents they cut the slot narrower at the front than against the wall and carved the block accordingly. So it could not be turned out at the front and must go back through the top.

That left only one way out of the problem.

Slowly Mark started to thrust upwards with his hands and shoulders while his powerful leg muscles fought to straighten him up. At first nothing happened, the block remaining exactly where it had been when the braves released the windlass handles. Then slowly, so slowly at first that even the eagle-eyed Bear Killer failed to detect the movement, the mass of granite began to rise. Mark's legs straightened, bracing apart on the rocky ground. Gradually the weight on his shoulders eased but it grew upon his arms.

Much as he wanted, Mark knew he must not stop his attempt at lifting. If the weight sank down he could never raise it again. Before his eyes swam a picture of blazing cabins, screaming women and children being killed, all the horrors that would be turned loose should he fail. He could not hear the excited chatter of the braves as they watched that great block of granite slowly move upwards.

Pegler's eyes bulged in disbelief as he watched the darker mass of the block show above the level of the ledge. First an inch showed, then two, three and more. The trader realised what Mark's actions meant. If the blond giant lifted the block back on to the ledge, the Kaddo would consider their medicine bad. Even now only the young, hot-headed bucks called for war. Older, wiser heads debated long, with many calls to follow the Comanche's lead in making a permanent peace. Given the sight of their prime war medicine broken, those who sought peace could present an argument even the most hot-headed buck understood.

That could not be allowed to happen. With a fortune in silver waiting, nothing must happen to ruin Pegler's plans.

Forcing himself to act calmly and walk with a nonchalant air, Pegler stepped away from Bear Killer. Then he made his way towards the wall, eyes on Mark all the time. Already the block stood well over halfway out of the slot. Strain contorted Mark's face and his muscular frame quivered in its giant effort. If anything happened to ruin his concentration, the granite would crush him to the ground. With that thought in mind, Pegler slid the knife from his belt sheath. He held it so the Indians could not see the blade in his hand.

Mark saw the knife and understood its purpose. Gathering himself, he put every last ounce of strength he possessed into a final surging thrust. Up shot the block, tilting forward at the top of the slot. For a moment it hung motionless and then the weight dragged it over. Mark felt the pressure leaving his arms and heard the wild shouts of the crowd.

Knife held for a belly-ripping slash, Pegler lunged towards the slot. Then he sensed rather than saw the black mass tumbling towards him. Maybe if he had continued forward he might have saved himself. Instead he dug in his front foot and tried to throw his body back to safety. Down came the block, four hundred pounds of granite, on to Pegler. He screamed once, then bones crashed and blood burst from ruptured flesh as the block squashed him into the ground.

Weak with exhaustion Mark fell against the back of the slot. Though sweat half blinded him, he saw and heard enough to tell him what happened to Pegler. Much as he felt the man deserved to die, Mark pitied him and nausea rose at the sight of what lay under the block.

The sight caused even the Indians to draw back and stare with horror-filled eyes. Before any of them recovered, hooves drummed loud, coming along the canyon.

A huge white stallion thundered up. Seated on it was a tall, lean man who wore only a blue breechclout and moccasins, with a gunbelt supporting a Dragoon Colt at one side and bowie knife on the other about his waist. Maybe he had shorter hair than any Indian brave, but he carried a war lance in his right hand and his face bore the savage lines of a warrior on the rampage.

Bringing his stallion to a rump-sliding halt, the rider landed on his feet between Mark and the Kaddo. Amazement showed on their faces as they stared at the apparition and superstitious awe rose in every breast for none could think from where the newcomer sprang.

On back-tracking Mark's stallion, the Ysabel Kid had read the story of its flight and finally reached the trading post. Again the sign told him all he needed to know, that his *amigo* had been taken a prisoner by the Kaddo. Then the Kid stopped being a white man and turned into that most deadly of fighting machines, a Comanche Dog Soldier.

Although he travelled light, he carried, as always, a pair of moccasins and the breechclout of his mother's people. Stripping off his white man's clothing, he donned the dress of a *Pehnane* who rode to war *Pukutsi*—and when a *Pehnane* rode that way he aimed to raise all hell and shove a chuck under it. Dressed and armed in a fitting manner, with his other clothes bundled on the blood bay's saddle, he set off to rescue the blond giant or die in the attempt. When a *Pehnane* went *Pukutsi* there were no half measures, he could only succeed or be killed to stop him.

To a man of the Kid's ability there was no difficulty in following the tracks of Mark's captors. Even when it became too dark for him to read sign, his ears showed him the way.

On arrival at the canyon, the Kid saw Mark take Wycliffe's place under the block and guessed what might be happening. Before leaving his grandfather's new camp, the Kid heard a medicine woman tell of the unrest among the Kaddo. How she knew, he could not imagine, but she claimed the other tribe believed they possessed medicine to crush the white men. If Mark knew of that, he might be trying to break the medicine.

Another alternative came to mind. Occasionally Indians would give a prisoner they admired a trial of strength or courage by which he could win his freedom. In such trials the chances of success were negligible, but the Kid knew better than interfere. To charge down in a do-or-die rescue attempt might distract Mark, cause him to weaken his hold and bring the rock upon him. So the Kid sat and watched, amazed despite his knowledge of Mark's great strength. From his place the Kid could not see Pegler clearly enough to recognise the danger. Before he realised what the trader intended, the rock fell and saved him from further concern on that score. Setting his horse running, he charged down to make sure that Mark received his winner's due.

'Who are you?' demanded Moon Watcher, first to recover from his surprise at the Kid's appearance.

'My people call me *Cuchilo*, the Knife.'

'Who are your people?' the medicine man inquired.

Releasing his hold of the lance with his right hand, the Kid turned it palm downwards. With his forearm bent before his chest, he moved it to the right in a wriggling motion.

'The Snake Going Backwards!' breathed Moon Watcher.

'I am of the *Nemenuh*,' agreed the Kid.

'The Enemy People,' said Bear Killer, nodding in acceptance.

Three names, but they all meant one thing—Comanche. The tribal sign came from an old Comanche legend.* No matter to which band he belonged, any Comanche said he was *Nemenuh*, one of *the* People. To all other tribes the last name proved most correct. Even those tribes, like the Kaddo, who occasionally lived at peace with the Comanche used the name *Tshaoh*, the Enemy People.

While the older men present showed signs of being impressed, a couple of young bucks let out derisive laughs. Fresh from their first war trail, each showed signs of successful encounters. One wore Sandel's gunbelt with the Coopers in the holsters, although the bow he used to deliver the *coup de grace* to Tejas had been left in his tepee. The other cradled Tejas' Spencer carbine on the crook of his arm and a scalp of long Indian-black hair dangled from his belt.

'The *Tshaoh* used to be fighting men,' jeered the buck with the Spencer. 'But no more.'

'Now they are like old squaws,' his companion went on. 'Begging for food and shelter from the white m——'

The first part of the conversation had been in Spanish, a language most Texas Indians understood. While the Kid spoke some Kaddo, he wanted Mark to be able to follow what was said. Hearing the mocking words, the Kid acted as would any Comanche *tehnap*† when insulted by a youngster barely beyond the horse-herding age.

Pivoting smoothly around, he drove the butt of the lance shaft up and on to the jaw of the buck with the Spencer. In continuation of the move, as the buck reeled backwards and

* Told in *Comanche*.

† *Tehnap*: an experienced warrior.

dropped his weapon, the Kid met the other's challenge. One glance told him that he did not need to worry even though the second buck grabbed for the Coopers. Before either revolver cleared leather, the end of the lance rammed with some force into the buck's belly. A strangled croak broke from him and he doubled over with hands clawing to his middle instead of continuing to draw the guns. With the lance still gripped in both hands, the Kid swung it up. He hooked the shaft under the offered jaw and heaved. Lifted erect, the buck went on over backwards to sprawl on the ground. Fast as a cougar leaping to its kill, the Kid straddled the buck's body.

'The choice is your's,' he growled in the Kaddo language, holding the lance ready to strike. 'Do you live or die?'

Any lingering doubts as to the Kid's right to be called a Comanche died after his masterly display of lance handling. To the horse-Indians in general, and the Comanche most of all, the lance held a special position as a weapon. Only the bravest warrior carried one, accepting that he might be first into a fight and last out of it. Nor could he throw the lance, but must keep it in his hands and go close enough to use it.

Lying on the ground, the young buck suddenly realised just how precious life could be. He looked up, by the needle-sharp point and razor-edged blade of the lance to the savage face beyond and knew any hesitation would see the weapon thrust home. No man present would blame the Comanche—the Kid was all of that—for doing so under the circumstances.

'I live!' the buck croaked.

His companion came to a halt, standing dazed for a moment. Then, letting out a snarl, he dived for the carbine. Through the exhaustion which filled him, Mark recognised the Kid. All wonder at how the Kid came to be on hand departed as Mark saw the danger to his friend. Shoving himself forward, Mark reached the Kid's side and curled his hand about the grips of the old Dragoon. Handling a strange weapon, from an awkward position, Mark could not produce his full blinding speed. Yet he drew fast enough. The buck's hands closed on the Spencer when the Dragoon boomed in Mark's hand. Dirt erupted into the Kaddo's face, temporarily blinding him. While Mark did not shoot for such an effect, it served his needs better than had the lead sunk into the buck. Spluttering, the brave dropped the carbine and sat knuckling his eyes in an attempt to clear them. When he finally managed to focus again, he found himself faced with the yawning muzzle of the Dragoon and lined blade of the lance. Again the Kid gave the choice and once more the recipient elected to live.

Holding the Colt, Mark expected the rest of the braves to

jump him and the kid. None of the crowd moved but admiration flickered on more than one face. The Kaddo respected courage or dexterity in the use of weapons, both of which the two Texans had demonstrated.

'Are you all right, *amigo*?' asked the Kid.

'I'll do. Lifting the rock didn't trouble me, but shooting off this fool cannon like to bust my arm.'

'Leather it, *pronto*. We can't fight our way through this bunch, so we'll have to talk our way out. Act like you expect your warrior's due.'

'You're the Injun,' Mark said dryly and dropped the Dragoon back into its holster. 'Now let's see what happens.'

'Get my brother a drink of water,' the Kid said to Bear Killer. 'He passed the test and is a free man.'

'Do it,' the chief ordered and a girl ran to obey. 'You say your name is Cuchilo. Are you the grandson of Long Walker?'

Once more the conversation went into Spanish. 'I am,' agreed the Kid.

A low mutter passed around the crowd for all knew the story of the treaty council at Fort Sherrard, especially the Kid's part in it.

'What brought you here, *Cuchilo*?' asked the old medicine man.

'I heard there were foolish words of war being spoken among the Kaddo and hoped to see you make lies of them.'

Moon Watcher nodded, showing no surprise that the Kid had heard of the war talk. It had been the medicine man who told of the Kid's exploits at the treaty council, although Moon Watcher never went near the Fort.

'Why should we go the way of peace?' demanded Bear Killer.

'Because you will all be killed if you make war,' the Kid replied.

'We have guns like the soldier-coats now,' a young brave pointed out, waving his Winchester.

'Guns need bullets. You have few, the white men can get many. And they have wheel guns that can fire from where no rifle can reach them. They have guns which shoot bullets faster than a hundred men with rifles. The *Nemenuh* saw they could not fight such weapons. Do as my people did, ask the White Father in Austin to make a treaty with you. Go to him while you can still fight, not after you are beaten and must take whatever they offer.'

'Already the white men come to take our land——' Bear Killer began, indicating the scared-looking Wycliffe who crouched on the ground with two lances lined on him.

'That's a lie,' Mark interrupted and waved a hand towards the granite block. 'That one lied to you. He planned to take the silver from this place and the men came to steal it from him.'

'And why did you come, big one?' Moon Watcher wanted to know.

'They killed a man who had been like a father to me. I followed them.'

Every man present could understand Mark's motives and heartily approved of them. To hunt down the killer of a close friend ranked as a prime virtue and did nothing to lessen the esteem he gained by his actions. Moving forward, Moon Watcher looked at Mark with his head cocked on one side.

'Why did you listen to Hair Face's words in the tepee?'

'No man loses by listening to talk,' Mark answered. 'He told me much, but I did not say I would help him.'

'That I know,' Moon Watcher stated. 'My son lay outside the tepee listening and he speaks your language.'

A grin flickered across Mark's face, mirrored for a moment by the Kid. No matter that some Texans regarded Indian medicine men as fakes, both knew some to be remarkably shrewd, capable and with powers that no white man could fully understand. Certainly old Moon Watcher did not strike either as a charlatan and he seemed to have out-foxed Pegler.

'So you knew what he meant to do?' Mark said.

'I knew it well,' agreed the old man. 'And so did Bear Killer.'

'That was why I let Hair Face have you,' the chief went on. 'So that Moon Watcher's son could listen as you talked.'

'Do you want war, Bear Killer?' Mark asked bluntly.

'If the Great Spirit gave us medicine I would fight,' the chief admitted.

'Was that why you put that one to the test?' Mark inquired nodding to where Wycliffe sat on the floor under guard.

'He came to our land to rob and killed Kaddo braves. One had a brother who called for revenge. I could not refuse.'

'And what now, chief?' demanded the Kid. 'Do you still lead the braves to war?'

'The medicine is broken, *Cuchilo*,' Bear Killer replied. 'We do not ride.'

'Then meet the White Father in Austin. His heart is good to the Indian and he will treat you fairly.'

'Will you and the big one speak for us if we do?' asked Moon Watcher.

'We will,' agreed Mark. 'We will arrange the day for you to come, but then we must ride. Our chief wants us with him as soon as possible.'

'Don't he just,' drawled the Kid in English. 'Ole Devil'll be spitting eagle feathers and's like to have us on the blister end of a shovel for weeks if we don't get back to home real soon.'

'Stay the night with us,' suggested Bear Killer. 'There is much to say.'

'One thing I want, chief,' Mark answered. 'Him.'

'He is your's, my brother,' Bear Killer replied, following the direction of Mark's finger and eyeing Wycliffe in disgust. 'Take him when you leave in the morning.'

'Y—You saved my life, friend,' Wycliffe said as Mark came towards him.

'Is Billy dead?' Mark growled.

'Not as I know of.'

'Then, mister, you'd best hope I find him. If I don't, I'll see that you hang for Sailor Sam's murder in his place.'

CHAPTER SIXTEEN

NOT THE WAY TO USE A LANCE

STANDING behind a clump of bushes, with Rags' hand clamped over her mouth, Winnie wondered what had happened to make the men act in such a manner. She watched Billy Wycliffe and Augie moving cautiously down the slope, making use of every bit of cover available and carrying their rifles. Then a distant movement caught her eye and she looked in its direction.

Three men rode into sight through the trees and along the opposite side of the rolling ground before her. In the lead came a bare-headed Churn Wycliffe, seated on his fine bay mare, wearing an Indian buckskin shirt instead of his previous clothing. Slightly behind and to the right of Wycliffe rode a tall, slim youngster clad all in black and afork a magnificent white horse. At the left of Wycliffe, also just to the rear of the bearded man was—and Winnie could hardly believe her eyes— Mark Counter.

In some way, how she could not imagine, the blond giant had not only escaped from the Kaddo but met up with a friend and captured Churn Wycliffe. Even a naive country girl could figure that out. From the position they rode and the fact that they wore weapons while Wycliffe had none, it was obvious that the party did not travel as friends.

Then the meaning of Augie and Billy's actions became clear to the girl. They planned to rascue Wycliffe and probably kill the two men with him. Unless she sadly misjudged Mark's nature, killing him would be the only way to take away his prisoner. In addition to her aversion to standing by and watch murder done, she owed Mark her life. He saved her from the Kaddo and she saw a chance to repay him.

Feeling Winnie sag against him, Rags relaxed. Her lack of opposition lulled him into a sense of false security, so her next act came as a complete surprise. Twisting her head, she managed to put her mouth into position and sank her teeth around the base of his thumb. At the same moment she hacked back at his shin with her foot, a trick learned in childhood scuffles, further weakening his hold. With a jerk she tore free from his grasp and started to race down the hill at an angle to take her behind the other two men but towards Mark's party.

'Look out, Mark!' she screamed, shocked to see how close he had come. 'They're waiting for you!'

'You lousy bitch!' Rags howled, shaking his hand then charging after her. 'Just let me lay hands on you.'

The last part of his speech was all but drowned in the crack of shots and a scream of a man in pain. Snarling in fury, he plunged after the girl and ignored what happened to his companions.

Mark and the Kid had been treated as honoured guests by the Kaddo. In addition to admiring his strength, they respected what they thought to be Mark's tolerance in merely throwing dust into the young buck's face instead of driving the bullet into him. After a good meal they had talked long on the subject of making peace and had arranged for word to reach the Governor. At dawn Mark and the Kid had collected Wycliffe ready to return to Austin. The Kaddo had even given Wycliffe's mare to the Texans so that he would not slow them down.

Clear of the canyon, the Kid had changed back into his normal clothing. While they allowed Wycliffe to ride with his hands free, he made no trouble. Watched over by two men highly skilled in the use of weapons, any attempt to escape would end in failure. As he rode along Wycliffe had wondered where Billy might be. Knowing his nephew, heading for the safety of Austin had seemed the most likely place.

The Kid never relaxed when on the trail and kept constantly scouring the rolling wooded country through which they passed, eyes taking in every detail. In his growing years he had excelled at the game of *Nanip'ka*, Guess Over The Hill, played to teach Comanche youngsters how to locate hidden enemies. That early training served him well. He had seen the partially concealed Rags and read significance in the man's withdrawal. While he doubted if either of his companions saw the watcher, the Kid decided to take precautions.

'Hold my lance, will you, Mark?' he said.

'Sure. What's up?'

'Nothing.'

Which did not fool Mark for he had noticed that the Kid bent and slid out his rifle after handing over the lance. Wycliffe had heard the conversation and accepted it at face value. If he found the other two rode up closer to him, he thought little of it. Nor would looking back have told him anything, for the Kid held the Winchester hanging down out of sight on the far side of the horse.

Having ridden many dangerous trails with the Kid, Mark

knew the signs. A slight jerk of the head directed Mark's attention towards the slope down which the two men made what they imagined to be an unobserved advance. Mark had recognised Billy Wycliffe and tensed in his saddle. However he made no attempt to draw a weapon; to do so would warn the men that they had been discovered and might scare them off.

Up on the slope Billy felt worried and uneasy when he saw that his victims moved at an angle which would carry them past his hiding place at a distance of some thirty yards or more instead of coming straight towards him. Augie had halted in a position about forty yards farther along the slope, kneeling behind a rock and lining his rifle. Sure the approaching men suspected nothing, Billy had cradled the butt of his Winchester against his shoulder and had aimed past his uncle at the broad chest of the blond giant.

Suddenly Winnie had screamed out her warning. Finger on the trigger of his rifle, Billy stiffened at the sound. Then panic hit him. Already he knew how fast Mark could move and did not want to tangle with him in a gun fight. So he had aimed and begun to squeeze the trigger. Farther along the slope Augie had lined his rifle at the Kid, but twisted around with an angry growl on hearing the girl.

When the Kid heard Winnie, he knew the game was going to burst wide open at the seams. Jerking his left foot from the stirrup, he booted Wycliffe's bay hard in the ribs while starting to flip himself from the saddle. Taken by surprise, the mare leapt forward and carried her rider between Mark and Billy. Just an instant too late Billy saw the danger. Already the rifle's trigger had depressed far enough to free the hammer. The primer spat its flicker of flame into the bullet's powder charge, turning the black grains into a cloud of gas that hurled the bullet along the barrel. Lead meant for Mark ripped into Churn Wycliffe's body and tumbled him out of his saddle.

Landing cat-footed alongside his horse, the Kid darted forward. He threw up his rifle and fired in one fast move. Turning back to his work, Augie saw flame lick from the Kid's Winchester. Then something hot struck and seared across Augie's skull. His hat spun away and he staggered into the open before collapsing and lying perfectly still.

Mark also flung himself from his saddle but the lance he held prevented him from collecting the rifle from its boot. On landing he prepared to toss the primitive weapon away in favour of one of Colonel Colt's improved life-savers. Then he saw Billy turn without making further attempts at fighting.

Cold rage welled up inside Mark, the deadly anger his great

strength caused him to control most times. There fled the murderer of Sailor Sam; a coward without the guts to face an armed man. Gripping the lance between his two big hands, Mark hurled himself up the slope after Billy. The Kid also started running, levering another bullet home as he made for where Augie lay. There would be time enough to cut across and help Mark, should that prove necessary, after making sure the man could not take a further part in the affair.

Winnie fled down the slope with the speed of a cougar-spooked pronghorn. Behind her, pain from his bitten hand filling him with such rage that he forgot caution, Rags followed. Neither paid any attention to Billy as he went by them in the opposite direction. Nearer came the sound of Rags' running feet and Winnie stumbled around a large clump of bushes. A big shape loomed up in front of her and she swerved desperately without recognising Mark for the moment.

Following the girl, Rags saw the blond giant before him and sent his hand grabbing for a gun. Like a flash Mark lunged, driving forward the lance. Steel sliced into Rags' belly, ripping it open. Picking up the screaming man on the lance's head, Mark flung him aside like a cowhand forking hay into the corral. Then, without a glance at either his victim or the girl, Mark took up the chase once more.

With the ambush chance ruined, both his enemies alive and his friends out of the game, Billy had the fear of death to spur him on. From the corner of his eye he saw the black dressed young man bounding up to cut him off. Behind him heavy feet thudded on the ground, drawing closer. Catching his foot on a root, he stumbled and, in trying to prevent himself from falling, dropped the rifle.

Reeling against the next tree, Billy flattened back to it and glared through wild eyes at the approaching blond giant. Snarling terrified curses, the young killer gripped his revolver's butt. The holster turned on its swivel and the Colt fired through the open bottom. While allowing a real fast first shot, such a holster made re-cocking its revolver difficult and did not lend itself to accuracy at any but close range. So the bullet missed but Mark knew better than chance going any closer.

Back swung his right arm, carrying the lance over his shoulder, then hurling it forward. Its head struck Billy just under the centre of the breast bone, penetrating with such force that it sank into the tree trunk behind and pinned him to it.

Slowly the red fighting rage ebbed from Mark and he stared at what he had done. Coming up, the Kid cradled his rifle across one arm and took in the scene with no great show of emotion.

'Damn it,' he said indignantly, looking at Mark. 'You're not supposed to *throw* a war lance.'

'It seemed the best way to get rid of the fool thing,' Mark replied. 'How about his pard?'

'He's one lucky *hombre*. My bullet only creased his skull and he'll live to hang.'

While Augie lived, he did not hang or even stand trial. He had not been present when Sailor Sam was murdered and Winnie pleaded for him, saying that he had saved her from Billy. Guessing what would have happened to her had Billy been alone, Mark patched up Augie's skull, saw him safely back to Lake Travis and let him go free.

That came later.

Mark looked at the writhing body on the lance then growled to the Kid, 'Go stop the gal coming here until I've got that lance out.'

'Sure,' the Kid replied. 'We'll not tell her about the silver. The less who know about it the better.'

Mark nodded grimly. The silver had cost Sailor Sam his life. Eleven of Churn Wycliffe's gang, Pegler and his hired help had all died through that ill-fated mine. As far as Mark was concerned, the silver could stay in the ground for ever.

THE END